Dear Readers:

I don't know about you, but for me, high school wasn't smooth sailing. There were many times I felt I didn't fit in, many times I didn't feel pretty enough, thin enough—the list goes on. I know a lot of you can relate.

And how many of us had a crush on that special someone, yet he didn't have a clue? Mmm hmm. Well, that was the inspiration for Alice's character, and her story.

It was a treat to write about an "ugly duckling" turned beautiful swan—who, of course, gets her man this time around. Not for being beautiful on the outside, but for being beautiful from the inside out. Sure, it's fiction, but I'm also an incurable romantic and believe such a story can really happen. I'm sure it's happened for some of you. I hope you enjoy Alice's and Marcus's story!

To all my fans, thanks for your continued support! This is my first story for HarperCollins, and I'm thrilled to be writing for them. I'd love to hear your comments, so feel free to contact me. You can e-mail me at *kayla@kaylaperrin.com* or visit my website at *www.kaylaperrin.com*. You can also send snail mail to:

Kayla Perrin
HarperCollins Publishers
10 East 53rd Street
New York, New York 10022

I look forward to hearing from you! Until next time, keep believing in love!

Warm wishes,

Kayla

If You Want Me

Kayla Perrin

HarperTorch
An Imprint of HarperCollins*Publishers*

This is a work of fiction. Names, characters, places and incidents are products of the author's imagination or are used fictitiously and are not to be construed as real. Any resemblance to actual events, locales, organizations, or persons, living or dead, is entirely coincidental.

HARPERTORCH
An Imprint of HarperCollins*Publishers*
10 East 53rd Street
New York, New York 10022-5299

Copyright © 2001 by Kayla Perrin
Excerpt from *Gotta Get Next to You* copyright © 2001 by Margaret Hubbard
ISBN: 0-7394-1504-2

Printed in the United States of America

*For every woman
who has ever felt uncomfortable
about her weight or her looks,
may we all realize our true beauty
that comes from within.*

*And to two very dear childhood friends,
Allette Brown and Cheryl Falardeau—
two women whose beauty radiates
from the inside out.
I love you both.*

If You Want Me

Prologue

"Alice Gayle Watson."

Alice froze as she stepped into the foyer of her house, as if her legs had turned to ice. Her mother never called her by her full name unless she was angry. "Yes, Mama?"

Rosa Watson appeared at the living room entrance. Stepping into the foyer, she calmly said, "This came in the mail for you."

It was a simple enough statement, nothing to get upset over, but one look at the envelope her mother extended and Alice's stomach dropped to her knees.

"Thanks, Mama." She took the letter from her mother, then stepped past her, heading for the stairs.

"Wait one ever-loving second." The calm voice was gone, replaced by a stern tone.

Alice turned. "Mama—"

"Alice, how many times have we talked about this?"

They never *talked* about it; her mother dictated and Alice listened. But Alice was almost eighteen, almost a high school graduate. Wasn't it time she made her own decisions?

Telling her mother that was easy when she rehearsed it in the privacy of her own room—but not when her mother was looking down at her with such raw disappointment.

"It's only a letter," Alice finally said.

"From the Screen Actors Guild," Rosa said with contempt.

"It's just—"

"I know what it is. I opened it."

Alice's mouth fell open in shock, but her words of protest died in her throat. Why couldn't she tell her mother how she felt? That she deserved some privacy and respect?

"It's a list of agents," her mother continued, then huffed. "In *Los Angeles*. What are you planning to do, move there?"

Maybe it was her mother's mocking tone, or maybe the reality that she finally had to make her mother understand. But Alice found the strength to boldly reply, "Yes. Yes, I am."

Her mother's laugh was full of pity. "You're going through with this silly dream of yours to be an actress?"

"It's not a silly dream. I want this more than anything." From the time she was little and she'd watched movies on television and the big screen—movies like *The Wizard of Oz* and *The Sound of Music*—she'd known she wanted to be an actress. Movies were magical. They took her to another time and place, gave her a chance to live out the happy ending she hadn't found in her own life. She wanted to be a part of that magic. Only her father had understood that, but now he was gone.

"Look at you," her mother replied, staring down at her with scorn. "Who's going to hire you, let alone represent you?"

Alice choked back a sob. It was the worst thing her mother had ever said to her. She knew her weight had always been a sensitive issue with her. "I'm gonna work out. Eat better."

"Oh, Alice. When are you going to learn? You have to stop living in a dream world and face reality."

Why didn't her mother believe in her? "I can do this."

"For someone with a decent grade point average, you certainly aren't acting like you have the sense God gave you."

More harsh words, like a knife plunging into her heart. If her father were here, he wouldn't let her mother do this to her. He would protect her. Yet her mother's attitude made her even more determined. "I'm going." Her voice wavered, but she went on. "You can't stop me."

Rosa's eyes grew wide with surprise, then narrowed. "I'm telling you this for your own good, Alice. You're setting yourself up for failure. Just like you've done with Marcus."

"You don't know anything about Marcus," Alice replied, louder than expected. How dare her mother mention Marcus, her one true friend? He was the only one other than her father who believed in her.

"It's obvious you're in love with him. But in all this time, has he reciprocated your feelings? You live in this dream world where you actually believe

a boy like Marcus would fall for a girl like you."
Rosa sighed. "You are going to get your heart broken, mark my words."

Her mother almost sounded like she wished it would happen. Alice stared at her in shock, wondering how they could even be related. Where was her motherly love, her compassion?

At that moment, the phone rang, saving Alice from this horrible conversation. She hustled past her mother to the living room, where she grabbed the receiver. "Hello?"

"Alice."

She closed her eyes as warmth rushed through her. It was Marcus. What perfect timing. "Oh, Marcus."

"What is it? What's wrong?"

He knew her so well. "Everything," she whispered.

"Why don't you tell me about it when you see me. Can you meet me in twenty minutes? At Maxi's?"

"Yes." She needed to get out of here. "Yes, I can." She hung up and hurried out of the house, ignoring her mother's protests that they hadn't finished their discussion.

Marcus was already sitting at a table when Alice arrived at Maxi's, a doughnut shop and café, and a local hangout for teenagers. Despite the buzz of chatter from the throng of students, he seemed to sense her arrival and looked up as she entered. He smiled. Just one of his sexy smiles made her entire day.

Every time she saw him, Alice's heart did a little dance in her chest. He was so incredibly attractive. Six-foot-two, Marcus was athletically built and had smooth, dark brown skin. His black hair was short and wavy. He had a strong, chiseled jaw and beautiful, thick lips—lips that Alice always wished she could kiss. But his eyes were the most striking feature of his oval-shaped face. Always intense, his eyes were so dark they looked almost onyx.

Alice walked toward him, noting the sneers she got from a group of students, but she ignored them and held her head high. She had Marcus. She didn't need anyone else.

"Yo, Alice." Willie Thompson, a fellow senior who picked on her every day, jumped in her path. "When are you gonna go out with me?" His tone was mocking, as were his actions as he folded his hands before her as if pleading. His group of friends at the adjacent table, mostly jocks, howled with laughter.

Suddenly, Willie whirled around, so fast it startled Alice. Marcus had him by the collar of his T-shirt.

"You want to pick on someone," Marcus said, his eyes black as coal as he glared down at Willie, "pick on me."

The whole shop went quiet in anticipation of a fight.

Willie held up his hands in surrender. "Relax, man. I was just kidding."

Marcus shoved Willie toward his table. "Don't let me have to tell you again."

It was amazing how Marcus's expression changed from one of hardness to softness as he moved his eyes from Willie to Alice. Like he had on so many occasions before, Marcus had come to her rescue. "Thanks," she said.

"No problem." He placed a hand on her back and led her to his table. "Willie's a loser. Ignore him."

Alice wished she could use that excuse for the kids in school who made fun of her simply because she wasn't pretty and was a little overweight. Including Marcus's girlfriend, Tanisha. How could he be with someone who was so mean when he was so good?

Tanisha was a cheerleader. Marcus was a star running back for the school's football team. After weeks of cheering for him from the sidelines, Tanisha had approached him after a game and they'd started talking. Soon after that, they'd started going out. Yes, Tanisha was beautiful, but that's all she had going for her. Her beauty hid a cruel and manipulative side. Alice always hoped Marcus would see that for himself, but whenever they were together, Tanisha acted so sweet and loving, and Marcus hadn't yet figured out her true nature.

"What's going on at home?" he asked as they sat.

She told him about the fight with her mother. "She thinks I'm crazy. That I'm gonna fail." Her eyes searched his desperately. "Do you think that?"

"No, I don't. You're a great actress."

Marcus's praise meant so much to her, but her mother's disbelief had shattered her confidence. "You're not just saying that, are you?"

He reached for her hand and squeezed it. "I've seen you in every play you've done in the past two years, remember? When I say you're good, I mean it."

"Thank you." Most recently, Marcus had watched her perform in *Misconceptions*, a play at a local community theater. Her mother hadn't wanted her to take the acting class—Alice had no clue why—but she'd worked hard and saved her money. In the end, she'd been devastated when the director had given her the role of Amy, a fat, unattractive kid who was picked on in school. Alice had gone to Marcus, unsure if she should accept the role. He'd been angry at the director's narrow-mindedness, but had convinced her to do the role because it was a chance to showcase her skills to local agencies. In the end, she had done so well she'd received a standing ovation—and a personal commendation from the director.

"I say go for it."

Marcus was the only thing that could keep her here in this sorry town where people judged her because she wasn't model-thin and gorgeous. Even her own mother favored her sister, Marie, over her, simply because Marie was beautiful and she was not. So she had to admit that part of her was a little upset when Marcus didn't tell her to stay in Chicago, that he would miss her if she went away.

Every so often, Alice wondered if she should risk telling Marcus how she really felt about him. Should she tell him now? Tanisha was supposed to be going to some school in New York to study drama. With Tanisha gone, she might have a chance.

"There's something I want to discuss with you." His whole body was tense, his forehead scrunched thoughtfully. What could it be?

"What, Marcus?"

"It's Tanisha."

Alice's heart leapt. It was foolish to immediately feel hope, but she did. God, if she could only have a chance with Marcus, her life would be complete. "What about her?"

"I need your opinion. As a woman."

"Okay."

"We've been going out for a year and a half now."

Don't remind me. Alice still didn't understand how Marcus couldn't see Tanisha for what she was— evil, manipulative, and self-centered. "She's going to New York, isn't she? Are you two still gonna see each other?"

"We said we would, but . . ."

"But?" The hope burned brighter.

"Oh, I should just say this. What do you think about me proposing to her at the grad party?"

Propose? God, no. Alice's head suddenly started spinning, like she was being thrown around in a tornado. This couldn't be happening. He couldn't actually consider marrying Tanisha. *Oh, Marcus, you can't do this. She's only gonna hurt you.*

She'd tried to tell him that before, but he was so in love with the gorgeous Tanisha that he couldn't see her faults.

"If you were Tanisha," he continued, "and I asked you to marry me, would you leave for New York? Or would you stay here in Chicago with me?"

Of all the questions to ask. Alice almost couldn't answer, she was doing everything to keep from visibly shaking. If Marcus married Tanisha, he wouldn't have time for her anymore. She knew that. Tanisha hated her.

"Alice?" he prompted when she remained silent.

"If it were me?" She met and held his eyes. "Yes, I'd stay wherever you are."

He didn't catch her double meaning, but his shoulders drooped with relief nonetheless. "That's what I thought. I'm gonna do it. Right after the grad party. I can only get her a small ring, but she loves me, right?"

I *love you.*

"I don't want to lose her," Marcus said determinedly. "She means everything to me." After a moment, he asked, "Alice, what's wrong?"

"Hmm? Oh, I'm thinking about my mother."

"I know, it's tough. But like I said, go for it." His lips curled in a small smile. "I will miss you, though."

She almost wished he hadn't said that. Not now that he'd told her he was going to marry Tanisha.

"But we'll keep in touch, right?"

"Oh. Sure." Alice bolted to her feet. "I've got to go."

Marcus looked at her with concern. "So soon?"

"Yeah. I have to talk to my mother. Work this out." But she really needed to get away from him.

"Okay then. See you at school tomorrow."

"Yeah." Then Alice got out of Maxi's as fast as she could.

Tears poured down her face as she walked home. It hurt more than it should, but she couldn't stop the pain in her heart. No, Marcus had never been anything other than a friend to her, but she'd held out hope that one day he would love her.

But now he was going to marry Tanisha . . .

Reality came crashing down on her, heavy and devastating. Her life wasn't going to get any better here. No Prince Charming would come along and rescue her from her painful existence. No Prince Charming would ever love her. Not while she was Alice Watson, Chicago's ugly duckling. Marcus was the closest she'd ever come, and he was in love with someone else.

Her mother's words echoed in her mind. *You have to stop living in a dream world.*

But it was that dream world that had saved her from depression. In her dreams, she always had a happy ending. She had Marcus's love. When Marcus was simply dating Tanisha, she'd held out hope. A long shot, but hope nonetheless. Now, she had nothing.

The last thing she wanted to do was watch Marcus marry Tanisha and she wasn't going to stay here and prove her mother right. And she certainly didn't have to stay in this city where people had hurt her since childhood and would hurt her until the day she died. She was going to make something of herself, put the bad memories behind her—even if it killed her.

Harden your heart.

The moment school was over, she was outta here. And when she left, she wouldn't look back.

Not ever.

One

Thirteen years later . . .

"Hey, isn't that . . . ?"

"Oh, my God. Is that Desirée LaCroix?"

Alice heard the hushed whispers and buzz around her as she walked purposefully through the corridor. She saw the curious stares. Even with dark sunglasses on and her hair pulled back in a ponytail, people often recognized her in public.

Today, that public place was a crowded Chicago hospital.

Her brisk pace made it clear that she wasn't here to sign T-shirts or notepads or anything else. Who in a hospital was? Like everyone else in these packed corridors, she was here to visit a patient.

Not just any patient. Her mother.

Alice's pace faltered for a brief moment as the realization of the situation dawned on her again. She could hardly believe she was truly here, that her mother had actually had a heart attack. The last time she'd talked to her mother, she'd told Alice never to come back to Chicago, and Alice had heeded her command. Until now. Now, the hard, cold woman Alice had considered indestructible could actually die. When her sister, Marie, had called to tell her the news, Alice had felt something she hadn't felt in years—remorse and regret, and the overwhelming feeling that she needed to see her mother before it was too late.

If for no other reason than to finally look her in the eye and ask her why she didn't love her.

"Psst. Look."

Alice didn't break her stride as she rounded the corner and headed for the elevators. Marie had told her the room number and wing where her mother was in Cook County Hospital. The woman at the information desk had pointed her in the right direction.

Her anxiety built as she rode up in the elevator, watching the numbers illuminate to indicate which floor they were on.

When the elevator doors finally parted, Alice was filled with a sudden sense of dread. What if her mother didn't want to see her? What if she'd come all this way for nothing?

She turned right, glanced at the first few doors, saw the numbers were going up, not down, then pivoted on her heel and headed in the other direction. As she reached room 612, she slowed and inhaled a shaky breath, praying she could compose herself. Even after all this time and how far she'd come in her life, Alice was actually afraid to walk into the room and see her mother.

She opened the door and stepped inside.

Alice wasn't prepared for the emotions that overwhelmed her as she looked inside the room and saw an empty bed. *Not yet,* she thought. *Oh, God, not yet.*

She stepped further into the room, her head now aching from the urge to cry, but the tears wouldn't come. There was a vase of yellow carnations on one side of the bed and two cards on the other. Lifting a card, she saw it was from her niece, Mia, to her mother. Yes, this was her mother's room.

But her mother wasn't here.

Oh, God. Was she too late?

At the sound of someone entering the room, Alice whirled around. Marie stood in the doorway, a Styrofoam cup in her hand, and a startled expression on her face.

"Marie." Alice could hardly breathe. "Where's Mom?"

"In surgery. You didn't think—"

"I didn't know what to think. Oh, Marie." Alice practically flew toward her and wrapped her in an embrace. It was an instinctive move, but awkward nonetheless. She and Marie weren't exactly close.

"Alice."

Alice pulled back and looked at her sister for the first time in years. Her hair was drastically shorter than it had been the last time Alice had seen her, slicked back off her face and held in place with gel. It was no longer black but auburn. It suited her oval-shaped face. Marie had put on weight over the years, but it had all gone to her hips and waist, not her face.

One side of Marie's lips lifted in a half smile but her expression was wary. There were dark circles under her eyes, proof that she'd spent a sleepless night.

"Last night you told me that she didn't want the surgery."

"The doctors were finally able to talk some sense into her. I called you a couple hours ago to tell you she'd changed her mind, but you'd already left."

"Triple bypass?" Alice asked.

"Yeah." Marie's voice was faint.

"So this is serious."

"Pretty much so. There's extensive blockage in her heart. Thank God Mia was with her at the time. If we'd all gone to bed . . ." Her voice trailed off and ended with a sniffle.

"Was she conscious before she went to surgery?" Alice asked.

"Yeah."

"Did she ask for me?"

Marie shook her head.

Alice turned then and walked to the window. She stared outside but barely registered anything other than the bright sky. What had she expected? That her mother would have clutched Marie's hand before surgery and begged her to call her? Scenes like that only played out in Hollywood movies, not real life.

Alice faced her sister. "Where's Mia?"

"In school. I didn't want her to miss the day."

Silence fell over them, heavy and oppressive. There were so many things Alice wanted to say, so many things she was afraid to say. The truth was, her sister was a virtual stranger. She knew she'd married her high school sweetheart, Chad Greenley, had one child, then divorced three years later. That was about it.

"I can't believe how good you look," Marie finally said, a hint of wonder in her voice. "I guess the cameras don't lie."

"Thanks," Alice told her, a feeling of disappointment tickling her nape. But she should have known Marie would make some comment about her weight, even though she'd been slim and trim for over ten years now.

"I'm glad you're home, Alice. I'm not sure I can deal with this by myself. The doctor said that Mama's going to need to take it easy for at least six weeks. Virtual bed rest."

"Six weeks?"

"While she recovers. With both of us taking care of her, we should manage just fine."

"Both of us? I can't stay for six weeks." Maybe not even six days.

"You're not working on a film, are you?"

"Not now." Alice had walked off the set of her latest movie after a fiasco with the director. She'd asked him for time off to see her mother and he had used her mother's illness as an excuse to proposition her for sex. A favor for a favor, he'd said. In fact, the whole scenario had left Alice with a bad taste in her mouth. For a long while, she hadn't felt quite the same optimism she'd once felt about Hollywood. She'd struggled so hard to succeed, yet that success was often soured by the downside of the film industry. The kissing ass. The sucking up. The endless diets and low self-esteem. The back-stabbing from people she'd considered friends. Knowing that her best often wasn't good enough, that even though she'd worked her butt off to earn respect, she was seen by some men as a toy to be used for their pleasure—however they wanted, whenever they wanted. Sebastian Charles's tactless proposition had been the icing on the cake.

She needed a break from the Hollywood scene.

Still, returning to Chicago and taking care of the mother she had never been able to please wasn't something Alice had considered. Something she didn't want.

"Mama needs you, Alice."

"I doubt that."

"She's still your mother."

Alice bit her tongue, refusing to ask why their mother had never treated her as a daughter. Marie had never understood Alice's unhappiness at home. How could she, when their mother had showered Marie, the beautiful one, with the love and attention she had denied Alice, the ugly duckling?

"Yes, she is. But this is so . . . sudden. I haven't even told my agent that I'm away. And I'm waiting to hear back on a couple of roles I'm up for."

"We know. You have a life; it's not here." Marie didn't hide her bitterness.

"That's not what I'm saying."

"Then what are you saying?"

"Marie." Alice's voice was harsher than she intended. "I need to think, that's all."

"I can't believe you'd run away again. At a time like this."

"I'm here, aren't I? Look," Alice began, her voice softening. "I don't want to argue with you, Marie." That's not why she was here. If Alice was in Los Angeles or Toronto or even France on a film set and her mother died, she'd never be able to forgive herself. "Mom's gonna be in surgery for a while, right?"

"Mmm-hmm."

"And after that she'll be recuperating for a while."

"Yes."

Alice blew out a frustrated breath. She couldn't believe she was actually considering this. "All right, I'll stay as long as I can."

"Thank you." Marie sounded relieved.

"But if I'm gonna stay here and help take care of her, then I have to make some calls now. Take care of some business." What she really needed was some time alone to collect her thoughts and accept the situation. She'd come home to see her mother, make sure she was all right, and if she wasn't, be there for the rest of the family. She'd left Chicago thirteen years ago and had had no plans to return. Certainly not indefinitely.

"All right. I'll stay here and wait for word."

Alice nodded tightly. "I'll be back in a bit."

Then she walked out of the hospital room in search of a quiet spot to make some phone calls.

It was a bad idea, of course. Marcus just wasn't the kind of man to pick up and bed strange women, especially not in this day and age. And even if he wanted to be that kind of man, he had no clue where to start. He'd dated only one woman seriously, had married her, and since their divorce two years ago he had thrown himself into work. Hell, he could hardly remember what women looked like naked, it had been that long.

The only time he'd come close to getting involved with anyone else was seven months ago, and that had ended in disaster. Even now, that situation was tough to swallow, so as Marcus accelerated his cruiser on the JFK Expressway, he pushed the thought from his mind.

Last night, Marcus's former brother-in-law and a fellow cop, Khalil Barrett, had told him that he was too uptight and needed "help" unwinding. Marcus respected Khalil, so much so that he'd joined the force years ago at his suggestion, but he didn't always agree with him. Especially when it came to women. Marcus knew he didn't need *that* kind of help. If he needed to unwind, he'd spend more time at the gym. It was that simple.

He did miss sex, though. It was just the complications he could live without. For whatever reason, he always chose the wrong women. He was drawn to pretty faces, and that had gotten him into trouble. The first time he could live with. The second he wasn't so sure.

The April day couldn't have been more perfect, with a bright, cloudless sky and warm sun, but Marcus's mood was far from perfect. Even the fresh air whipping against his face didn't clear his mind as it usually did. There was no mystery as to why he was in a funky mood; though he'd officially been cleared of any wrongdoing in the Melissa Reynolds case, recently he couldn't stop replaying that day seven months ago when everything had gone horribly wrong.

Forget it, Quinn, he heard Khalil say. *What could you do?*

It was that question that haunted him. Could he have done something differently? *Would* he have done something differently if he hadn't crossed the line and gotten involved with her?

Marcus frowned as he glanced in the rearview mirror. Immediately, he saw the royal blue BMW Roadster convertible approaching at breakneck speed. Damn, didn't the idiot behind the wheel see his marked cruiser? Obviously not, because the car sped past him as though he were going backward.

He immediately hit his lights and gave chase. As he neared the car, he saw black hair flying with the breeze and realized that it was a female driver. That fact made him feel somewhat better; women tended to be more reasonable than men.

Most of the time.

This one he had to wonder about. Either she was hell-bent on not stopping, or she still hadn't noticed him behind her. He blasted the siren once, then relaxed as the BMW began to decelerate. Seconds later, the driver pulled the car onto the left shoulder and came to a stop.

He should have called dispatch and run the tag, but his gut said the woman behind the wheel wasn't dangerous. She just wasn't particularly bright.

Still, as he made his way to the car, he did so cautiously, with his hand on his gun. Just in case. More than one Chicago area cop had been killed at a routine traffic stop.

"Place your hands where I can see them," he said as he approached the car.

The woman's hands immediately went into the air. A good sign.

He stopped at the passenger door, towering over the occupant, whose hair was in disarray. "License and registration, please."

She lifted her head to face him. "Officer, I . . ."

Even behind the sunglasses, he could see her eyes

widen, her surprise mirroring his own. He would know her anywhere. *"Alice?"*

"Marcus?"

"In the flesh."

God, that voice. Alice took a deep breath. It was smooth and sexy, like velvet. She'd heard the phrase *rock your world* before, had listened to her female friends use it when describing men, but not until this moment in time did she actually understand its true meaning. But as a tremor passed through her body from the top of her head to the bottom of her feet, followed by what could only be described as a white-hot flash, she knew that her world had been more than rocked. It had been sent into orbit— which surprised the hell out of her. She'd gotten over her crush on Marcus Quinn ages ago.

"Oh, my God." She pushed her sunglasses into her hair. "Marcus!"

A smile crept onto his face, which surprised him almost as much as seeing Alice out of the blue. He'd always thought that if he ever saw her again, he would feel anger, or at least annoyance. When she'd left Chicago in pursuit of fame, she'd forgotten all about him and their friendship.

He leaned forward and rested an arm on the window frame. "I can't believe it's you, Alice. Or should I call you Desirée LaCroix?"

Alice felt a stab of pain in her fingers and realized that she was gripping the steering wheel as if it were a lifeline. It was just that seeing Marcus here, on the side of a highway, looking even more gorgeous than the last time she'd seen him, had unnerved her. She dropped her hands to her lap. "It's Alice, Marcus. That's my name."

"Hmm," he said thoughtfully, standing to his full six-foot-two-inch height. His smile vanished and Alice didn't have a clue what was going through his mind.

Marcus stared at Alice, taking in the sight of her. He knew from the magazines he'd collected, from the interviews he'd watched on television, from the images he'd seen of her on the big screen that she was beautiful. Yet he didn't really know if her beauty was real or a trick of lighting and makeup, because he hadn't actually seen her in the flesh for almost thirteen years.

Now he knew without a doubt. Alice Watson had in fact blossomed into a beautiful swan. There'd been no tricks with makeup or lighting. In fact, with no makeup on now, she looked even more beautiful than when he'd seen her on the screen, which he never would have imagined was possible. It was hard to believe she was actually the same Alice he'd known in high school.

Not that he couldn't tell she was the same person, but man, this version was literally stunning. Full, sexy lips. Clear, honey-brown skin. Bright, cinnamon-colored eyes. Silky black hair that kissed her shoulders. She was quite slim now, maybe seventy pounds lighter than she'd been when he'd last seen her. A little too skinny, perhaps.

Except for those breasts, he realized, as his eyes ventured lower.

His gaze went back to her face. Those bright eyes were wide with surprise as she looked up at him, and Marcus's face went warm with embarrassment. Damn, what was wrong with him? Checking her out like she was a piece of meat. He remembered what Khalil had said about him needing to unwind, and for the first time Marcus conceded that his friend might be right.

"So," Alice began, "we meet again."

"Yeah."

One word, but at least he was talking. Talking was better than this strained silence between them. Though with the way he'd looked at her, Alice had to wonder if he hadn't just been checking her out.

"How are you, Marcus?"

He shrugged. "I'm all right."

If he'd been checking her out a moment ago, he certainly wasn't now. And he didn't sound all right. He sounded . . . annoyed, maybe? Maybe he simply felt as awkward as she suddenly did. Trying to make conversation with a man who she'd once considered a dear friend after thirteen years of not seeing or speaking to him—of course that was awkward. She forced a bright smile. "How's Tanisha?"

"We're divorced."

"Divorced?" Alice nearly choked on the word. She had always known Tanisha would hurt him.

"Yep. I thought I knew her, but I didn't. But then, I thought I knew other people, but was wrong about them too."

The brusque tone of his voice combined with the way his eyes narrowed slightly made Alice realize he *was* annoyed with her. And truth be told, she couldn't blame him.

"I'm surprised you came back," he said when she remained silent.

"My mother." The reality of it all washed over her once more. Would it ever feel real? "She's had a heart attack."

Marcus's eyes grew round with shock. He leaned forward, once again resting his arm on the window frame. "I'm sorry."

"I guess word doesn't spread around the neighborhood like it used to."

"I wouldn't know. I've been living in East Rogers Park for the past ten years. And I work downtown."

"Oh. Well . . ." Her voice trailed off as she couldn't think of anything to say to him that wouldn't sound lame. Or reinforce the fact that she didn't know him anymore. East Rogers Park was miles away from the southern suburb where they'd grown up. Finally, she sighed. "I don't know what's going to happen. If she'll be okay. She's having triple-bypass surgery at Cook County Hospital as we speak. I . . . I had to get out of there." Once again, Alice realized her mother might actually die.

"Damn. That's serious. Are you okay?"

"It doesn't quite feel real yet."

"Is there anything I can do?"

She considered his question, then frowned. "No."

"How about a coffee somewhere? Maybe on the waterfront?"

"With you?"

He shrugged. "Why not?"

Alice recognized Marcus's old protective instincts kicking in, and maybe, if their friendship hadn't died, she would have taken him up on his offer. But after thirteen years, it would be too awkward to lean on him for support the way she once had.

She asked, "Aren't you working?"

"I can take a break."

"I don't think that's a good idea, Marcus." Disappointment passed over his features, and Alice quickly added, "I just need to be alone right now. I need some quiet time before I head back to the hospital."

"Sure." He thrummed his fingers on the window frame of her car, then stood. "I'll see you around, then."

"Yeah."

"Just slow down, okay? Another cop won't be so nice."

She smiled her thanks, and as he turned and headed back to his cruiser, she watched him through the side-view mirror. Well, he definitely did the police uniform proud. He looked both powerful and sexy. But even seeing him in uniform, she could hardly believe he was actually a cop—which once again drove the point home of just how far apart they'd drifted.

She started the car and eased into traffic. Only as she drove off did she realize that she hadn't told Marcus a way to reach her. And he hadn't asked.

As Marcus slipped into his cruiser, he watched the sporty BMW merge into traffic. He kept it in his sight until it became a blur up ahead, then disappeared around a curve.

Alice Watson. Desirée LaCroix. Whoever. He shook his head ruefully. He shouldn't be disappointed, but he was. Hadn't he known she had changed? He didn't need to physically see her to accept that fact. Practically from the day she had left Chicago and headed for Los Angeles, she'd forgotten about him—and he had been one of her best friends. Or so he'd thought.

He'd sent her two letters the first month she'd

been away, then an invitation to his wedding in the fall. She'd responded to the two letters, but hadn't responded to the invitation. Just in case she hadn't gotten it, he'd sent another one. When he still didn't receive a reply, he hadn't worried about it, figuring she was busy, but he had been certain she'd come back for the event. She was, after all, his best friend. But not only had Alice not come home for his wedding, she hadn't even called to explain why she hadn't been there on one of the most important days of his life.

He hadn't tried to reach her after that, waiting instead to hear from her, but she hadn't written him. Hadn't called. There were many times he had missed his friend and wanted to contact her, but, wondering what the hell was going on, he played the stubborn game and continued waiting. Finally, when he'd graduated from the police academy the following spring, he'd sent her a brief letter, but again, no response. Marcus had finally figured out that she wanted nothing to do with him now that she was on her way to stardom.

Just like that, their friendship was over. And Marcus had felt a sense of disillusionment. He could understand her not contacting her mother, since her mother had more or less thrown her out. And her sister had never been much of a sister from what he'd seen. But him? He had never expected she'd cut him out of her life.

Though he never would have believed it if someone had told him it would happen, Alice Watson had "gone Hollywood." She'd even gotten herself a stage name once she'd become successful—Desirée LaCroix. How pretentious was that?

Maybe he was judging her too harshly. Maybe she simply wanted a new name to reflect her new image. She had changed dramatically over the years, shedding several pounds, changing her hair, her clothes. She'd grown into a beautiful woman, no doubt, and her new image spoke of flair and success. It was what she'd always wanted—and what she had achieved.

So why didn't Marcus feel happier for her?

Alice continued her drive at a steady pace, careful to stay within the posted speed limit. What an unbelievable twenty-four hours this had been! First her mother's unexpected heart attack, then Marcus's sudden reappearance in her life.

Her heart pounded furiously, and while she told herself that was because she had yet to call her agent and tell her about yesterday's disaster on the set, deep down, she knew Marcus was the one who had caused the reaction. After all this time, one look at him and her heart had gone into overdrive.

It wasn't that she wanted him. But maybe the fact that he looked so good—even better—after all this time made it easier to remember the feelings she'd once had for him.

Or perhaps it was feelings of guilt. She could see the hurt and a hint of anger in his eyes when he'd looked at her. He didn't understand why she'd cut him out of her life.

It wasn't that she'd forgotten him, though for her sanity she'd known she should. She just hadn't been able to remain friends with him while he was married to Tanisha. What was she supposed to do, call his matrimonial home and ask Tanisha if she could speak with Marcus? And even if she could bear hearing his wife's voice, she wasn't sure she could bear it if Tanisha told her to go to hell, or that Marcus didn't need her anymore.

Bottom line, Alice hadn't been able to deal with the fact that Marcus had married Tanisha. Plain and simple. It had been easier to stay away and mend her broken heart.

Alice's thoughts were interrupted by the sound of loud music, and her gaze flew to the rearview mirror. Behind her, a car approached at an extremely fast speed. As it gained on her, the convertible veered into the left-hand lane and sped up alongside her. She glanced to her left. The Jaguar carried a group of young black males, who, when they saw her, tooted the horn, howled, and waved. Grateful for the diversion from her thoughts and flattered by their attention, Alice flashed them a smile, then turned her attention back to the road. But as the catcalls continued, she looked back at them. One of the men literally hung out of the car gesturing toward her, trying to get her to pull over.

Alice wasn't about to do that, but she was smart enough not to offend them. So with a shrug and a smile and a gesture to her watch, she told them without words that she couldn't stop. The driver pouted and the front seat passenger blew her a kiss before their Jag accelerated and left her in the dust.

Alice shook her head, a smile playing on her lips. Funny how life was. Now that she was attractive enough to get the attention of most men, she didn't care if she had it. Sure, she appreciated a respectful smile or a wave or even a cheap pickup line—*if* the men were harmless. Once, she'd thought that being beautiful would solve all her problems. The truth was, being beautiful had brought its own set of headaches, including countless sexual propositions in Tinseltown from young men and men old enough to be her great-grandfather. She'd had to prove herself more than an average-looking or older woman would because people tended to assume she'd been hired for her looks, not her talent. And there were so many times she'd been sent in for bimbo roles that she'd lost count.

The irony of her reversed situation didn't escape her.

Alice glanced at the Chicago skyline as she drove, once again contemplating the circumstances that had brought her home. With chagrin, she realized that driving around all day wouldn't make the issues she had to deal with disappear.

If she was going to stay in Chicago, she might as well find a hotel for now and get settled. And though she was dreading it, she had to call her agent about what had happened yesterday.

And finally, the greatest challenge of all: She had to head back to Cook County Hospital and face her mother.

Two

Alice turned left after entering the hotel lobby and walked several feet with her small suitcase to a less crowded area where she could use her cell phone. She'd left her rented BMW with the valet, then fought to hold on to her luggage when the bell captain offered to tag her suitcase and have it brought directly to her room upon check-in.

"No," Alice had said. Yes, she'd come this far, but as she'd pulled up to the entrance of the Sheraton Hotel, she suddenly hadn't been sure she should check in.

On the drive here, she'd made up her mind that this was the right thing to do. The hotel was closer to the hospital than her mother's house was; she could get to her mother quicker if anything drastic happened. But now that she was here, she realized that she could reason all she wanted, she simply didn't want to go back to the house where she had grown up.

The house her mother had told her never to return to.

Until now, she'd never thought she would return. She'd heeded her mother's command and had planned to do so forever. Thirteen years ago on a gray day, she'd walked away from her home and the family that didn't love her, and had moved on with her life. But now . . .

Now, checking into a hotel seemed like running away from her problems. If she was here, and if she was here for her mother, then she should go to her house. Certainly it wouldn't kill her.

But for right now, she used her cell phone to call her agent in Los Angeles.

"Come on, Connie. Pick up."

"Connie Frum."

Alice gripped the phone. "Connie, hi. It's me."

"Alice, I've been trying to reach you since yesterday. I keep getting the voice mail on your cell phone."

"I know. I meant to call sooner."

"What on earth happened?"

Alice's shoulders drooped and she leaned her back against the wall for support. "My mother's in the hospital. She had a heart attack." Connie didn't speak, waiting for her to continue. "I asked Sebastian for some time off the film, and he . . . he came on to me. Connie, he cornered me in his trailer and tried to get in my pants. Forcefully." Remembering the whole incident made her cringe. "I kneed him in the groin and walked off the set."

"Damn," Connie muttered. "I guess there's nothing I can do to smooth this over."

"No. I'm not going back." The ugly scene played

out in her mind—Sebastian naked from the waist down and doubled over in pain, screaming expletives at her. Even as she'd walked out the trailer door, he made sure to tell her that she'd never work for him again—as if she'd ever want to. Alice loved acting, but she wasn't about to compromise herself for anyone. She'd worked too hard over the past thirteen years for that.

"I'm sorry to hear about your mother," Connie said after a moment. "How is she?"

"She's in surgery right now. She's expected to survive, but it'll be weeks before she fully recovers." Alice couldn't help thinking of her father, how he hadn't been as lucky as her mother. He'd had a heart attack while driving, and had spun into oncoming traffic. The accident had killed him.

"When will you be back?"

"I don't know. Maybe next week. Or the week after. I'm not sure."

"Edmond Minter sent a script for you. It arrived yesterday. Get this—he wants you for the lead female in a big-budget action feature, starring opposite *Ryan Gray*. He said you're the only one he has in mind for the role."

"You're kidding!" Alice's heart leapt at the news, excitement washing over her. Edmond was a well-respected producer and director for whom Alice had worked twice before. And Ryan Gray was one of the hottest box-office draws in Hollywood—*white* box-office draws. To have a chance to work with him could take her career to an even higher level.

"I kid you not." Alice could hear the ear-to-ear smile in Connie's voice.

As quickly as it had come, the excitement fizzled.

How could she even consider the role when her mother was so sick? "I don't know when I'll have a chance to look at it."

"They're only in preproduction now, with plans to shoot in the fall or winter."

That was several months away. Her mother would be better by then.

"I don't have to tell you what a role like this could mean for your career."

"No, you don't."

"Where will you be staying?"

Again, Alice considered whether she should stay here at the Sheraton or at her mother's house. "I'm not sure yet."

"Let me know as soon as you've settled. I know you're dealing with a lot right now, but I can send you a copy of the script as soon as you're ready."

"Sure." Connie was a typical Hollywood agent—shrewd, but considerate at the same time. She'd give Alice some space now, but she didn't want her client to lose out on such a wonderful career opportunity.

"Look, Connie. About Sebastian—"

"Don't worry about it. He's lucky we don't slap his ass with a harassment suit."

"Thanks." Walking off the set meant Alice had forfeited her pay, and right now, she had no desire to fight for it on the grounds that Sebastian was a sexist pig. Connie could be more upset, but she was no doubt seeing dollar signs with the Edmond Minter offer.

"Call me as soon as you're settled."

"I will."

Alice hung up, closed her eyes, and dropped her head forward. So much to think about. Too much.

But right now, she had to get back to the hospital. She couldn't put off seeing her mother forever.

Rosa Watson was out of surgery and sleeping in ICU when Alice returned to the hospital a few hours later. Marie sat in a chair by her side, holding one of her hands and talking softly to her. Alice couldn't hear what she was saying. When Alice stepped further into the room, Marie noticed her and quickly rose.

"I'm glad you're here."

"What is it?" Panic spread through her body, like flames burning her flesh. "What's wrong?"

"Nothing," Marie quickly clarified, realizing Alice had misread her statement. "The doctor said the surgery was a success, but Mama will probably sleep through the night. She's definitely gonna need to take it easy for the next several weeks, as well as take all kinds of medication. But you know Mama. She'll probably fight us on this all the way."

No, Alice thought, *I didn't know Mama. Not really.* Thirteen years had passed since they'd last spoken. What did she know of her anymore? What had she ever known about her?

"Anyway, I don't want to leave her, but it's almost three and I have to pick up Mia. I already called the school and she's gonna wait for me. So will you stay with Mama?"

"Are you coming back?"

"I couldn't reach Chad, and right now, I don't think there's any point in bringing Mia here yet. That's why I want you to stay. I know visiting hours are limited in ICU, which means you'll have to spend a lot of time in the waiting room, but it's comfortable—"

"You want me to stay the night?" Alice asked, surprised.

"I think one of us should. In case something happens."

Alice's gaze rested on her mother, who was sleeping. She certainly couldn't hurt her in this state. And Marie was right; if their mother took a turn for the worst, one of them should be by her side.

"All right . . . I'll stay."

"And if Mama wakes up, at least one of us will be here."

"Marie, do you think she'll want to see me?"

"She's your mother," was all Marie said.

Alice settled in the chair beside her mother's bed after Marie left. The years hadn't been good to her mother. Her narrow face was drawn, old. Her black hair had thinned and was now filled with several gray strands. She looked nothing like the headstrong matriarch of the Watson family who had told Alice to leave and never return that June day almost thirteen years ago.

Sitting here, watching the rise and fall of her mother's chest, listening to the constant beep of the heart monitor, didn't seem real. Alice's mind kept imagining this as a scene in a movie, where her mother would wake up, see her and immediately try to make amends for all that had gone wrong in their relationship. But this wasn't a movie. In reality, Alice held no delusions that the scene would be anything like that when her mother finally woke up.

Though she'd once told herself to harden her heart, to forget that her mother didn't love her, or at least didn't love her enough, a part of her heart ached as she regarded her mother now. The part that wished they could have had a normal, loving mother-daughter relationship. The part of her that was still a dreamer and still believed in happy endings, even though a happy ending had eluded her in her own life.

As far back as Alice could remember, her mother had been cold and distant toward her. Mostly, Rosa hadn't seemed to understand nor have patience for Alice's numerous questions that stemmed from her endless curiosity. Questions like "Mama, what if when we dream, we're really visiting different places? I mean, *really*?" Her mother would roll her eyes and ignore her or tell her that she was too much of a dreamer, like being a dreamer was the worst thing in the world. Which, in turn, left Alice feeling like something was wrong with her. But those questions were so much a part of her, and over the years, Alice had realized that if her mother shunned her curious nature, she was shunning her. Her questions had fueled her creative mind, which had fueled her dream to be an actress, a dream her mother had balked at from the first moment Alice had told her that's what she wanted to do, when she was merely eight years old.

Alice extended her hand, let it hover over her mother's for several seconds, then finally returned it to her side. The ache to touch her mother surprised her, especially considering the last conversation they had ever had . . .

"Because you *had* to take those acting classes, your father is dead. Now you're going to abandon me. I hope you're happy."

Anger washed over Alice. Implicitly blaming her for her father's death was the final straw. Now more than ever she knew she had to get away. Her mother didn't understand her, didn't love her. For a while, Alice had blamed herself for her father's death as well, but that was because her mother had drummed that blame into her head with endless talk of how her father could have survived his heart attack if he hadn't gotten into a car wreck. Now, Alice knew better. It wasn't her fault that her father had had a heart attack while en route to pick her up from her acting class.

"I'm going, Mama. It's all arranged."

"Is that so? Where will you stay?"

"Aunt Sara said I could stay with her."

"My God." Surprise flashed in Rosa's eyes, and maybe even a hint of pain. "You're gonna stay with her?"

Alice knew that her mother hated her sister-in-law, but she couldn't understand why. But it wasn't only Aunt Sara she had a problem with; when Uncle Winston was alive, her husband's brother, she'd never seemed to like him, either. Whenever Uncle Winston and Aunt Sara had come to visit from Los Angeles, Rosa had always been cold toward them. If everyone was in the living room, Rosa was in the kitchen. When they all sat together for dinner, Rosa barely looked at Uncle Winston and Aunt Sara, let alone said more than two words to them. And when Uncle Winston spoke about his various roles in films and commercials, Rosa never said a word, but Alice could tell by her eyes and body language that she was angry.

Was that where Rosa's animosity toward Aunt

Sara stemmed from? Because Aunt Sara had supported Uncle Winston's career in Hollywood? And if so, why did her mother think that acting was the worst career in the world?

"Yes, I'm staying with Aunt Sara. She's happy I'm going for my dream and said she'd welcome me with open arms."

Alice had hoped her last comment would draw a reaction from her mother—guilt, pain, something—but she remained as cold and unfeeling as ever. Instead, she said, "If you leave this house and go to L.A., Alice, don't come back. You hear me? I'm wiping my hands of you."

Alice fought with all her might not to cry. She had to be strong, accept the fact that her mother didn't love her and get on with her life.

Even if it was the hardest thing she'd ever have to do.

"Mama—"

"I'm serious, Alice."

With that, her mother turned and stalked out of Alice's bedroom. And at that moment, Alice knew there was no point in staying in Chicago and trying to win her mother's love and support. It would never happen. That night, she packed her bags. The next day, she would leave Chicago, never to return.

Not even Marie offered any sympathy after Alice told her what happened. Instead, she said, "I don't know what happened to you. Maybe Dad's death made you crazy."

"I'm leaving, Marie. Are you gonna say good-bye or not?"

Marie frowned as she stepped toward Alice in the

foyer. She gave her sister a brief, stilted hug. "I hope what you're looking for is worth what you're doing to this family."

Then Alice left, determined to prove to them that she could make her dream come true . . .

Alice's mind drifted back to the present, where she found she was squeezing her eyes closed so tightly her head hurt.

But not even physical pain could erase the painful memories of the past.

Alice was in a state between full consciousness and total sleep, her body powerless to move while her mind was active.

She recognized immediately that she was dreaming, yet she couldn't pull herself out of it. It was a dream she had had several times over the past thirteen years. In the dream, she was sitting cross-legged in a garden, surrounded by thousands of different flowers in a dazzling array of colors. It was a gorgeous day, so the fact that she was crying always startled her at first. Then, out of nowhere, her mother appeared and walked toward her, extending a hand. And she said, "Alice, I love you. I've always loved you."

The voice in her dream sounded so real that it jolted Alice awake. For a moment, the bright sunlight streaming through the window blinded her and she didn't recognize her surroundings. Where was she? The next instant, her eyes flew to the right as she remembered she was in the hospital.

To her surprise, she found her arm stretched across the side of her mother's bed, her hand clutched in her mother's. Alice sat upright, realizing this wasn't a dream.

Her back ached from sleeping on the chair in the waiting room most of the night, then in this one beside her mother's bed. A blanket lay bunched up around her waist. She had a vague memory of a nurse bringing it to her last night in the waiting room, yet didn't remember carrying it into her mother's room less than an hour ago.

Careful not to wake her, Alice freed her hand from her mother's. Rosa stirred, moaned softly, then settled back into sleep. Alice watched her for several minutes, making sure she rested peacefully. Finally, she walked to the door and exited the room. Outside, she dropped her head and began massaging her neck as she walked toward the nurses' station.

"Morning."

Instantly, Alice's head whipped up, her stomach fluttering. "Marcus," she said, hating how breathless she sounded. "What are you doing here?"

He smiled. In one hand, he held a bouquet of purple tulips. In the other, he held a large Starbucks coffee cup.

"I figured I should drop these off for your mother."

Her eyes roamed over his body as he moved away from the nurses' station and strolled toward her. He wore black jeans and a black turtleneck, which showcased his incredible physique to perfection. He'd become more muscular over the years. His chest was broad, his biceps huge. No doubt his powerful body was a result of his rigorous training as a police officer. As he stared at her with his dark eyes, she stared right back, memorizing the face she hadn't seen in years. His lips were still sensuous and full. His eyes still had the power to pierce her skin and make her flush. But his hair was different; he wore it so short now that he was almost bald. A trim goatee framed those damn full lips. Lord, why did her gaze keep coming back to his lips?

"How's she doing?" As Marcus handed her the flowers, Alice got a whiff of his musky cologne. The scent woke her up. She realized she was staring and immediately jerked her gaze away.

"As far as I know, she's been asleep since the surgery." Had Rosa awakened and taken her hand, or had that simply been a reflex action? "The surgery was successful."

"I'm glad to hear it." Marcus gave her a quick once-over, noting she wore a pair of fashionable high-heeled boots that probably cost as much as his week's salary. He passed her the Starbucks cup. "This is for you."

She looked at the cup he held before her. "Coffee?"

"I didn't know how you take it, so it's black, but I've got creamers and sugar in my pocket."

"Oh, there is a God." Cradling the flowers in one arm, she accepted the cup. She closed her eyes and inhaled the heavenly aroma. "Thanks."

"No problem. Cream and sugar?"

"No thanks. I just want the caffeine." She took a sip. "You didn't have to come."

"I know." He'd been certain he would find her here. And while he'd told himself not to come, that he should simply stay away from Alice, he had somehow gotten into his car this Saturday morning and driven here in search of her. Yes, he had wanted to check on Rosa because he'd known her for years. But something in his heart made him come here for Alice, because he knew that seeing her mother would be hard on her and he still felt the need to protect her. Old habits died hard.

"Well, thanks."

"No problem," Marcus said.

Silence fell between them, then Marcus asked, "How are *you*?"

Alice understood the question, and immediately felt thankful for Marcus's presence. How thoughtful of him to come here for her, the way he would have back in the day. Coming here would undoubtedly bring up sad memories over his own mother's death to cancer seventeen years ago, which made his trip that much more selfless. But that only made her feel more guilty for letting their friendship die over the years. "It's been strange, really. I'm not even sure she will want to see me."

"I know it's got to be hard, but all I can say is hang in there."

"I'm trying." Her eyes met and held his. She shifted uncomfortably beneath the weight of his gaze. She spoke to break the tension. "I do appreciate this, Marcus."

"No problem." He paused, then said, "Look, I'm gonna get out of here. I just wanted to pop by and say hi."

"Wait," Alice said as Marcus turned. He stopped and faced her with a curious expression. "Your number." Alice gave him a tentative smile. She didn't like this wall between them and knew she had to do whatever possible to break it down. She appreciated him thinking about her, caring about how she must feel now, even though she'd more or less turned her back on him thirteen years ago. "Maybe you could give me a way to reach you—in case I need to talk."

"Oh." Marcus's eyes betrayed no emotion. "Sure."

"Just let me get a pen."

Alice went to the nearby nurse's station, placing the flowers and coffee on top. Snagging a pen and paper, she turned around, took a step, and nearly collided with Marcus. She didn't realize he'd followed her.

"Sorry," they both said at the same time.

"Here," Alice said after a moment. She didn't meet his eyes as she handed him the pen and paper. Time and distance had made them polite strangers.

He jotted down his number and passed the pen and paper back to her.

"Who knows, I may call on you to do your civic duty sooner than you think." He merely shrugged, and Alice realized that he wasn't buying into her attempt at humor. She stuffed the number in her pocket. "Thanks, Marcus."

He turned and took a few steps, then stopped and faced her again. His gaze roamed over her body, taking in the changes. Her legs were slim beneath flowing black pants. Her waist was tiny, but at least her hips were full. He hated that anorexic-waif look where women didn't even have a figure. Alice definitely had one. She looked good.

Yes, she had changed, and if it was just physical, it wouldn't bother him. But her character had changed as well. She truly wasn't Alice Watson anymore. She was Desirée LaCroix, Hollywood diva.

"How long do you plan on staying in town?" he asked.

"I'm not sure yet. Apparently my mother will need help for the next several weeks. But I've got a couple of film roles I'm considering . . . God, that must sound shallow. I just mean that if my mother gets better sooner than we expect . . ." She let her statement hang in the air.

"I hear you," Marcus said, though he didn't believe her. Why wouldn't she run back to Hollywood as soon as she could? Her own words indicated that her career was more important than being here for her mother.

Not that he didn't understand how hard coming back was for her. But deep down, he knew there was nothing keeping her here in Chicago. "Well, if you feel like calling me before you take off, you know where to reach me."

His tone said he expected her to head off in the next day or two. Certainly, that was tempting, but she couldn't. Not yet. She was here, and she'd deal with her mother. Come what may.

He turned to leave again and she realized with surprise that she didn't want him to go. Maybe it wasn't fair to ask him to stay, but she suddenly craved his comfort. She craved a gentle squeeze of his hand or the soft smile he used to give her so many years ago. So, as he reached for the handle, she asked, "How's your father?"

Marcus paused then faced her again. "Fine." Until she'd asked the question, Marcus hadn't realized how much he wanted to stay and chat with her.

Like he'd done so often in the past. After Alice had left, he hadn't had another friend quite like her with whom he could share his feelings and concerns. In high school, she had understood his pain over losing his mother to cancer because she'd lost her father. They'd formed a connection he thought would never break.

But it had, and right now, it wasn't only the several feet of ceramic floor stretching between them. "Dad's retired and living in Florida now. Tampa."

"And your sister?"

"Janice is in St. Louis. Fell head over heels in love with some football player from Canada she met at a wedding. I've never seen anyone pack up and move out of here so fast."

"You're kidding!" The thought of Marcus's younger sister, who'd always had her head in the books, falling in love with a jock made Alice smile. Being a dreamer, she was a romantic at heart and loved to hear stories of instant love between seeming opposites. Besides, such stories always made her believe that dreams could actually come true in real life, not just in the movies.

"Nope. They've been married for seven years now and have two children. Every time I talk to her, she sounds like she's on cloud nine."

"That's nice."

Hearing footsteps, Marcus glanced over his shoulder. Marie and Mia walked toward them. "Hello, Marie. Hey, Mia!"

Mia threw her arms around his waist and hugged him.

Alice's mind spun with so many questions she couldn't find a voice. Hadn't Marcus said that he'd lived in the north end for the past ten years and that he worked downtown? So how did he know Mia?

"Marcus, what are you doing here?" Marie glanced between Marcus and Alice.

"I heard your mother had a heart attack. I just came by to see how she's doing."

"Aunt Alice!" Mia broke away from Marcus and ran toward her. Alice scooped her niece into her arms and hugged her warmly.

Thank heaven for Mia, pulling her back to the present, to the shore where she could hold on to her sanity. Alice kissed her cheek.

"Hey, sweetheart. It's so good to see you." Though they spoke on the phone several times a year, the last time she had seen her was three years ago when Mia was seven. Marie had surprised her by allowing Mia to come to Los Angeles and spend a week with her.

"I missed you a lot, Aunt Alice."

"I missed you too, sweetheart," Alice said. And she did. Right now, it felt so good to hold her in her arms.

Alice gave her niece another squeeze, then patted her bottom. Mia dropped to the ground.

"How's Grandma?" Mia asked.

It was a simple question, yet it made Alice wonder what type of relationship Mia and her mother had. Did Rosa love her grandchild unconditionally, the way she'd loved Marie? The thought caused a lump of emotion to form in Alice's throat, so she forced it from her mind.

"She's doing well, Mia. But she's still sleeping."

"I'm gonna go see her."

"Okay."

Mia gave Alice and Marcus a warm smile before heading toward Rosa's room with Marie.

"You two know each other?" Alice asked glancing at Marcus, then at Mia's back.

"I help out at the Bartlett Theater House where Mia takes acting classes. Just a little volunteer work from time to time," Marcus explained.

Surprise, surprise. So he'd left the neighborhood but he still had ties there.

He glanced at his watch. "Listen, I have to go, but I'll see you later." His gaze swept over her again, leaving her feeling breathless.

Then Marcus was gone.

Three

"Mama?" There was excitement in Marie's voice and Alice immediately hopped off the window ledge. Was her mother finally awake? She started for the bed, then paused, fear gripping her. What if her mother didn't want to see her?

"Hey, Mama," Marie said. "You're gonna be all right, you hear? You're gonna be just fine."

"Aunt Alice is here," Mia announced proudly.

A shudder passed over her as one, then two, then three full seconds went by. Her mother hadn't responded to Mia's announcement. Oh God, her deepest fears were true. She *had* made a mistake coming here.

"Alice?"

The voice was weak, but it was Rosa's. Alice didn't move.

Marie whirled to face Alice with a firm stare. "Alice."

Alice found the strength to put one foot in front of the other until she was at her mother's bedside. But she couldn't summon a smile right now even if her life depended on it. It took all her power to swallow the nervousness rising in her throat.

"Is it really you?"

"Yes, Ma—Mother." *Mother* seemed less personal somehow than *Mama*. "It's me."

Rosa's head moved ever so slightly to the left. "Come closer. Let me look at you."

Alice made her way to the side of the bed. Her mother gazed up at her as she lifted a hand to her face. "Were you here with me last night?"

"Mmm-hmm."

"I thought I was dreaming." Rosa ran a hand over her face, and Alice remembered a time in the long-ago past that had been filled with warmth, when she'd been a little girl, no more than five or six—before she'd started to gain extra weight, and before she'd expressed an interest in acting. Then, Alice had truly believed that she'd had her mother's love just as much as Marie had. "I've missed you."

Her mother's confession broke the dam of emotion within Alice, and she realized just how much she had missed her mother over the years. She didn't miss the bad times, but she did miss the few good times they'd had when she'd been a young child. Maybe from now on they would have only good times. If one could will that to happen . . . Alice took her mother's hand in hers. "I missed you too, Mother. How are you feeling?"

"Just tired, but I've been used to tired in my life. I can handle this."

"Promise me you'll take it easy." She may not

have had the best relationship with her, but Rosa Lynn Watson was the only mother she had, and Alice didn't want to lose her.

"I guess it took something like this to bring you home."

Alice couldn't deny the truth, so she didn't even bother to try. "Yes."

Rosa's hand fell onto her stomach and she closed her eyes. "Well."

Well what? Well, at least she was here? Well, she shouldn't have bothered coming? Alice searched her mother's face for answers, but found none. She had the feeling she'd just been dismissed.

Hurt, Alice stepped away from the bed. "I need to take a shower. Get something to eat. Maybe even sleep."

"Of course. Go on back to the house," Marie told her. "I'll stay with Mama."

The house. No one would be home now, yet she dreaded the thought of going there. If she went there now, she couldn't very well move to a hotel at a later date without it looking like she didn't want to be around her family. "Actually, I was thinking of just going to a hotel. Something close to the hospital. That might be easier."

Marie looked at Alice with disdain. "You're not planning to stay with us, are you?"

"I didn't say that."

"How are you going to help me with Mama if you're living in some fancy suite at the Ritz?"

Marie's mocking tone made it clear just what she thought of the idea. But it also made it clear to Alice what she thought of her life. The few times she'd spoken to her over the years, Marie had always made some snide comment about her money or her assets. Alice still didn't understand why her sister couldn't be happy for her.

Feeling the beginnings of a headache, Alice reached for her purse from the foot of the chair. She dug out the bottle of Advil she never left home without, unscrewed the cap, and shook the bottle until two pills fell into her palm. She popped the pills into her mouth and washed them down with saliva.

"I only meant that I could go to a hotel to shower and change. But forget it. I'll go to the house. Do you have the key?" Alice had long since thrown hers away.

"Mia, do you have your key handy?"

Mia dug a key chain out of her jeans pocket, skipped over to Alice, and handed her the single key. "Here, Aunt Alice."

"Thanks, sweetheart."

"We'll see you at home later," Marie said.

Home. The word gave Alice pause. She wasn't going home. The small house on London Street hadn't been a home to her in years.

Nearly thirteen years after the day she had left and vowed never to return, Alice Watson's life came full circle as she parked her car in the driveway of the small Chicago house where she had lived most of her childhood years.

Home, Marie had said.

She killed the engine and held on to the steering wheel as though it were a lifeline.

Home.

A mix of emotions washed over her as she sat in

her car, not yet ready to cross the threshold to the past. Being here she couldn't help remembering once again the last argument she'd had with her mother when she had told her that if she left her house to go to Hollywood, she should never return.

Alice closed her eyes to force the memory away. Her mother wasn't here; she wouldn't greet her with a pitiful look. It was just her and her memories.

Yet Alice didn't move.

Thirteen years. It seemed both like ancient history and only yesterday. Was that possible?

Alice took a deep breath, opened the car door, and got out.

Marie had been living in this house with their mother for the past few years, since her divorce from her high school sweetheart. How could Alice stay here with both of them? If she stayed in Chicago for any length of time, she'd be better off getting her own place. Given the history of tension among them, how could they all stay here together and keep the peace?

As Alice walked to the back of her sports car and opened the trunk, her mind drifted to her father. He had been the one bright spot in this house, in her life, always making her smile and laugh, making her believe that he could chase all the demons away. This house had never been the same after his death, as if it lacked the warmth of his heart and soul.

Alice lifted her small suitcase from the trunk, then closed it. Six weeks? There was so much she would have to do if she was going to stay even half that long, including getting some more clothes.

She felt weird going up to the house, like a

stranger, and she even glanced down both ends of the street to see if anyone was looking. *Silly,* she told herself, then climbed the stairs.

She dug the key out of her pocket and opened the door.

The house was still, almost eerily so. It was exactly the way she remembered, which she also found a little creepy. She almost expected her father to come hurrying down the stairs.

Alice swallowed. Not all of her time here had been bad. She did have some good memories, all of them before her father had died and when she'd been much younger.

She wished she could pass off her mother's indifference years ago as a mere inability to understand her and her dreams. But it was more than that. During the last few years she'd spent in this house, especially the years after her father had died and she'd become more determined to be an actress, Alice had come to realize that her mother no longer loved her.

Marie hadn't understood her, but she also hadn't tried. She'd been too concerned with Chad Greenley, the love of her life, and all her friends. Marie had been involved in almost every school activity, while Alice had been involved in none. Ultimately, Alice accepted the reality that her sister ignored her because she didn't fit in the way Marie did. She was an embarrassment to her, especially in public.

A loner, Alice had found happiness in movies and fairy tales. She remembered a game she used to play, and to her surprise, a smile spread over her face as she stepped inside the house. Her mother couldn't be bothered with all her questions in the

Do You Believe? game, but her father had always listened and answered thoughtfully.

One summer night as she and her father had sat on the porch steps, staring up at the dark sky, Alice had asked, "Daddy, do you believe it's true, what they say about wishing on a star? That your dreams will come true?"

Her father had looked down at her from big brown eyes, eyes that seemed to hold the answers to all the world's secrets. Then he'd given her a warm smile. She loved the way his salt-and-pepper beard moved when he talked and smiled. "Yes, sweetheart, I do."

"So they're magical?"

"I guess you could say that." He draped an arm over her shoulder. "All I know is that when I look at the stars, I feel peaceful. I feel like my parents are looking down on me, watching over me. I feel very close to them."

"You mean their spirits are up there?"

"Mmm-hmm."

"Wow." She looked up at the stars in wonder, imagining which ones represented the grandparents she hadn't gotten to know.

"The key is believing, sweetheart. Anything's possible, if you believe."

Alice had believed her father without question.

She would ask her mother questions like that as her mother braided her hair at night. "Mama, do you believe that when we go to sleep, the ceramic dolls and stuffed animals come to life?" At the time, Alice had recently seen *The Nutcracker Suite,* and had been fascinated by the play.

"Oh, Alice," her mother had replied. "I don't have time for that nonsense."

Alice had dropped the matter but had asked Marie the same question that night as they brushed their teeth in the bathroom.

"Why would you think something crazy like that?" Marie had asked her.

"I saw it, in a play. And it made me think . . ."

"You know what I believe?" Marie placed her toothbrush in the holder, then stared at Alice. "I believe Todd is in love with me. Isn't that cool?"

Alice didn't even know who Todd was, but that didn't matter. What mattered was that Marie had dismissed her, just like her mother had.

Now, Alice shook her head to toss the memories from her mind. Funny how some things never changed. And funny how much life changed you. Her secret dream that Marcus would fall in love with her never happened. And when she lost her father, she'd been so devastated she hadn't believed that any of her other dreams would ever come true, until one night she'd looked up at the sky and seen a star brighter than the rest. She'd remembered her father's words that night as they'd sat on the porch steps looking up at the starlit sky and she decided his spirit lived in that star, that he was telling her not to give up on her dreams because from wherever he was, he still had faith in her.

Alice had gone to Hollywood and made her dream of becoming an actress come true. She'd lost weight, blossomed into someone people would no longer laugh at, built a dream career. She'd ultimately come to learn that just like there was good and bad in life, some dreams would come true while others wouldn't.

Alice walked into the living room and sat on the

sofa. It squeaked slightly in protest. The happy memories of her father and pride in her success vanished as doubt over her current situation took hold of her heart.

What would happen now that she was back in this house? Would the dream she'd had for years that she could resolve her differences with her mother come true? Or would her time spent here turn into the biggest nightmare of her life?

And what will happen with Marcus? she suddenly wondered. Was there a chance they could rebuild their relationship and become friends again? Or had she killed their friendship when she'd left this house, and Chicago, thirteen years ago?

Four

Two weeks after surgery, Rosa was released from the hospital. Days after that, she continued to comply with the doctor's order of bed rest, though she complained and fussed as if lying still would kill her before any activity would.

"Humor us," Alice told her every time she protested the doctor's instructions.

"And all these pills can't be good for me."

Rosa kicked up the same fuss every time she needed to take her medication. In the beginning, Alice had told her how important it was to take the pills, but ultimately she had started to ignore her mother's complaints. Considering she didn't resist swallowing the pills, there was no point in verbally sparring.

Her mother alternated between being demanding and indifferent. There hadn't been another soft moment like the one in the hospital, when she'd told

Alice that she'd missed her. Instead, the wall between them seemed as insurmountable as it had years ago. Alice didn't know how to break the barrier between them, and she wasn't sure she wanted to make the effort for fear it would be a waste of time.

And yet another unfulfilled wish.

Alice and Marie took turns setting the bath for Rosa, preparing food for her, sitting with her while she slept. Alice made most of the low-fat, low-cholesterol meals because she'd been making them for years. Marie spent more time sitting. The arrangement was working out well so far.

This Saturday morning, Alice had stayed in bed longer than she'd planned because the past two weeks had finally caught up with her. If it wasn't for the fact that her belly started growling, she might have been tempted to sleep another few hours. Getting out of bed, she stretched, slipped on a robe, then made her way downstairs.

"Aunt Alice, is that you?"

Mia's cheerful voice always filled Alice with warmth. She hadn't seen much of her all week because of school, so she was looking forward to spending this weekend with her. As Alice stepped from the landing into the foyer, Mia flashed her a bright smile from the kitchen table at the back of the house.

"Hey there, sweetie," Alice said. "Morning, Marie."

"It's almost afternoon," Marie told her. She stood over the stove making a grilled cheese sandwich.

"I know." Alice sank into the chair beside Mia. "I was extra tired this morning."

"Can I fix you something, Alice?"

"I'm gonna have coffee to start."

"No wonder you're so thin. Skipping breakfast can't be good for you."

Alice chose to ignore Marie's comment. She *did* eat. Just not the moment she woke up.

"Aunt Alice, are you going back to Hollywood soon?"

"Mia," Marie said, her voice stern. "What did I tell you?"

Alice glanced at Marie, then back at Mia. She understood immediately that something was going on, yet she had no clue what it could be. "No, Mia. I'm not going back to Hollywood yet. Why do you ask?"

Mia's eyes dropped to the table. "I just wondered."

"Are you sure there's nothing else?" Alice asked her, sensing that there was.

Marie placed the plate with the grilled cheese sandwich on the table before her daughter. "Your aunt is not going to have time."

"Time for what?"

Disappointment shone in Mia's eyes as she faced Alice. "The acting coach at my theater quit last week. I was hoping . . . maybe you could be the new acting teacher."

"Me?" Alice was flattered that Mia had thought of her.

"I told you she wouldn't be able to do it," Marie said with a dismissive shrug as she sat across from her daughter.

"Wait a second," Alice said to her sister. "I haven't even had a chance to think about it."

"We're doing a play in two months. I think you'd

be the best teacher in the world," Mia said, her voice trembling with excitement.

"Two months?" That was more time than she wanted to spend here, but Mia looked at her with such longing that it was hard to dismiss the idea. Helping out at the theater would definitely help keep her mind off her problems with her mother.

"Why don't you come to the theater with me today? Check it out. You can decide later."

"Wow. Today?"

"Mia, you heard your aunt."

"Please, Aunt Alice."

Alice hated to disappoint her niece. "I guess I can go with you to the theater."

Mia beamed then. "Oh, thank you! Everyone's gonna be so excited."

"I'm not making any promises."

Mia continued as if she didn't hear her. "They're thrilled that you're my aunt. Everyone thinks you're a great actress. Me, I loved you in that TV movie, *Hailey's Secret*. You even made me cry during that movie. It was like you weren't really my aunt, but really Hailey."

Mia's honest praise made Alice's heart soar. "That's my favorite of all the parts I've played." And the one that had launched her career. Playing a woman whose obsession with having a baby had ruined her marriage had garnered her rave reviews.

"I want to be an actress so badly." Mia threw a quick glance at her mother. Marie sat with her face resting in her palm, her lips pressed tightly together.

"I know."

"Mom doesn't like that idea, but I don't see what's wrong with it."

"You seem to have a good head on your shoulders, so I'm sure you'll do all right."

"Mom didn't even want me to take acting lessons, but Dad let me."

Marie humphed. "That man would say the sky was pink just to argue with me."

Thirteen years ago, Marie could only sing Chad's praises. Alice wondered what had gone wrong in their marriage. Marie had never told her. "What time is your class today?"

"One o'clock. I better call Dad and tell him not to pick me up. I can't wait to ride in the BMW!"

Mia flew from the kitchen table and disappeared in the living room.

"I hope you know what you're doing," Marie said when she heard Mia speaking to her father.

"I'm simply taking my niece to her acting class."

"I hope so," Marie said, but her tone was doubtful.

Mia returned. "It's all set. You can take me to class."

"Then I'd better get ready," Alice said, rising. She felt Marie's eyes boring into her as she casually walked out of the kitchen, heading for the stairs.

"Come on, Aunt Alice," Mia said excitedly as she jumped out of the BMW.

Alice sat for a moment before opening her car door. It was the same theater her father had taken her to years earlier, the Bartlett Community Theater, a theater owned by and for black folk. Alice felt a moment of fondness at the memory. It seemed fitting that Mia should go here too.

There was so much about Mia that Alice recognized in herself. The drive to be an actress at that young an age, and not simply because it was a cool thing to do. Alice could see it in Mia's eyes—her niece's passion stemmed from her soul.

Mia was already at the front doors when Alice stepped out of the car. She waved her over. A smile touched Alice's lips. She knew her niece wanted to 'show her off', and it was a nice feeling. At least someone in her family was happy for her success.

Alice joined Mia at the theater's entrance. Placing her hand on Mia's shoulder, she opened the door and led her inside. It was dark at the back of the theater, but lights illuminated the stage up front. Parents and children milled around the stage chatting.

Mia took Alice's hand and tugged on it, hurrying her down the aisle. "Hey, guys," she announced.

Everyone turned, but given the lighting it would be hard to recognize her and Mia. As Mia hustled forward with Alice and they came into the light, an excited buzz emanated from the crowd.

"Hey, it's Desirée LaCroix!" one boy said.

Children swarmed Alice and Mia.

"I told you she was my aunt," Mia told the other children, leading Alice to believe she'd tried to convince them of this fact before.

"Hi, guys." Alice hugged the children who wanted to get close, smiled at the others who looked at her from wide eyes. She was so absorbed in greeting them that she hadn't noticed the parents. So when she looked up and met a woman's eyes, a shock passed through her body.

"I don't believe it."

"Carmen Keller," Alice said. Carmen was an old classmate. They'd been in the same drama class at school for two years. Never in that time had Carmen said two kind words to her. She had, however, said plenty of awful things.

"Wow. I can't believe you're here."

"Just bringing my niece to her acting class."

"My son, Jeremy, is taking classes here. I never did bother pursuing acting, but I've followed your career. Very impressive."

"Thanks." Having no desire to make polite conversation with a woman who had never been her friend, Alice turned. And saw Terry Wright. God, not Terry. Terry had been downright cruel, picking on her whenever he saw her. He and Willie Thompson had been two of her worst nightmares.

"Hello," he said, offering her a smile that didn't quite reach his eyes. "Desirée LaCroix."

"Alice Watson," she replied tightly. She didn't know why it was important, but she wanted him—and Carmen—to know that they were looking at the same Alice they had treated as less than human when they were in school.

"Nice to see you again," he told her.

Alice bit her tongue and offered him a tight smile.

"We're all so proud of you," Carmen said.

There were others. Stacy. Melody. Scott. Not all of them had been mean to her, but none had been her friends. Now, they were all smiling and eager to talk to her.

Mia returned to her after making the rounds with her friends. "What's happening?" Alice asked her.

"Nothing. Our teacher didn't come, just like he said he wouldn't."

"Oh." Alice felt a sinking sensation in her gut,

feeling unspoken pressure to fill in where the teacher had left off.

"Why don't I take you to meet the director of the theater?" Mia asked.

"I don't know, Mia."

"Maybe you can just be our teacher until she finds someone new. Please? You'll be great."

"Okay, I'll talk to her. But she may not want me."

"Who wouldn't want you?" Mia asked. She took Alice's arm. "Come on."

Mia led Alice through the crowd of children and parents toward the right of the stage. Before they could round the corner into the semidarkness, a figure appeared out of the shadows. The person took a couple more steps toward the light, then stopped dead in her tracks.

And Alice's stomach dropped to her knees.

Tanisha Barrett, her old nemesis, stood two feet in front of her.

"Hi, Tanisha," Mia said. "Aunt Alice, this is Tanisha, the theater's director."

No, not Tanisha. Anyone but Tanisha.

"If it isn't Desirée LaCroix," Tanisha chimed, her tone sarcastically sweet.

"Tanisha."

Tension filled the air between them, but thankfully, Mia didn't notice. "Tanisha, is there a new teacher yet?"

"Not yet, Mia. But I'm working on it."

Hearing her niece address Tanisha so familiarly was strange. She'd done the same with Marcus at the hospital. When Alice had been young, she'd never have called an elder by his or her first name. But times had changed.

Yes, times had changed, and she was Alice Watson, successful actress, not the school joke. She squared her shoulders, determined to present the confident image she'd worked so hard to hone.

"My aunt's back in town and she'll be here for a while, so I was thinking maybe she could be our new teacher."

Tanisha chuckled, a hollow sound. "I can't imagine Desirée wanting to work here." Her eyes met Alice's. "A busy Hollywood actress like yourself."

Tanisha's voice held a note of jealousy, and Alice couldn't help it—a sense of power washed over her. Tanisha had always wanted to be an actress, but she had never quite been able to make it.

Alice had to agree with the saying—success *was* the best revenge.

"Actually, I'll be in town for a while," Alice told her. "I'd be happy to help out."

"Oh, that's right. A bit of trouble in paradise, hmm?"

"Excuse me?"

Tanisha ignored her. "I do appreciate your offer, Desirée, but I don't think that will be necessary. In fact . . . Oh, here he is now."

Alice turned, looking in the direction Tanisha's eyes went, and her heart instantly went into overdrive.

Marcus Quinn was hustling down the aisle.

Marcus was slightly out of breath after running from the parking lot into the theater. Tanisha had called him at the last minute and asked if he could help her out at the theater today. Why she had waited until the last minute to ask if he could teach the students he didn't know, but hadn't Tanisha always done things last minute? Marcus had never figured her out.

Marcus supposed it was his fault that she still felt she could turn to him. After he and Tanisha had split, he'd continued working at the theater because he really enjoyed working with the kids, despite his feelings for Tanisha. The theater meant a lot to him, and he knew funding was tight, so he didn't mind helping out when he could.

As he hurried down the aisle toward the stage, he saw Tanisha walking toward him. Then he noticed Alice and Mia right behind her.

The sight of Alice caused him to pause midstride. He hadn't expected to see her here. He hadn't expected to see her at all. He'd expected her to be on the first plane back to Hollywood now that her mother was back home.

Yet she was smiling at him from behind Tanisha, as though she was happy to see him.

He continued walking toward them.

Today she wore a long, pink dress imprinted with tiny blue flowers. It was a simple dress, but it hugged every curve of her body and made her look like a million bucks. She folded her arms beneath her breasts, and his eyes were immediately drawn to their full lusciousness. The next instant he glanced away, uncomfortable that he was seeing her in a way he never had years ago.

It was just that every time he saw her, he couldn't believe how much she'd changed.

Tanisha stepped in front of him. "Marcus, finally."

"I got here as quickly as I could."

"What's going on?" Behind Tanisha, Carmen spoke. "The children fooled around last week because there was no teacher, and you assured us he would be back this week."

"Yeah," another parent complained. "We're paying for these classes."

"The prices have gone up, yet what are we getting for the money?" Scott asked.

Tanisha held up her hands as the grumbling grew louder. "Please, everyone. If you'll just give me a chance to explain."

"I want my money back," a woman said from among the crowd.

"Please," Tanisha repeated, more firmly this time. "I apologize for the inconvenience. I've made every effort to resolve the situation with Mr. Thompson, but unfortunately, he won't be returning."

"*What?*" Angry murmurs erupted.

"But," Tanisha quickly interjected before the crowd got too loud. "I have a replacement teacher. Some of you already know him. Marcus Quinn."

Marcus narrowed his eyes as he shot an angry look at Tanisha, but she ignored him.

"Marcus?" Carmen asked. "How can he be the new teacher? He's got a full-time job."

"I enrolled my kid in this class because of the summer play," Stacy whined. "She deserves a qualified teacher."

"Uh . . . Well, actually, Marcus came today to help out. As you know, he's helped out with the classes before, so he's certainly qualified." More grumbling. "But I've also asked Desirée LaCroix if she'll be their new teacher. Since she's taking a break from Hollywood for the next several months."

Marcus turned to look at Alice in shock, as did everyone else. She seemed as surprised as he did at the announcement.

He took a few steps through the crowd until he was standing just feet from Alice and her niece. Was the diva really going to be here for the next several months?

"That would be great," Carmen said, relief flowing from her voice. "Someone with actual acting experience."

"A *lot* of experience," Melody agreed.

"Did she say yes?" another parent asked.

Tanisha moved through the crowd to stand at Alice's side. "I've asked Desirée to think about it, and she promised she'll give me an answer this week."

Alice's eyes widened as she threw a sideways glance at Tanisha. It was as he figured. Tanisha was lying to save her butt. He had to hand it to his exwife; the woman could lie with the best of them.

"I hope you'll do it," Melody said to Alice. "I've seen all your films. You do decent, wholesome roles. You're a good role model for children, and I think you'd be a great teacher."

"Yes, please," another woman urged her.

The room soon erupted with pleas like "Will you?" "Please do it," and "Come on" from the parents and children alike. Soon, the children were chanting "Desirée, Desirée," and giggling.

Alice met Marcus's eyes, as though seeking his approval. The gesture reminded him of their high school days when she had often asked his advice before making a decision. He wondered why she'd seek his advice now. Strangely, after all this time, he felt a surge of warmth that she would turn to him. But he didn't know what to advise and shrugged in response to her silent question.

"See, Aunt Alice," Mia said amidst the noise. "Everyone wants you to be our new teacher."

Tanisha placed an arm around Alice's shoulder and smiled brightly. Marcus was close enough to see Alice stiffen. He wondered if anyone else had noticed. Probably not.

He knew there was no love lost between Tanisha and Alice. In high school, Alice had told him on more than one occasion that Tanisha didn't like her, but he'd been so blindly in love with Tanisha that he'd always told Alice she was mistaken. After all, before they married, Tanisha had never said a bad word about his best friend. It was only after they'd been married for a while that Marcus had noticed Tanisha's animosity toward Alice. When he'd mention her name, wondering aloud why she hadn't been in touch with him, Tanisha always said something snarky like, "I don't know why you're friends with that loser anyway."

He gave Alice credit now. She smiled for the children and parents as though she and Tanisha had been the best of friends.

"As I said, Desirée is going to give me an answer in a few days." Tanisha turned to look at Alice. "But maybe she can help out today?"

There were more enthusiastic pleas and Alice finally spoke. "All right. Since I'm here, I don't mind helping out. Today."

As the room got loud with excited chatter from the children, Marcus wondered if anyone had heard her say "today." And he wondered if she would actually consider being the new teacher. Maybe the Alice he had known years ago would, but the star she had become? He couldn't see it. Why would she work for a theater that had been struggling to stay afloat for a few years now, when Hollywood could call at any time with a six- or seven-figure offer?

He'd have to see it to believe it.

Marcus watched her run a hand over Mia's hair in an intimate gesture. And suddenly he wondered what it would be like to have her hands on his body, caressing his face, his chest, his back.

Whoa, where had that thought come from?

As if Alice sensed he was staring at her, she looked up from Mia and met his eyes. The laugh she'd been sharing with Mia died on her lips. She gave him a startled look, almost as if she knew where his thoughts had ventured.

Uncomfortable, Marcus looked away, then clapped his hands together loudly, getting everyone's attention. "We've got a class to teach," he said. "Let's get started."

Two hours later, Alice said good-bye to the last parent and child, then watched as they slowly made their way up the aisle to the back of the theater and to the exit. Her shoulders sagged and she exhaled a slow, relaxing breath.

She couldn't believe how exhausting the afternoon had been! The children had been bundles of energy, and trying to control their excessive giggling and over-the-top acting as she'd led her group in an improvisation lesson had proved harder than she would have imagined.

The parents had also been a concern. She was used to working in front of a director and film crew, but teaching these children while their parents watched had been extremely unnerving. She'd worried that they might expect some type of spectacular acting instructions, simply because she was Desirée LaCroix.

She needn't have worried. Every single parent not only thanked her for her time, but praised her techniques. It made her feel what she never had in high school: accepted.

"You're quite the star." Marcus spoke behind her at the same time that he placed his hands on her shoulders. Alice's head snapped up. Marcus had disappeared with Tanisha while she'd chatted with the last few parents and she hadn't heard him return.

"Oh." The feel of his hands on her shoulders, gently massaging, made her mind go blank. "Well, thanks."

Marcus worked his thumbs up the back of her neck while his fingers worked her shoulder blades. Just as she began to relax at his touch, he took his hands away from her shoulders. Alice heard him slap them against his thighs.

She grasped the back of her neck, still feeling the warmth of his hands there as she turned to face him.

His eyes roamed the length of her body, slowly, lingering a moment too long on the gentle swell of her breasts before returning to her face. A current of heat passed through her. Was she mistaken, or had Marcus just looked at her like . . . well, like he wanted her?

That was crazy.

He glanced toward the back of the theater, and Alice followed his gaze. Mia was returning from outside. "Get some rest," he said gruffly. "That's the best medicine for tension."

She didn't like this. One minute, he seemed like the old Marcus she had known in high school, wanting to talk to her or be near her. The next, he pulled away and shut down.

"There's something I want to ask you," he said after a moment. "I know that you came back here because your mother is sick, but is there something else going on?"

Alice frowned. "No. Why would you ask that?"

"Tanisha mentioned you'd be here for several months. I just wondered why."

"Oh. No, I didn't tell Tanisha that. I told her I'd be here till the summer."

He didn't respond. Instead, he stared at her as if she was a puzzle he was trying to figure out.

"Hey, guys. I'm locking up now." At the sound of Tanisha's voice, they both looked to her. She stood across from them at the beginning of the other aisle, dangling keys in one hand.

"Yes, of course." Alice was glad to escape Marcus's overwhelming presence. "Mia, you ready?"

Mia grabbed her backpack from a front-row seat and slipped it onto a shoulder. "Uh-huh."

Alice grabbed her purse, then placed an arm over Mia's shoulder as they walked to the exit. Marcus walked a few steps behind them, and she couldn't help wondering what was bothering him.

Forget it, she thought. She couldn't very well pretend she knew him anymore, and trying to read his mind would only make her crazy.

Tanisha held the back door open. She smiled at Mia, but didn't even acknowledge Alice.

"Thanks for coming today, Marcus," Tanisha said when Alice and Mia stepped outside. A surge of anger shot through Alice's veins at the realization that Tanisha hadn't even given her a token thank-you. Funny how she wasn't acting chummy-chummy with her when the audience was gone. But then she reminded herself that Tanisha had never liked her. Her actions now shouldn't be a surprise.

"Tanisha," Marcus said harshly.

"What?" Tanisha turned to lock the door.

Alice and Mia were down the theater steps when Marcus replied, "What's happening with Willie?"

Tanisha's back stiffened. "I fired him."

Marcus gave a brief nod. "I think it was great of Alice to stay and help out today. Don't you?"

Alice turned in time to see Tanisha roll her eyes. Realizing Alice saw her, she tried to mask her reaction with a fake smile. It didn't work.

"Yes," Tanisha replied reluctantly as she stared at Marcus. Her gaze went to Alice. "Desirée, I appreciate you helping out today."

"No problem," Alice said, casually placing a hand across Mia's shoulder. "As I said, I did this for my niece. You mentioned that you want me to consider teaching the class on a permanent basis?"

"Oh, well." Tanisha waved a hand in the air, dismissing the idea as she made her way down the steps. "I'm going to talk to Willie, see if he'll agree to some changes and come back."

Alice was slightly disappointed. Not so much because she wanted to be the new teacher, but because Tanisha was dismissing her the way she had done so many times in the past. After all this time, she didn't think anything Tanisha did could bother her anymore, but apparently she was wrong.

"Wait a minute," Marcus said, placing his hands on his hips. "You told all the parents today that Alice would be taking over the class."

"*Possibly* taking over the class," Tanisha clarified.

Marcus glanced at his watch. "What happened in the last two hours and ten minutes?"

Tanisha shot an anxious glance at Mia. "I just figured I should try and convince Willie first before I offer his job to someone else."

Marcus frowned, then walked down the front steps. He bent before Mia. "Hey, sweetheart. Do you mind waiting at the car while we adults talk a few things out?"

"Sure," Mia said.

Alice watched her stroll toward the BMW, then turned to face Marcus and Tanisha. Before she could speak, Marcus did.

"Just what kind of game are you playing, Tanisha?"

"It's all right, Marcus," Alice said. She was a big girl; she didn't need him fighting her battles.

"No, it's not okay. This is classic Tanisha. Lie when it benefits you—"

Tanisha looked wounded.

"Marcus, it really doesn't matter." Though the fact that he was standing up for her with *Tanisha* was almost worth the trip back to Chicago. At least he'd figured out her true colors.

"If you must know," Tanisha answered, "I have some concerns. About her *reputation*. It could hurt the theater."

"What the hell are you talking about?" Marcus asked angrily.

Alice shot him an exasperated look. If Tanisha didn't want her help, that was fine with her. She certainly wasn't going to beg the woman.

"*She* knows what I'm talking about," Tanisha said with a flip of her head in Alice's direction.

"I have no clue what you're talking about," Alice replied dryly.

"For goodness' sake, it's all over the papers."

"What papers?" Alice asked her, getting more confused by the second.

Tanisha finally looked at her. "*The Intellect*, Desirée. You're featured on the front cover."

Five

"Oh, my God." Alice groaned as she scanned the picture of herself on the front cover of one of the nation's biggest tabloid papers and the blurb beneath it. The picture was actually flattering; it had been taken at this year's Golden Globe Awards right after she'd received her award for best supporting actress in a dramatic series, and she looked stunning in a shimmering gold gown. But no one would remember that wonderful moment in her career, not when the caption below screamed: *Sex-Starved Desirée! Find out why this hot actress was fired from her latest film. More on page three.*

"This was the only one?" Alice asked.

Marcus nodded. "There was no mention of you in any of the other tabloids."

After leaving the theater, Marcus had insisted on following Alice to her house in his car to drop Mia off, then the two of them had gotten into his Mustang and driven to the nearest variety store. Marcus had gone inside and purchased the paper, then returned to her, a frown marring his handsome features as he dropped the paper onto her lap.

"For now," Alice said glumly. "If *The Intellect* has printed this story, it can't be long before the rest of the nation's tabloids report their version of it."

She seemed genuinely shocked and mortified by the story, but Marcus couldn't help wondering if the story was true. After all, she was an actress. She could easily be acting surprised now.

"You want to talk about it?" he asked. No matter the situation, he felt the old need to be there for her.

Alice rolled up the paper into a tube shape, effectively hiding the front cover. "Not really."

"Who's the guy in the picture with you?"

"Oh, him," Alice replied, wishing Marcus hadn't reminded her of that sour chapter in her life. "That's Noel Sanders."

"You were engaged to him, weren't you?"

As a celebrity, her private life had been public knowledge, so she shouldn't have been surprised that Marcus knew about her brief engagement, yet she was. She wondered if that meant he had followed her career. "*Was* is the key word. Talk about a lapse in judgment."

Marcus started the car and drove along the tree-lined street in silence, heading in a different direction than they'd come. Alice wondered where he was taking her and was about to ask until she saw the familiar old building in the distance.

She chuckled, a hint of fondness in the sound. "Maxi's is still there?"

"Yep."

He pulled up in front of the old building, which sat on the corner of the street. The yellow awning was still there, though the *x* in *Maxi's* was fading, making the sign look like it read Mavi's.

"There are a few more choices here," Marcus told her as his eyes met hers across the front seat. "No longer just doughnuts and coffee. They've got soup, salads, sandwiches. Frozen yogurt."

"Wow. This place *has* changed." It had been a junk-food junkie's haven years ago.

"It's Saturday, so it'll be quiet. The kids still hang out here during the week."

Marcus opened his door and got out of the car, and Alice did the same. They met at the front of the Mustang and he gently rested his hand on her back as he led her inside.

Alice couldn't shake the odd sensation at his touch.

Maybe it was simply the memories she couldn't shake. The fact that she and Marcus had once been close but she'd let time and distance come between them. Still, at this moment, it was like nothing had changed between them. He was bringing her to their old hangout to talk, just as he had so many years before.

"You want coffee, juice?"

"Frozen yogurt sounds nice," Alice told him. "Strawberry, if they have it."

Three elderly women sat at a table several feet away, so Alice seated herself at a table near the front door. She didn't want anyone getting a good look at her. Just in case.

Folding her hands in her lap, she looked out the window. Sitting here was like taking a step back in time. She could almost see the smoke as it lingered in the air, almost hear the chatter of a roomful of students. She glanced around the store and her gaze caught the NO SMOKING sign. So much for the vision of students puffing away on cigarettes. Indeed, times had changed at Maxi's.

It was right here at Maxi's that Alice had fallen in love with Marcus. They'd first started talking after her father had died. Every day for a full week after his death, Marcus had brought her here to talk about how she felt. He had held her hand as she talked and cried, had let her rest her head on his shoulder. He'd comforted her and assured her that he understood what she was going through because he'd lost his mother.

Unlike the kids who picked on her because of her weight, Marcus was never ashamed to be seen with her. He didn't mind when everyone saw her rest her head on his shoulder, knowing full well his jock friends could tease him for being such close friends with someone who wasn't part of the "in" crowd. And when she was with Marcus, other kids didn't bother her. It was like being with Marcus gave her a certain level of respect. When she was with him, everything about her life seemed perfect.

But it wasn't only the sad time after her father's death and how Marcus had been there for her then that she remembered now. She and Marcus had shared many laughs at Maxi's over a hot chocolate or a soda. He'd share with her all the crazy things his friends did for various girls' attention, or something funny that had happened in one of his classes. She'd shared with him her passion for acting. Not only had he understood her dream like her father had, he'd encouraged her to pursue it. Spending time at Maxi's after school had come to be the highlight of Alice's days.

Her old high school was a couple of blocks away, a place she had never cared to see again. Today she had seen a handful of her former classmates, people she'd never thought she would see again. People she didn't *want* to see again. But it hadn't been as bad as she would have expected. To her, she was the same old Alice, but to them, she was different—successful Desirée LaCroix—and for the first time, they had treated her like a person who had feelings.

"It's strawberry," Marcus told her as he appeared at the table and placed the clear plastic cup holding the pink frozen yogurt before her. He sat down with his own chocolate doughnut and cup of coffee.

"Great." Alice took in his firm stomach and broad shoulders. "I guess it's true what they say about cops and doughnuts."

"That's one stereotype I'm not going to deny." He smiled.

Nostalgia washed over Alice at the sight of that smile. How many times had she and Marcus sat in this place, maybe in these very same seats, talking about what was going on in their lives? How many times had one of his smiles made her feel so light she felt she could fly?

"It's been a long time, huh?" he said, reading her thoughts.

Alice swallowed a spoonful of the strawberry yogurt before answering. "Yes, it has."

"I thought I would have heard from you in the past two weeks."

"I know. I've been . . . preoccupied. With everything."

"Guess you don't have much time for your old friends, hmm?" He softened the comment with a playful grin, but Alice realized for the first time that he probably thought she felt she was too good for her old friends. Not that she'd had many here, but she certainly didn't feel that way about him or anyone else. Until now, she'd figured he was simply upset with her because she'd let time and distance come between them. "I meant to call, Marcus. Honestly. It's just that it's been weird adjusting to being back here."

He took another bite of his doughnut and sip of coffee without saying anything. Alice wondered if he believed her.

"What's with this story in *The Intellect*, Alice?"

Alice gave him a grim look. "You don't believe that story, do you?"

As much as Marcus wished he could tell her what she wanted to hear, he couldn't be entirely sure. She had changed over the years, and who knew what she'd done while in Hollywood? Back in high school, he never would have thought she'd disappear from his life, but that's exactly what she had done. He said, "The Alice I knew thirteen years ago wouldn't have done something like that."

"You think I've changed."

"You *have* changed." His eyes roamed over her face and body. "I'm not saying I believe the story. I guess what I'm saying is that if there's anything you want to tell me, I'm here to listen."

"You're not going to get a confession out of me, if that's what you think," Alice said defensively.

"I'm not expecting one." But he was prepared to deal with the reality that she might tell him something he didn't want to hear. Hell, maybe he *was* hoping for a confession about how the Hollywood scene had corrupted her—anything that would explain how she could so easily forget about him.

"I was beginning to wonder," she said.

"It's quite the story, Alice."

"Sebastian Charles is a liar and he'll be lucky if I don't slap him with a lawsuit," Alice snapped angrily.

"Were you working on a film with him?"

"Yes, but I didn't leave because I propositioned him for sex. Hell, I wasn't *fired*. I know that some people want to believe the worst about people in show business, but not everyone in Hollywood does drugs, or drinks too much, or sleeps their way to the top. I certainly didn't need to sleep with Sebastian to secure my job on that set. And God knows I wasn't obsessed with him." She met his eyes with a steady gaze.

The look she gave him said she desperately wanted him to believe her. "Is that what your mother thinks?"

Her gaze fell to the table. "I don't know what she thinks."

"It's been tough, hasn't it?"

"We're barely talking. I don't know why I'm surprised."

"So what happened on the set?"

"I was working on a feature in L.A. Oh, it was such a wonderful role. The kind of role people wait all their lives for. I was cast to play a doctor who discovers a breakthrough in medicine, a medicine that will save some lives, but most likely not my daughter's. Not in time, anyway. It's deep, it's meaty. It's every serious actor's dream." She paused. "When Marie called to tell me that my mother had had a heart attack, I knew I had to come home. I . . . I kept thinking about my father, how he was here one second, then gone the next. If I was going to have to say good-bye . . . I didn't want to miss my chance again."

As though it were yesterday, Marcus remembered Alice walking into their sophomore English class in early October, quietly crying. She'd sniffled throughout the entire class, and he'd found himself watching her from several rows away. She hadn't noticed. At the end of class, their teacher, Mrs. Gallagher, had asked someone to share their notes with Alice, yet all the students had walked out, ignoring her. Alice had folded her arms across her desk and buried her face.

Seeing her in pain had struck a chord with Marcus. Though they hadn't been friends up until that point, he couldn't help feeling angry that everyone had snubbed her. So he had approached her and offered to lend her his notes. She'd given him one of the warmest smiles anyone had ever given him, despite her tears, and he'd felt a stab of guilt that he hadn't made a point of befriending her before, other than the brief nod and smile or verbal hello he usually gave her.

He walked with her out of the class, and after a few moments of trying to compose herself, he'd asked her what was wrong. Alice had immediately told him about her father. That he had died suddenly of a heart attack the week before. How guilty she felt because he'd been driving to pick her up at the time, and had ended up in a car accident. When he'd told her not to blame herself, she'd confided in him that she *hadn't* blamed herself, not until her mother had told her that if it wasn't for her, her father would still be here. Her mother believed that if her father hadn't been driving while he'd had his heart attack, he would have had a chance of surviving.

Marcus had suggested that they go to the school cafeteria, where they'd spent the remainder of the afternoon talking. Their rapport had been instant and easy, and Marcus had felt comfortable telling her that he, too, had suffered tragedy in recent years—his mother had died of cancer the week before he'd started his freshman year. Her quick deterioration and death was something that still haunted him.

"You still miss your father, don't you?"

"Terribly."

Pain flickered in her eyes, and Marcus found himself wishing he could take away that pain, just as he had wished years before.

"Anyway," Alice continued. "After my sister called me, I asked the director, Sebastian Charles, for some time off. He made a big deal out of how there was so much money invested in the film, like it would be impossible to rework the shooting schedule. It happens all the time on film sets, and considering the circumstances, it wasn't an unreasonable request. Besides, I only wanted a few days. Max. When he finally agreed to give me the time off, he told me I first had to do something for him."

Marcus's heart pounded wildly from a sudden surge of anger. He could only imagine what the director had asked her to do—and it was just the kind of horror story Hollywood was famous for, if his instincts were right. "Tell me it's not what I think."

"It's worse." Alice sighed. "It got ugly, Marcus. Ugly enough for me to know I couldn't continue working on the film."

"Did he hurt you?" The extent of his anger surprised him. But if the man had hurt her, he didn't care if he was a Hollywood director, he'd go out to Los Angeles and pound the crap out of him.

Alice shook her head. "No. I didn't let him."

He settled back in his chair, realizing just how crazy his thought had been. That Alice had held her own didn't surprise him. While he'd often come to her aid when other students were picking on her, she had always put on a brave face for the world. But he knew how vulnerable she had truly been. Between fighting for her mother's love and trying to live in her sister's shadow, not to mention the jerks at school who always picked on her, her life had been a living hell.

"Sebastian seemed completely baffled that I turned him down. I did worse than that, actually," she said, a victorious smile spreading on her lips. "I . . . well, I kneed him in the groin and walked off the set."

"Ouch."

"I thought that was the end of it. I didn't care how great the role was, I wasn't about to step foot on that set again and work for that pig." Alice realized that her chest was heaving as she spoke, she was so livid. She drew in a deep breath to calm her nerves. "I guess this is his idea of payback."

"But to say you turned on him after he rejected your sexual advances?"

"I know we haven't been in touch over the years, but I assure you, Marcus, I'm the same Alice Watson I was when I left Chicago. Sebastian had to come up with some story to explain why I was no longer working on the film, and he did this when he knew I wouldn't be around to defend myself. To make everyone believe I ran away. To make it seem more credible."

"You did what was most important."

"God, Marcus. What if this is the beginning of the end of my career? Just a couple weeks ago, my agent told me another director wants me on a major feature in the fall. But now . . ."

Marcus felt entirely out of his element, talking to a successful actress about tabloid articles and future film projects. He knew nothing of that world. He was a beat cop whose job could hardly be classified as glamorous. "Your career means the world to you, doesn't it?"

"It did." Alice was surprised at her words. "It *does*. Oh, Marcus. I know this won't make sense. There are people who would kill to have my career, but I've been feeling restless for some time." She shrugged. "I don't know."

"But you've always loved acting."

"I still do. It's the Tinseltown BS I can live without. It's all about who you know. And as far as Sebastian's concerned, it's about who I didn't blow."

Alice paused, surprised by her bitterness. She hadn't meant to sound so crass, so sour. She did have happy memories of Hollywood. Winning the Golden Globe Award this year had been the high point of her career. She was proud of what she'd accomplished. She'd done well for herself and intended to continue doing well for herself. It was just this crazy story that had her in a funky mood. "Actually, I don't know why I'm even saying this. Maybe it's just being back here, dealing with my mother's health crisis. I really can't imagine a life outside of the film business."

"I'm sure you can't," Marcus said in a supercilious tone.

"It's my life, Marcus. I can only hope this tabloid trash doesn't affect my career in a negative way."

"I'm sure you can get some spin doctor to save the day. Besides, in the showbiz world, negative attention is often better than no attention, isn't it?" Wasn't that what these stars did when things didn't quite go their way? Hire spin doctors to turn all the facts around and have them looking sweet? Besides, so many actors had gotten themselves into ugly situations, yet their careers flourished almost *because* of their flaws. Especially the beautiful ones. They could get away with almost anything.

Alice was looking at him like she couldn't believe what he'd said. "You don't understand," she said after a moment.

"Hey, what do I know about caviar and ritzy parties and designer outfits? I'm just a cop."

There was no mistaking the sarcasm in his voice, and Alice finally understood the extent of his feelings—he was *angry* with her. And while part of her could understand his feelings, she didn't appreciate him ragging out on her, right here in their old hangout. "Marcus, if you have something to say, why don't you just say it?"

He stared at her long and hard. "Obviously your career means a lot to you."

"Too much?" Alice asked, cocking her head to the side in a feisty gesture.

"Hey, it's your life."

"Damn it, Marcus."

"Don't push this, Alice. I'm not sure you'll like what I have to say."

The bell above the entrance sounded as a teenage couple entered the shop. Alice watched them walk past their table and to a far corner, then turned back to Marcus. She blew out a ragged breath. She didn't want to fight with him. But she did want to hear what he was feeling. "Talk to me."

Marcus glanced through the window. "I'm sorry about Tanisha. How she used you today when it suited her."

A frown creased Alice's brow. Marcus was clearly avoiding the issue. "It's all right."

"No, it's not. I intend to talk to her."

"What good will that do?"

"It will let her know she can't treat you the way she did."

"You haven't changed, have you?"

"Meaning?"

"You were always so serious. Always seeming to carry the weight of the world on your shoulders. Marcus, you're not responsible for what everyone does." When he didn't say anything, she continued. "I can handle Tanisha."

"I'm sure there's nothing you can't handle, Desirée. A successful actress like you, you don't need anyone."

Alice raised an eyebrow. Her stage name on his lips sounded sour. "Now what's *that* supposed to mean?"

"Let's just say that not all change is good."

"And what does *that* mean?"

Marcus shrugged.

"Don't you dare judge me, Marcus. We haven't been friends for years. You don't know me anymore."

"Exactly," he said, meeting her eyes with a level stare. "And whose fault is that?"

His question stopped Alice cold. He was right, of course. The death of their friendship had been her fault. But coming to Maxi's now and talking the way they had years ago, she'd felt as though they'd made headway in terms of reestablishing their friendship. Clearly she was wrong.

As if in response to her frustration, he said, "You know, I never thought thirteen years would pass without even a phone call or letter from you."

Though Alice had wanted him to tell her what was wrong, she suddenly wasn't ready to deal with it. She swallowed a spoonful of the yogurt, stalling for time. What could she say that would seem reasonable? "I just . . . Trying to establish a career in Hollywood is very difficult. Between working to survive and auditioning, there wasn't much time for anything else."

"Hmm."

He wasn't buying it. She couldn't blame him. The explanation was lame. But the last thing she wanted to do was admit she'd been head over heels in love with him and absolutely crushed when he'd told her he was going to marry Tanisha.

"You ready?" he asked as he stuffed his napkin into the paper cup.

Alice scraped the sides of the plastic container

to capture the last bits of yogurt. She swallowed the last spoonful, but she was too concerned with the distance between her and Marcus to enjoy the taste.

"Yeah, I'm ready." She stood. She may as well head home.

At least there, she knew what to expect. Marcus was too unpredictable.

"I heard," Marie said as Alice walked into the house and sank onto the sofa in the living room.

"Evening to you, too."

Sitting with her legs curled up on the armchair, Marie shook her head with disdain. "God, Alice. A sex scandal? What's going on?"

"If you're asking whether or not the story is true, no, it's not."

"I don't like this. It's exactly this type of thing I want to spare Mia from. But you come back here with a snazzy car, fancy clothes, looking like a glamour queen—that's got to influence her."

The hint of envy in Marie's voice surprised Alice. Considering Marie put down Hollywood on almost all the occasions they'd talked in the past, it never occurred to her that her sister might be jealous of her success.

Alice said, "Mia has a mind of her own."

"I don't think you realize how much of an influence you have on her. I don't want her getting caught up in the amoral vacuum that we call Hollywood."

Alice raised one perfectly sculpted eyebrow as she regarded her sister. "*Hollywood* isn't bad, Marie.

There's good and bad in everything but it's the bad stuff that sells papers. I'll talk to Mia about the article, if you want. God knows you can't shelter children from this stuff."

"No. If she doesn't know about it, I don't want you to say anything. God, you'll defend that place till your dying day. You were always so obsessed with being in the spotlight."

"That's not true." Alice had never craved the spotlight, though that came with being a successful actress. She'd simply had a burning passion to act— as real to her as the need to breathe.

"Of course it's true."

This wasn't what Alice needed right now. Her day with Marcus had already ended on a sour note and she wanted merely to relax. Still, Marie's comment hurt. Like her mother, her sister had never supported her.

She felt the beginnings of a headache and reached into her purse for her bottle of Advil. "How's Mother?"

"Sleeping. A couple of the neighbors came by to see her, but I didn't want them staying too long. Mama seemed extra tired today."

"I'll check on her later. Where's Mia?"

"Her father picked her up. He'll have her until tomorrow."

Alice dry swallowed two pills, then stood. "I need a nap."

"Oh, I almost forgot." Marie jumped up from the armchair. "Something came for you via FedEx." She hustled through the dining room to the kitchen, then returned with a package and handed it to Alice. "It's from Los Angeles."

Alice looked at the package. The return address was from Connie Frum.

"Any idea what it is?" Marie asked.

She knew exactly what it was. "It's a script from my agent. Something she wants me to look over."

"For a part?"

"Yeah."

"Guess you'll be taking off to Hollywood again for your next big film and we won't hear from you for a few years." Gone was the envy, replaced by bitterness.

"I'm not going anywhere," Alice replied, unable to keep the annoyance from her voice. "At least not until Mom gets well."

With that, Alice slipped the script under her arm and headed upstairs to her room to read it.

Six

Alice awoke with a start, then bolted upright when she realized someone was knocking on her bedroom door. Glancing at the digital clock beside her bed, she saw that it was eleven minutes after ten. The daylight filling the room indicated it was morning, which meant Marie was at work at the dental office and Mia was at school.

Alice threw the covers off and darted to the door. "Mother!" she exclaimed when she opened it. "What are you doing out of bed?"

Her mother wore a scowl. "Someone had to answer the phone."

"There's a call for me?"

"Not anymore."

Alice wore a silk and lace nightie that reached her midthigh, and her mother took in the outfit with distaste.

Not bothering to go to her closet for a robe, Alice

placed her arm around her mother's waist to give her support. "Mother, you know you're not supposed to be out of bed."

"I wanted to talk to you," she said.

Slowly, Alice led her mother down the hallway to her bedroom. "You could have waited until I came to you."

"No, this couldn't wait."

Alice opened the bedroom door with her free hand and entered the room with her mother. Her mother might object to the bed rest, but even now she walked with more effort than was normal, and her breath came in quick gasps.

Alice noticed the bed was neatly made, and looking at her mother, she frowned. "You've barely been out of the hospital for two full weeks. The doctor said bed rest, Mother."

"I needed to get up and stretch my legs."

Alice released her so that she could turn down the bedspread. "Next time, wait for me. All right, get back in."

Sighing, Rosa sat on the bed's edge. Alice helped her put her feet under the covers. Then she propped up the pillows behind her mother's head so she could sit up comfortably.

"You don't have to pretend that you care."

Alice's hands stilled on the cover she was adjusting around her mother's hips. A painful lump instantly formed in her throat.

"Of course I care," she managed, though her voice was stilted.

"If you cared, you wouldn't have told Sara about my private business."

Alice's heart was pumping so hard from the myriad of emotions she tried to suppress—anger, disbelief, sadness, bitterness. She did a breathing exercise, one she often did before a performance, to subdue the unwanted feelings. "Aunt Sara called?"

"Yes, she called. And she knew about my heart attack. I don't see why you had to tell her."

"I didn't know it was a secret."

"That woman has never liked me, so I'd appreciate it if you would keep my private business from her in the future. Oh." Rosa's hand flew to her chest.

"Mother." Panic washed over Alice as she watched her mother's eyes squeeze shut. She placed her own hand over Rosa's. The contact felt foreign, bringing home to Alice once again the reality that she and her mother had never been close. It made her fear over her mother's health sharper, keener. What if they never got the chance to make things right between them?

"What do you need? Should I call the doctor?"

"No," Rosa replied. She blew out a weary breath and opened her eyes. "It was just a pain, but it's passed."

"Do you see why you're supposed to stay in bed? Have you taken your medicine?"

"Marie made sure I took it this morning."

"Can I get you anything?"

"Fruit."

"All right." As Alice went downstairs to the kitchen, her hands trembled. Seeing her mother in pain had scared her more than she'd expected. She whispered a silent prayer that she wasn't about to have a relapse.

Minutes later, she had a bowl of cantaloupe,

honeydew melon and apple pieces arranged. She brought it to her mother.

"Thank you," Rosa said softly.

A wave of sadness washed over Alice. It was hard to see her mother, who had always been so strong, weak and stuck in bed.

She couldn't risk upsetting her again. This stage of her recovery was critical, and Alice didn't want to do anything that might cause her more harm. She didn't know how her mother would react to the story in *The Intellect*, but she'd make sure she didn't tell her about it, and would swear Marie to secrecy on the subject as well.

She left her mother with the bowl of fruit and a novel, a romantic comedy she'd been reading, and went back to her bedroom. She would have to call Aunt Sara.

Aunt Sara had kept in touch with the family for years after Uncle Winston's death. She'd been a godsend for Alice in the beginning when she'd left home, providing her with a place to live and money to get by. She had also supported her unconditionally, something Alice had not gotten from her own mother. Aunt Sara's love had made leaving Chicago seem like the right thing.

For some reason, Rosa didn't like Aunt Sara. From the time Alice was a young child, she remembered her mother complaining when her father told her that Uncle Winston and Aunt Sara would be in town. Considering they saw them once a year at the most, Alice could never understand why her mother was so against seeing them. Her father would insist, but her mother couldn't hide her discomfort even for the few short hours her aunt and uncle visited.

That was just one more thing Alice didn't understand about her mother. From what she knew of Aunt Sara, she was a good, decent, and loving person who'd lost her husband too soon and had never remarried. She and Rosa had more in common than her mother thought.

Alice strolled to the bedroom window and peered outside. The sky was a bleak gray, yet across the street, May flowers sprouted from the ground in a few gardens. Her mother always used to enjoy planting flowers in the spring, but with her heart attack, she wouldn't be able to plant anything this year. Maybe Alice could pick out some impatiens and marigolds for her.

As soon as that thought came to her mind, Alice dismissed it. She wasn't here to play house and plant flowers and pretend to the world that all was okay. She was here to help her mother while she got well. Then she would go back to Los Angeles and continue with her life.

She looked to where the script from her agent lay on the small desk she'd used as a child. When she'd opened the package last night, she'd planned to skim through it, but from the first page she was hooked and she'd stayed up late reading it. It had taken her longer to get through it than she'd anticipated because she'd read, then stop, and imagine herself in the lead role of Tina playing opposite Ryan Gray, one of America's best-loved heartthrobs. It was a suspense thriller about a cop turned serial killer in Los Angeles. If she accepted the role, she and Ryan would play FBI agents who worked together to solve the crime. God, what this part could mean for her career.

The phone rang, interrupting her thoughts. "I'll

get it," she called out, hoping her mother wouldn't exert any effort to reach for the phone. It rang a second time as she made it to the hallway. Alice snatched up the receiver. "Hello?"

"Hello, Desirée."

"Who is this?"

"It's Tanisha Quinn."

Tanisha Quinn. Good Lord, was she still using Marcus's name?

And if she was, why should she care? It wasn't like she still had feelings for Marcus. She'd gotten over him years ago.

"I didn't expect to hear from you," Alice said.

"I've left several messages for Willie and haven't heard back from him, so I'm hoping you'll reconsider my offer that you teach the class."

"Really?" Alice shook her head with chagrin. One minute Tanisha wanted her, the next she didn't. Now she wanted her again. "What about my *reputation?*"

"Actually, I spoke with some of the parents, and they don't seem to mind at all if you take over the class—despite that nasty story. But you have to understand I'd be concerned."

Alice doubted Tanisha had spoken with anybody. Except perhaps Marcus. And she was more than tempted to say no. In fact, she would have, if it weren't for Mia.

"Look, I need someone, and if you're willing to do the job . . . You are, aren't you?"

Tanisha sounded almost desperate. "All right, Tanisha. I'll do it."

"Great. Can you come to the theater and see me today so we can talk details?"

"Sure. What time?"

"Say, in an hour?"

"All right."

An hour later, Alice pulled into the parking lot of the Bartlett Theater. She had made sure her mother was okay, then assured her she wouldn't be gone long.

There were two cars in the parking lot. The Sunbird belonged to Tanisha, she knew from the past Saturday. As she climbed out of her car, she wondered who owned the Honda.

It looked like it might rain any minute, but Alice still wore sunglasses. And a baseball cap. It was the best she could do to keep a low profile after that tabloid report.

Unlike Saturday, when she'd brought Mia here for her class, the theater was well lit when Alice stepped inside. Tanisha, however, was nowhere to be seen as she scanned the vast area. Alice took a few steps toward the left aisle, then remembered that Mia had led her to the right of the stage when she'd been bringing her to meet the director. When Alice had taken classes here years ago, the offices had been to the left of the stage while an off-limits storage area had been to the right. She hadn't noticed yesterday but obviously there had been renovations to the theater.

Crossing the back of the theater to the far right aisle, Alice made her way to the front in search of Tanisha. The back of her neck tingled with apprehension. It wasn't that she was afraid, but she had never dealt with Tanisha in a civil, one-on-one capacity, and the fact that she was about to spend some time alone with her now made her uneasy. She knew they'd never be friends.

When she got to the front of the theater, she saw double doors that led behind the stage, no doubt to the offices. She pushed her weight against one door and walked through. That's when she heard the voices. While she couldn't quite make out what they were saying, she could distinctly make out male and female voices. She moved closer.

"God, you are impossible," Tanisha said, frustrated. "This conversation is over."

"Why won't you listen to me?"

"I don't have time for this."

"You need me. You know you do."

"What I need is for you to leave."

"Damn you, Tanisha!"

Alice contemplated turning around and going back out the doors, and was about to do just that, when someone whizzed through the office door like an out-of-control freight train. Alice quickly flattened her back to the wall. Seeing her, the man stopped momentarily, clearly surprised.

Their eyes met.

Willie Thompson.

He was angry, no doubt about it, and after a brief pause, he continued on his way, stalking through the double doors into the main area of the theater. Then he was gone.

Alice stayed where she was, her back pressed against the wall. She wondered if he'd recognized her. Willie Thompson had always hated her. Marcus had come to her defense against Willie more times than she could remember.

What was he doing here? And what had he and Tanisha been arguing about?

Alice counted to five, then continued to the open

office door. Tanisha, who sat with her elbows propped on a cluttered desk, her face in her hands, didn't see her. Alice softly rapped on the door.

Tanisha's head whipped up, anger flashing in her eyes, followed by relief when she saw it was Alice. "Oh, Desirée. Come in, come in."

Alice stepped into the room. "Was that Willie I just saw?" she asked. She knew it was, but she merely wanted a conversation opener.

"Yes," Tanisha replied, punctuating the statement with a groan.

"He's not coming back, is he?"

Alarm flashed in Tanisha's eyes. "You heard us?"

"No, not really," Alice quickly said. "I didn't hear what you were saying. But I did hear loud voices."

Tanisha's shoulders sagged, as though a burden had been lifted. "No, he's not coming back. I don't even know why he bothered coming here today." Sighing, she lifted some papers from a spot on the desk and added them to an already massive pile. "Please, have a seat."

Alice sat in the black chair across the desk from Tanisha. It was well worn, with a tear through the fabric of the seat, revealing the yellow foam beneath.

"All right," Tanisha said as she straightened a pile of folders. "What can I tell you about this job? Well, as you know, you'll be teaching children. They range in age from nine to thirteen. We used to offer a class as well for older students, but we didn't get enough enrolled in the last couple years to continue with that. Maybe we will in the future, but for now, the older kids seem more interested in video games, computers, and school sports.

"Anyway, each child in the class pays a nominal fee. A hundred and fifty for a session, which is spring and summer. A total of ten weeks."

Alice remembered. It had been the same when she'd taken classes at the theater, except that all those years ago the fee had been fifty dollars.

"We try to keep the costs low with sponsorship so more children in the community can benefit from the theater, but I have to tell you, we haven't been very successful in getting major sponsorship in the last few years."

"Why not?"

"I don't know." She folded her arms across the desk and stared at Alice. "In the spring, the children meet here once weekly for ninety minutes and learn different aspects of acting. They do monologues, improvisation, role playing. Stuff like that. Once school is out, they have classes three times a week in preparation of the summer play. God, not even that's picked out yet."

"You don't know what play you're doing?"

"Willie was in charge of all that, but he left us high and dry."

"I see."

"I have some ideas. Maybe I could give you some of the plays to look over and you could decide."

"Me?"

"Might as well."

Alice shrugged. She didn't have anything better to do in the daytime anyway, and while her mother recovered, reading a few plays would be preferable to sitting around the house twiddling her thumbs. Or trying to avoid confrontations with her mother. "Okay."

Tanisha searched for something among the mess of papers on her desk, then groaned and buried her face in her hands. "I could kill Willie."

Alice hadn't heard their entire argument, but she'd had the distinct feeling that it wasn't altogether work-related. If at all. The brief snippets she'd heard, and the intensity of the exchange, had made her wonder if Tanisha and Willie were involved. Was that why he had walked out on her and the theater, because of a lover's spat?

"I'll be honest with you, Desirée—"

"Alice."

"Whatever."

Alice raised an eyebrow.

Tanisha ignored her and went on. "Look, Willie wanted more pay, and frankly, the theater's struggling to stay afloat as it is. I don't know what you expect, but I definitely can't pay you anything near the kind of money you earn on one of your films or TV shows."

Alice chuckled softly. "I didn't think so, and I wouldn't expect that kind of payment. In fact, I don't expect anything at all."

"I have to pay you."

"Consider it a favor." For Mia, not for her.

Tanisha shook her head, dismissing the offer. "No, I'll have to draw up a contract and present it to the other board members. We have to pay you something."

"Then how about a dollar a week?"

Tanisha's mouth nearly hit the desk. "You're joking."

"I don't need the money, Tanisha. That's not why I'm taking the job. I'm doing this for my niece."

"If you're sure . . ."

"I am."

"All right. I'll draw up the contract. I don't think the board will object, not when we need all the money we can get. You can sign it later this week and officially start on Saturday."

"Great."

"Now, I'm going to send out some press releases to let the world know that you're the new teacher. I'd also like to schedule a press conference. The media will no doubt be interested in this. Do you think you can be available sometime, answer questions for the media?"

"Just tell me when."

"This is great." Tanisha's lips curled in a smile. "I can capitalize on the fact that you used to take classes here, and how you went on to great success. With a name like yours attached to the theater, maybe we can finally get some big corporate sponsors."

Tanisha was tactless, but Alice wasn't offended. She understood that the theater was struggling to survive, and she would do what she could to help out. For Mia. And for herself, she acknowledged. Because this place brought back so many happy memories. Besides, she would need something to occupy her thoughts while she stayed in Chicago.

And that, she just realized, was what she'd committed to doing. At least until the summer.

Alice glanced around the office. Framed pictures lined the walls. Pictures of children posing for the camera. Candid shots of children performing on stage. There was a picture of Tanisha with a group of children, her arms spread wide around them. A picture of Tanisha and Marcus.

Alice's stomach clenched at the sight. Marcus stood beside Tanisha, his arm snaked around her waist, and they were both smiling brightly for the camera. In one hand, Tanisha held some type of plaque.

It shouldn't disturb her. Hadn't she had years to get over Marcus's marriage to Tanisha? Still, Alice wrenched her gaze away from the photo and turned her attention to the other side of the office, where she perused the pictures on that wall. Unlike the left wall, which boasted color pictures, this side had several black and white photos. More candid and posed shots.

And, she realized with surprise, a picture of herself.

Alice got up and strolled over to the picture. She hardly recognized her image, though she remembered exactly when the photo had been taken. It was the summer before her father had died, and in the picture, she was standing beside that year's teacher, Mrs. Stoffman. The picture had been taken at one of the rehearsals for the play they were doing that summer, and they were both smiling from ear to ear.

A smile touched her lips at the memory. She'd loved Mrs. Stoffman, who had been the teacher for three of the four years she'd taken classes at the theater. Mr. Noble had replaced her in Alice's last year of classes, and it had been he who'd given her that horrible role in the play from hell. Thank God that had been her last experience at the Bartlett Theater, rather than her first. She may well have given up acting if that had been the case.

But while the memory of the picture with Mrs. Stoffman was pleasant, the image she saw of herself was not. She found it difficult to look at the way she had been, because it made her remember things she wanted to forget. The awful names she'd been called by her classmates, like "Miss Piggy," and "Tub of Lard." She remembered the horrible jokes.

"Hey, Alice. How many people does it take to roll you out of bed in the morning?"

"About ten sumo wrestlers!" Ha ha ha ha.

"What's it like rolling around in the mud, Alice? That's what pigs do, right?"

Bile, pungent and bitter, rose in her throat at the memories. She tried to block them from her mind the way she had done for years. She had learned to forget as a way to survive. But the truth was, in the years since she had left Chicago, she hadn't truly forgotten, nor left the pain behind. The constant jeers had haunted her as she'd worked damn hard to shed her body's extra pounds and change her image.

"Desirée?"

"Hmm?"

"I asked if there's anything you'll need for the class? Props, reading material, et cetera."

"Oh." Alice swallowed, hoping to dislodge the painful lump in her throat. "No, I don't think so. You said you had some ideas for the summer play."

"Yes. We've got several books of children's plays."

"I'll take as many as you have to lend me." God, she couldn't believe she was actually going to do this.

Standing, Tanisha went to the bookshelf behind her desk and removed two thick volumes. "These are new so they should have fresh material." She passed the books to Alice. "I do appreciate you helping the theater out of this bind."

That was probably the nicest thing Tanisha had ever said to her, but Alice wasn't naïve enough to believe Tanisha was truly grateful to her. She was grateful to Desirée, whose reputation as a star she hoped would attract attention—and money—to the theater.

She needed to get out of here. "I'll go through these, see what I like." Pushing her chair back, she stood. "I've got to get back to my mother."

"Yes, Marcus told me. I hope she'll be okay."

"Thanks." Alice walked toward the door. She couldn't help wondering how close a relationship Marcus and Tanisha still had. Were they like some divorced couples who remained close despite their separation? Why did they divorce? Whose decision had it been? And . . . was Marcus still in love with his ex-wife?

She didn't want to think about that.

"I'll call you about the press conference."

"You do that."

Alice turned on her heel and headed out the office, wondering what the hell she'd just gotten herself into.

Seven

"Come on, man. One more."

Grunting from the effort, Marcus lowered the bench press to his chest, then forced himself to do one more repetition. "All right," he managed to say between clenched teeth.

Khalil reached for the bench press and helped guide it into its cradle. Marcus's arms burned, and as he lay back, he stretched them to ease the ache in his muscles.

"That was great, man," Khalil told him. "Three hundred pounds."

Marcus sat up and rested his elbows on his knees as he caught his breath. He'd been pushing himself hard lately, adding more and more weight to the bench press. Normally, he was content with 225 pounds; that kept his arms trim and powerful. But the extra pounds had served to relieve stress.

"All right, spot me."

Marcus heaved himself off the bench and let Khalil take his place. He was taller than Khalil by a good two inches, but Khalil had a larger frame. He looked like he could be a linebacker.

"How much weight you want on here?" Marcus asked him, moving to the back of the bench to spot Khalil.

"Add a hundred pounds."

Like him, Khalil had been testing his own limit lately by adding more and more weight. The two had always competed to see who had more testosterone. "You sure you can handle that," he joked.

"Put it on. I haven't got all day."

Marcus spotted Khalil as he bench-pressed four hundred pounds ten times. By the end, he was groaning loudly, and Marcus held a hand under the bar, just in case Khalil needed extra help. It took a major effort to lift the bar the last time, but Khalil did it slowly but surely.

Sitting up, Khalil's eyes roamed the gym. They worked out every weekend at a gym near Navy Pier come hell or high water. While Marcus enjoyed getting a good workout, he knew that Khalil enjoyed the added perks the gym offered—namely the women.

Now, his eyes followed an attractive dark-skinned woman with a knockout body.

"Which machine do you want to head to next?" Marcus asked.

"Gimme a second, hmm? A guy needs to stop and refuel."

"Seems to me you spend most of your time 're-fueling.' "

Khalil looked up at him and grinned. "Isn't that

an inalienable right? Life, liberty, and the pursuit of hot bodies?"

Marcus chuckled. Khalil was pushing forty, had never been married, and seemed content to spend the rest of his days as a player. If that was his choice, he respected that.

"There's more to life than women, man."

"Yeah?" Khalil's face twisted with skepticism. "Like what?"

"Like good friends," Marcus replied, his tone syrupy.

"You sound like a damn Hallmark card. I told you you need to find a woman. Damn, look at her. Mmm mmm mmm. Isn't she fine?"

Marcus's eyes followed Khalil's gaze to another ebony beauty. He shrugged. "Yeah, she's fine."

"Don't sound so excited."

"It takes more than just a pretty face to get me excited these days," Marcus told him.

Khalil stood. "You're scaring me."

"You're forgetting I was married to your sister."

"Touché."

Marcus had known Khalil for fifteen years, had worked on the Chicago police department with him for twelve. He knew him well enough to talk candidly about his failed marriage to his sister. Unlike some people who would take their family member's side in a divorce, Khalil had examined the facts with an open mind. Where Tanisha was concerned, he didn't sugarcoat her behavior or try to justify it.

Together they walked to the water fountain. Marcus loved a beautiful woman as much as the next guy, but he wasn't in the mood for a relationship these days. Nor a casual fling. He'd already made a couple big mistakes by falling for pretty women and he didn't plan to make another.

As boring or clichéed as it sounded, he was concentrating on his career. He hoped in the next year to move from being a beat cop to working in drug enforcement. If it weren't for that whole mess with Melissa Reynolds, he'd no doubt already be working in DEA. He'd gotten involved with Melissa, a woman he was supposed to protect from her crazy estranged husband, and now she was dead. His lapse in judgment had cost a woman her life and had gotten him reprimanded at his precinct. Now he had to prove himself again.

When Khalil moved from the fountain, Marcus bent over it and drank several mouthfuls of water.

"Speaking of Tanisha," Khalil began, "she tells me Desirée is in town."

"Yep."

"You've seen her?"

"I ran into her at the theater."

"Does she look as hot in person as she does on film?"

Marcus gave him a look.

"Hey, it's my curious nature, man. So, is she?"

"Alice definitely looks hot." Knockout figure, full hips, sweet kissable lips, and the best breasts he'd ever seen. Marcus still had a hard time believing her drastic image change. But he suddenly realized that what he had a harder time with was the fact that he suddenly found her sexually attractive in a way he hadn't before. Before, they'd been strictly friends.

But with her fame, fortune, and good looks, Alice had become a different person.

More proof that just because a woman was beautiful didn't mean she was attractive in the way that mattered most.

When Tanisha had called Marcus yesterday and asked him if he could help out at the theater Saturday afternoon, he had said yes, like he usually did. He helped out for the kids, because he wanted to provide a positive role model for them. As a cop, he knew how important it was to keep children occupied in extracurricular activities to prevent them from being tempted by the lure of the streets. But as he pulled up in front of the theater early that afternoon, he was stunned to see the parking lot so jampacked with cars he couldn't even get a space. He parked behind a van on the street. Only when he got out of his Mustang and began walking toward the theater did he realize that the van belonged to a local television station. So did two more across the street.

What was going on?

He took the steps to the theater's double doors two at a time and opened the heavy door.

He hardly recognized the place. It was crammed with people. There were definitely more parents and children here than there had ever been, and as he scanned the object of the various television camera spotlights, he suddenly knew why.

Desirée LaCroix stood on the stage before a throng of reporters while parents and children packed the theater seats, watching her.

As Marcus made his way down the aisle, he couldn't quite swallow his annoyance. The place was a media circus. There Desirée was, basking in the spotlight as she chatted onstage before numerous cameras, when this theater was supposed to be about the kids.

You could take the star out of Hollywood . . .

Christ.

Tanisha stood at the foot of the stage, watching the whole spectacle. Marcus strolled to her side. "Tanisha, what's going on?"

"Hey, Marcus." She flashed him a bright smile. "Isn't this great? I sent out a few press releases announcing that Desirée would be teaching the class, and look at all the interest in the theater. There are even more parents here to sign their children up for classes."

Marcus felt a modicum of guilt that he'd immediately blamed Alice for soaking up the attention. He should have known Tanisha was behind this show. And he couldn't entirely blame her for doing what she could to garner attention for the theater. It badly needed funding.

". . . at least until midsummer," Alice was saying when Marcus turned his attention to her.

"Ms. LaCroix, we understand you have roots in Chicago. Is that true?" one reporter asked.

"Yes, I do." Alice smiled cheerfully, as though she'd loved this city. But Marcus knew better. She couldn't wait to get the hell out of Dodge. "I was born and raised here in Chicago."

"I understand you studied drama at this very same theater. Is that why you've decided to come back here and work?"

Alice didn't even blink as the flash from various cameras went off in her face. "Yes, that's part of the reason."

"Is there any truth to the recent story that you propositioned Sebastian Charles for sex and when he turned you down, you became obsessed with him?" another reporter asked. "Is that why you've returned to Chicago—because your career in Hollywood is on the rocks?"

Alice's smile faded and a muscle in her jaw twitched. "That is categorically untrue. My relationship with Mr. Charles was never anything but professional." Her eyes scanned the group of reporters. "Thank you for your time."

"Ms. LaCroix—"

"One more question—"

"I wish I had more time, but the reason I'm here is to teach the children, and they've been patiently waiting. Once again, thank you."

She was polite yet diplomatic, and Marcus was proud of the way she'd handled herself.

Alice stepped from the podium as photographers and cameramen continued to catch footage of her. She strolled to stage right and descended the stairs. Tanisha walked over to her and Marcus trailed behind her.

"No, Tanisha," Marcus heard Alice say when he neared them. "I'd prefer that they leave now. This has already been enough of a circus, and I don't want this to be about me. This is about the children."

"They're going to want to get some shots of you working with the students," Tanisha told her.

"Then why don't we do that now so they can leave and we can get down to business."

"She has a point," Marcus said from behind Tanisha.

Alice's gaze flew to his. He saw surprise there—

clearly, she hadn't expected to see him here. But after a second, she offered him a faint smile.

Tanisha whirled around and faced Marcus. "You don't understand. This is exactly the type of attention the theater needs. With Desirée teaching the children, just think of the type of corporate sponsors we can attract."

"There's a fine line between attention and exploitation."

"Tanisha, please tell them they have a few more minutes to get whatever they need." Alice sounded impatient. "This has already taken up too much time."

"Fine," Tanisha snapped, then walked off toward a reporter and her cameraman.

Marcus stared at Alice as she shook her head and placed a hand on her hip. He had expected her to lap up the attention, but perhaps he had judged her too quickly.

"What?" she asked, when she realized he was staring. "Do I have something on my face?"

"No." Marcus's eyes lingered over her oval-shaped face, her high cheekbones and full, sexy lips, her perfectly arched eyebrows. Her raven-colored hair that fell in soft waves around her shoulders. Damn if she wasn't one of the most beautiful women he'd ever seen.

"Then why are you staring at me like that? Did I make a fool of myself up there?"

Marcus glanced away, once again uncomfortable with the thought of Alice as a sex symbol, rather than the friend he'd had so many years ago. It seemed inherently wrong to be checking her out the way he was.

"You sounded great up there. I think you handled the last question very well."

"I didn't expect that, but I guess I should have."

There was still a vulnerable quality to her, one he hadn't noticed before. In some ways, he could still see his old friend, the one who'd needed his protection, needed him.

For one thing, the question about her being obsessed with that director had truly startled her. He would have expected an actress not to falter at all and show nothing but the cool and confident façade. But although she had quickly recovered, she'd been mortified for a second.

She'd been like that years ago. When other students picked on her, pain would flash in her eyes for a moment before she tried to hide the emotion.

As much as it had disturbed him to notice her the way a man notices a woman, he couldn't prevent his eyes from moving lower. Today she wore black leggings that hugged the curves of her hips and thighs and a cream-colored knit top that hugged her large breasts. Thank God she wore a black blazer over the ensemble, or she'd look like a walking, talking vixen. He was sure at least some of the parents wouldn't appreciate that image in their child's drama teacher.

Hell, who was he kidding? It was him who had a problem with the image, not anyone else.

"I better get started," she said, interrupting his thoughts.

"Sure."

She glanced at him nervously, then scooted past him toward the children and their parents.

*　　*　　*

As Alice walked past Marcus, she couldn't help feeling flustered. Her face was hot; her thoughts were scattered. For a brief moment, she didn't remember why she was even here.

She hadn't expected to see Marcus staring at her the way he had been. There was no doubt about it—he was checking her out. For three years in high school she had dreamed Marcus would one day look at her like that, but he never had.

Until now.

He was still so incredibly handsome, and his lazy gaze roaming over her had definitely made her body tingle in a way it hadn't quite tingled before. But it had also disturbed her. Who was he seeing when he looked at her with that hot, lazy gaze—sexy vixen Desirée LaCroix or his old friend Alice Watson?

She was still the same person she'd always been, so in a way it hurt to know that he now found her desirable, simply because she'd shed some pounds. It didn't quite make sense to feel hurt, she knew, but in her jumbled thoughts, all she could think was why wasn't she good enough before?

She turned and looked back at him. He wasn't looking at her. Her heart dropped a notch with disappointment.

Make up your mind, she told herself. *You can't have it both ways.* How could she want Marcus to check her out but not want him to check her out?

"All right, everyone," she said, forcing Marcus from her mind. "Last week I didn't really get the chance to know you all, so that's how we'll start the day. Though there are considerably more people here this week."

"Who wasn't here last week?"

Alice's head whipped to her right at the sound of Marcus's deep, sexy voice. How had she not sensed his approach?

Several children raised their hands in response to Marcus's question.

"You all come with me," he told them. "You need to register before you can take the class, and I'll be taking all your information and answering your questions." He glanced at Alice and smiled. "We'll be working together."

"Are you here every week?" she asked.

"Considering how short-staffed this place has been, pretty much every week."

Great, Alice thought. Just what she needed.

"Everyone loves you, Aunt Alice!" Mia exclaimed when the last parents and children were making their way out of the theater. It was the first moment Alice was able to spend alone with her niece.

"I just hope I can do the job."

Mia giggled as if the idea of her aunt not doing a good job was ridiculous. "Of course you can."

"Oh, Mia." Alice pulled her close. "You have so much faith in me."

"Of course. You're the best."

Alice remembered her sister's words, that Mia idolized her. She prayed she was able to present a level-headed, positive image for her niece.

"Dad!" Mia exclaimed. Breaking free from Alice, she ran up the aisle and met her father as he walked toward the stage.

Chad was picking Mia up after the class today. Normally, he picked Mia up from home and brought her to her class, then picked her up afterward and she spent the rest of the weekend at his house. It was an arrangement both he and Marie were happy with.

Her feet clad only in stockings, Alice wandered up the aisle to meet her ex-brother-in-law. She'd worn her high-heeled boots today—a mistake she wouldn't make again. Barely an hour into the class, her feet had started to kill her and she'd taken the boots off.

Chad greeted her with a warm grin, followed by a kiss on the cheek. "Hello, Alice."

"Hello, Chad." While he hadn't paid much attention to her in high school, he hadn't been evil either, which had scored him points in her book. It was years later that she'd had the chance to get to really know him and form an opinion of him as a person. When he and Marie had visited her in Los Angeles, Chad had been genuinely sweet to her, congratulating her on the small successes she'd achieved and encouraging her not to give up. Finally getting to know him during that visit, Alice had ended up wondering why he had married her sister. They were complete opposites.

"You look wonderful," Chad told her.

"So do you." He was tall, lean, and unlike the last time she'd seen him, bald. The look suited him.

"I saw you on the news."

"Already?"

"Yep. One of the local channels gave a snippet of what would come up later, and you were right there, front and center."

"Wow." Even though she was used to being in the spotlight, she was surprised by the attention she was receiving here.

"I've got to run, but it was nice seeing you again."

"Likewise, Chad."

"And hey, don't be a stranger. If you ever want to get together for a drink or anything, let me know."

Alice nodded. "Sure." She wondered if that was a subtle come-on. "See you tomorrow, Mia." She bent to hug her niece.

"Bye, Aunt Alice."

Alice watched Chad wrap an arm around Mia's shoulder and lead her up the aisle. It reminded her of her and her own father and the many times he had done the exact same thing when picking her up from this theater.

Lord, she missed him.

"Hey."

A hand flying to her heart, Alice whirled around. And found herself facing Marcus's broad chest. God, he'd snuck up on her again! Slowly she lifted her gaze to meet his.

One side of his mouth lifted in a grin. "Sorry. I didn't mean to scare you."

Alice told herself that her heart was beating this erratically simply because of the scare, *not* because there was something about Marcus, something powerful and exciting. Something dangerous.

"It's all right."

"You're not so tall anymore."

"Excuse me?"

His gaze fell to her feet. "Without the heels."

"Oh. Yeah. I took them off."

"Not quite practical, huh?"

"No, not quite. Speaking of which." She turned and walked back to the foot of the stage where she'd placed her stylish but impractical boots. When she bent to slip them on, she saw that Marcus had followed her. For a tall man with a muscular physique, he certainly moved as quietly as a cat!

"I thought you'd left," she said after a moment.

"I was in the office."

"With Tanisha?" Alice hoped her sudden jealousy couldn't be heard in her voice.

"She needed me to help her with some filing."

Alice zipped up her second boot and stood. "You two are still close, aren't you?"

Marcus shrugged. "Not really. But we've learned how to tolerate each other." His smile didn't quite reach his eyes. "She's not the most organized person, and since I'd hate to see this place go downhill, I help out whenever I can. It's a better alternative to kids finding entertainment on the street."

"Serious Marcus who wants to save the world."

"I do what I can."

Alice slipped her purse onto her shoulder. "Well, it was nice seeing you again." She'd hoped to sound friendly, but instead her voice had sounded pompous. She just felt so confused around Marcus. Unlike years ago, she didn't know what to say, how to act. From some of his comments, she had the feeling he thought she was some sort of prima donna. Again, she felt a moment of sadness that she'd put distance between them. "Next week?"

"Maybe."

"All right, then."

She turned as quickly as she could, determined to escape. Never in a million years would she have predicted this, but being around Marcus made her uncomfortable.

Maybe it was the fact that every time she looked

at him, she remembered her silly dream that he'd one day love her. It was a dream she had long thought buried and one she certainly wanted to forget.

Outside, she hurried down the steps to her car. But as she rounded the driver's side and reached for the handle, she froze as her gaze dropped. Then she pivoted on her heel and ran back to the theater as if the devil himself were chasing her.

Eight

Run, Alice, run, Marcus thought sardonically as he watched her shapely form flee up the aisle to the exit. It was ironic that they'd once been close friends, considering she could barely stand to be around him now.

Maybe he shouldn't blame her for running. He hadn't exactly been the nicest person to her. He knew he had been goading her with his subtle comments about her acting, but he wanted to break through that tough exterior and finally reveal the vulnerable Alice Watson he had known and loved.

Sighing, Marcus made his way to the back of the theater and the exit. It had been a long day and he was ready to go home.

He opened the door and *oomph*. Alice ran right into the thick wall of his chest. He reached out and gripped her arms, steadying her.

Even before looking down at her face he knew something was wrong. She was trembling.

"Oh, God, Marcus."

Concern sweeping over him, his hands moved up her arms until he grasped her by the shoulders. His eyebrows bunched together as he noted her quivering lips. "Alice, what happened?"

"My car. Somebody . . ."

Easing her aside, Marcus ran out the theater exit and down the steps to her BMW. Standing in front of her car, he checked out the rag top, the bumper, but didn't notice anything wrong. He turned back to her. "What?"

"The front tire on the driver's side."

Marcus moved to the right and immediately saw what had scared her. A pocket knife was jabbed into the front left tire, holding a folded piece of white paper in place. "Christ."

He dropped onto his haunches and examined it closely. Usually people just slashed tires, but someone had clearly wanted her to notice this. Digging into his back pocket, he pulled out the handkerchief and reached for the knife.

"Don't," Alice quickly said.

He paused, then turned to face her. "We need to see what the note says. Whether it's meant for you or not."

Alice dug her cell phone out of her purse. "Then I should call the police."

"Lucky for you, a member of Chicago's finest is right here."

"It's probably best you don't get involved. I mean, you'll have to do a report, and I'm sure you have better things to do."

Marcus felt a spurt of anger. She was always pushing him away. "I don't patrol this area, so no, I won't be writing any report. Been playing a cop on television a little too long, hmm?" Marcus added with a hint of sarcasm. Cop dramas rarely got their facts straight.

"The show was called *Code of Honor*, and they happened to research everything in the script. I'm proud of my work on that show."

"Really? I heard you quit because you wanted twice the pay per episode. Which would average out to about five years of my salary."

Ignoring him, Alice shoved a pair of sunglasses on, then started punching digits on her phone.

"You certainly have your priorities straight. Can't make a call if you don't look like a glamour queen. I bet you have a different pair of sunglasses for every day of the week."

Her bottom lip puffed out in a pout at the same time her fingers froze. "That's exactly what I mean."

Marcus stood. In the doorway of the theater, she'd been scared. She'd run back to him for help. But now the fear in her eyes was gone, replaced by stubbornness.

"What are you talking about?" He reached her in two quick strides.

"I don't need your help," she said, evading his question. She moved past him and bent to examine the damaged tire.

"Damn it, you don't think you need anyone's help, do you?"

"I don't need yours."

That infuriated him. "Why the hell not?"

She shot to her feet. "Because it's obvious you don't like me."

"What?" Marcus asked, giving her a puzzled look. "Who said I don't like you?"

"Marcus, you don't have to deny it. I know our friendship isn't the same anymore." Her shoulders sagged and her voice softened. "I . . . I should just deal with this on my own. I didn't mean to bother you." She turned away.

He grabbed hold of her by her upper arms and forced her to look at him. But he was suddenly at a loss for words because he'd pulled her too close. Damn, he couldn't think with her soft breasts pressed against his chest!

He wanted to feel those beautiful mounds of flesh against him, skin to skin.

Alice's breath snagged as Marcus held her to him. Her nipples hardened against his strong chest and her heart pounded wildly. Being this close to him, her body couldn't help reacting to his overwhelming sexual aura with excitement.

Slowly, she raised her gaze to his. Marcus's onyx eyes sent a bolt of heat through her body. God, to be lost in that heat . . .

As suddenly as he'd grabbed her, Marcus released her.

Alice was silent and Marcus looked away. She didn't understand what had happened between them any more than he had. All he knew was that something had felt incredibly right about holding Alice against him. But it had been so long since he'd had such intimate contact with a woman that he hadn't been able to stop his groin from tightening. Before he embarrassed himself, he'd had to step away from her.

"See. That's exactly what I mean." A hint of disappointment sounded in Alice's tone. "One minute, you communicate with me, the next you shut down."

"That has nothing to do with not liking you," he said from clenched teeth. He realized his tone would do nothing to comfort her.

She was staring at him, he knew, but with those dark designer sunglasses, he couldn't see her eyes. He wanted to snatch them off her face. Still, he didn't need to see her eyes to know she had sensed the sexual path his thoughts had taken.

"It's not that I don't like you. It's just that you're so . . . different now."

She huffed and turned back to her car, and he was reminded that there was a bigger issue to deal with here.

He walked back to the car and once again bent beside the tire. She didn't protest as he plucked the knife out. He unfolded the sheet of paper with the tips of his fingers. Written in red crayon was: *We don't want you here. Go back where you came from or else.*

Marcus gnawed on his bottom lip. The handwriting was large and sloppy, which led him to believe it had been exaggerated so no one would recognize it.

"What does it say?"

The fear had returned. Though he still couldn't see her eyes, he could read her body language. She hugged her torso and shifted her body weight from one foot to the next. "You're gonna have to report this."

"What does it *say*?" Her tone went up a pitch, not from anger, but alarm.

He couldn't very well keep this from her, though he felt the strongest urge to protect her as he once had when bad things happened to her.

Before he knew what was happening, she moved toward him and snatched the letter from his hand. Her lips pulled in a firm line as she read it. "Well," she said, as though she'd just read an ad for fertilizers. Then she crumpled the paper into a ball.

"Damn it." Marcus reached for the crumpled paper and grabbed it from her. "This is evidence."

"Forget it. I don't want to call the police."

"Whether you want to or not, you have to. For one thing, there's a gaping hole in that tire, and you'll need a police report for insurance purposes. And like it or not, this is obviously a threat."

"God."

"Alice, I know you've only recently returned to Chicago, but do you have any idea who would do something like this?"

She shuddered, and he wanted to wrap his arms around her and make her fear go away. But he didn't touch her.

"No. But this *is* Chicago. I didn't exactly have many friends here."

"You had me."

"I know. I didn't mean you." She rested her butt against the car's front hood and exhaled a shaky breath.

At that moment, Tanisha stepped out the front door of the theater. Seeing Marcus and Alice still in the parking lot, she flashed them a confused look, then slowly made her way toward them.

"What's going on?"

"Alice's tire was slashed," Marcus told her.

"Oh, dear." Her tone was almost mocking.

Alice narrowed her eyes as she gazed at Tanisha. She certainly didn't sound surprised, nor truly sympathetic.

Marcus must have picked up on her tone, for he said, "You don't know anything about this, do you?"

"Of course not!" Tanisha exclaimed, her back stiffening with indignation. "Besides, why would I do something like that?"

Alice regarded Tanisha carefully, wondering. Truthfully, she couldn't put anything past this woman who had never liked her. But considering Tanisha seemed glad to have her teaching the class, the idea of her slashing her tire didn't make much sense.

"You didn't see anything or any*one* suspicious?" Marcus further queried.

"Marcus, this place was a zoo today. Well, I doubt I can be of any help, so if you don't mind, I've got a ton of things to do." She lifted the pile of binders in her hand as proof.

"Fine by me," Alice said.

"I'll see you both later."

Marcus gave Tanisha a tight nod, then she turned and strolled to her car. He didn't say another word until she drove past them and out of the parking lot. Marcus faced Alice. She frowned at him and he sighed. He recognized the stubborn tilt of her chin. Were all actresses this testy? She certainly was doing her best to give him a hard time.

"Listen, as I said, I don't patrol this area, so I can't do an official report, but I am a witness. I'm gonna call the police so they can come out here. You'll also need a tow."

"There's got to be a spare in the back."

"This is serious, Alice." He remembered Melissa, how she hadn't taken her situation seriously either, and now she was dead.

"How long will all this take?"

"Why? Hot date?"

She pushed her sunglasses into her hair and scowled at him. "No, but I do have to get home to my mother. Marie won't be happy if I'm gone too much longer."

"I'm sure Marie will understand."

Alice raised a skeptical eyebrow.

"Pass me your phone."

She shoved it in his hand, then sulked. For the life of him, he couldn't understand why she was being so difficult. She was too damn stubborn to appreciate his help.

Women. He'd never understand them.

Alice knew she was being difficult, but she was helpless to stop her behavior. She was dealing with the whole gamut of emotions right now, and it was hard trying to maintain a cool, calm exterior. And the last thing she wanted to do was break down in front of Marcus.

She was frightened. Who would stab a knife into her car tire with a note telling her to stay away? As much as she wanted to pretend otherwise, it was clearly no prank.

The incident, and Marcus's question as to who would have done this to her, also had her feeling pain she thought she'd long ago buried. It didn't matter that she'd worked so hard to change; someone here still didn't like her. Had one of the very parents who'd smiled at her in the theater been the one to sabotage her car?

The thought that she still wasn't liked frustrated her, and she glanced at Marcus from behind her sunglasses. Talk about the ultimate irony; now that she'd finally achieved a look she was happy with, one men appreciated, Marcus could barely stand to be around her. It was like he'd prefer she was the former Alice—fat, ugly, unloved, and miserable.

The police came and took her statement, and now, Marcus spoke with the tow-truck driver who was hooking her rented car to the back. She still couldn't believe this had happened.

She walked over to him. "You're gonna take it to Specialty Rentals right away?"

"Yes, ma'am."

Alice had called the rental company and told them what had happened. They'd instructed her to have the car towed to them. The official police report would follow, but in the meantime, she had to pay the enormous deductible.

"Then I may as well ride with you," she said to the driver.

Marcus's head whipped around at her comment. "You'll ride with me."

She glared at him, but he glared right back. Clearly, she wouldn't win this one. "Fine." She marched to his Mustang.

God, what was wrong with her? She was ready to ride with a strange tow-truck driver, just to avoid being around Marcus?

A little voice told her it was because he'd hurt her pride. Even now that she was beautiful, she clearly still wasn't the type of woman Marcus wanted.

But as soon as that thought entered her mind, she couldn't believe it. Was that why she was so . . . irritable? Because Marcus didn't appreciate her new look? That didn't make a lick of sense. She had gotten over Marcus Quinn a long time ago. The only thing she regretted was the loss of their friendship, and that was her fault.

By the time Marcus opened the door for her, she had convinced herself that her belligerence had nothing to do with any type of sexual frustration, but with the fact that she was angry over the reality that they couldn't seem to connect once again as friends.

The silence between them was stifling as Marcus followed the tow truck. By the time they hit the expressway, Alice couldn't take it anymore.

She turned to him and said, "Marcus, I want a truce."

He didn't look at her. "All right."

"No, I'm serious. I know we haven't exactly connected the way we once did, and I'm sorry for that. I want to get past this."

Marcus didn't respond for several seconds, then faced her with a bleak expression. "I feel like I don't know you anymore."

His words hurt, but she bit back the pain. "Thirteen years have passed, Marcus. We've grown apart."

He glanced at her. "I guess I miss my friend."

Her lips lifted in a faint smile. "I miss you, too. Marcus, I know I'm the one who let time and distance come between us. And I'm sorry for that. But some of the things you've said make me wonder if you even *like* me anymore."

"I suppose I've been acting a bit childish, but I was trying to figure you out by pushing your buttons. Figure out if the Alice I knew was still there."

"I'm still the same Alice. Yes, I have more money now and I look different, but I don't think I'm better than anybody, Marcus. I'm just trying to enjoy my life. I wasn't always able to do that."

"And I always supported that. So why did you cut me off, Alice? I was your best friend. How could you move away and forget about us?"

Because I was in love with you and you were in love with someone else. But she could never tell him that. "I'm sorry, Marcus. When I left, I was dealing with all these ambiguous feelings about my mother, my painful memories from school . . . I know it wasn't right, but I guess I put everything behind me. Including you. But I swear, Marcus, I never forgot you."

"And what about my wedding?" Marcus's tone held both disappointment and disbelief. "Why didn't you call or come back for that?"

Alice paused. "Truth be told," she answered softly, "I didn't want to see you marry Tanisha."

He met her eyes, giving her a puzzled look.

"She never liked me, Marcus. And you were always so wonderful. I thought you were making a mistake and I didn't want to be there to witness it."

Once again, he looked at her, then back at the road. He didn't say anything, and Alice wasn't sure if he bought her explanation. She leaned her head back against the head rest.

Silence fell between them. There was so much left unsaid, but for now, this was a start.

Hopefully while she was here in Chicago, they could work at being friends again. Especially since he helped out at the theater and there was a good chance she would see him every week. She didn't want them to feel awkward around each other. Not after how close they'd once been.

His marriage to Tanisha had been part of the reason she'd let their friendship fade the first time. That and the fact that he hadn't returned her love. But she was over him now, and she was a much stronger person than she'd been thirteen years ago, so Alice didn't plan to make the same mistake twice. If they managed to recapture the friendship they'd lost, this time when she returned to Los Angeles, she'd make sure they always stayed in touch.

She wouldn't let distance come between them again.

Nine

Alice's head itched from a mixture of heat and sweat, but she refused to take off her baseball cap as she ran. In the four days since the attack on her car at the theater, there hadn't been any more incidents, and she felt relatively safe. But she still didn't want to take any chances, which is why she made sure she was as unrecognizable as possible when she went on her morning jog.

Her Baldwin Hills neighborhood in California was so completely different from this south Chicago neighborhood where she had grown up. In California, the homes were brighter, in various shades of creams, pinks, and yellows. Warm colors. The homes here were dark-colored brick, which seemed to suck up all the sunshine. Her modern Baldwin Hills home rested in the hillside, overlooking the Pacific Ocean. It was a beautiful view to wake up to every day, certainly more beautiful than looking out the bedroom window at the old houses in this neighborhood.

That was why Alice couldn't understand the fondness she felt as she jogged through these south Chicago streets every morning.

She always ventured outside after the children had gone to school and the streets were quiet. But as she jogged, it was as if the streets were alive with action as memories played in her mind like an old movie reel.

She could see a group of girls playing double-dutch on the street corner, laughing and having a wonderful time. She hadn't thought about it in years, but there was a time when she had been one of those girls. Granted, she'd been about ten or eleven at the time, before she'd started to put on all that weight, but she *had* had some friends. She had been happy.

The year before high school, her very best friend, Lynette Jackson, had moved south with her family. She'd been crushed because she and Lynette had both had a fondness for acting. After jumping rope for a little while, she and Lynette would always take off and venture around the neighborhood, conjuring up exciting stories about where they lived. Then they would act them out.

"I swear that house is haunted," Lynette had said once when they passed a house that had been boarded up for years. "Gosh, what do you think happened?"

That was all Lynette had to ask to get Alice's mind churning with ideas. "I know. Everything was peaceful there. Everyone was happy. Then one day, the family just disappeared. No bodies, no nothing.

And everybody is afraid to go in the house now because they fear they'll disappear too."

"Creepy," Lynette had replied, her eyes dancing with excitement.

Alice had never found a friend like her again, except for Marcus. By the time she went to high school, she was at least thirty pounds overweight, which made her an oddball. Other students had immediately ostracized her. She'd further retreated into her own comfortable shell, because in that shell, she could dream that the world was the way she wanted it to be. But as her high school years went on, people picked on her more. And she'd gained more weight.

Only in her fantasies, at the theater, with Marcus and with her father did she find some type of comfort and happiness. Then her father had died, and her mother had blamed her for his death and more or less completely cut her off emotionally.

Alice took a deep invigorating breath as she increased her speed. It was weird going through the neighborhood and seeing familiar landmarks. The park she walked by every day from school. The church they'd attended every Sunday. It was sad to see that a few more places had been boarded up, like Mr. Harris's ice cream shop, where on many a Saturday afternoon her father had taken her for a sundae. Now, she had no desire to conjure up some silly story about what mysterious thing might have happened to the place. She was too old for that.

She rounded the corner onto London Street and slowed to a fast walk. Several seconds later, she was at her mother's house. She stuck the key in the door but as she turned it she found it was already open.

Her heart went haywire. She knew she'd locked the door when she left for her jog. When she'd left the house, her mother had been taking a nap. Marie was at work and Mia was at school, so who was inside her mother's house?

Cautiously, she stepped inside. Her alarm turned to curiosity when she heard boisterous laughter and chatter coming from upstairs. She climbed the stairs two at a time and followed the laughter to her mother's bedroom.

Inside, her mother sat up with her back resting against the headboard while another woman sat on the edge of the bed. As Alice stepped into the room, her mother's laughter faded, and the woman turned to face her.

"Oh, hello. Rosa, this must be your daughter." A smile spread across the woman's face.

"Hello," Alice said, though she wasn't quite sure who the woman was. Wait. There was something familiar about her. Was that Mrs. Ellery? The woman who had once been so thin you could see her bones through her skin? The voice sounded the same, but . . .

Her mother answered the question for her. "Yes, Clara. This is Alice."

"Look at you!" the woman exclaimed. She stood and walked over to Alice, taking her hands in hers. "You're so beautiful. Just like you are on TV. I always wondered if it was just makeup and lighting, but honey, you look good!"

"Mrs. Ellery?"

"Yes, baby, it's me. And you can call me Clara."

"Wow. It's been ages." And she looked completely different. No longer skin and bones, the light-skinned woman was heavyset. Her hair had gone from vibrant black to completely gray. Instead of the thirteen years it had actually been, Clara looked like she had aged thirty years or so. It was such a drastic change, Alice could hardly believe it. "How have you been?"

The older woman sighed. "Life has been hard, but I'm still hanging in there. With God's help, I make it from day to day."

"Amen to that," Rosa chimed.

"You be thankful for the time you have with your mother, you hear?" She looked from Alice to Rosa. "I know how quickly you can lose it all."

Alice glanced past Clara to her mother and found her staring at her. But after a second, her mother looked away.

"Well, I won't keep you, Rosa. I only came to say hi."

Alice expected Clara to walk back to her mother, but instead she surprised her with a hug. The woman seemed to put all her heart and soul into it, and Alice felt warm.

"It's so good to see you home," Clara said.

"Thank you." It was one of the warmest welcomes she'd received since her return to Chicago.

Clara then slowly walked back to the bed. Bending, she pressed her cheek against Rosa's. "You take care, you hear? I'll come back and visit you soon."

"I'll see you out," Alice said.

"No, I'm fine. You stay with your mother."

Alice watched the older woman's retreating form. She definitely walked much slower, and she favored her left leg. She wondered what had happened to make her age so quickly in such a short time.

From what Alice remembered, Clara had had a son who was a couple of years younger than Alice. But the woman's words about being thankful for the time she had with her mother had a haunting quality and Alice couldn't help asking, "Did something happen to her son?"

Rosa shook her head ruefully. "Leukemia. The poor thing. One day he was healthy and strong, heading off to college on a football scholarship. The next . . ." Rosa's voice ended on a sigh.

"No," Alice gasped. Staring at her mother, the reality of just how fragile life was hit home. She wondered if she and her mother would ever make amends before it was too late.

"I feel so bad for Clara. He was her only son. After he died, she got so depressed that she just ate and ate and didn't stop. That's why she's so big now. Poor thing. If she can just pull herself together, I know she can lose all that weight and be pretty again."

You have such a pretty face. Sweetheart, if you would just lose some weight . . . She had heard those words and others like them so often in her life that hearing them now made her want to scream. Why couldn't people accept others for who they were, not how they looked?

Why hadn't her own mother been able to accept and love her for who she was?

Alice held her tongue. Rosa was weak and didn't need her anger. Still, she couldn't help wondering if her mother had always been ashamed of her when she was young for being so fat. If she was even good enough now.

She felt a heavy pressure on her chest, squeezing

the air from her lungs as she tried to push back her tears.

"Alice?"

Alice looked to her mother, hopeful. "Mother?"

"Can we talk?"

Her heart thudding in her chest, Alice approached the bed and sat. "Yes. I'd like that."

Rosa folded her hands in her lap. "I have a couple things to say, and I hope you'll hear me out."

"Okay." Alice wondered if her mother was finally going to say what she'd always wanted to hear: that she was sorry, that she hadn't meant to love her less than Marie, and would she forgive her?

"Marie and I have talked about this, and we're not sure you should be doing that job at the theater."

Alice's heart sank as shock washed over her. *This* was what her mother wanted to talk to her about? "It's too late," she told her matter-of-factly, hoping she kept the disappointment from her voice. "I'm already doing it."

"You were always too stubborn to listen, but hear me out. Marie doesn't think you're setting a good example for Mia, and I can't blame her."

It was like Alice had stepped back in time thirteen years. Once again, her mother was disapproving of her career choice, even though she'd made a success of herself. The reality hurt. "I am showing Mia that if you put your mind to it, you can make your dreams come true." *Even if you don't have the support of your family.*

"Marie doesn't want her pursuing Hollywood dreams. And neither do I."

"Why not?" Alice stood. It felt like troops were doing battle inside her stomach.

"I know you don't want to listen, but what about the recent tabloid story? Don't you think something like that will affect Mia in a negative way, give her all sorts of bad ideas?"

Alice gasped.

"Yes, I know. Marie told me."

Her sister had betrayed her. God, how could she do this? Alice had specifically told her not to tell her mother about the story to spare her any unnecessary anxiety.

"It's not true," Alice felt compelled to tell her mother. But there was doubt in her mother's eyes as she stared back at her. "I'm telling you the truth."

"The point is this is an example of the type of thing that can happen when you get caught up in the Hollywood lifestyle. I already lost you to that. I don't want to lose my granddaughter too."

You lost me long before I left, Alice wanted to retort, but didn't dare. How could she argue with her mother when she was recovering from a heart attack?

Alice took a deep breath to calm herself. "I *like* working at the theater. You should see the kids, Mother. They're so full of life and dreams—"

"Why do you insist on hurting me?"

Her mother's words stabbed at her like a knife. "I'm not trying to hurt you."

"I've lost so much already. You'd think you could do this one thing for me."

Alice spun around and faced the window. The weather had changed from bright and sunny to dark and gloomy, almost as though it had been scripted to match this scene.

"Did you tell Sara what I told you to tell her?"

"Not yet."

"I'd appreciate it if you would."

God, her mother was impossible. Not even her aunt could call to wish her well and be appreciated for the effort.

"Don't worry. I will." Alice crossed to the bedroom door. Aunt Sara would no doubt be offended, but if that's what her mother wanted, so be it.

"Alice?" Gone was her mother's strong voice, replaced by a soft, almost weak-sounding croak.

As Alice stared at her, emotions warred inside her. She was frustrated that her mother wasn't well enough for them to have the kind of discussion she craved. But every time her mother seemed weak or in pain, Alice's heart ached for her.

"Yes, Mother?"

"Can you get me some water? All this talking has made my throat dry."

Disappointment washed over her like a cold morning breeze. Alice hugged her torso to fight off the chill. But it was pointless. The chill came from the inside out.

And as she made her way down to the kitchen, she reminded herself that the happy endings she often dreamed of didn't truly happen in real life. Only in the movies.

Alice was sitting on the living-room sofa with her legs curled beneath her, one of the thick volumes of children's plays in her lap. But her mind wasn't on the selection of plays, and when she heard Marie enter the house, she jumped to her feet and met her in the foyer.

"Hello, Alice."

"You told Mom about the tabloid story?"

"Oh, that." Marie slipped off her leather jacket and placed it on the coat tree. "Yeah, I did."

"Why would you do that, Marie? You promised me you wouldn't tell her."

"She's our mother. Don't you think she has a right to know?"

"This wasn't about her not knowing. This was about her health." Alice was glad she'd told Marie a white lie about the car. Instead of telling her about the knife and note stuck in her tire, Alice had told her that the tire had blown while she'd been driving.

"It just came out. We were talking about you teaching the class at the theater, and . . ."

"You don't want me teaching the class."

Marie folded her arms across her chest as she faced her sister. "No. I don't."

"Why not?"

Marie didn't answer right away, leading Alice to believe she didn't have a good reason for such a wish. What harm could come of her giving her time to the theater? In fact, just yesterday, Tanisha had called her with the wonderful news that a major computer software firm had learned of the theater's plight and was giving them a very generous donation. She'd told Marie that, but her sister hadn't been impressed.

"I don't think you're presenting an accurate picture of Hollywood to my daughter," Marie said.

"This has nothing to do with Mia. This has to do with the fact that even now, after I've made something of myself, you can't be happy for me."

"That's not what this is about."

"Then what is it about?"

"Mia's future!"

Alice and Marie glared at each other for a long moment, then Marie stalked past her to the stairs. "Forget it," Marie said as she charged to the second level. "There's no point talking to you."

When Alice heard a bedroom door shut loudly upstairs, she dropped onto the landing and let out a frustrated groan. God, what was she doing here in this house? Her mother was barely talking to her. Marie didn't seem to want her around. Why was she willingly putting herself through this torture? She could always stay in a hotel and come to the house when necessary to take care of her mother, who, thankfully, was getting stronger every day. Then, after her mother no longer needed her, she could go to the theater and teach the children until they performed the play. After that, she could go back to Los Angeles and kiss this place good-bye once again.

Placing her palms flat on the landing, Alice pushed herself up. She felt an unexpected and very strong urge to call Marcus. Leaning her hip against the banister, she wondered why. But she knew. How many times had she called him from this house after an ugly argument with her mother or sister?

Too many to count.

But she couldn't very well just pick up the phone and call him now to complain. For one thing, things had changed between them. For another, she was a big girl now and quite capable of fighting her own battles.

If this were years ago, she never would have outright questioned her mother and sister's opinions. Except for the day her mother had opened her letter from the Screen Actors Guild and Alice had finally felt compelled to defend her dreams, she had always protested silently, so as to avoid a confrontation. In her years in Hollywood, she'd quickly learned that she had to fight for what she wanted, and that meant being vocal. She wasn't about to revert to the way she once was just because she was back in this house.

But she certainly didn't feel like dealing with anyone, and since Mia was spending the evening at a friend's, Alice retreated to her bedroom to continue searching for a children's play the students could perform.

There were so many to choose from, so many of which would be wonderful, but she could choose only one. Automatically she dismissed the ones with fewer than ten characters. The class had twenty-five students, almost twice the normal limit of fifteen, because there had been so much more interest in the class once the word had gotten out that Desirée LaCroix would be teaching it. Tanisha was content to continue registering students, but Alice had insisted they limit the class to no more than twenty-five. Even now, she wished she had told Tanisha twenty. She could only hope that she could give each child adequate attention.

Alice was so absorbed in going through the thick volume of plays that she was startled when she heard the knock on her bedroom door. She closed the book on her lap. "Come in."

Marie opened the door a crack and peeked in. "Marcus is downstairs."

"Marcus!" Alice's heart thumped in her chest.

"Mmm-hmm," Marie replied in a singsong tone.

Alice bolted to her feet, smoothing her T-shirt as she did. A quick glance in the mirror and she groaned. Her hair was pulled back in a ponytail, she wore no makeup, and she was dressed in an over-sized T-shirt and shorts. Hardly appropriate attire for visitors.

But she certainly didn't have time to change, and she wasn't going to keep Marcus waiting. As she made her way downstairs, she wondered what he was doing here in the middle of the week.

In the foyer, Marcus stood facing the door. When he heard her, he turned. His eyes met and held hers, and Alice's breath snagged in her chest. Wearing black slacks, an olive-colored shirt, and a black blazer, he looked as if he had come from a modeling shoot. He could easily rival Denzel Washington on the big screen any day.

She felt even more conscious about her appearance, and as she walked toward Marcus, she crossed her arms over her chest.

"Marcus." She gave him a warm smile. "Hello."

His eyes swept over her in a quick perusal. "I hope this isn't a bad time."

"No. What are you doing here?"

"I was in the neighborhood. And I figured I'd see how you were doing."

"I'm okay."

"No other problems?"

Marie sat in the living room with a magazine on her lap, but Alice wasn't naïve enough to believe that her sister wasn't eavesdropping. "Uh, maybe we can step outside."

She placed an arm on Marcus's bicep, immediately feeling the bulging muscles beneath. He was definitely an incredible specimen of a man. Pushing that thought out of her mind, she led him to the front door and onto the porch.

Dusk settled over the city. There was a chill in the air, so Alice hugged her arms.

"Cold?"

"No, not really."

Marcus's eyes swept over her again, lingering on her legs and feet. Alice couldn't believe it, but her skin actually tingled beneath his gaze. God, he was staring at her legs. And judging from the look on his face, he liked what he saw.

Which thrilled her down to her very toes.

"You should at least put on some shoes."

"I'm fine. Really."

"Here." He slipped out of his blazer. "Take this."

His chest muscles bunched and expanded, and Alice was helpless to tear her eyes away from him. He'd always been incredibly sexy when they were younger, but now that he was a man . . .

He looped his arms around her as he placed the blazer on her shoulders. His fingers barely grazed her body, but where they did she felt prickles of warmth. The blazer held his body heat, and it enveloped her. The faint scent of his musky cologne floated to her nose. "Forever a gentleman."

"I try my best."

"You asked if anything has happened. No. But

I've had time to think, and I'm not convinced that note wasn't pure coincidence."

Marcus raised an eyebrow, his expression dubious.

"Okay, maybe it was intentional, but I guess I just think it was someone's crazy idea of how to get a laugh."

"And you thought it was funny?"

Despite Marcus's jacket, Alice suddenly shivered as she remembered the knife protruding from her tire. "If you wanted to scare me, you have."

"I didn't mean to scare you. I just hope you take this seriously. You have to pay attention to everything, Alice. If you see anything or anyone that seems strange—"

"Call you and you'll come save me?" Her lips curled up in a smile.

"I don't want anything bad to happen to you," Marcus said seriously.

"Thank you."

She met his eyes and for a long moment, he simply stared at her. Then he jammed his hands in his pants pockets and dropped his gaze to the artificial turf covering the porch.

"By the way, congratulations. I heard about the cash donation to the theater. There's no doubt that happened because your name is now connected to the theater."

"I'm just glad the theater has gotten some of the money it clearly needs."

"Wanna celebrate? Maybe get a bite to eat?"

"Right now?"

He shrugged. "Why not? Two old friends . . ."

"Uh, well, this isn't exactly the best time." For one thing, she certainly couldn't go out dressed as she was. Other than that, she really wanted to go through the plays so she could narrow down her options to a few.

But it was the thought of going out with Marcus when she couldn't quite stop looking at him like he was the sexiest man alive that made her fearful of spending time with him. Maybe it was better she limit their one-on-one time together.

"Oh."

If Alice wasn't mistaken, he looked slightly crushed. She wondered why. "Rain check?"

"Sure. Well, I'm glad you're okay. Did you get a different car?"

"Mmm-hmm. The black Saturn."

"Good. Nothing flashy."

"I don't think whoever slashed my tire knows where I live. And if he or she does, they haven't come here."

"Good to hear. Hopefully, it's nothing to worry about. But just in case, please be careful."

"I will."

"All right, I won't keep you."

"Here's your jacket." She shrugged out of it and passed it to him. And when his eyes flickered over the length of her body again, her heart pounded against her ribs.

Their gazes met, held. Something changed between them in that moment. A spark ignited and Alice's skin grew hot as Marcus's gaze once again went lower, lingering on her lips.

Almost as if he wanted to kiss her.

Alice's mouth suddenly went dry, and she flicked her tongue out to moisten her bottom lip.

Marcus watched the simple action, and Alice realized that she *wanted* to feel Marcus's lips on hers—slow, wet, and hot.

God, what was wrong with her?

"What was that?" Marcus asked, turning his attention to the road.

"What?" Alice looked behind him.

"I . . . I thought I heard a noise." He shrugged. "Guess it was nothing."

Alice's heart fluttered as Marcus looked at everything but her. Goodness, he was actually avoiding her.

She hadn't mistaken the desire she'd seen in his eyes any more than she could deny the rush of passion she'd felt beneath his gaze.

Days ago, she was irritated because Marcus hadn't looked at her with the spark of interest that said he thought she looked good. Now that he had, she suddenly wished he wouldn't.

Maybe she was going crazy.

"Well, I guess I'd better go," he said.

"Good night." Alice smiled brightly.

"Good night." He turned and headed down the steps.

As Marcus started his car and backed out of the driveway, he saw Alice peer through lace curtains of the floor-to-ceiling window beside the door. He frowned, and not simply because he was wondering why the hell he couldn't read her.

He hadn't quite been prepared for seeing her so casually dressed. And *barefoot*. Christ, he hadn't expected her to look so good so dressed down.

She *was* beautiful. Damn, she was more than

beautiful. She was exquisite. From those wide, brown eyes to her ruby red toenails, the whole package was gorgeous.

He thrummed his fingers against the steering wheel. Today, she looked like the girl next door, but she was hardly that. And he still wasn't entirely sure her stardom hadn't gone to her head.

At least he had eased his mind. She was all right.

The knife incident had disturbed him more than he'd thought it would. It had brought the memories of Melissa back with striking force.

He had met Melissa Reynolds almost a year ago when he was assigned to drive by her house while she was under police protection. She had filed for divorce from her husband and walked out on him. As a result, he had threatened on numerous occasions to kill her. Twenty-two years her senior, her husband was enraged at the thought that she'd married him for his clout and money, and that once she didn't need him, she was getting rid of him without a second thought.

Melissa was afraid, which was why she reported the threats to the police. She had gotten a restraining order, but when she claimed she'd seen her husband hanging around her new house on several occasions, the captain of Marcus's precinct ordered police units to drive by her house at regular intervals to make sure she was okay.

Marcus knew the captain was attracted to Melissa and couldn't fault the man; he had seen pictures of her, and she was absolutely stunning in person. But he didn't expect her to show an interest in *him*.

He was parked outside of her house writing down some notes when she first came out to see him. Instantly, he was smitten by the dark-skinned beauty.

"Hey there," she said, smiling down at him as she glanced through his car window.

Marcus closed his notebook. "Hello, Mrs. Reynolds."

"Please, call me Melissa."

"All right. Melissa."

Bending, she leaned her elbows against the window frame and stared at him directly. "You must get pretty lonely out here. All by yourself."

Her playful pout made it clear she was flirting. Marcus suddenly felt flustered. "I've got a lot of work to keep me occupied."

"Hmm." Bringing one hand to her hair, she twirled a dark tendril. In moving her arm, she gave Marcus a clear view of her cleavage—and he knew it was no accident. But he was helpless to stop his body's reaction to her raw sensuality.

"Did you need something?" he managed to say.

She giggled. "That depends."

"On what?"

She answered him with a heated look. Marcus glanced away.

"Why don't you come inside? For some juice, or maybe a sandwich?"

"No. That's all right." The last thing he needed was to go into this woman's house. He knew exactly what she wanted. Maybe if they had met under different circumstances he might be tempted, but this was wrong.

She'd stood then, sighing wistfully. "Well, if you change your mind."

"I won't." He spoke in a businesslike tone, and he was proud he'd pulled it off. He thought that would be the end of it.

He was wrong. Over the next two weeks, she always came out to see him. When her subtle and not so subtle attempts to seduce him failed, she resorted to playing on his sensibilities as an officer. "I'm afraid," she'd say. "I think Peter is at the back of the house."

Marcus would do a search of the area and find nothing suspicious. But to make her feel better, he sometimes went inside her house and share a coffee with her or a piece of fruit. Soon, he admitted to himself that he liked spending time with her as much as she liked spending time with him. She was vivacious, her laughter refreshing. And she was beautiful. He was flattered by her attention.

One time when they were in her kitchen, as they laughed over some silly joke, Melissa edged closer to him and placed her hand on his thigh. He knew exactly where she was heading, and this time, he wasn't about to resist her. She ended up in his arms, her body pressed to his, his lips smothering hers. But after a very quick and heated exchange, he regained his sanity. He knew better than to cross the line with someone he was supposed to be protecting, and he got out of there fast. He had many more opportunities, but aside from that one time, he never touched her again. It wouldn't be right. He was there to serve and protect, not do the nasty.

Which is why in the days before her death, he began pulling away altogether, refusing to go inside her house for a coffee or a quick bite. Not only was he worried about the appearance of impropriety, he was worried about getting himself tangled in a web he couldn't get out of.

He still regretted the events of that last day. It was precisely because he was trying to keep their contact to a minimum that his judgment had been clouded. That day, she came to the car and begged him to come inside. She said Peter had called her and she was afraid for her life.

Reluctantly, he had gone inside, checked the house and the property. Finding nothing amiss, he became frustrated. Melissa was clearly trying to seduce him again.

Still, there was something in her voice that evening when she pleaded with him not to leave her, not yet—a hint of fear in her eyes that was genuine. If he had only believed her. Stayed a little while longer. Trusted his instincts. But he hadn't. He figured she was manipulating him, and he left her even as she begged him with tear-filled eyes not to go.

An hour later, he was back at the house, staring in disbelief at her lifeless body. Peter had shot her, then shot himself.

The ensuing mess was ugly. Peter had left a note saying he had been driven to such drastic measures because his wife had been in love with and was having an affair with someone else. It went on to say he hoped the guy was happy.

There had been many questions about the note, and after a couple of days, Marcus confessed to his captain that he was the man Peter had referred to. He told him how he had flirted with Melissa, had gone into her house on more than one occasion and spent time with her when he should have been outside, watching the house. He admitted to Captain Greer that he had been flattered by Melissa's attention, which had contributed to his lapse in judgment, but he also promised him that he had *not* had an affair with her, only that the husband was deranged enough to believe he had.

In the end, nothing had come of it. Marcus hadn't been reprimanded because there simply wasn't enough evidence. But in his heart, Marcus knew he was guilty of crossing a line. If he had kept things on a strictly business level with Melissa, she might very well be alive today.

The whole ugly incident had proved to be a learning experience. He would never compromise his role as police officer again. And he would keep a level head around pretty women.

He wasn't going to make another mistake.

With that thought, his mind came back to the present. Back to Alice. She definitely exuded a powerful sexuality, one he had been trying to ignore from the first moment he'd seen her again. But something inside him had stirred when he'd seen her tonight in a way it hadn't before. Maybe it was the fact that her beauty seemed to shine from the inside out.

Marcus gazed out at the water as he drove north along Lake Shore Drive toward his home. He didn't care if Alice looked good in a burlap sack. He wasn't going to lose perspective around her.

She'd once been a good friend, and he didn't mind working to rebuild that friendship. But that's all this relationship was about.

Nothing else.

Ten

If someone had asked her two months ago if she'd consider teaching a class of children the basics of acting, Alice would have said no. It simply hadn't been part of her vision in terms of an acting career. But to her own surprise, she found she was enjoying the job tremendously.

Two weeks had passed since the tire incident, and nothing else had happened. The parents all seemed pleased with her efforts, with the exception of Terry, who always grumbled and complained about something. So Alice felt comfortable chalking the tire incident up to a childish prank.

Alice clapped her hands together to get the children's attention. After forty minutes of role playing, they'd become restless, so she'd given them a break. They were slowly making their way back onto the stage.

"Come on, everybody," Alice said. "It's time to get back to work."

They congregated around her, sitting cross-legged on the floor. In the first couple of weeks, they had taken longer to settle after a break, but as the classes had progressed, the children had become more serious. Probably because last week Alice had let them all know that they would have to audition for parts in the summer play—the best actors would get the best parts. She had worried that the concept of competition might cause disputes among them, but they were all acting like little professionals.

Alice sat on the stool. "All right. We've been doing a lot of role playing and improv, which you have all been wonderful at. But right now, I want to try a different kind of exercise. It'll still be role playing, but with a twist." Her glance took in the whole group. "I want you to think of someone you don't like."

"That's easy," Devin said.

A few of the children giggled, and Alice gave them a stern look to quiet them once again. "This is serious," she explained. "Now, this can be someone at your school, someone on your street, someone from anywhere. But it has to be the person you like the least."

"What if they're old?" Jenna asked. "There's this really mean old lady on my street."

"If that's the person you like the least, that's fine."

"What do we get to do? Act out what we'd like to do to them?" Brian's eyes danced with mischief, and his comment made the children laugh once again.

"There's this girl in my class I'd like to—"

"No, that's not what you'll be doing," Alice

quickly interjected, wanting to quell the kind of negative thoughts that had given her this idea. During the break, she'd walked past Linda and Carrie, and she'd overheard them talking negatively about another girl. What she'd heard had made her think of her own childhood, how people had shut her out because she was different and how she wished they could have spent a day in her shoes. That's exactly what she had in mind for the children now.

"In fact, you'll be doing the exact opposite. You are going to pretend to be this person. You have to imagine what it's like to be them, try to feel what you think they feel and think what they think."

Clearly surprised, the children looked around at each other, mumbling words Alice couldn't quite hear. She had the sense that the thought of pretending they were their least favorite person was not a popular one.

"The fact is, when you work in plays or in the movies, sometimes you have to play the part of someone who is totally different from you." Her eyes scanned the group, settling on Brian. "For example, suppose you know someone who's a racist, so you don't like them because of that. But what if one day you get hired to play a bad guy who *is* racist? How would you do it? You'd have to get inside the head of that person, even though in real life, you're nothing like him.

"So I want you to take a few minutes to think about that. Then, we'll discuss who you've chosen and go from there."

"What about you?" Michelle asked. "Are you gonna choose the person you like the least as well? That way, you can show us exactly what you mean."

Michelle's question gave Alice pause. In proposing this idea, she had never expected the tables to be turned on her. It was an exercise she'd thought of spontaneously, and given her own past, it seemed fitting at the time.

"Yeah," Devin chimed.

"Well . . ." she hedged. "I'll think about that while you all think about it. And we'll see." But the thought of getting into the mind of her least favorite person was harder than she'd imagined. There were several people she could choose, but Tanisha stood out above the rest because she had a calculating, manipulative way about her. Slimy, like a slug. To your face she could pretend she liked you, when behind your back she did what she could to make your life miserable.

Not that Tanisha had ever gone out of her way to pretend she liked Alice. Only when Marcus had been around. When he hadn't been, she had consistently picked on her like the other students had. But she'd been able to fool Marcus, because she'd been a good actress.

Knowing that about her, and remembering the way Tanisha had tried on more than one occasion to sabotage her friendship with Marcus, Alice didn't particularly want to get into her head. Never in a million years would she understand why Tanisha had been hellbent on making her life miserable, and at this point in her life she didn't even want to try. Because trying meant remembering. And remembering meant pain.

Tanisha had done her best to make Marcus choose between her and Alice. If Marcus told Tanisha he was going to walk Alice home because some guys had been picking on her, Tanisha would suddenly be ill. There was a time Marcus had promised to take Alice to a movie on a Friday night, just a friendly date, and she'd had a rough day at school and home and was looking forward to an evening where she could pretend Marcus was hers. He'd called that evening to tell her that Tanisha had some crisis and needed him. Marcus was always apologetic when breaking a date with Alice, but he hadn't recognized the pattern in Tanisha's manipulation.

"Okay," Alice said. "Are you ready?"

Suddenly the theater was pitched in blackness. Excited shrieks erupted from the children, followed by laughter.

"Everybody stay where you are," Alice instructed them. She fully expected the lights to come on at any moment, but in the meantime she didn't want any of them getting hurt by wandering around when they couldn't see a thing.

She waited several seconds, and when the lights didn't come on, she called out into the darkness. "Hello? Anybody out there?"

More giggling. Then, "Woo."

Damn. This was not her idea of fun. Well, she would have to do *something*. She didn't trust herself to go down the side stairs, but she could probably find her way to the back of the theater in the dark and open the door. "Okay, guys," she said to the children. "Take a seat and *stay* seated. I'm gonna go see what's going on."

Boy, was she glad she was wearing jeans and a T-shirt. Going down on all fours, Alice crawled in the direction of the stage's edge. Once there, she went onto her butt and slid off the edge to the floor below. It was a short distance, but as she landed, her legs wobbled. The darkness had disoriented her.

She walked forward slowly, feeling for the first row of seats. Her knee made contact with a chair before her hand did and she stumbled. Recovering, she felt her way around to the aisle, then continued on. She didn't like this one bit, and as she carefully made her way to the back, her heart did a series of somersaults in her chest.

Her shoulder brushed against something, and Alice screamed. A few of the children roared in laughter just as she realized she'd collided with a body.

"Alice?"

"Marcus!"

"Yeah."

Marcus's voice was coming from a distance away. So if he wasn't the one who'd bumped into her, then who was?

She felt a swoosh of air as the body moved past her. Was that one of the students, or someone else? And was someone deliberately trying to scare the crap out of her?

Goosebumps popped out over her skin. "Marcus, where are you?"

"Here." His voice was closer. "Keep talking."

"I'm about halfway up the aisle on the right."

"All right. I'm almost there."

Alice's heart thudded so hard in her chest, she was certain the sound reverberated against the theater walls. "Marcus?"

"Right here."

One strong hand touched her breast, and she jumped about a foot.

"Sorry," Marcus said, a hint of embarrassment in his tone. "I didn't see you."

"I know." But her heart still raced from the brief contact. Marcus's hand on her breast had made her body tingle all over.

"What happened to the lights?"

"I don't know. I was heading back to open the door." But if Marcus had just come in, why hadn't she seen a stream of light when he opened the outside door? "When did you get here?"

"I've been here for a while. I was watching you with the kids, then I went to the back office. The lights went off there and I figured I'd come out here to see if the theater was dark too. That's when I heard you scream."

"Someone brushed against me, Marcus. That's why I screamed. I thought maybe it was one of the kids, but they didn't say anything." She giggled nervously. "Maybe I imagined the whole thing."

"You're okay?"

"Yeah. But I'd be better if I could see something." Alice linked an arm through his and held on to him tightly. She was relieved he was here.

"All right. Let's get to the back door and let in some light."

"Yes." Alice clutched Marcus tighter. "Let's."

Marcus's heart raced. He liked the way Alice felt against him, her breasts pressed against his arm. Hell, he'd liked the charge that shot through him as he accidentally touched her. But mostly, he liked the way she held him so tightly, which made it clear she trusted him to protect her. And he knew he would do anything to keep her safe.

God, he had to get over his complex with beautiful but vulnerable women.

As Alice and Marcus moved up the aisle, the back door opened. The silhouetted shape of a man appeared. After her encounter with the unknown person in the aisle, Alice found she was more afraid than she wanted to admit. Instinctively, she clutched Marcus's arm a little tighter.

"Hold that door open," Marcus said. But the very next instant, the lights came to life.

Terry stood in the doorway. "What's going on in here?"

"The lights went out," Alice explained a bit defensively. Every time Terry looked at her, she felt like she'd done something wrong and needed to justify her actions. "Why are you here so soon?"

"It's almost four o'clock. I came for my son."

Alice glanced at her watch. It wasn't quite three-thirty. She'd given the parents strict instructions to drop their kids off and give her the three hours for the class with them alone. When the parents were around, the children were more easily distracted, as was she. Terry was the only one who gave her a hard time on the issue.

As an afterthought, Alice realized she was still clutching Marcus's arm. She loosened her grip, smiling at him sheepishly.

"I'm gonna head to the back," Marcus said. "Check the breaker switch to see if I can figure out what happened."

"Okay." She walked toward the stage and the children—then paused midstride as she saw Willie. When had he gotten here?

Apparently, Marcus was wondering the same

thing, for as Willie approached them, he asked, "Did you just get here?"

"No, I was in the office when the lights went off."

"I didn't see you back there," Marcus said.

"I was with Tanisha. Ask her."

Marcus wasn't sure what to believe. Willie could be telling the truth. He had been in the wardrobe room, not in the office, so he couldn't account for Tanisha's whereabouts nor Willie's.

Perhaps he was making too much of this. But something in his gut told him something was wrong.

He wrapped an arm around Alice's shoulder and led her several feet to the left, out of earshot of Willie and Terry. "Alice, I think you should wrap up the class for today. I don't like this."

Alice met his eyes with concerned ones of her own. "What? Do you think—"

"I don't know what to think. But I'd rather not take any chances."

"Oh." She spoke casually, though Marcus's concern had her scared. She knew he was considering the possibility that the lights going out hadn't been an accident.

Which made her remember the person she'd brushed against.

She shivered, and to her surprise, he cupped her chin. Her gaze flew to his, wide and curious. He held her gaze, his eyes dark and mysterious. Alice's pulse raced with the realization that she wanted him to trail his fingers along her skin, tangle them in her hair, kiss her senseless.

Marcus suddenly glanced away, dropping his hand to his side.

Leaving Alice with more questions than answers.

"Go on," he said. He was back to being the professional cop. "You round up the kids. I'll go to the back and see if I can't figure out what happened."

"Sure."

As Marcus made his way to the back office, he tried to push the question of why he had spontaneously touched Alice out of his mind. Instead, he focused on Tanisha. Where had she been in all of this? And where was she now?

He found her in the office, sitting at her desk.

"Marcus, what happened?" she asked as he walked toward her.

"I thought maybe you could tell me."

"Me?"

"Don't try to pretend you sat at your desk the entire time the lights were out."

"Actually, I did. Willie had just left the office, and I certainly couldn't see a thing back here. I figured I was better off staying where I was."

"What's up with Willie anyway? I thought you fired him."

"I did . . . but we had some things to iron out."

"I'll bet," Marcus said, his tone sarcastic.

She batted her eyelashes. "Excuse me?"

"Forget it." He'd known for a while that Tanisha and Willie were sleeping together. He certainly wasn't jealous, but he did wonder when his ex-wife was finally going to grow up. And he wondered if her involvement with Willie had gone sour and if that was the reason she'd fired him as the theater's teacher.

The way he saw it, the children had gained when Willie had walked out. He'd never been as gentle with them nor as encouraging as Alice. Watching her today, he'd seen a side of her he hadn't expected. She treated them as if *they* were the most important people in the world, not herself. She laughed while she instructed them, something he'd never seen Willie do. She gently placed a hand on their shoulders, or framed their faces when they had difficulty getting the exercise right. Willie was known to bark out orders to control them, while Alice simply gave the children a look and they calmed down.

"Marcus?"

"Hmm?"

"I asked if you could check the fuse box or the breaker. Whatever it is."

"Sure. I'll do that now."

"In any case, this is an old building. I'll probably have to call someone in to check the circuits."

"No doubt," he said, then strolled out of the office. He had a feeling he wouldn't find a damn thing out of order.

Marcus's instincts were right. He didn't find anything strange. If someone had messed with circuits, they seemed to be in good working order now.

Still, he told Tanisha to make sure an electrician came in and checked the wiring. It *was* an old building, so he couldn't be one hundred percent certain that the blackout hadn't been an accident.

Leaving Tanisha in the office, Marcus went back into the theater, hoping to catch Alice before she left. But a quick perusal of the area told him she was gone.

Damn it.

He didn't know why he was so out of sorts. He hadn't asked her to wait for him, but he had assumed she would. He had hoped to catch her to ask her a few more questions. Maybe he was overreacting, but he was worried about her. It wasn't a feeling he could describe, other than a gut instinct.

Like the one he'd ignored with Melissa.

God, he didn't want to make that mistake twice.

Realizing that Alice might still be outside, he jogged up the aisle to the back door. When he opened the door, he saw a couple of parents and their children in the parking lot. And he saw Alice's black Saturn making a right out of the parking lot.

"Alice!" he called, but she didn't hear him. Of course she didn't.

As he watched the rear of her car disappear, he told himself to get hold of his emotions. Why was he acting like this? It didn't make sense. At least she was on her way home, away from this theater. It was here he was most concerned for her.

He waved at Carmen as she got into her car with her son. Then he descended the steps and made his way to his own car. But the nagging worry about Alice didn't leave him, not even as he backed out of the driveway and sped off down the street.

Amidst his thoughts of whether someone was truly out to get her, he remembered the electric jolt he'd felt when his hand had touched her breast. To his utter surprise and frustration, he found he had an erection. Lord, what was wrong with him? He had to admit that ever since he'd seen her at her house, he thought about her quite often. Damn, he *wanted* to touch her again, to see if she'd moan and purr if he put his hands all over her.

God, that was all he needed. Yeah, she looked like a goddess now, but did that mean he had to think about what it would be like to get her between the sheets?

Maybe Khalil was right. Maybe it had been too long since he'd last had sex.

Which was, he thought with chagrin, just over a year—a short-term affair with a colleague months after his divorce, which hadn't worked out because she had picked up and moved to Denver. After that, he couldn't be bothered with casual romps just to satisfy his sexual craving.

But maybe it would be different with Alice.

No, no, it wouldn't. It would be a mistake. Damn, but a year was a long time. No wonder he was looking at his old friend-turned-goddess and thinking about getting her naked!

No matter how hard he tried to get the image out of his head, he kept seeing her standing before him in her baggy T-shirt and shorts, those slim, smooth legs exposed, those beautiful large breasts jiggling as she moved—and he found himself wanting to strip her naked and just feast on her luscious body until they were both left sweaty and so satisfied that neither one of them could move. His erection stretched painfully against his jeans. Damn. Two hard-ons in one day.

What was wrong with him?

He pictured Alice's big, brown, doelike eyes staring up at him. Maybe something was finally right.

His mind was so absorbed with Alice that when he heard the loud *pop!* he only had time to veer toward the curb and hit the brakes. Experience and instinct made him duck for cover even as he reached for his holster, only to realize it wasn't there. He didn't carry his gun while off duty.

The next instant the sound of laughter made him cautiously lift his head. On the sidewalk beside his car, he saw a group of young boys. They were laughing hysterically—at him.

That's when he saw the old, gray Chevy pass him with smoke billowing from its tailpipe. Damn, a stupid car had backfired!

"Quinn, get a grip," he told himself. Which meant he had to find a way to stop thinking about Alice.

The first order of business when he got home would be a cold shower.

Hell, the way he was feeling, he may as well fill the tub full of ice and set his ass in there.

Maybe that would do the trick.

Eleven

As she did every morning, Alice awoke with the hope that somehow she and her mother would make some headway toward repairing their relationship. But like every morning since her return to Chicago, that hope quickly dwindled. Why a little flame of hope continued to burn in her heart, Alice didn't know, and she wished there was a way to snuff it out.

Not caring would be so much easier. Her mother's indifference and cold attitude wouldn't hurt her if she simply didn't care. During her thirteen years away from home, she'd thought she *had* stopped caring, but being home proved to her that she still did.

Bright and early, Alice prepared a breakfast of fresh fruit pieces for her mother and brought it to her in bed. Rosa didn't even thank her. Instead she asked her once again if she'd called Sara. Apparently, Sara had called yesterday but, seeing the number on the Caller ID, Rosa had let the phone ring, so Sara had left a message. Rosa reiterated to Alice that like the first time Sara had called, she didn't appreciate Sara's interference in her private business. She wanted Alice to put a stop to it.

"Why, mother?" Alice asked. "What did Sara do to make you hate her so much?"

"Just tell her I don't want her calling me. As far as I'm concerned, we stopped being family the day Winston died."

Alice was tempted to tell her mother that if she wanted Sara to stop calling, then she should tell her herself. But Alice didn't do that; she couldn't. Not while her mother was still recovering.

"And you can tell whichever of your friends that keeps calling here and hanging up to stop that nonsense," Rosa added. "Though it's probably Sara, just trying to get on my nerves."

Alice didn't even bother to reply to that. Good grief, Sara was fifty-two years old. She certainly had better things to do with her time than crank-call her sister-in-law. For all Alice knew, her mother was making that story up.

Alice left her mother's room feeling more frustrated than ever. Each day she spent in this house made it more and more clear she didn't truly know Rosa. How was it possible for people who were flesh and blood to be so completely different?

Now, back in her own bedroom, Alice sat cross-legged on the twin bed. Reaching for the phone, she brought it onto her lap. God, she hated to do this, but she had put it off long enough—hoping her mother would come to her senses—which she hadn't, so now Alice had no choice. She punched in the digits to Sara's Los Angeles number.

It rang three times before Sara picked up. "Hello?"

"Aunt Sara. Hi."

"Alice?"

Alice could hear a smile in the woman's voice, which made what she was about to tell her even worse. "Yeah, it's me."

"Child, do you know what time it is?" she teased.

Alice threw a quick glance at the digital clock beside her bed. It was 9:23, which meant it was two hours earlier on the west coast. Gosh, she hadn't even thought when she'd picked up the phone!

"I'm sorry. I completely forgot about the time difference."

"That's all right." Her yawn sounded over the phone line. "I was getting up anyway. Have to open up the shop."

"How are you, Aunt Sara?"

"I've been fine. Busy, but hanging in there."

Aunt Sara hadn't remarried after her husband, Winston, had died. She'd loved him dearly, something even as a child Alice had noticed, and later Sara had confided in Alice that she didn't think she could give her heart so completely again.

While living with her for three years, Alice had known that she'd brought immense joy to the woman's life. She hadn't had any children of her own, and she'd easily fallen into the role of mother with Alice. For that, Alice would be eternally grateful.

"So, the business is going well?"

"The shop is growing every day. I've even got one of those dot-com addresses on the Web so I can sell flowers that way. Now, if only I was computer-literate."

Alice chuckled softly. She missed her aunt. In the last ten years that she had been on her own, she had seen her aunt often, but as she got busier in the film industry, their contact lessened. Still, she'd tried to show her appreciation to her aunt for taking her in at a time when she'd desperately needed someone. Sara had always derived great pleasure from planting flowers, and had dreamed of the day she could quit her job as a housekeeper and open a flower shop. The moment Alice had the money, she'd made that dream come true for her aunt.

"I'm sure you'll do just fine."

"It's good to hear your voice."

"It's always good to hear yours too."

"Did your mother tell you I called? I called yesterday too, but no one was home."

"Yes . . . Aunt Sara, I have to talk to you about that." Alice blew out a frustrated breath. "I don't know what's wrong with my mother, but she . . . well, she doesn't want you to call here for her again. She's being real bullheaded about the whole thing. I think she's too proud to admit that she's sick."

"Oh, brother." Sara sighed.

"I'm sorry, Aunt Sara. I wish I understood her, but I don't."

"It's not your fault, sweetheart. For some reason, she still sees me as a threat."

"A threat? That doesn't make any sense."

There was a brief pause. "You left her, came to live with me."

"Yeah, but you had nothing to do with that. She's the one who pushed me away. Told me to go."

"Hmm."

Aunt Sara was upset, Alice could hear it in her voice, and she didn't blame her. Her mother had always been cold toward her aunt, and from what Alice knew, she'd never had just cause.

But then, what had been her just cause to tell her own daughter to leave and never return?

"It's probably best I call you from now on," Alice told her aunt. "Since Mom's health is still delicate, and I don't want to upset her."

"You have a wonderful heart, Alice. That's the one thing I love most about you. Despite all you've been through, you still find it in your heart to give."

"Oh, you give me too much credit."

"It's true, and I hope one day your mother is able to give you the love you deserve."

"That's very sweet of you. Thanks." A beep sounded on the line. "Oh, hold on a sec. Another call's coming through."

"I'd better get going, hon. Love you."

"Love you, too. Bye." Aunt Sara had succeeded in doing what she did best—filling her heart with warmth. Alice clicked over to the other line. "Hello?"

There was only dead air. "Anybody there? Hello?"

Alice hung up. Just as she was replacing the phone on her night table, it rang. She snatched the receiver. "Hello?"

"I'm watching you," a muffled voice said softly.

"What? Who is this?"

Click.

A chill swept over her. Alice stared at the receiver in her hand as if it could give her answers. But of course it couldn't.

When she'd had a phone installed in her room last week, she hadn't gotten a Caller ID box. But she could still find out who had just called. She hit the star button, then punched in number 6 followed by 9. A recording came on that told her the last number that called her line was unknown.

Damn. Alice replaced the receiver, an uneasy feeling in her gut. She didn't know what to make of the call, but passing it off as a prank would be too easy. God, what if someone actually *was* watching her?

She reached for her purse beside the bed and dug out her wallet. She'd placed the scrap of paper with Marcus's number there. As soon as she found it, she called him.

His phone rang four times before a machine picked up. At this time in the morning, he was no doubt at work. But as he didn't live in the neighborhood anymore, she didn't know which precinct.

"Hi, Marcus. It's Alice. Call me, please. As soon as you get this message."

She hung up the phone and walked to the window. Standing to the side of the frame, she peered outside. She saw nothing but two red-breasted robins in the oak tree opposite her window.

Was someone really watching her? And if so, was that person outside right now, hiding somewhere? In a house across the street?

The voice had been so muffled that she couldn't make out if a woman or a man had called. God, she prayed this was some type of prank.

If it wasn't . . .

Did someone know where she lived? Where her mother lived?

Finding that thought disturbing, Alice hustled

from the window and returned to her bed. Maybe she should keep a low profile.

And until she heard from Marcus she needed something to keep her mind occupied. She reached for the volume of plays on the floor beside her bed. Tanisha had given her the okay to do something that would require a bigger budget, made possible by the donation from the computer graphics firm. And she was constantly making more phone calls to solicit funding.

Alice had narrowed the choice down to two plays: *Out of This World* and *The Big Adventure*. Both plays had fairly large casts, which would provide roles for all the students.

As she re-read *Out of This World,* a charming little mystery about a ghost that haunts a classroom, Alice felt more and more certain that this was the play the children would perform. Yes, it was perfect. She would announce her decision at the next class.

Alice was reading the last pages of the play when the phone rang again. Startled, she could only stare at it. She couldn't believe she was actually afraid to pick it up.

When it rang a third time, she grabbed the receiver. "Hello?"

"Desirée, hi. It's Tanisha."

Fleetingly, Alice wondered if Tanisha would ever call her by her real name. Whatever her reason, Alice had long stopped correcting her. It just wasn't important.

"What's up, Tanisha?"

"I received a call from Darin Walburg today. He's one of the city councilors I usually meet with to solicit funding for the theater. In the past, they've given us a substantial amount of money, but over time, that amount has decreased considerably. Anyway, I was speaking with him today about increased funding for the fall season and he told me he would like to meet you, Desirée, so the two of you can discuss your vision for the theater's future. Oh, and he's a real fan of yours."

"Why on earth would he want to meet with me about the fall season? And I don't have a *vision* for the theater. I'm only helping out until the summer."

"All right, so I wasn't totally honest with him. But he doesn't need to know that. Tell him anything you want, as long as he ends up giving us a nice big fat check."

"I can't believe you'd even ask me to lie."

"You're an actress, aren't you? I thought you told stories for a living."

Alice ignored the snide comment. It was meant to get a rise out of her, and she wouldn't give Tanisha the satisfaction. "I won't lie to him. *My* reputation is on the line here."

"Then at least meet with him," Tanisha quickly said. "Tell him what you think this theater means to the community. That shouldn't be too hard a stretch for you."

Tanisha's snarky tone led Alice to wonder, not for the first time, what Tanisha was doing at the theater herself. Surely she could have found a job elsewhere, for more pay. Did she even care about the children? Perhaps it was being in charge that made her work there so appealing.

Remembering the picture in the office of Tanisha with her arms spread wide around a group of students, Alice prayed Tanisha was doing it for the children, not for any selfish motives.

"He wants to get together with you for dinner on Friday. I told him around seven."

"You said I'd be there?"

"You told me you'd do whatever you could to help the theater."

"Yes, but I'd appreciate a call first!" Alice snapped. "Where?"

"Downtown somewhere. I told him you'd call him today."

"Fine." Alice was angry with Tanisha's thoughtlessness, but she thought of Mia and the fact that she didn't want to see the theater go downhill, and realized she'd do what she could to help out.

"Here's his number."

Alice wrote down the number Tanisha recited. "All right. I'll call him. Bye."

When Alice hung up, she was about to call Darin, but instead decided to check on her mother. It was just about noon. Time for her to take medication.

Alice rapped softly on her mother's bedroom door, then opened it. Inside, her mother, sitting on the edge of the bed, scrambled to shove some kind of box she'd been holding beneath her pillow.

Walking into the room, Alice frowned. She'd caught a glimpse of the silver box, and knew it was her mother's jewelry box. Why hide it?

"What is that?" she asked, despite the closed expression on her mother's face.

"I need a refill of a prescription."

"What? Why didn't you tell me?"

"Because I didn't realize until now."

"Let me see the bottle." Alice approached her

mother and her mother passed her the pill bottle. "You've got one refill. I'll call the pharmacy."

"I can call the pharmacy myself. I'm not helpless."

Alice bit her cheek, determined not to say anything, but finally she couldn't hold her tongue any longer. "I'm trying to help you, Mother, yet you act like I'm the enemy."

"If you give me a few minutes, I can call the pharmacy, then you can go pick up the pills."

Just like that, her mother had dismissed her once again. Alice didn't know how much more of this she could take.

"Whatever you want, Mother." She palmed the pill bottle so that she could take it with her to the pharmacy. "By the way, I spoke with Aunt Sara. I told her not to call here anymore. I hope you're happy."

Alice didn't wait for her mother's reply. Instead, she marched out of the room and to her own bedroom, where she slipped out of her cutoff jeans and T-shirt and put on a summery dress. Then she grabbed her purse and headed out of her house to her car.

As she settled behind the wheel, the feeling of frustration disappeared and was replaced by a sudden feeling of fear.

Was someone out here, watching her? If so, who was it?

But the bigger question was, what did this person want with her?

Hours later, Alice was surprised to open the front door and find Marcus standing on her mother's front porch. Worry lines creased his forehead as he stared down at her.

"Marcus," she said, unable to keep the happy note from her voice. "What are you doing here?"

"You called."

"And you came over? You live clear across town. Why not just call me back?"

"Your message sounded urgent."

Alice glanced at her watch. It was just after six in the evening, and he'd probably come right over after work to see if she was okay. Why did that thought make her pulse pound wildly? She could get used to his heroics.

But she wouldn't. The last thing she wanted to do was fall for Marcus once again. She may have succeeded in the tough arena of Hollywood, but her heart was still fragile. Besides, romantic entanglements had a way of ruining friendships, and right now, she wanted to rebuild their friendship more than anything.

"I . . . It seems silly now that I even called you."

"Humor me."

"You want to come inside?" Marie and Mia had gone out for dinner, and Alice had turned down their offer to join them, feeling that mother and daughter needed some time alone.

Marcus considered her carefully. "Actually, I'd like to cash in on that rain check since I'm here. I haven't had any dinner yet. Have you?"

"No."

"Good. Why don't we get a bite to eat somewhere?"

"Oh." Dinner with Marcus. That was harmless enough. And a good way to work at rebuilding their friendship. "Okay. Gimme a second."

She ran up the stairs to her bedroom, where she gave herself a brief once-over in the mirror. At least she was decently dressed today. Letting her hair loose from the scrunchie holding it in a ponytail, she fluffed it with her fingers, then frowned at the disheveled look. She pulled her hair back into a ponytail once again, applied a dab of burgundy lipstick to her lips, then stood back to look at her reflection.

Acceptable.

She grabbed her purse and was on her way out of the bedroom when she remembered perfume. She spent a fortune on the stuff, she may as well use it. Grabbing her favorite fragrance from her dresser, she sprayed some on her neck and wrists.

She peered in her mother's bedroom, found her watching television, and told her she'd be out for a little while, then went back downstairs to meet Marcus.

"Ready," she told him, with a smile. Bending, she slipped into casual sandals. When she glanced up at him, she saw him looking at her. At her feet, to be precise.

Her face flushed. She stood. "Let's go."

"Are you going to tell me why you called?" Marcus asked as she locked the door.

"Oh. In the car." She followed him to the Mustang. He opened the passenger door for her and she slipped inside. Then he rounded the car and got behind the wheel. As he started the car, he said, "All right, tell me."

"I got a crank call," she explained. "I probably just overreacted."

"What did the caller say?"

Alice was silent for a moment as her fingers played with the fabric of her dress. "He said, 'I'm watching you.' "

"He?"

"Actually, I don't know. The voice was muffled. I couldn't say for sure if it was a man or a woman."

"I don't like this."

Alice swallowed. She didn't like the situation either. She'd been trying as much as possible to pretend it didn't exist, but that wasn't going to make it go away.

They drove for several minutes in awkward silence, Alice watching the dazzling array of oranges and reds as they met the darkness on the horizon.

When they pulled on to the JFK Expressway, she turned to him. "Where are we going?"

"I figured we'd go to Navy Pier. There's a lot of variety there, so if we don't like one place, we can go to another."

"Sounds like the place has changed since I was last there."

"Big time."

Twenty minutes later, they were parked and walking through the gates of Navy Pier. The place was crowded—with tourists, Alice supposed—which was fitting, in a way, since she suddenly felt like one herself. It had been so long since she'd been here, and Marcus was right, the pier had changed considerably from its former industrial nature. It was now a tourist attraction. It had several restaurants with both indoor and outdoor seating, and at the front there was a listing of movies, indicating there was a theater inside.

"Where do you want to go?" Marcus asked.

"Doesn't matter to me."

Marcus placed a hand on the small of her back and led her along the sidewalk, through the crowds. Alice stiffened at his touch. He'd touched her like this years ago, yet now it seemed different somehow. And damn if she didn't like how his fingers felt on her body.

A mere few feet up the enormous strip, Marcus veered to the left, pulling her body to his as he did so. She was too close. She could smell the musky fragrance of his cologne, mixed with the faint hint of soap and Marcus's own unique, one hundred percent male scent.

Alice pushed the thought from her mind. It was exactly that kind of thinking that could get her into trouble.

As Marcus led her into Joe's Be-Bop Café, the sounds of Dixieland jazz greeted her. Despite the coolness of the evening, several people enjoyed the seating on the outdoor patio.

"You want to sit outside or inside?" Marcus asked.

"Inside."

Like the outside, the interior of the restaurant was crowded. On the stage a band of men played to an attentive crowd. Already she liked the place.

A hostess greeted them. "Smoking or non?"

"Non, please," Alice replied, then glanced at Marcus when she realized she'd made the decision for both of them.

"Fine with me. I don't smoke."

All the tables close to the band were filled, so the hostess led them to the very back of the restaurant, the only spot with a few open tables. As they sat, she placed the menus before them, then informed them that their server would be along shortly.

Marcus lifted his menu. "I don't know about you, but I could eat a horse."

"I'm starved."

They both checked out the menu in silence, then Marcus asked what she was going to have.

"Probably a burger. Smothered with cheddar cheese. And fries. You've got to have fries with a burger."

Marcus lowered his menu and raised an eyebrow at her. She knew exactly what he was thinking. He was surprised that she didn't eat tofu and salads to keep her slim figure. It annoyed her, because everyone seemed to think she'd starved herself into thinness. She once was fat, but now she was slim and everyone needed to get over themselves.

"Wow, a woman with an appetite. My kind of girl."

Immediately, Alice felt guilty for jumping to conclusions about him. It was just that between her sister and everyone else's disbelief that she'd lost so much weight in a natural, healthy manner, she expected him to feel the same way.

"Tanisha didn't eat more than a few pieces of lettuce whenever we went out," he added, as though he'd read Alice's inner thoughts.

"The key to weight loss is eating a balanced diet and working out. And every once in a while, a big, juicy burger. 'Cause the body definitely needs that too."

She flashed him a smile that Marcus found contagious. Her smile seemed to spill out from her very soul, which made her even more beautiful than she already was. "If I haven't told you already, you look great."

"Thanks."

She blushed, and he was surprised. Surely she heard every day in Hollywood just how gorgeous she was. But the more time he spent with her, the more he realized she didn't have a conceited bone in her body.

"Would you like some wine?" he asked.

"Sure. A Chardonnay would be great."

The waiter appeared and Marcus ordered a half carafe of Chardonnay. Then he settled his elbows on the table and simply looked at her.

He didn't say a word, and Alice shifted uncomfortably. Why did he have to look at her like that? As if he were trying to strip her naked with his eyes. That very thought made Alice's heart jump with excitement. She remembered high school, how in love with Marcus she had been. She would have given anything for him to look at her that way, to have his arms wrapped around her in a lover's embrace, to feel his lips caress her mouth, her neck, her breasts.

Alice's body thrummed with the direction of her thoughts. God help her, she was aroused.

And Marcus wouldn't stop looking at her.

He was her *friend*, not her lover, but any stranger here would think he was more than that. She tried to hold his gaze, to pretend she was just as bold, but she ended up blushing and looking away.

"Do I scare you?"

"What?" Those incredible cinnamon-colored eyes widened.

"You tend to look away when I look at you. I was just wondering if I scare you."

She laughed. "Of course you don't scare me."

He kept his eyes on hers, steady, but she met him with an equally steady gaze of her own. The vulnerability he'd noticed before was gone. Days ago, he hadn't been able to look at her in such a bold way because seeing the new and improved Alice reminded him how little he knew her now. But after spending time with her at the theater, he'd seen that she was still his old friend.

"I'm sorry," Marcus said. "I just find you fascinating to look at."

"Fascinating?"

"Yes. I still can't believe how much you've changed."

"Oh." She knew it didn't make sense, but she was disappointed. She didn't want to think that every time Marcus looked at her, he saw Desirée, not Alice.

"Does it embarrass you when I look at you?"

Alice responded with part shrug, part shake of the head.

Marcus definitely sensed some discomfort on her part. But the fact that she didn't think she was an all-important diva endeared her to him even more.

He wondered how she saw him, and was about to ask, until he came to his senses. He did *not* want to go there.

Instead, he changed the topic to business. "Did you happen to get a number of this person who called?"

Alice folded her arms across the table. "I tried. But it was unknown."

"Hmm."

"Hmm what?"

"Has this happened to you before? Someone stalking you, I mean?"

"Stalking!" she cried, then glanced around when she realized she'd raised her voice enough for others to hear. She spoke in a hushed tone. "Stalking? You think someone's stalking me?"

"What would you call it?"

"I . . . I don't know."

The waiter appeared with their wine, breaking the seriousness of the moment. Marcus ordered two cheeseburgers with fries for both of them. As soon as the waiter was gone, Marcus said, "Look, Alice, I know this isn't a comfortable topic. It never is. But for whatever reason, someone's determined to scare you."

"But who? Why?"

"I don't know. Do you have *any* idea?"

"No. None at all. I haven't been here for thirteen years. I know I wasn't the most popular person in high school, but who would want to actually hurt me? And after all this time?"

"One thing you learn as a cop is that some people are just plain crazy, Alice. We'll never understand what motivates them."

That thought made her shudder.

"There was someone in Los Angeles," she said after a moment. "A guy who used to send me weird letters. He used to tell me all the sexual things he wanted to do to me. But the letters always went to my agent, not me, thank God. Marcus, I never let anyone know where I lived. I never let the media know my true name. I'd heard the stories of obsessed fans stalking actors and I wanted to be safe, just in case." Fear tickled her spine. "You don't think this guy could have followed me here?"

"Anything's possible."

"But how would he find me at the theater? Here in Chicago, so far from Los Angeles?" She shook her head. "No, someone I know is doing this. Someone who knows I'm working with the kids." She remembered bumping into someone in the darkness of the theater. "And someone who isn't a stranger to the theater. That's the only thing that makes sense." She shrugged. "Maybe it's all some sort of sick joke."

He stared at her in disbelief. "It would be one thing if you didn't get that note, Alice. But you did. And the incident at the theater? You know this is more than a joke."

"All right, but what am I supposed to do? I'm not going to live in fear, Marcus."

"Damn it," Marcus said, his voice rising. "It's exactly that type of attitude that can get you killed."

Her eyes widened with fear, and Marcus immediately regretted his words. He hadn't meant to say that. But he'd suddenly thought of Melissa, how she'd so stubbornly refused to take the precautions that could have saved her life. Sure, she'd gotten a restraining order, but after a while she had acted like the whole "Peter's gonna kill me" threat was a game, a game where the prize was snagging her favorite cop, not saving her life.

Marcus shook off the memory. "I'm sorry, I didn't mean to say that."

"Do you honestly think someone wants to"— she leaned forward—"*kill* me?"

"I didn't mean to say that. I was thinking about another case."

She studied him, noting the tension in his features, the way his fist clenched on the tabletop. This case must have been a bad one to affect him so deeply. "What happened?"

"There was a woman," Marcus answered matter-of-factly. "She didn't take her situation seriously enough. Now she's dead."

"Marcus, I'm sorry."

"Yeah, well, life goes on." He reached for the wine glass the waiter had filled and took a liberal sip.

Though he didn't offer more details, Alice could tell this case had gotten to him. No wonder he was hell-bent on playing the hero.

Which made her stomach knot. Marcus was looking out for her because he wanted to right some wrong from the past, not because he cared about her. No, that wasn't right. He did care, just not as deeply—or as exclusively—as she once thought.

Alice blew out a shaky breath. "I don't want to talk about this anymore."

"I didn't mean to scare you." Marcus's eyes gently caressed her face. "I just want you to be careful."

"I'm not scared."

She was either lying, or one stubborn woman. But as she ran a hand through her shoulder-length ebony hair, angling her head to the right as she did, he lost all thoughts of how stubborn she was or how afraid for her he was. All he could think of was the incredibly beautiful woman sitting across from him.

He swallowed hard, his mouth suddenly dry, his eyes following her tresses to their tips, and lower, to her ample bosom. As she shifted in her seat, his eyes followed the slight, gentle motion of her breasts. His entire body tingled with sexual awareness, and an arousal stretched against his jeans.

Damn. He had to get a grip. They were only breasts. Spectacular breasts, full, lush, and luscious, and right now the only reason to get a hard-on in a public place. Alice seemed completely unaware of her effect on him and he wondered if she had any idea just how sexy she was.

She heaved a sigh and he couldn't help noticing how her breasts rose and fell in his peripheral vision. She was going to drive him mad, he was sure.

Marcus was glad when the waiter arrived with their burgers, and they dug in. But the thick, calorie-filled burger didn't do much to douse his libido. Because watching Alice eat proved to be an erotic experience. The way her tongue flicked out to catch the stray juices of the burger . . .

"What?" she asked, staring at him.

"Nothing." Damn, he was losing it.

They ate the remainder of the meal in silence. Marcus suggested dessert, but Alice was too full. And since all he could think about was getting her out of this place and into his bed, he didn't bother to order any dessert for himself.

"Excuse me." Both Alice and Marcus looked up to see a young black man standing beside their table.

"Yes?" he asked.

"I hope you don't think this is a weird question, but my girlfriend and I were wondering . . . are you Desirée LaCroix?"

Alice nodded slowly. "Yes. Yes, I am."

"Wow. I've never met an actress before." He

glanced over his shoulder and nodded, and Alice saw a young woman a few tables away grinning at her. "Do you mind if my girlfriend says hi? I wanted to be sure it was you before she came over."

"Sure."

When the girlfriend practically did the hundred-meter dash to their table, Alice became uncomfortable with the attention. Others started staring and wondering. Alice ducked her head, hoping no one else would recognize her.

"Hi," the woman said, excitement bubbling from her voice. "I'm Trina, and this is my boyfriend, Clay. I told him it was you!"

"Nice to meet you both," Alice said.

"Do you mind . . . could we get your autograph?" Trina passed her a napkin.

Alice autographed the napkin for the couple.

"We love your work," Clay told her. "You were great in that series, *Code of Honor*."

"Thank you." She smiled politely. They apologized for taking up too much of her time, said their good-byes, and walked away.

"Let's get out of here," Alice quickly said. "I'm not really in the mood for this."

"Do you get that a lot?" Marcus asked.

"What? People who appreciate my role in the cop drama?" she asked, giving him a pointed look.

"That still doesn't make it accurate," he retorted playfully. "But no, that's not what I'm talking about. I'm talking about people recognizing who you are."

"It happens a fair amount. Mostly, people just look at me like they *think* they know who I am, but they're not sure, so they don't approach me. They don't want to feel foolish in case it's not." Alice glanced around, saw the curious stares coming from other patrons. "You ready?"

"Sure."

Marcus stood and extended his arm. She accepted it.

God, what a beautifully strong arm.

Marcus settled the bill with the hostess, then they headed outside.

Night had fallen over Chicago, but the pier was alive with action. She released Marcus's arm.

She looked out at the water and hugged her torso, but after a moment she sensed Marcus's eyes on her, and she turned back to him. And stared. Perhaps she stared a little too long into his dark, enigmatic eyes, because the energy between them changed in a heartbeat.

"Let me show you the rest of the pier," he said, his voice low and seductive. He nodded his head toward the back of the pier, where the crowds were sparse, and Alice highly doubted there was anything to see back there.

She wanted to say no. Heard the word in her head, but she couldn't seem to form it on her lips. "Why not?"

Marcus closed the distance between them and placed a firm arm around her waist. Turning her, he led her down the walkway toward the back of the pier. So many thoughts were flying around in her brain, it was hard to make sense of any of them.

Maybe the alcohol had clouded her judgment. She wasn't much of a drinker, so the two glasses of wine she'd drunk had made her a little lightheaded. But that was a lame excuse, she realized, because the cool breeze on her skin had sobered her the moment she'd stepped outside.

Marcus's fingers curled around her waist as they continued to walk. Away from the light. Away from the crowds.

This is dangerous.

Her brain sent off warning bells, but she was powerless to step out of Marcus's embrace. She was powerless to stop him from leading her around the corner to the darkest part of the pier.

Oh, God. Why was she letting him do this? This had nothing to do with rebuilding their friendship!

As he slowed and stopped before a tree, whirling her so that her back rested against it, they were suddenly the only two people in the world. Behind him, the moon glistened on the water. The sight would almost be romantic if the thought of being in such a romantic, dimly lit place with Marcus didn't scare her to death.

Marcus blew out a long, audible breath, and she saw it dance around her face before she felt it. Smelled it. The sweet scent of his breath tantalized her, and damn if she didn't know the wanton person she'd become.

She wanted to feel those full, sexy lips on hers.

"Alice," he said softly, yet the word reverberated through her body, causing her to shiver. She saw his eyes flick over her hair, and then his hand did the same thing, finally resting on her cheek. "Alice, Alice, Alice."

The energy between them was so charged, it robbed her of her voice.

"I can't believe we're here like this." There was no mistaking the intent in his voice, in his eyes.

"I can't believe it either," she whispered, surprised at the raspy note in her voice.

"I've been trying to fight it, but I'm not doing a very good job."

Alice swallowed.

"It's like you've put some hex on me. Looking at you isn't enough. I want to touch you." He trailed a finger from her cheek to her chin, and a soft moan fell from her lips. His other hand found her face. "I know. I feel the same way."

What way? she tried to ask, but again her voice betrayed her. She was literally paralyzed right here on the spot, unable to refute what he was saying, unable to pull out of his embrace.

Unable to think.

But hell, she didn't want to think. Not if thinking would ruin this inexplicable excitement she felt at his touch.

His thumbs intimately brushed her cheeks, then trailed to her lips in synchronized formation. They stroked her mouth from the outer edges to the middle, then back again.

And as though Marcus had been an old high-school love and they'd done this a million times, her mouth parted on a soft sigh. She couldn't stop herself from tipping on her toes, from arching up to meet his luscious mouth.

God help her, she was lost.

"Alice . . ."

His lips met hers with the faintest of contact, yet she felt a jolt unlike anything she'd ever experienced before. She tensed, and he paused, holding his face still, his lips a mere fraction of an inch from hers, their breath mingling as their gazes locked.

"It's okay," he murmured.

He gave her another brief kiss, then took her bottom lip between his and suckled. Softly. The feeling was so incredibly erotic. His tongue played over her lip while his teeth nipped, and her eyes fluttered shut. The exquisite delight was pure torture. If his mouth and tongue could make her lips feel this way, how would they make her breasts feel?

The thought shocked her. It wasn't like her to think of getting naked with a man the first time she kissed him—but this was no ordinary man. This was Marcus Quinn, the man she'd been crazy in love with in high school.

She wanted to feel his tongue everywhere. Because she knew he'd know what to do with it. Just how to please her, make her cry out in ecstasy.

At last, he covered her lips with his, slowly, sweetly. His hands crept around her waist, holding her to him as his hot tongue slipped inside her mouth. Moaning softly, she accepted it. This was pure pleasure. Pure heat.

She couldn't get enough of him.

Wrapping her arms around his neck, she pulled him closer, savored the taste of him, the feel of his hard body against hers.

This was dangerous, because Marcus had the power to hurt her, yet she couldn't pull away, couldn't stop the soft mewling sounds escaping her lips.

Couldn't stop kissing him.

The kiss grew more urgent and he brought his hands to her face again, holding her firmly in place, leaving her no avenue of escape. If she died from lack of breath now, it would be the best kind of death she could ever imagine.

Lord have mercy, Marcus Quinn was kissing her! And this time, it wasn't a dream.

Twelve

As abruptly as the kiss began, it ended when Marcus tore his lips from Alice's. To her chagrin, she ushered a soft moan of protest.

His eyes met hers, dark, intense. For a moment, neither spoke.

"Man." He rested his forehead against hers.

"Marcus . . ." Her voice sounded so husky that it was almost an invitation to kiss her again.

Pulling his head back, he smiled at her. "You're delicious."

Just like that, heat pooled between her legs. Never ever had anyone said she was delicious.

"I . . . am?"

"Mmm-hmm. Sweet. Hot."

God, he was making her hot and wet just whispering those words to her. It was all so unreal, it seemed like a dream, but the frantic beat of her heart and the urgent rise and fall of her chest told her that this was very real.

Marcus Quinn had kissed her!

He glanced toward the water, breaking the intimacy of their heated gaze, and Alice inhaled a much needed breath. Slowly, she regained her sanity. This was wrong. She'd screwed up their friendship when she took off years ago. She didn't want to ruin their chance at rebuilding it by letting her emotions get the best of her again.

Squirming a little, she moved out of his embrace and walked toward the railing. The water was tranquil, offering her a chance to collect her thoughts.

Marcus knew he'd crossed the line, but for the life of him, he didn't know what to do to stop his raging hormones. Damn, but she was gorgeous. Her smile, her body. She had felt so good pressed against him that if they weren't on this pier, he would have been tempted to take her right here.

He watched her as she stood at the water's edge, and walking up to her, he placed his hands on her shoulders. "What are you thinking?"

So many emotions swirled through her, she couldn't define exactly how she felt. Scared, excited, confused, exhilarated and depressed all at the same time. "Why did you kiss me?"

He hesitated. "I don't know."

She wished Marcus's hands didn't feel so right on her body. She wished he'd given her a different answer.

"All I know is that I'm attracted to you," he added.

Alice said nothing. Surely it wasn't really *her* he wanted, but Desirée LaCroix. She was used to that. From the moment her body had changed, men had been attracted to her new image, even though she was the same person she'd been before. Not even Noel, the man she'd planned to marry, had been able to see past her looks.

But Marcus was supposed to be different, and the reality that he wasn't seeing her for her made their moment of passion harder to bear. She shouldn't have strolled back here with him, shouldn't have kissed him. No matter how tempted she was, she had to make sure nothing like this ever happened between them again. How could she put her emotions on the line once more? She'd dared to believe he might be her Prince Charming, but he'd fallen in love with Tanisha. He hadn't found *her*, Alice Watson, attractive. And beneath her makeover, she was the same person.

Clearly, Marcus liked her new look, and for that reason, he could probably have a casual fling with her. But Alice couldn't let that happen. Because deep in her heart, the place where she'd locked up her feelings for Marcus, she could feel them starting to escape once again.

"Alice—"

"I think we should go," Alice said brusquely.

He sighed. "You're probably right."

Marcus wasn't even going to put up a token protest. She tried, but failed, to fight the sense of disappointment.

He rubbed his hands up and down her arms to warm her, and Alice quickly stepped to the right, moving past him. His touch was too distracting.

They walked in silence to the car. Once inside, Marcus spoke. "With all the weird stuff that's been happening, I was thinking maybe you should move in with me."

Alice whipped her head to the side, staring at him in disbelief. "What?"

"I'm a cop, Alice. I can protect you."

"I'm perfectly capable of protecting myself," Alice replied testily.

"But what about your mother?" Panic flashed in her eyes, and he knew he'd made his point. "If someone out there actually wants to hurt you, and he or she knows where you live—"

"No." Alice wouldn't consider the idea.

"I think you should give it some thought."

"I just did."

Marcus sighed. "I'm trying to help, Alice. As your friend."

"And if I need your help, I'll call you. But I'm not moving in with you."

Clearly she was determined, so Marcus didn't bother to press the issue. He could only hope that whoever was harassing her didn't mean her serious harm.

Even after she watched Marcus's car disappear into the night, Alice's heart didn't slow to its normal pace. The memory of how his full, sexy lips had felt on hers kept invading her mind. Every time it did, she felt a rush of warmth and an exquisite pulsing at the center of her being. The memory of his hands possessively wrapped around her waist led to another level of daydreaming she knew she ought to be ashamed of.

Alice sighed. She wasn't ready to go inside. She feared that with one look at her, her mother, sister, and niece would know her innermost erotic thoughts. So she stood on the porch with her back resting against the door, wondering what it would be like to have Marcus as a lover.

She pictured him naked, powerful, with that sly smile dancing on his lips and in his eyes as he taunted and teased her to arousal. Then she pictured him walking toward her, covering her lips with his as he slowly unzipped her dress . . .

"Enough," Alice said aloud, heaving herself off the door. She had to put Marcus out of her mind. Still, he had such strong hands and a wickedly sensual way about him that Alice knew he'd be an amazing lover.

Shaking her head, she dug in her purse for the key to the front door. As she slipped it in the lock, she thought she heard the sound of someone crying. Had something happened? God, was her mother all right?

She threw open the door and rushed inside in time to see Mia charging up the stairs, sobbing loudly. Marie was on the landing, fast on Mia's heels, but, hearing Alice come in, she paused.

Alice stared at Marie, then glanced upstairs again. Mia's bedroom door slammed shut.

"What is going on?" Alice asked her.

Ignoring her, Marie stomped up the stairs. Alice followed her, sensing major trouble brewing. Upstairs, Marie opened Mia's bedroom door, but Alice darted past her, heading into Mia's room before she could. She didn't like her sister's lethal body language.

Mia was nowhere to be seen, but the sounds of whimpering came from the closet. Alice approached the closet door and knocked softly. "Mia, honey. What's wrong?"

Mia opened the closet a fraction and snapped, "Ask her!"

Alice's head went back to the doorway, where Marie now stood with both hands planted on her hips. Alice almost expected steam to come from her sister's ears, that's how angry she was.

"You come out here, child!"

Opening the door, Mia released a sob and threw herself into Alice's arms. She wrapped her arms around her waist in a viselike grip.

Marie's eyes flashed fire. "Come here."

Mia buried her face in Alice's stomach.

"Your aunt can't protect you, Mia. Get your butt over here!"

Marie started toward them, but Alice shielded Mia and turned her body so that her back faced Marie. Mia lifted her head and as Alice stared down into her tear-filled eyes, she saw herself there, the way she had been years ago. The helplessness. The fear that no one understood nor loved her. The sight broke her heart.

Finally, she looked over her shoulder at her sister. "Marie, maybe what you both need is a cooling-off period—"

"And how would you know? You're not a mother."

The comment was like a slap in the face, but Alice paused, deliberately holding her angry retort in check. "No, but I was a child." Gently, she rubbed Mia's back. "Sweetheart, why don't you go wait in my room?"

"Alice—" Marie began in a warning tone.

"Marie," Alice replied, her tone just as serious. Then to Mia, "Go on."

Mia was hesitant, but eventually darted past her mother and down the hall. When she heard a bedroom door open and close, Alice asked, "What on earth is going on?"

"That child is too old for her years, that's what's going on."

"She's a child, Marie. What did she do that was so horrible?" Memories of her own troubled relationship with her mother flitted through her mind.

"She needs to learn her place, instead of lipping off."

Her sister looked as if she were about to explode. "Calm down, Marie. From what I've seen, Mia is a good child. I don't know what happened—"

"You're right, you don't know what happened."

There was a time when her sister's confrontational attitude would have made her back down, but not anymore. "Then why don't you tell me?" Alice asked gently.

Marie scowled. "She's mad at me because I won't fund her acting classes."

"I thought Chad paid for that."

"So did I."

"What happened?"

Marie walked further into the bedroom and dropped herself onto Mia's bed. Alice sat beside her.

"He's the one who's gotten her all excited about acting classes—and he knows I can't afford it. The fee for the second half of the class is due now for those who paid in installments, if Mia's going to stay in the class through to the summer. Chad called at the last minute and said he doesn't have the money. He says that since he's paid for the classes in the past I should pay for them now. He knows I don't have extra money for this."

Alice looked at her sister with a dumbfounded expression. "That's the problem?" When Marie didn't answer, Alice smiled. "Why didn't you just ask me? You know I have the money."

"I don't need a handout."

"This isn't a handout. It's a hand up." In her own stubborn way, Marie had always refused any money from Alice on the few occasions they'd communicated over the years. She knew it was pride, but Alice didn't think pride should be a factor with family. "Besides, it's the least I can do for the niece I haven't seen in years."

"Alice, you know how I feel about this!"

"Yeah, but I don't understand. I'm your sister."

"My *baby* sister. Do you know how it looks if I can't take care of my own child?"

"You have been taking care of her." Where was this coming from? "I'm offering to give her a gift. Last I heard, it wasn't against the law for an aunt to give her niece a gift."

"I guess not."

"Then why are you being so stubborn? Unless this isn't about the money . . ."

Marie buried her face in both hands, then slapped them against her thighs. "Chad did this deliberately—to make *me* look like the bad one."

"Why would you look bad?"

"Because I'm the one who's saying no to the classes. Not because I don't want her to take them, but because I can't afford it. It's another hundred dollars, Alice. Mia isn't going to think about the fact that her father isn't coming up with the money now;

she's only going to think that *I'm* the one saying no to her. I swear, all Chad cares about is proving to her that he loves her more than I do."

Alice's hand hovered over Marie's back, wanting to offer comfort with a touch, but let her hand drop to her lap. "Maybe . . . maybe you're wrong. Maybe Chad just doesn't have the money."

"Because he's spending all his money on the women he's seeing doesn't mean my daughter has to go without!"

She finally touched Marie's back soothingly. "Is that what this is about? You're still in love with Chad?"

Marie's eyes flew to hers. "God, no."

"Then what's the problem? I said I'd cover it."

"So now you get to look like the good one. Again, I'm bad. Everyone else is good."

At her sister's comment, Alice took her hand back. Her subtle comfort clearly meant nothing to Marie—and that hurt more than she cared to think about. But for the first time, Alice realized that her sister had insecurity issues, and that realization surprised her. Marie had always seemed so secure and together. What had happened over the years to shake that confidence? Her breakup with Chad, the man who'd been the love of her life?

Alice continued in a gentle tone. "Marie, we're talking about acting lessons. I'm hardly taking your place."

"Aren't you?" She gave her a pointed look. "You're teaching the class, everyone's fawning all over you, especially Mia. Pretty soon she's gonna want to pack her bags and head to Hollywood with you."

"So, this is about Hollywood again? Big, bad evil Hollywood that's going to corrupt your daughter?"

"It changed you. It could easily change Mia."

"*Hollywood* did not change me. *I* changed me. You don't like the fact that I'm not the same timid Alice I was years ago, do you?" The one who had lived eighteen years in her sister's shadow.

Marie ignored her. "You know how I feel about this subject."

"But I don't understand. Mia's ten years old, Marie. Nobody's talking about Hollywood here. We're talking acting classes. It's hardly a life commitment."

"But with you encouraging her—"

"All right," Alice said, holding up a hand, "you need to stop." As her sister looked at her with a startled expression, Alice stood. "You know, you never did support my dreams when I was younger. Neither did Mom. And I felt so damn alone that I felt the only place I could find happiness was thousands of miles away. Is that what you want to do to your daughter? Make her sad enough that you push her away to look for happiness somewhere else? Trust me, Marie, you do not want to do that. Show her your love. Show her your support. And teach her to make responsible decisions. If you try to hold her down, you'll lose her. And you may never get her back."

Surprisingly, Marie didn't say anything. Merely sighed softly and looked away.

"You're probably right."

Unable to believe her ears, Alice spun around and faced her sister. "What did you say?"

"I said, you're probably right." She ran both

hands through her hair, pulling it tightly off her face. "I don't want to lose her."

Alice was so taken aback by her sister's quiet response that she didn't know what to say. She sat back down. "Let me pay for the classes, Marie. I want to do this because I . . ." She suddenly felt an ache in her heart, an ache to tell her sister that she loved her and finally close the distance between them. "Because I love Mia. And because I love you."

The phone rang, but both Alice and Marie ignored it.

Marie's eyes misted. "Oh, Alice. I love you, too." She reached for her hand. "I don't mean to get down on your career. I'm just frustrated with everything. My life. My failed marriage. I'm thirty-three years old and I'm back at my mother's house with my daughter." She sighed. "I don't know if or when I'll ever get my life together."

"Of course you will. And like I said, I can help you. Because you're my family and I want to be here for you." When Marie remained silent, Alice said, "At least let me pay for the classes, Marie."

"Okay, Alice." A small smile formed on Marie's lips. "I'll let you do this. But can I ask a favor?"

"Sure."

"Please keep this between us. That you're paying for the classes. I want Mia to think . . . well, to think I'm paying."

"No problem."

"Thanks, Alice."

Marie surprised her with a hug, and the place deep inside her where she'd locked her emotions opened. She felt the sting of tears, but sucked them back by inhaling deeply through her nose.

"You're welcome."

There was a light rapping at the door, and both women looked up. Mia stood there, a frown still pulling at the corners of her lips.

"The phone's for you, Aunt Alice," she said, then quickly disappeared.

Alice stood, and Marie followed her example.

"I'll give Mia some time alone, then I'll tell her," Marie said as they walked out of the room.

Alice couldn't help wondering if she should buy a lottery ticket. If her sister could agree to two of the things she'd suggested in one day, her odds of winning a multimillion dollar jackpot couldn't be too bad.

Alice picked up the receiver, which lay on her bed. She suddenly wondered if Marcus was calling to say he'd made it home safely, and her pulse raced. "Hello?"

"Hello, Alice."

"Oh, Connie. Hello."

"I thought I would have heard from you by now."

Alice twirled the phone cord around her finger as she lay back on the bed. "Actually, I meant to call. I've just been busy."

"Edmond Minter keeps calling me about you, Alice. This is big, I'm telling you."

Alice sucked in an uneasy breath. She suddenly wasn't ready to deal with the question of whether or not she would work on their upcoming film. That reality disturbed her, because two months ago, she would have jumped at such a chance. Maybe she'd needed more of a break from Hollywood than she'd imagined. And with her relationship with Marie starting to look better . . . She didn't want to jeopardize that.

"What have you told him?"

"That you're considering the script and several others. Doesn't hurt to make it look like you've got a dozen projects to choose from, especially with that ridiculous story in *The Intellect*. I've done some damage control along with your publicist, which included telling Sebastian Charles we'll slap him with a lawsuit if he so much as breathes your name in public circles again, but there's no doubt *some* people will believe that story." She sighed. "You know, I thought maybe we could set you up with an interview. Maybe *Good Morning America*, where you can show the world just how together you are, that you're hardly sex-starved. Maybe even mention the real deal, that your mother had a heart attack."

"No," Alice said emphatically. "I'm not going to do that." She wasn't about to use her mother's brush with death to gain public sympathy. Besides, she didn't want to go on any show to refute Sebastian's bogus claims. She hadn't done anything wrong, so why defend herself like she was guilty?

"I think it could help."

"But it could also hurt. If I do an interview, the press will just dissect it and look for signs that I'm lying. No, I'm not doing any interview."

"All right. I've told Edmond that you're still out of town on personal business, but they're going to want to hear from you soon. Did you read the script?"

"Not in its entirety," Alice replied, wondering why she was lying. She'd read the whole thing and had loved it. "But as I said, I've been busier than I expected with my mother, and I'm helping out with my niece's acting class."

"Well, please try to get to it soon. I'd hate to see this opportunity pass you by. This is a mega opportunity, Alice."

"I know."

"All right. Talk to you later."

"Yes, soon," Alice promised.

As she hung up, she wondered what had happened to her. Why she wasn't jumping up and down over the chance to be in this film the way she had done somersaults on her aunt's lawn when she'd landed her very first role.

She lay back and closed her eyes. It was this whole precarious situation with her mother's health and their relationship. And now things were looking better with Marie. And then she was absorbed in teaching Mia's acting class, something she was enjoying immensely. Plus, she and Marcus were recapturing their friendship.

But acting was as much a part of her as breathing was.

She'd be back in Hollywood just as soon as her mother was well. Until then, she wasn't prepared to make any decisions about her future.

Thirteen

Despite the darkness of the room, when Marie opened the door and crept inside, Alice was instantly alert.

"You awake?" Marie whispered.

"Yeah." Though she wished she were dead to the world. Thoughts of Marcus and their passionate interlude had kept her awake most of the night, and now she was exhausted. Her dreams had become even more erotic during the night, leaving her thoroughly unsatisfied when she'd awoken and realized his magnificent body was not in bed beside her.

Marie went to the window and pulled up the blinds in one fast movement. Bright sunlight suddenly filled the room, offending Alice's eyes. Groaning, she threw the covers over her head.

The bed squeaked as Marie plopped down on it and yanked the covers from Alice's face. "What are you doing today?"

Alice groaned in response.

"Oh, come on. It's after nine. You can't still be tired."

Knowing that there was no way her sister was going to leave her alone, Alice sat up and stretched. "Aren't you supposed to be at work?"

"I've been doing so much overtime lately, they let me have the day off. So do you have plans?"

"No," she replied, covering a yawn. "Why?"

"Great."

"Great why?"

"You can help me get some things for the party."

"Party?" Alice asked, surprised. "What party?"

"Oh. Of course you have no idea what I'm talking about. But I did remember that it's your birthday on Monday, and I figured we could have a party on Sunday. Kinda a birthday and homecoming party all in one."

Alice crossed her legs beneath her, then rested an elbow on each knee. "Don't bother going to any trouble, Marie. I don't need a party."

"I've already invited everybody."

"*What?* When?" Butterflies danced in Alice's stomach.

"This morning. Our talk last night got me thinking. I know you think I never supported your dreams, but that's not . . . that's not true." Marie gave Alice a small smile. "I just wanted to do something for you."

That her sister was actually making an effort to mend the rift between them melted Alice's annoyance. And her resistance. "A party."

"Mmm-hmm. Everybody I talked to is absolutely thrilled with the idea."

Alice rolled her eyes. She couldn't imagine the people Marie invited being thrilled to see her. They'd never been her friends.

"I'm serious. It's been almost thirteen years since you left Chicago. A lot of people want to see you again, especially now that you've become a big-time Hollywood actress."

"I'm not big time." She'd had some great roles and great exposure, but mostly in television as opposed to on the big screen.

"Are you for real? That TV series alone made you a local celebrity. A Chicago girl who made good." Marie smiled tentatively. "Everyone from Smithfield High is curious about Desirée LaCroix. Especially since word has spread that you're teaching the class at the theater. People want to see you again and say hi. Tell you how proud they are."

"Why do I find that hard to believe?" Alice asked, frowning.

"Alice." Marie spoke softly yet firmly. "I know I was pretty blind and self-absorbed years ago, but I realize that you had a tough time during high school. However, you're not the same person anymore. Don't you see? You're beautiful, successful, confident. Maybe you weren't close with the people I'm inviting—"

"Close? Marie, we weren't even nodding acquaintances, let alone friends."

"Okay," Marie agreed. "I'll give you that, but what I'm trying to say is that they're curious about you. If we have this party, you can show everyone how far you've come. And you can show them— and yourself—that they can't hurt you anymore."

Her sister *did* have a point and a smile touched

Alice's lips at her sister's thoughtfulness. Still, she wasn't sure. "I don't know."

"You may not believe it, but a lot of people ask about you. They've changed, Alice, and not just because you're a star now, but because they've grown up. Debbie mentions you every time she comes in for a cleaning. And there are others. I think they truly care about you and are interested in your success."

Alice's stomach fluttered with nervousness. The idea of spending an afternoon with the people from her high school was daunting at best, even though Marie was right. She *wasn't* the same person now, so why should it bother her? "Look, Marie, I'm not objecting to the idea of a party. But it should be something small. Something between the family. Remember, Mother's still recovering."

"Actually, I asked her about it and she said she doesn't mind. She's dying to get out of that bedroom."

Alice knew her mother was growing restless, being a virtual prisoner in her own home. She was able to get up on her own now, bathe on her own, but Alice and Marie made sure she did nothing at all strenuous, and for a woman who had once been so active with work in and outside of the home, that was like a punishment.

"Sounds like it's a done deal," Alice said, resigning herself to that fact. "What did you have in mind for today?"

"I figured we could pick up some decorations. Nothing much, but you may as well choose what you like since the party *is* for you."

Marie smiled, and Alice found it contagious.

More than anything, she knew this wasn't about simply having a party, but about Marie trying to make amends and show her that she cared. Her heart filled with warmth. "Sure. When do you want to go?"

"After breakfast?"

"Okay."

"Great. I'll be downstairs." Marie hopped off the bed. When she reached the door, she turned and said, "We're gonna have a good time."

Shopping with her sister, something she'd never done. Alice was suddenly looking forward to this simple task.

Yeah, it was going to be fun.

"Hmm. I dunno. Maybe a couple curls. Right here."

They were in the upstairs bathroom, and Alice stood behind the chair upon which Mia sat. She met Mia's eyes through the mirror. Her niece indicated the long strands of hair at her temples. Until now, Alice had been loosely curling Mia's hair in layers to give it volume. "What kind of curls?" Alice asked.

Mia shrugged, then a spark lit up her eyes. "I know. Maybe I can pull it off my face." Holding the hair atop her head, she indicated what she meant. Her eyes met Alice's in the mirror. "Like yours."

Today, Alice wore her hair in a bun with two drop curls on either side of her face. Clearly, Mia wanted the same look. It was harmless, Alice knew, but she suddenly wondered what Marie would say if she saw her daughter looking like a replica of her sister. Alice reached for the curling iron, then paused. Instead, she crossed her arms over her chest. "Mia, may I ask you a question?"

"Uh-huh."

"Why do you want to be an actress? Is it because of me?"

She frowned. "Is that what my mom said?"

"Kind of."

"Well, it's not true. My mom doesn't believe me, but I do have a mind of my own." Staring ahead, Mia fluffed her shoulder-length hair.

"I've got an idea." Alice pulled back some of Mia's hair, testing variations of the look. She hadn't noticed it before, but Mia really did resemble her. "I think it will look really nice if we pull the top back and give you some ringlet curls by your ears. What do you think?"

Mia nodded with enthusiasm.

Reaching for the curling iron, Alice picked it up and went to work. Chad had called and asked if he could have Mia tonight, since she'd be spending Sunday with her mother and Alice for the birthday party. Marie had agreed, and now Alice was getting Mia ready for her dinner date with her father.

"I've been working with you for the past several weeks," Alice said as she continued to curl Mia's hair, "and you're definitely a good actress. But what do you like about acting?"

Mia's face lit up. "Everything. I love getting to pretend I'm someone else. I love making people laugh. I love getting to act in a story that always has a happy ending."

She was more like Alice than she knew. But it had nothing to do with Alice's influence on her. Perhaps it was in the genes.

"What about you?" Mia asked. "What do you like about acting?"

"Pretty much the same things you said." She wound more hair onto the curling iron. "I've just always loved stories. Ever since I was a child, I enjoyed movies and fairy tales and . . . I don't know. It's just always been a part of who I am." Completing the last curl, Alice replaced the curling iron on the bathroom counter and pulled the plug out.

"This looks great, Aunt Alice!" Mia said, smiling. "Thanks."

"Let me just finish up." Alice placed a few hairpins in her hair to hold the style. "There."

Rising, Mia struck a dramatic pose with one hand on a cocked hip, the other at the side of her head. She giggled.

Alice giggled too. As their laughter faded, Mia turned to face her. "Mia, you think you'll pursue an acting career?"

She shrugged. "You did."

"I know. But it's a tough job. To most people it looks glamorous, but it's not always like that. It's hard work, long hours. And sometimes your best still isn't good enough."

Mia's lips curled in a frown. "You don't want me to be an actress."

"No. That's not what I'm saying. I'm just saying that you're young and you have a lot of options. Don't do something because you think it's cool. You have to really like what you're doing."

"I really do love acting."

"You do, don't you?"

"Mmm-hmm. But like you said, I'm still young, so who knows?"

Alice wrapped Mia in a long, tight embrace. Marie didn't give her daughter enough credit. The child had a good head on her shoulders, and Alice trusted her to make the right decision for her life.

Bending, she gave her a kiss on the forehead. "I'm so proud to have a niece like you."

Mia hugged her. "And I'm so proud to have an aunt like you."

Fourteen

When the doorbell rang shortly after three on Sunday afternoon, Alice was suddenly tempted to run upstairs and hide in the closet. She knew the thought was childish, but the last thing she wanted was to spend the next few hours with the very people who had made her life a living hell in high school.

She saw some of them briefly when they dropped off or picked up their children from the theater, which didn't bother her, because she didn't have to spend any real time with them. She enjoyed teaching their children. At least their children respected her, looked up to her. But their parents—she had prayed she would never have to see these people again, and now it was like a nightmare coming true.

She should have insisted Marie cancel the party.

As Marie cheerfully answered the door, Alice straightened her spine. She was Desirée LaCroix, wonderfully successful actress, after all.

And wasn't success supposed to be the best revenge?

Damn straight.

She'd dressed the part. Wearing a cream-colored designer pantsuit that hugged her curves in the right places and flared around her ankles to give the illusion she was wearing a skirt, she knew she looked stunning. The bodice hugged her generous breasts, revealing a good dose of cleavage. At her wrists, the delicate crepe material flared again to match the pant legs.

Classy, yet sexy.

She wasn't naïve enough to believe her former classmates were interested in Alice Watson, so she'd give them a good dose of Desirée.

One by one, the party guests entered. Carmen, Heather, Jill, Karen, Felicity. Many of them had been cruel to her in high school. Had laughs at her expense. Others had simply acted like she was a nonentity. Where had Marie found them all, anyway? Were they all patients at the dental office where Marie worked?

Or perhaps they were all members of the Ultimate Bitch club. Maybe they'd taken a blood oath to stay friends for life . . .

While Alice's heart pounded, her brain told her she was judging them all by their past actions. Carmen had seemed genuinely friendly to her at the theater the times she saw her. Wasn't it possible they had changed?

Still, just being around her old nemeses made her more than a little uncomfortable.

Heather, Karen, and Felicity were still divas. The rest had put on varying degrees of weight over the years. It was still a shock to see that Jill, who'd once been a cheerleader, was now about two hundred pounds.

My, how times had changed.

Alice's mind wandered to Marcus. She wondered if he was coming. At least seeing him would make these few hours bearable.

"Guess who it is?" Marie asked, stepping into the living room with the latest guest. "Sherry."

Alice nearly choked on a breath. God, not Sherry. She was a year older than Alice and she'd never said anything nice to her in all her high school years. Sherry was most definitely Marie's friend.

I just don't get it, Alice had overheard her saying once. *How could your parents have someone as beautiful as you, then have her?*

To Marie's credit, she hadn't laughed when the other girls had. In fact, she had come to Alice's defense, telling her friends to shut up.

But for a person who had shown some sort of familial instincts then, why on earth would she invite someone like Sherry to this party now?

"Hey, Alice." Sherry approached her with open arms and Alice let her hug her. "How ya doing?"

"Wonderful," Alice replied, hoping she didn't sound as flaky as a pie crust. "Life has been great for me. What about you?"

Sherry shrugged. "Oh, I'm okay. Nothing like you. I'm not famous or anything."

Alice chuckled, the same, fake Hollywood chuckle that she hated. "I'm hardly famous."

"Of course you are. You put Smithfield High on the map. You've done us all proud."

The doorbell rang again, and Marie practically

floated toward it. She was truly in her element as hostess.

While Marie ushered the next guest into the room, Sherry greeted Rosa, who sat on the living room's loveseat. Alice was thankful that she didn't have to exchange any more small talk with a person she most definitely did not consider a friend.

As person after person entered the party—Dawn, Betty, Juanita—Alice marveled at just how fake people could be. The way Felicity and the others greeted her with exuberant hellos and kisses, the way one might greet a long-lost relative, one would think these people had been in her corner from day one, that they weren't the same people who had endlessly ridiculed her during her school days.

Almost everyone brought a pot with some sort of food, and Alice helped bring it all to the kitchen. Keeping active kept her mind off the fact that she felt like she was in the Twilight Zone.

"Alice."

Hearing her name, Alice whirled around to see Carmen.

"I wanted to give you this," Carmen said, extending her a small, elaborately decorated box. "Happy birthday."

"Oh . . . you didn't have to."

"I wanted to." Her lips curled in a soft smile. "You've done wonders with the class. Devin is so excited."

Alice carefully undid the gold foil wrapping, then pulled open the box's flap. A huge candle sat in a crystal cylinder. Lifting the candle to her nose, Alice inhaled the sweet scent of vanilla.

"Thanks, Carmen. How thoughtful."

"You're welcome."

As the counters and table were covered with food items, Alice placed the candle on top of the fridge. Afterward, she was surprised to see Carmen still standing in the kitchen.

"You can go ahead and dig in," Alice told her.

"Actually, I wanted to say something."

Alice tensed. "All right."

Carmen glanced at the floor, then back at Alice. "I know this is a little late. But I want to apologize. I'm sorry for the way I treated you in high school."

Alice was so surprised, her eyes nearly popped out of their sockets. But years of training as an actress allowed her to hide her shock.

"Alice, I really hope that we can put those days behind us. When I look back, I'm just so embarrassed at my behavior and I have no other excuse than I was young and incredibly stupid."

Maybe she was a sucker, but the fact that Carmen was trying to make amends made the resentment she'd felt dissolve like snowflakes hitting warm pavement. "High school was a long time ago. I don't really remember much of it," Alice told her. It wasn't exactly a lie. For years, she'd suppressed the memories so they could no longer hurt her.

Carmen let out a relieved breath. "I'm glad to hear that."

She had similar experiences with Felicity, Jill, Sherry and Juanita, though they didn't come right out and apologize. But they all were extremely nice, and in their eyes she could see a hint of regret. Alice was filled with an odd sense of joy. It wasn't like she'd call them or anything in the future, and certainly not hang out with them, but this was one day.

She was surprised—and proud of the strength she'd found to face the very human demons of her past.

And it didn't matter that Karen and Heather didn't pay much attention to her, though this was her birthday party. Their indifference now surprisingly didn't hurt her. Marie had been right. The party was healing for her.

Alice went to the washroom, and when she returned, she saw Mia on the sofa beside Rosa. Chad must have dropped her off in the past few minutes.

"Aunt Alice!" Mia jumped to her feet and ran into Alice's arms.

"Hey, sweetie." Alice sat in the spot Mia had vacated beside her mother, and Mia snuggled up beside her.

"You okay, Mother?" Alice asked.

"I'm just fine."

Surprising her, Rosa reached for and squeezed Alice's hand. It was this kind of mixed signal that always pained her. Sometimes it seemed like she was breaking through the cold wall her mother had erected around her emotions, other times she felt completely shut out.

Marie and the rest of the women stood by the dining room table, nibbling on various appetizers. Absentmindedly, Alice watched them as Mia chatted to her about the role she hoped to land in the play.

Felicity and Marie laughed at something, then Felicity turned and saw Alice. She waved her over. "Alice, come over here. You've been so quiet about your movie star life. We want details."

"Yeah," Dawn added. "Who'd you meet? Who's really a hunk, who's not? All that stuff."

Alice rose, and Mia rose with her. Putting on the

air of Desirée, Alice made her way to the group. There she told them the stories they wanted to hear. And they laughed at everything she said, seeming for once, to laugh with her—not at her.

A loud clapping sound reverberated in the room, followed by a "Quiet everybody!" All the women in the room turned to face Rosa, who stood just beyond the living room at the head of the dining room table.

The chatter slowly died, and when everyone was quiet, Rosa spoke again. "It's nice to see—and hear—that everyone is having a wonderful time. I, for one, am happy to have some excitement in this house." She smiled, and there was laughter among the group. "But now that we're all here, I say we acknowledge the guest of honor."

A chorus of "hear hears" rang out.

"I would just like to say how proud I am of my daughter, and how happy I am that she is home." She directed a loving smile at Alice.

The smile would have warmed her, should have. But Alice felt confusion instead. Her mother was *proud* of her? Was she saying this simply because she had an audience, or did she mean what she said? And if she meant the words, why on earth hadn't she said them to *Alice* before now?

Grinning from ear to ear, Marie and Mia approached her mother and stopped at her side. It was only then that Alice saw the large box.

"Alice," Marie said. "Will you come here, please?"

Stunned, her feet propelled her across the living

room until she reached her family's side. In fact, she was so stunned that not even Tanisha's unexpected appearance at the party had jarred her more.

Rosa, Marie, and Mia all passed the box to Alice.

She couldn't imagine what it was, but as she looked down at the unwrapped box, she heard people saying "Open it."

"Yeah, open it."

Her head whipped up at the sound of that voice.

His voice.

He'd come.

Marcus's eyes met and held hers across the room. Those dark, intense, stunningly sexy eyes. She literally shivered, and she only hoped those standing around her hadn't noticed.

Her eyes strayed then to what he held in his arms. In one hand, he had a bouquet of red roses. In the other, a wrapped gift.

But it was the flowers that made her heart leap. Marcus had brought her red roses! God, the thought thrilled her. She wondered if this was the way all the girls in high school felt when they received red roses from their beaus. While she'd received expensive trinkets from interested men in Hollywood, this simple luxury was something she'd never experienced.

"Don't keep us in suspense," Jill said.

Jill's voice startled her, reminding her that she was in a room full of people. "No," Alice said, her voice almost a croak. "Wouldn't want to do that."

Slowly, she lifted the lid off the box. Inside lay a large scrapbook with the words A BRIGHT AND SHINING STAR engraved on the cover in gold.

Alice brought a hand to her mouth. She lifted it

out of the box and opened it. It was a scrapbook of articles about her career. Alice brought a hand to her mouth as it fell open.

Who had done this? Mia? Her sister and mother had never supported her career, so she couldn't imagine them putting this together.

"What is it?" everyone seemed to ask at once.

Her hands now shaking, Alice closed her fingers around the scrapbook and lifted it to show the crowd.

And noticed that Marcus had moved closer to her.

For a moment she couldn't breathe, let alone speak. Maybe it was because he was the only male in the room, but the energy had suddenly changed. He was like a candle in a dark room, glowing brightly, giving warmth.

"Well?" he asked.

Alice cleared her throat. "It's a scrapbook."

"With memories of her career over the years," Marie added. "News clippings, rave reviews, pictures she sent me of her with various stars."

Alice couldn't believe her ears. Why, if they hadn't supported her career, would they have done this?

God, had she been wrong about them all this time?

She glanced at Marcus and found him smiling at her, silently sending her support.

"Is Denzel in there?" Alice heard someone ask, not sure whom. Right now, all she could think was that Denzel had nothing on Marcus.

"You bet," Marie replied.

God, why was he looking at her like that? Like he wanted to snare her soul with his gaze alone.

And he could, but Alice would never let him know that.

"Alice?"

"Huh?" Her eyes found Heather's.

"I said," Heather began slowly, "is he as hot in person as he is on film?"

"Oh, yes," Alice replied, but her gaze roamed to Marcus as she said the words. "He's very hot."

"Oh, I'm so jealous!"

She looked away before he had her totally within his power and she lost her heart to him once again. Glancing down at the scrapbook, she opened it— but she didn't see much beyond a mix of colors and newsprint.

"Will you pass it around?"

It was him again, his voice wrapping around her like silk. She didn't dare look at him as she handed the scrapbook off to Betty, who was closest to her.

"And now," Rosa announced, "we have a cake."

Alice's eyes widened with surprise. "A cake?"

"Yes, a cake. I was hoping you didn't see it."

"I didn't."

Rosa disappeared into the kitchen, then returned with the large cake to the table. It was covered with white icing, pink roses in the corners, and pink wording that spelled out HAPPY BIRTHDAY, ALICE. YOU'RE A STAR IN ALL OUR EYES.

"This is so . . . unbelievable," Alice said.

"We are proud of you," Marie said to her.

Alice didn't know what to think. This pride and support was too sudden to believe it was real. But the articles over the years were real, and Alice felt even more confused.

She truly felt like she was in the Twilight Zone as

she watched Marie dig the knife into the soft cake. Perhaps that's why, though she saw him approaching, she jumped when she felt Marcus's full lips on her temple.

Flustered, she turned and gave him a smile.

"Sorry I'm late. Happy birthday. These are for you." He passed her the bouquet of roses, and Alice's knees actually went weak.

"Roses," Marie whispered in her ear, then reached for the card. Alice quickly plucked it from Marie's fingers. "They're for me."

"Sorry." Dramatically, Marie let her empty fingers dangle in the air, then looked at Marcus. "They're beautiful."

"Like the birthday girl."

Alice fingered a delicate flower. Somehow, she was able to contain her smile, though inside she was beaming brighter than a neon sign.

Marie passed Alice a slice of cake. "You want a piece, Marcus?"

"Oh yeah," he replied. But he was looking at Alice.

Her throat was suddenly so dry, she wondered if it would be suicide to take a bite of the cake. She very well might choke to death.

"This is for you, too." He passed her the wrapped box.

"Marcus, you didn't have to. Thanks."

"It's not from me. I found it on the porch."

"You're kidding." Who would leave a gift on the porch? "Tanisha, you came in shortly before Marcus. Did you bring this?"

She shook her head. "Not me."

Alice shrugged and placed it on the table. When

she turned back to Marcus, she found him staring at her. "Wow," he said, "You look great."

At that moment, she remembered exactly what she was wearing, and realized that from his vantage point, he no doubt had a great view of her cleavage. Her body suddenly felt hotter than she feared was normal. Or healthy. She'd never felt like this when any other man had looked at her.

She blushed. "Thanks." Needing something to fiddle with, she reached for the mysterious gift box and began unwrapping it. She'd opened the other gifts and may as well open this one.

Discarding the wrapping paper, she lifted the lid and looked inside the box.

Then screamed.

Fifteen

Marcus's throat constricted at the sound of Alice's scream. As the box fell from her hands onto the table, he quickly grabbed it and looked inside.

"Jesus," he muttered. Inside the box was a brown stuffed teddy bear with a rope tied so tightly around its neck the head was almost severed. There was no mistaking the threat.

"Who left this box on the porch?" Marcus asked, his eyes scanning everyone in the room.

People shrugged and shook their heads as they glanced at one another.

"Someone has to know something." His gaze settled on Tanisha. "Alice said you came in just before I did."

"I have nothing to do with this," she protested.

"You didn't see this box on the porch?"

"No!"

He eyed her suspiciously a moment longer, wondering if she was lying. She'd always been so good at it that she'd fooled him often.

Tanisha angled her head to try to see inside the box from across the table. "What is it?"

Marcus couldn't tell if the question was sincere or not. Did Tanisha already know?

"Marcus, please get rid of it." From her chair, Alice looked up at him with pleading eyes. Eyes that held fear.

He'd do anything to erase that fear. He reached for the lid and replaced it over the box, but not before Rosa and Marie had crowded around him to peer inside.

"Oh, my." Rosa inhaled a shaky breath and placed a hand on her heart. "Alice, why would someone send you something like that?"

Her mother's frightened question drove Alice into action. She couldn't crumble, though she wanted to. She needed to shelter her family from this, put on a brave face so they wouldn't be scared. Pushing her chair back, she stood and placed an arm around her mother's waist. She urged her into the chair she'd just vacated. "Mother, sit down."

"I don't understand," Marie whispered, her voice trembling. "Who would do this?"

Alice looked at Mia, who was staring at her with a terrified expression. "Mia, it's all right. It's just a . . . a crazy joke."

"Are you sure?" she asked, her voice shaky from fear.

"Yes, sweetie. Now please get a glass of water for your grandmother."

The party guests mumbled amongst themselves for several minutes, offered apologies, then slowly dispersed as it became clear the festivities were over. Alice glanced around the living and dining rooms and realized Marcus was no longer here. She suddenly felt like a deflated balloon.

But moments later he returned, no longer holding the box, and a wave of relief washed over her. Why did the mere sight of him calm her? Maybe because he was a cop and she felt safer with him around.

He called to her from the living room entrance several feet away. "Alice, may I speak with you?"

"Sure. Mother, are you okay?"

"Yes, I'm fine."

When Alice reached Marcus, he said, "I checked the area around the house. I didn't find any more suspicious packages."

Alice hugged her torso. "Marcus, I'm scared."

Marcus surprised her by wrapping an arm around her shoulder and pulling her close—and Alice instantly felt protected in his arms.

"I promise you, I'm going to find out who did this." As a cop, he knew the danger of making such promises, but this was Alice, and it was a promise he intended to keep.

"I didn't want to believe it before, but someone really wants to hurt me."

"Alice, I suggested this once and you didn't consider it, but I'm going to suggest it again. I think you should stay at my place." He paused as his pulse accelerated. Nerves. "I'd feel much better if I could keep an eye on you."

Alice looked up at him and offered him a smile, but it wavered, and the sight nearly broke his heart. He couldn't let anything happen to her.

"At least let me get you out of here for a while."

"Yes, please. Get me out of here." She stepped out of his arms. "Give me a second."

Marcus waited for her while she disappeared into the living room, where he heard her tell her family she'd be heading out for a little while. A couple of minutes later she returned.

"You ready?"

"Mmm-hmm." She grabbed a leather jacket from the coat tree and slipped into it.

He opened the front door and let her pass, then he stepped onto the porch after her. Once again, he placed a hand on her shoulder. "Damn, you're shaking."

She nodded in response.

Marcus led her down the front steps to his car. He let her in the passenger side, then seconds later, got behind the wheel.

Alice wrapped her arms around her body while Marcus started the engine. She couldn't stop shaking. As much as she tried to forget the image, she kept seeing the strangled teddy bear. There was no doubt the bear was meant to represent her.

Someone was seriously threatening her. But who? Tanisha *was* the last person to enter the party before Marcus arrived, which made her a suspect as far as Alice was concerned. Maybe she was jealous because she thought Alice was pursuing Marcus.

But Tanisha hadn't said anything to Alice about her relationship with Marcus until yesterday, and there had been threats before. And Tanisha seemed so grateful for her help at the theater that Alice couldn't truly imagine her doing this.

"You cold?"

His voice startled her out of thoughts. She nodded. Marcus turned on the car's heater.

She watched him while he drove. His lips were set in a tight line, his forehead scrunched. No doubt his cop mind was going a mile a minute trying to solve the situation.

"Marcus, I don't know what to do. All this time, I figured that if someone was trying to scare me, at least they didn't know where I lived."

"That's exactly why I want you to stay with me. If this person knows where you live, then your family is at risk as much as you are."

She wished it were that simple. But the truth was, staying with Marcus would be extremely difficult. Dangerous. It would be so easy to fall for him again if she spent every day with him. "Do you really think that's the best thing?"

"I've got an extra bedroom," he replied, as if sensing her concern.

"That's not what I mean. My mother . . ."

"She's recovering from heart surgery. Needless to say, something like this can't be good for her health."

"You're right." Alice frowned as she lay her head back. She needed to think about the situation. In the meantime, it couldn't hurt to stay with Marcus tonight while she contemplated the best course of action. "Are we going to your place now?"

"May as well."

"I didn't bring anything to sleep in."

"I've got T-shirts."

The idea of wearing one of Marcus's T-shirts seemed way too personal. "No toothbrush."

"We can stop at a drugstore and buy one."

"Okay." Alice tried to sound cool. They were both adults. She wasn't going to his place for a romantic rendezvous, but to escape a very real threat to her life. "Don't you think I should go to the police?"

"I'm gonna solve this, Alice."

He was so adamant, Alice wondered if he was trying to prove something. Or make amends. Maybe for the case he'd mentioned the other day, where the woman had gotten killed. She didn't ask about it.

They drove along Lake Shore Drive in silence. Alice didn't pay much attention to the scenery until Marcus turned left off the main road and onto a side street, then another. He pulled up in front of a small, red-brick house.

They got out of the car and Alice followed him up the steps. It was a quiet, picturesque neighborhood with mature trees, the type of neighborhood where young husbands and wives began building their lives together. And here she was, about to enter the home of the one man she'd loved.

Alone.

When Marcus opened the front door and let Alice pass, he suddenly felt self-conscious. Not only was the house a small bungalow, it needed a good cleaning. The place was dusty and the linoleum floors could use a wash. "I know it's not what you're used to," he announced as he followed her into the house. "Not fancy at all . . ."

She faced him, giving him a dumbfounded look. "You think I care about how your house looks?"

"Well, I know you're used to posher places than this."

Did people really think she had lost touch with

her roots? That she was some prima donna? "I like it. I think this place suits you."

"Thanks."

"It does. The colors." They were strong, like him. "The smell." She could literally smell his masculine scent in the air.

"Have a seat." He gestured to the living room. "Can I get you a drink?"

She shook her head. "I'm fine."

"You sure you're okay?"

Alice sat on the sofa, and Marcus sat on the loveseat across from her. "You're gonna think I'm weird, but you know what I keep wondering about?"

"What?"

"I know I should be concerned about who wants to hurt me, but instead I keep thinking about the gift my family gave me. Marcus, it was a *scrapbook* of my career. My mother disowned me for going to Hollywood to pursue my dream. Why on earth would she care what I've done over the years?"

"Obviously, she's loved you all these years."

"She hardly talks to me. She won't tell me how she feels, even when I try to get her to open up. Sometimes she's deliberately difficult, like she's trying to push me away. Then she'll suddenly be nice, or reach for my hand—she did that today—and I don't know what to think."

Alice sighed. "I want to understand her, but she's a complete mystery to me."

"She loves you, Alice. That much I can see."

Alice shook her head, her mind still trying to digest it all. "Except for my father, sometimes I really do wonder if I dropped from another family tree."

"Clearly, while they haven't been able to show

you their support outwardly, deep in their hearts they must support you. I think they're proud of you."

"Maybe they are," Alice conceded.

"Well, I'm proud of you."

Alice raised her gaze to his. "You are?"

"Of course."

"I wasn't sure what you thought."

"I'll admit when we first met again, I wondered if you'd 'gone Hollywood,' but after spending time with you, I realize you're still down to earth." He smiled. "You're still my girl, Alice, and I'm proud that while you achieved success, you didn't lose your sense of self."

"Thank you." His comment meant more to her than he knew.

Alice glanced around the living room, at the afro-centric paintings on the walls. Photos of him and his father, his sister. A large portrait of his mother. When she looked at him again, she was jarred to find him staring at her with narrowed eyes, as though studying her. She glanced away.

"You don't want to be here, do you?"

She looked at him again, surprised. "Excuse me?"

"You feel uncomfortable around me."

Alice laughed her disbelief. "Of course I'm comfortable around you."

He shook his head slowly. "No, I don't think you are. Every time I look at you, you either give me that deer expression or you look away."

Her eyes widened. "Deer expression?"

"*That*," he said, gesturing to his eyes and imitating the wide-eyed look. "Your eyes widen like a deer trapped in headlights."

Alice flashed him an incredulous look, then immediately looked away—and realized her mistake.

"See. You just looked away—"

"What is your point?"

"You're uncomfortable with me because I kissed you."

Her gaze flew to his in that classic deer look. God, she had such sexy eyes. Marcus's mouth went dry as he realized how turned on he suddenly was. He had hoped to discuss what had happened between them in a mature fashion, but the mere mention of their kiss jump-started his hormones. All he could think about now was how wonderful and soft her lips had felt crushed beneath his, how aroused he had become when her nipples had hardened against his chest.

She was so damn beautiful. Even that deer expression made her look more incredible—fiery, passionate, vulnerable. And damn if he couldn't avoid dropping his gaze to her full, luscious breasts. They were firm yet soft, and his mouth very nearly watered at the swell of her cleavage. He forced his gaze back to those cinnamon-colored eyes. God, how could he live in the same house with her and manage to keep his hands off her?

"Look, Marcus, I realize the kiss just happened. I've already forgotten about it."

"Oh." His ego deflated. "I just thought . . . maybe we should discuss it. You know, in case you were worried that staying here . . ."

"I'm not worried," she said matter-of-factly.

"All right. I guess I didn't need to bring it up." Had she really forgotten their kiss already? Marcus tried to tell himself that it didn't matter, but disappointment the size of a golf ball stuck in his throat. Anxious, he stood. "You sure you don't want a drink?"

"I'm fine. But I will use the phone, if you don't mind."

"No problem. I'm gonna take a shower."

Upstairs, Marcus closed the bedroom door behind him and rested his forehead against the wood. Damn, he'd made a fool of himself bringing up their kiss! He'd thought that Alice might have given it a second thought, but clearly she hadn't. Hell, she'd spent years in Hollywood with guys fawning all over her. Why *would* she think twice about a kiss from a lowly cop?

He told himself that was a good thing, that maybe they'd both fallen into each other's arms simply because they'd been curious. With their curiosity satisfied, Marcus wouldn't have to worry about his judgment being clouded while he did his best to protect her.

But as he stepped into the shower and let the cool water run over his body, he wasn't quite convinced of his own argument. Curious or not, he knew he wanted to kiss her again.

Alice waited until she heard the shower running upstairs before she lifted the receiver. Even then, she couldn't bring herself to punch in the number she wanted to call.

God, she prayed Marcus hadn't known she was lying! She didn't want him to think the kiss meant something to her, when for him it was no doubt a reaction to spending time with the woman he now knew as Desirée, not his once homely best friend, Alice.

Glancing at the ceiling, she listened to the sound of the shower. Marcus was naked upstairs. The mere thought was enough to make her body thrum with desire.

Get a grip!

She could sit here and fantasize about him all day, wonder what he looked like naked and dripping wet. But that would drive her crazy. Remembering that she held the receiver in her hand, Alice finally punched in Sara's number in Los Angeles, praying her aunt was home. She made a silent promise to pay Marcus for the call when he took her back home.

She was. "Hello, Alice, sweetie. How are you?"

"Confused," Alice admitted, her mind shifting from the man upstairs to what had happened at the party. She told Sara about the scrapbook, and how surprised she was. "I can't believe she's the same woman who told me that if I went to Hollywood, I should stay away for good."

"I don't think she ever meant that, Alice."

"Then why say something so . . . final?"

"I don't know, but what you've just told me proves something I've suspected for quite some time."

"What?" Alice asked, suddenly intrigued.

"Oh, sweetheart, I don't want to say anything if I'm wrong."

"Aunt Sara . . ."

"Remember me telling you how disillusioned your uncle became in Hollywood? He always appeared strong, but the rejections got to him. He ultimately got hooked on sleeping pills, then alcohol. It nearly destroyed him. I think your mother was always afraid that the same demons that got hold of your uncle would get hold of you. She didn't want to lose you, too. But deep down, she still loved you. I hope I'm making sense."

"Aunt Sara, I know all this." Her aunt had talked candidly with her about her uncle's struggles while they lived together in Los Angeles.

"Yes, I know. But . . . Oh, you're just going to have to discuss this with your mother one day. Let her tell you the truth."

"What truth?"

"You're going to have to talk to your mother."

Alice wanted to question her aunt further. For the first time, she wondered if Aunt Sara knew more about her mother's motives than she'd ever let on in the past. But Marcus appeared at the entrance to the living room, clad in a Chicago Police T-shirt and gray shorts—and Alice stopped thinking altogether.

"Aunt Sara, I've got to go."

"Sweetie, I hope you and your mother can work this all out."

"Thanks," Alice said absentmindedly as she surreptitiously ran her gaze over Marcus's muscular thighs, then his large bare feet. "Talk to you later."

She replaced the receiver and stood. Marcus's eyes swept over her, and her nipples hardened. Just one look and he could do that to her—make her tingle, make her . . . hot. Lord help her, how was she going to handle staying here with him?

She wanted to kiss him again.

"You hungry?" he asked.

Disappointment washed over her. Here she was

getting hot and bothered while Marcus was as cool as a carrot. "Not particularly," she told him. *Unless being hungry for you counts.* "There was a lot of food at the party. But maybe you can show me my room."

"All right."

Marcus strolled out of the living room and Alice followed him. As she walked behind him up the stairs, she couldn't help watching the way his firm butt moved beneath his shorts.

She was lusting after him! The realization shocked her, but also gave her relief. Lust was normal. And Marcus was certainly a gorgeous creature. It wouldn't be normal if she didn't look at him with some level of female appreciation.

Still, with visions of what his body looked like dancing around in her head, Alice couldn't help thinking that this was going to be one long night.

Sixteen

It was time.

The decision was made as simply as that, though the decision itself had not been simple. After Marcus had dropped Alice home on Monday morning, she had seriously contemplated the pros and cons of actually living with him. In fact, she hadn't returned to his house that night as planned, despite his expressed concern. She'd spent a restless night at his house, wondering if she was indeed doing the right thing.

But she had spent an even more restless five nights back at her mother's house. Though she talked to Marcus every day and convinced him she was fine and could take care of herself, she couldn't quite shake the feeling that whoever was trying to scare her might return to the house—and do something worse than leave an implied threat on her doorstep. But the final catalyst had come last night, when there had been three phone calls with heavy breathing after an otherwise quiet week.

Foremost in Alice's mind was the concern that she not let her emotions dictate her actions. And putting her emotions aside, she knew that moving in with Marcus was the best thing she could do to protect her family.

After last night, she knew now that she had no other choice.

She had to move out.

Alice lay under the covers, staring at the ceiling as she thought about the past week. In the five days since she'd been home, her mother had been anxious over the whole birthday gift fiasco. She worried every time Alice left the house. Alice had tried to assure her mother that the gift was a stupid prank—though she didn't believe that herself—and had failed. The last thing Alice wanted to do was give her mother cause for a relapse with all this worry. In a way, she was touched, because her mother's concern confirmed what Aunt Sara had said—that she cared a lot more than she was ready to let on.

Marie felt bad because the party had been her idea, but Alice had convinced her that the threat wasn't her fault. And she also told her that despite what had happened, she appreciated the party. Marie had been right; facing the people who had once hurt her in some way had not only been therapeutic, it had reinforced for Alice how far she had come. And that people could change for the better.

Like Rosa, Marie was also concerned for Alice's safety. And Alice was concerned for theirs. Maybe spending some time away would be the best thing for everyone. She would miss them and the new closeness she felt with her sister and mother, but now that Mia was out of school she would see her three times a week at the theater anyway. And she could always visit everyone here.

Bottom line, and emotions aside, she had to keep her mother, Marie, and Mia safe. With her gone, the person who was threatening her wouldn't have any reason to come back to the house.

Alice sat up, stretched, then yawned. A quick glance at the clock told her she'd awakened late this Saturday morning. She was still tired from a sleepless night, but hopefully with her decision made, she would finally find some peace.

The smell of fried eggs wafted through the house. The family was no doubt gathered for breakfast. In the last week, her mother had been going downstairs for breakfast instead of staying in bed, insisting that she needed to get moving again.

Alice slipped into a terrycloth robe and slippers, then headed downstairs to join them.

"The sleepyhead is awake."

Alice made a playful face at Marie as she sauntered into the kitchen.

"Morning, Mother. Mia." Alice pulled out a chair and joined everyone at the small kitchen table.

"Morning," Mia and her mother replied in unison.

"How are you feeling?" Alice asked her mother.

"Much stronger. I told you I needed to start moving again. Get the blood pumping."

Rosa did look better. She'd lost weight over the past weeks, but her skin had a healthier glow.

"Can we dig in?" Alice asked.

"Yeah, can we dig in?" Mia mimicked.

Alice looked at her niece. Mia gave her a smile and she smiled back. Marie might think differently, but what harm was there in Mia wanting to be like her?

"We were just waiting on you," Marie replied.

Alice drew in a deep breath. Crispy bacon, scrambled eggs, potato fritters. When was the last time she'd had a breakfast like this? Too long. Over her years in Hollywood and in the weeks she'd prepared breakfasts for her mother, she'd opted for fruit or yogurt, and right now, her mouth watered at the sight before her.

Only her mother wouldn't enjoy this. Rosa had two boiled eggs and fresh fruit on her plate.

Rosa graced the food, then everyone dug in.

"I have something to tell you," Alice said after a few minutes. She looked at them each in turn. "I'm moving out."

"What?" Rosa dropped her fork onto her plate. "What on earth for?"

"I've given this a lot of thought, and I think it's best if I'm not around. My presence here is putting you in danger."

Rosa looked confused. "I thought you said that gift was a stupid prank."

"Yes," Alice replied slowly, knowing her mother would make that argument. "But I've talked to Marcus about this, and he agrees. I shouldn't take any chances."

"So you're gonna let this person get the best of you and run away?" Marie challenged.

"I'm not running away," Alice said, giving her sister a pointed look.

"Where are you planning to stay?"

This was the hardest part. Both her mother and Marie knew how much she'd been in love with Marcus years ago. She doubted they'd believe her moving in with him was entirely about protecting them.

"Marcus suggested I stay with him. He's a cop—"

"*Marcus?*" Marie guffawed. "You've got to be joking."

"Oh, Alice," her mother said, her voice full of pity.

Anger filled her. "This is *not* what you think it is. High school was a long time ago."

"Then what *is* this about?" Marie asked. "I saw the flowers he gave you for your birthday. *Roses.* Maybe there's something you're not telling us."

"I already told you why I'm doing this."

"You've been here all week, and nothing's happened," Marie countered.

"You're wrong. Just last night, I got three hang-ups." She looked at her mother. "This is about keeping you safe."

Marie and Rosa exchanged glances, doubt passing between them.

"Do you have to go?" That was Mia, sweet little Mia, looking at her as though she were about to lose her best friend.

"Oh, Mia. I'm not going forever. And I'll still be around. I'm going to see you at the theater, remember? I just have to make sure you guys are safe."

Still, Mia frowned.

"Do you really think this is necessary?" Rosa asked, her eyes filled with worry.

"Yes. But hopefully it won't be for long."

"Hopefully not," Marie said, giving Alice a soft smile.

"I'll be back as soon as this is all resolved. I promise."

"We'll miss you," Marie told her.

"Yeah, we'll miss you," Mia echoed.

And for the first time, Alice felt like a part of this family in a way she hadn't since she'd been a small girl. Like she was loved and respected.

But mostly, loved.

After the day's theater class, Alice went home, showered, changed, and packed her suitcase. She'd seen Marcus at the theater and had told him that she would be over later, so he was expecting her. But now that she stood on his front porch, her stomach fluttered with nervous energy. She'd thought this out and was convinced it was the right thing to do, so why was she so nervous at the prospect of actually moving in with him?

Because every time she was near Marcus, her emotions went haywire. She wanted him yet didn't want him at the same time. Being around him made her confused.

Alice tugged on her hip-hugging skirt, but it edged back up her thighs. What the hell—she was already here, already dressed in a sexy tank top and skirt that said she wanted him. She may as well knock on the door.

She *liked* the way he looked at her with male appreciation. She wanted him to look at her like that again, make her feel beautiful. Wearing this outfit, she had no doubt that would happen.

She knocked, then waited, her heart in her throat.

"Hey." Marcus's eyes lit up when he saw her, then slowly took in the length of her body, from her face to her waist, over her thighs and down to her toes, then back up over her hips, lingering at her breasts before finally returning to her face. His gaze was so intense that she shuddered, then got hot between her thighs as if his hands had stroked and caressed her. No one else's gaze had ever been able to do that to her.

"Hey, yourself." Alice offered a small smile and tried to keep her eyes on his face, but he was top-less, and as he continued to stare at her, she let her eyes wander over his body. He was strong and hard, like she knew he would be. He had a light dusting of curly black hair on his stomach that went lower, to his navel. Why was he half-dressed?

For the same reason she was so scantily clad?

"You gonna invite me in?" Alice asked, all too aware that Marcus's eyes were still roaming over her entire body.

"Oh. Sure."

Alice felt self-conscious as she stepped past him into the foyer of his home. Try as she might, she could dress the part of the sexy Desirée, but it was the timid Alice who crossed her arms over her chest in a last minute attempt to cover her breasts.

He closed the door and turned the lock, sensing her wariness. He frowned. "What's wrong?"

For a moment, she didn't know what to say. She was in Marcus's home, alone with him, and he was shirtless, for God's sake. Again, she looked at his magnificent chest. His dark brown skin gleamed be-neath the shaft of sunlight streaming through the window. Other than the small scar over his flat stomach, he was perfect.

Too perfect.

"God, I'm sorry." She made a move toward the door, but he stepped in front of her.

"What's the matter?"

Did he really have to ask? Was she the only one who felt a jolt every time they looked at each other?

She looked away. "Maybe this isn't such a good idea."

"We already talked about this."

Finally, she met his eyes. But that wasn't much safer than staring at his naked chest. She didn't realize just how muscular he was until she'd seen him half-naked.

"Yes, we talked about this, but . . ." She shifted from one foot to the other, unable to concentrate. How could she, when he was half-naked? "Can you . . . uh, put on a shirt?"

He raised an eyebrow as he looked at her. "Bothers you that much?"

What was he trying to do, tempt her? She gulped, then forced a smile. "I'm wearing one. It's only fair."

Marcus grinned. "You could always take yours off."

As he watched, her eyes widened in that deer look he loved. For all he knew, if Alice took her shirt off, he wouldn't know what to do. It had been that long. Longer still since he'd actually felt the urge to make love, but being here with Alice, he couldn't deny that that's what he felt now.

He wanted Alice to take off her shirt and free her voluptuous breasts. He wanted to softly stroke them with his fingers, then with his tongue. He wanted to take a rock-hard nipple into his mouth . . .

Marcus took a deep breath.

It had been too long, he told himself. Way too long. He was a man, after all, and Alice was one hell of a woman. He'd have to be crazy or dead not to notice her, not to feel anything when she walked into the room.

"I'd prefer you put your shirt on," she said softly. He almost asked if that was what she really wanted, because if she did, then why the hell had she shown up on his doorstep dressed in an outfit that was clearly meant to turn him on? But the fallacy in that thinking didn't fail him. He was a cop after all, and knew better than that. Women today dressed how they pleased, and just because they wore provocative attire didn't mean they wanted sex.

Besides, hadn't he told himself he wouldn't be influenced by another pretty face, another gorgeous body? So why was it that every time he stared at Alice, he found himself wanting to break his own promise?

Perhaps because she always looked at him the same way he looked at her—as though she liked what she saw. And the idea that she wanted him was one hell of a turn-on.

"Right," he finally said in response to her comment. "Give me a moment. Let me take your suitcase."

She passed it to him.

"Go ahead. Take a seat in the living room."

"Sure," she replied. Her bottom lip quivered slightly and she drew it between her teeth.

Marcus's groin tightened at the sight and he made a hasty retreat. He'd seen other women's lips tremble, but never had it seemed sexual until he'd seen it on Alice. He wanted to sink his teeth into her bottom lip, make her surrender in his arms.

All this because her lip had slightly trembled. Man, was he that hard up or what?

Upstairs, he placed the suitcase in the spare bedroom, then slipped into a T-shirt. After a brief lecture to himself on the cons of getting involved with Alice, he made his way back downstairs.

Alice sat with her elbows resting on her knees, her face resting in the palms of her hands. Hearing him, she looked up and did that lip-quiver thing again. Though this time it resembled a smile. Once again, he marveled at how much she had changed. Alice Watson was sitting in his living room in a body-hugging black skirt and low-cut cherry-red tank top, looking very much like a diva.

Looking like she wanted him.

His self-lecture went out the window as he realized just how much he wanted her, too. It would be pure torture for her to stay here and keep his hands off her. Maybe if they got the lust thing out of the way . . .

Taking a seat beside her, he tried to keep things strictly business. "I'm glad you finally came over."

"My mother and sister are really worried about me." She turned to him and blew out a frazzled breath—and he couldn't help noticing how her breasts rose and fell with the motion. She seemed oblivious to the effect she was having on him, so he forced his eyes back to her face and hoped to hell she hadn't noticed his body's reaction.

"I don't want my mother worrying. Worrying can't be good for her. I'd hoped that if I left they'd feel better, safer."

He placed a hand on the back of her neck and gently massaged it. "That's the way it goes when people care about you. You can't stop them from worrying."

God, his hand felt wonderful on her neck, and not simply because he offered comfort. No, she couldn't deny that the air between them was charged with a chemistry she didn't understand. Her eyes fluttered shut.

"Turn your back to me. I'll give you a massage."

Her eyelids popped open. What was she doing? This was dangerous.

"I . . . I'm hungry." No, she didn't mean that. "I should change." Damn, she didn't mean that, either.

She made an effort to stand, but he clamped a hand on her shoulder and forced her to stay seated.

"No," he said, his voice gentle, like a lover's caress. Suddenly, both hands were tangled in her hair. "Not yet."

Her heart beat furiously, and as he edged his mouth toward hers, she closed her eyes. His warm breath fanned her face and she had no idea that it could feel so erotic. With her eyes closed, the anticipation was greater, for she didn't know when the moment of contact would happen. Nervous, she flinched as his lips touched the corners of her mouth, then melted as he softly suckled her lips. After what seemed like hours of torture, he finally covered her lips completely.

This was different from the night on the pier. Whether deliberate or not, Marcus was being more erotic. Bolder. This time, as his tongue delved into her mouth, his hands ventured from her hair down the expanse of her throat to her breasts. She moaned, his fingers setting her body on fire.

He pulled back to look at her, his eyes mere slits. "I have to know, Alice. Did you wear this for me?" He stroked his thumbs over her nipples. "Because you knew it would turn me on?"

She managed only a whimper in reply. The truth was she had thrown on the sexy outfit because she wanted to see if he'd look at her again the way he had at Navy Pier. But admitting that somehow seemed absurd.

"I like it," he continued when she didn't respond.

Back and forth he stroked his thumbs, until her nipples puckered and pouted beneath his hands. "Marcus . . ."

He trailed seductive kisses from her mouth to her ear. "Damn, you are so beautiful."

Her back stiffened. She couldn't help it. As much as she'd always wanted to hear those words from him, actually hearing them now made her freeze. Slipping her hands between them, she pushed him away. "I have to go."

Bewilderment flashed in his eyes. "Why?"

Her throat constricted and she couldn't form words. He'd just said she was beautiful, yet she cringed inside. Now that she was Desirée he could see her as beautiful, but he'd never been attracted to plain, homely Alice.

"This isn't right." Her chest heaved with each ragged breath.

Marcus ran a finger down her neck, to her cleavage. "It feels right to me."

"No," she said forcefully. Sliding across the sofa, she turned her back to him. "This isn't real."

"Yes, Alice. It's real."

Flustered, she desperately wished she hadn't said what was on her mind. She wished it more so when Marcus slid behind her and brushed her hair over one shoulder.

God, it felt good. It felt real.

"No." She buried her face in her hands.

She felt and heard him more than she saw him, but when she lifted her head and opened her eyes, he was crouched on his haunches before her.

"Don't . . . look at me like that." Pushing herself off the sofa, she shot to her feet. He got to his feet too, his tall frame towering over her.

"What did I do wrong?"

How could she tell him? How could she say what was really in her heart? That she wanted him to want her for her, not her new, sexy image.

"I can't stay here."

She tried to step around him, but he blocked her path.

She tried to be strong, for she couldn't afford to make the mistake of loving him again. "Let me go."

"Not until you tell me what's going on."

He was going to make her act like a complete fool in front of him. Already she looked like an idiot, one minute melting into his kiss, the next ready to have a fit because he told her she was beautiful.

Beautiful. Her stomach dropped. She had to leave. She stepped to the right. He matched her step as though they were dancing.

"Will you stop that?" he asked. He put his hands on her face to hold her in place, but she shook him off. With a frustrated sigh, he dropped his hands to his hips.

"Just let me . . . leave." God help her, she knew how pathetic she must seem, but she couldn't stop herself.

"Not until you tell me why."

Again, she tried to step around him. Again, he blocked her path.

"Marcus—"

If he was smart, he would let her escape. Lord knew he didn't need the complication of a woman in his life, and this one seemed like she was nothing but trouble. He didn't know what to say around her, how to touch her, and damn if she didn't send totally mixed messages. One minute, she seemed to want him, the next she clammed up.

But instead of letting her go, he closed the distance between them in one quick stride. And before he knew what he was doing, he smothered her mouth with his.

It was far from gentle, and when he pulled away, they were both breathless.

"Why did you do that?" Alice asked, her chest heaving. The soft mounds of her breasts quivered with each breath, and Marcus's groin ached at the sight. He had the craziest desire to take her right there on the living room floor.

"Because I like kissing you."

"*Why*, Marcus?"

Wasn't it obvious? "Because I find you incredibly attractive."

"No, you don't."

"What?" he asked, bewildered.

She didn't answer. Dodging past him, this time she escaped, and he let her go. What else could he do? He only wished he knew what he'd done wrong.

It didn't make sense, but he felt a pain so deep inside as he heard the front door open, then close. He felt helpless, like he'd hurt her, but he didn't know how or why, and it was the last thing he had wanted to do.

But seconds later, when he heard the crash, the pain dissipated and was replaced with fear. Then his cop instincts took over. He ran.

Seventeen

Lord God in heaven, could she do nothing right?

She'd tried to make a clean getaway, but in her haste, she'd put the car in drive instead of reverse and plowed right into Marcus's Mustang.

Emitting a groan, she dropped her forehead onto the steering wheel. The horn sounded, startling her, and she jerked her head back up in time to see Marcus storming out the front door. God, he was going to be livid. She'd just smashed into his car.

But instead of stopping to check out the damage on his bumper, he rushed to her door and yanked it open. "Are you okay?"

She nodded weakly.

Leaning into the car, he scooped her out. "Come here."

It took her a moment to realize that he wasn't at all concerned with the car. Only with her.

Putting her on her feet, he said, "I know it's been

a while for me, but usually when a man tells a woman that she's beautiful, she doesn't run out and smash his car."

"Damn you, Marcus." She pounded a fist against his chest.

"That's assaulting a police officer."

She pounded him again, this time giving it all her strength. "Like I care."

"Ouch."

She moved to strike him again, but he grabbed her hands and held them between his. And as he stared down at her, Alice thought he might kiss her senseless right there in his driveway. Instead, he groaned as he glanced at something over her shoulder. Whipping her head around, Alice saw his next-door neighbor—an older black woman—standing on her front porch, straining to see what was going on.

"Come on," he said. "Before people start thinking we're having a fight."

"We are having a fight."

"Not that kind of fight," he said, wrapping an arm around her waist and pulling her close with more force than was necessary. "Hello, Mrs. Brady," he said cheerfully as he led Alice up the steps.

"Everything okay?" the woman asked.

"Sure," Marcus replied. "My girlfriend just had a little mishap."

"*Girlfriend?*" Alice queried, sounding appalled.

Glancing at her, she even looked appalled, and Marcus wanted to ask if the thought of being his girlfriend was really that revolting. Instead he ignored her as he ushered her into the house. Inside, he led her to the living room sofa, ordered her to sit, then went to the kitchen. Moments later, he returned with a glass of water. "Here."

"I don't want it."

"Drink it."

"No wonder you became a cop. I don't remember you being this . . . pushy."

"Occupational hazard."

"No doubt."

"Come on, Alice. I'll feel better if you drink this."

Feeling very much like a loser, Alice accepted the glass and gulped down several swallows of the cold water. It didn't make her feel better. Neither did the fact that Marcus loomed over her, his arms crossed over that beautiful brawny chest, as if he were a scolding parent.

"Want to tell me what that was all about?"

"No." How fitting. She sounded like a defiant two-year-old.

"Damn it." He grunted. "You want to run away from me that badly?"

Sipping the water, she ignored him.

He blew out a ragged breath and sat beside her. "Alice, whatever I did, I'm sorry."

She sipped more water. Tried to compose herself.

"If you don't want me to kiss you again, just tell me, and I promise I won't do it again."

"I didn't say that."

"So you do like it when I kiss you?"

She glanced at him. "I didn't say that, either."

"Well, do you or don't you?" he asked in a matter-of-fact tone.

She ignored him.

"All right. I'll tell you what I think, and you tell me if I'm right or wrong. We were kissing, and you seemed to like that. Then I said you were beautiful, and you freaked."

"Why?" she asked, so low she wasn't sure she'd actually said the word.

"Why did you freak? You tell m—"

"No. Why did you say . . . ?" She stopped. "Do you really think I'm . . . beautiful? Me, Alice, or me, Desirée?"

He didn't answer right away.

"That's what I thought." She guffawed. "You are so shallow, Marcus Quinn."

"Wait a minute!" Marcus sounded annoyed. "What the hell are you talking about?"

"Everyone thinks that just because I've lost some weight, I'm a different person. I had hoped you could see me for who I still am. The same Alice Watson who was your friend years ago." *The one you were never interested in before—so why now?*

"Ah, I see."

"No, you don't see. You think you can just say that I'm beautiful now and it's supposed to make a difference. Like it's supposed to make me feel good, when you were never attracted to me in high school."

"Wait a minute—this is about high school?"

God, she'd said too much. He didn't know how much she'd loved him years ago. Why, oh why had she opened her big mouth? "Forget it."

"No, I won't forget it. What did you mean?"

He was looking at her curiously, making it clear he'd sensed where this was going. "I'm just . . . stressed."

"No, this is about more than stress. Are you saying . . . were you *in love* with me in high school?"

"I shouldn't have said anything."

"You *were*." He sounded genuinely surprised, if not flattered. "Why didn't you say anything?"

"What difference would it have made?" Alice asked, not bothering to deny the truth any longer. "You were so goo-goo ga-ga over Tanisha."

"I never knew."

All right, she'd told him. And it hadn't been that bad. He didn't seem mortified. Just surprised, which made her wonder if it would have made a difference if she'd confessed her feelings for him ages ago. Would he have loved her back?

Marcus reached for her face, gently stroked it. "Why don't we forget the past and concentrate on the fact that I'm extremely attracted to you now."

Her stomach did a nervous flip-flop at his words. "To Desirée."

"To *you*."

"Now that I'm Desirée." Even to her own ears, she sounded lame for belaboring the point. But she didn't want to shut up, because she knew if they stopped talking, they'd end up in each other's arms.

"Will you *listen?*"

Alice jumped to her feet and he did, too. When she turned away, he took hold of her arm and whirled her around. Her flesh tingled beneath his touch.

"I don't know what you want me to say." His voice had softened, and damn if it didn't sound like he was whispering words of love to her. "I want you." His gaze fell to her breasts. "I want to touch you, taste you—"

"Oh, God, stop it." She shrugged away from him and turned, but he whipped an arm around her waist before she could escape. Forcefully, he pulled her against him. Her round buttocks pressed against his hardness.

"You feel that?" His breath was hot on her ear. "That's how much I want you."

Her chest rose and fell erratically, matching the erratic beat of her heart. Marcus Quinn had a hard-on. For *her*. It was impossible.

Yet it was possible, for she could feel the proof.

There was another time when she'd dared to believe that Marcus thought she was beautiful. A time she'd dared to believe he'd find her so irresistible that he'd pull her in an embrace and kiss her senseless, then make slow, passionate love to her. That dream was coming true, so why was it so hard for her to accept it?

Because it had always been a dream, one she hadn't truly expected to make a reality, given the fact that Marcus had been in love with someone else. Now that the dream was playing itself out, it scared her to death.

She struggled to escape him, but he held her in place.

"Don't, Alice. Don't run from me. Not now."

And she was so tired of running. So she let him turn her in his arms until she faced him, let him mold her body to his, let him press his strong chest against her soft breasts. His thighs against her legs. His rock-hard penis against her abdomen.

Oh, God. He really did have a hard-on for her.

"I want you so damn much, Alice."

He kissed her before she could respond, before she could run. As his lips slowly covered hers, her resistance—and her fears—slowly melted away until there was only heat and need.

He broke the kiss and turned her around so that her back once again faced his front. Though the room was filled with heat, she shivered as he brushed her hair over one shoulder and stroked his nose across the back of her neck. Then again. The torture was so exquisite, Alice thought she might die from it. As his nose flirted with her skin, his fingertips pressed into the softness of her belly, urging her closer. And when his lips skimmed her nape, her legs turned to jelly.

"You're stunning, Alice."

"N-no. D-don't say that." She wanted to make love to him, but she didn't want to be reminded of the truth she knew—that this was about lust for Desirée, not any feelings for Alice.

"It's the truth. God, you must know that."

"No . . ." But in defiance of her own words, she whimpered and reached for his thighs. They were solid, strong, and she loved the feel of them. And she couldn't help thinking about how they would feel naked against her.

He moaned softly against her ear. "Yes, Alice. Touch me."

"No." She pulled her hands away. Then cringed as she felt like an idiot. She was so afraid to go after what she wanted. Because she wanted it to be more than just sex.

Realization crashed down on her like a ton of bricks. Lord help her, she was still in love with him.

"Yes." He turned her in his arms. Planting his lips on her chin, he suckled softly, and damn if her body didn't turn to pure putty.

"I want to touch you." He ran his fingers down her arms. "I want to taste you." His tongue flicked over the base of her neck. "I want to feel my body between your legs." Placing a knee between her thighs, he forced her legs apart, intimately pressing his thigh against her. "Stop me whenever you want."

She purred in response.

He slipped a hand beneath her skirt. "You want to know what else?"

"Hmm?"

His fingers tickled her skin as they trailed higher, making her hotter than she imagined possible. "I want to try things with you I've never done before. Like massaging you in body butter and slowly licking it off."

"Oh, God."

"Mmm." He cupped her through her underwear, then stroked his thumb over her. He had long passed the point of no return. "Would you let me?"

She squeezed her thighs around his hand. "Oh, yes."

Lowering his head, he brushed his mouth over the mound of her breast, all the while stroking her. Her body went up in flames. Arching into him, she dragged her top down past the breast he favored, exposing a hard nipple. Immediately his lips covered it and he suckled like a man who had found gold.

She whimpered. And when his fingers slipped beneath her panties, she threw her head back, a cry escaping her throat.

With his body, he forced her backward to the sofa. She collapsed against it and fell onto her back. He pulled at her top until her other breast was exposed, then he flicked his tongue over her other nipple until she cried out from the pleasure. He kissed a path down to her navel, then pushed her skirt up until it was bunched around her waist. He paused over her, simply staring at the treasure before him, and she watched him, waiting, desperately wanting this intimate pleasure more than she'd wanted anything else in her life.

He brought his mouth down on her, pressing his tongue against her through her panties. The pressure of his tongue sent her over the edge. Her body was so taut, so on fire, that she exploded at the slightest contact. But as she gripped his head and moaned and rocked her own head back and forth, he didn't relent. Instead, he pushed aside the lacy fabric and kept up the pressure, so much so that she thought she would surely die.

"Oh, God, oh God, oh God . . ."

When she couldn't stand it any longer and felt the tears run from her eyes, he lifted his head and brought his lips to hers. He ravaged her mouth like a man who'd been starved of affection all his life.

She wanted him inside her. Gripping his buttocks, she pulled him against her as he kissed her senseless.

"Wait," he said.

She lay on the sofa as he rose and ran up the stairs. He was back in less than five seconds, with a square plastic package. A condom. It shouldn't have bothered her, but it did.

"I bought them this afternoon," he said sheepishly, reading her thoughts.

"Oh." She smiled.

He sat beside her and ran a finger over one breast, watching as it puckered, then lowered his head and brushed his lips over the hardened peak. She whimpered.

"Let me take this off. I want to see all of you."

Sitting up, Alice allowed him to remove her top and her bra. It felt thrilling to have his hands skim her body as he stripped her slowly, leaving her only in her black panties. As she sat half-naked before him, as his eyes hungrily took in the sight of her, she felt like more of a woman than she'd ever been. And she felt beautiful indeed.

Beautiful. Closing her eyes, she drew in a deep breath, savoring the feeling. When she opened her eyes, she saw him watching her, smiling. So she reached for him, pressed her palms to his chest, let them stay there a moment. He felt wonderful. He was hard, strong, hot. And right now, he was hers.

She wanted him. Pulling at his shirt, she slipped it off his chest. Her eyes went to his nipples, dark and delicious. The thought shocked her, made her wonder what it was about Marcus that always made her weak with longing. It had always been him.

Her eyes ventured lower, to his flat, beautifully sculpted abdomen. She touched him there, enjoyed the feel of him as he trembled beneath her hand. For once, she felt powerful, so she acted like she had power. Power to thrill him, to make him hers. Trailing her hand lower, she reached for the button on his jeans. His arousal strained against his jeans, large and hard.

God, she wanted him.

She undid the button, but the jeans were too snug to force off his hips quickly. Marcus helped her, and when he stripped down to his black bikini briefs, her breath snagged in her throat at the sight of him.

"Come here."

He took her hand and led her to the dining room. Pulling back a chair, he sat, then urged her onto his lap. She straddled him and he ran his fingers through her hair, drawing her face to his. He devoured her lips until she struggled for breath. All the while she could feel him beneath her, heat against heat. He kissed her ear, then whispered, "Ease up."

She did, and not knowing who she'd become, she slipped her fingers beneath the waist of her panties, then gyrated once, twice, as she slowly dragged the black silk off her hips.

"Oh, yeah," Marcus moaned.

Then she reached for him, forcing his underwear to his knees. She didn't know how she'd become such a bold person, but she wanted to turn him on as much as he was turning her on. Leaning forward, she flicked her tongue over his lips, but pulled back before he could kiss her back. She heard the condom package tear as she planted soft kisses along his jaw from his chin to his ear. When she reached his ear, she ran her tongue over the flesh. Slowly.

Forcefully, he grabbed her hips and urged her onto him. He took a moment to guide their bodies together, but once he did, he filled her completely with one hard thrust, and she cried out.

He reacted with a long moan and another deep thrust, then another, until they found a rhythm. God, he was driving her wild. Arching against him, she pushed her breasts out to meet his face. Greedily, he took a nipple in his mouth, and with each suckle drove her nearer to the edge of the abyss.

The feeling was so wonderful, so completely

erotic, that it felt like the first time. And when he reached for her other breast and tweaked and tugged at the nipple, she shattered. Crying out, she rode the wave of passion until moments later he gripped her back and cried out with his own release.

Spent, their ragged breaths filled the air. He held her in place, running his hands over her slick back. Then his lips brushed across her cheek and she met his mouth with hers and they kissed until neither had any breath left.

I love you, she thought, and was immediately startled. Opening her eyes, she looked at him, at the sweat beading on his forehead, his closed lids, his content expression. Joy filled her heart.

God, it was true. She did love him. She always had.

He'd crossed the line—again.

And now he felt guilty as hell. The very thing he'd told himself to avoid he had pursued as if his life depended on it.

Rolling from his back onto his side, Marcus's gaze fell smack on the reason for his foul mood this morning—Alice's shapely form. He watched her while she slept. He watched the small movements she made as she inhaled and exhaled, relishing the soft sounds of her presence in his bed. Her smooth, honey-colored back was exposed right down to those beautiful hips, where the bedsheet covered her. She looked perfect.

He wanted to reach for her, trail a finger softly down the length of her spine from the top of her neck to the small of her back until she awoke. Then he wanted to make love to her again, slow and easy, like the morning sunrise, not like the hungry, sex-starved man he had been last night.

Marcus blew out a frustrated breath as reality smacked him hard in the head. What the hell was wrong with him? Why, even now, could he not resist Alice? He had promised himself he wouldn't let a pretty face get to him again, but he had done exactly that last night. Was Alice right? Was he only attracted to her because she had transformed into the stunning Desirée LaCroix?

Marcus could only hope last night wouldn't screw things up.

He was supposed to be protecting her. Plain and simple. Nothing else.

His eyes flitted over her incredibly sexy form once again. After having a taste of her, he didn't know if he could live without it. Even watching her sleep was strangely erotic in a way he'd never before experienced. There was something about Alice, something that drew him to her, more than just the physical attraction.

Maybe it was her stubborn determination to take care of herself. Or her gentle side as she dealt with the children. Or the way she seemed genuinely surprised when he'd called her beautiful. She'd made a success of herself in Hollywood, yet she didn't have an ego. She was real.

But maybe what drew him to her was their friendship. Even after all this time, it was still there. He still felt he could talk to her, ask her opinion about things, give her advice that she'd appreciate.

That was exactly why he needed to keep things in

perspective. Their friendship was most important. Her safety was paramount. Sex would only confuse both issues.

They'd gone too far last night, but he'd damn well make sure it didn't happen again.

Could her life be better than this?

Making love to Marcus had been everything she'd dreamed it could be—and more. That was why, as they sat together eating breakfast at his small kitchen table, Alice was not only wearing one of Marcus's T-shirts, she was wearing a goofy smile as well. Her scrambled eggs had no taste, not when she could only remember the taste of him on her lips, the feel of his hard body pressed against hers, the feel of him thrusting deep inside her.

She was in love with him, and though at first she'd been worried that he might only be interested in her image, after the way he'd held her so tightly in his arms as they'd slept last night, she felt certain there was something more between them.

Perhaps it was too soon to hope, but she couldn't stop herself any more than she could stop breathing. She'd wanted this for so long that it still felt like a dream, but she preferred to consider it a dream come true. Was it impossible to believe that what had started off as friendship years ago had now blossomed into love? Surely, after making love to her so passionately, like he was a man who had finally tasted water after a long drought, he had to have feelings for her.

"Marcus, can I ask you something?" When he

nodded, she said, "Why did you and Tanisha get divorced?"

Marcus scowled. "I never should have married her in the first place."

"Then . . . why did you?" Alice hoped she wasn't treading on holy ground.

Marcus considered the question for a long moment, then sighed. "I loved her. At least I thought I did."

"Meaning?" Alice asked, an eyebrow arched with curiosity.

"Meaning I was blind in high school. I didn't see her for who she really was. I saw a gorgeous face and little else. To me, she was always sweet and loving, but it didn't take long after I married her to see her true colors."

"She hurt you." It was a statement, not a question.

"Yeah. I realize now that she was never the person I thought she was."

"I'm sorry."

"Hey, it's over. You move on." Marcus grew quiet, but after a moment spoke again. "You want to know something interesting? She was extremely jealous of you."

"Yeah, right." Alice snorted her disbelief.

"I'm telling the truth. When the word spread that you had gotten your first role in a feature film, she had to be there to see it on opening night. For some reason, she hadn't paid much attention to your television roles, but this was a feature. Big time as far as she was concerned, I guess. She kept making comments about how you'd look, that it was going to be a laugh to see you. Of course, when you appeared on the screen, she almost didn't recognize you. And then you should have seen her face. She almost turned white, which is no small feat for a black woman. When she couldn't say anything bad about how you looked, she started with some garbage about your performance. I think it was at that moment, sitting in the theater with her, that I started to realize that I had no love for her."

Alice felt a surge of pride that Marcus, whom she hadn't seen for years at that point, had been offended on her behalf. "It's understandable that people would be surprised at seeing how much I'd changed."

"You see, that's how different you are from Tanisha. What I've admired about you most is that you've always been classy. Never stooping to her level, despite how she must have treated you when I was too blind to notice."

"How long were you married?"

"Almost six years."

"God, that long?"

He frowned playfully. "Can I plead temporary insanity?"

Alice giggled.

"Like I said, I knew pretty soon that things weren't quite right, but I'd taken a vow and I wanted to do my best to make the marriage work. I thought if I gave her a house, attention, she'd be happy. But she never was. Even now, I don't understand her."

"Well, I'm sorry things didn't work out," Alice told him, though she really wasn't. She'd always known Tanisha would hurt him, and it was better that their marriage had ended before children had come into the picture.

"What about you and Noel Sanders?" Marcus asked.

"Oh, God!" Alice giggled and threw a hand over her face. "No questions about Hollywood."

"Too late," he said, flashing her a devilish grin. "I already told you about Tanisha. It's only fair."

She groaned, though she was still smiling. "Oh, all right."

"What was that relationship all about? I remember when I first heard you were going to marry him, I wondered if you'd lost your mind."

"I don't know."

Placing an elbow on the table, he rested his cheek in his palm. "You were always such a nice person. From what I'd seen and read about Noel, he sounded like a jerk."

"Actually, he was a jerk. Full of himself. Thought he was God's gift."

"And that's why you were going to marry him?" He gave her a skeptical look.

Remembering made her grimace. It was the first year she'd gotten a few roles in Hollywood, one of them being in a TV movie with Noel. To this day, she didn't know how they'd gotten involved. He was selfish and self-centered, even in bed.

"In retrospect, it was stupid," she explained. "I never should have gotten involved with him. But he seemed really nice, down to earth."

"Nice?"

Her hands flew up. "Okay, I admit. I was really naïve then." She paused. "If you want to know the truth, he was the first guy to really pay any attention to me . . . once I started looking . . . okay. I figured I should go for what I could get, because until then, I hadn't gotten much."

"Alice."

"No," she said, placing a finger on his lips to quiet him. "I don't feel that way now."

He took her hand. Squeezed it. "Good."

"Anyway," she continued, "I had no clue Noel had a drug problem until a few weeks before the wedding. That's why I canceled the wedding so suddenly. Not because I was fickle and got tired of him, like the media said. Besides . . ." Her voice quieted. "I realized he was far more in love with the image of Desirée LaCroix than the real me—Alice Watson."

She took a deep breath. "I was caught up with the whole Hollywood thing, and I guess after hearing enough times that we looked good together, that we'd done so well in that last film, that when he asked me to marry him I had to wonder if we wouldn't be good together in real life. And of course, I didn't realize until after we were engaged how good an actor he was—on and off the screen. He was far from nice, had terrible mood swings and a terrible temper. Though for a while I didn't think I could break off the engagement because he really seemed to be in love with me and I didn't want to break his heart."

"*Way* too nice."

They fell into silence, then Alice asked, "Did you want a family?"

"With Tanisha? Never."

"What about now?"

He shrugged. "Honestly, I don't know if it's in the cards for me."

"Why not?"

"I'd want to be married if I have a family. And I'm not sure I ever want to do that again. I'm not sure I could use the insanity defense twice." He laughed.

Alice didn't want to look stupid, so she laughed too. Though she couldn't quite laugh down the disappointment. But it was so intense, her heart plummeted to her stomach. She knew it was crazy. What did she expect after one night of sex? A marriage proposal?

"You know," Alice said, changing the subject. "I was thinking that maybe we could go down to the waterfront again. Not for dinner, but maybe for a walk. It's a beautiful day, and I'd love to spend it outside. I do a lot of jogging. Do you? It's a great way to keep fit."

"Hmm."

"Or, maybe you could show me around your neighborhood. Some of the areas that have changed over the years."

He didn't respond, and Alice paused in her rambling to stare at him. Either he didn't sense her looking at him, or he was ignoring her, because he didn't look up from his plate of food. The absorbed expression on his face was clear.

A chill washed over her. She suddenly realized that things didn't seem right. Last night, he hadn't been able to get enough of her, but now . . . he seemed far away. Was it because she'd asked if he wanted to get married again? Did he think she meant to her?

"Marcus, did you hear me?"

"I've got to get ready for work," he said, still not looking at her.

He was dismissing her. "Oh. You're working today."

"Yeah." Setting down his fork, he lifted his head. "Alice, we need to talk."

Another chill. "All right."

He blew out a frustrated sigh as he rubbed one temple. "I take the blame fully for what happened last night, but . . . it can't happen again. God, that sounds cheesy. The point is, I'm supposed to be protecting you, not . . . not anything else. Making love is a distraction, and I broke my word when I said I wouldn't touch you, but you have it again. As long as you're here, under my protection, there won't be a repeat of last night."

For a long while, Alice stared at him, trying to figure him out. From hot to cold in the blink of an eye. "So," she began slowly, "if I wasn't staying here, it would be okay to touch me?"

"That's not what I'm saying."

"Then what are you saying, Marcus? Because I'm confused."

"You have every right to be upset, Alice. I know that. But we can't fall into bed again. We're *friends*. I don't want to do anything to complicate that."

Alice tried to read his expression. She saw a mix of guilt and frustration—but no blatant sexual desire like she saw last night.

No love.

God, how could she have been so stupid? Just yesterday she'd questioned his motives about getting her into bed, but she'd wanted him so badly, she'd given in to her lifelong dream of loving him.

And he'd given in to his attraction for Desirée LaCroix.

Last night, she'd forgotten one very important thing—this was real life, not a Hollywood movie. Marcus wasn't going to fall in love with her just because she had wanted him for fifteen years. And she realized that she had been waiting for this moment all these years.

But it had been no more than sex for him.

"I see," Alice said, quickly rising.

Marcus's chair scraped on the linoleum floor as he shot to his feet. "Alice—"

"For God's sake, don't treat me like some lovesick teenager. I don't need to be coddled and comforted. I'm a big girl."

Alice could have sworn she saw the light in Marcus's eyes snuff out, but she had to be wrong. He had no feelings for her, at least no feelings other than *friendship*, so why would he be disappointed?

No, there was only one fool in this room. And it was her.

She made a hasty retreat upstairs and was thankful that he didn't follow her. She couldn't let him know how much of a fool she actually was.

She couldn't let him know that she was in love with him, body and soul.

Eighteen

For the rest of the week, Alice and Marcus didn't say much to one another. They were nothing more than polite strangers as they coexisted in his house. They tried not to get in each other's way, and they spoke only about necessary things, such as Marcus telling Alice he would be working late, or Alice assuring him she'd call him from the theater to let him know she was okay. The distance between them hurt her, but Alice would never let him know that.

She still couldn't get past their night of incredible lovemaking—and the subsequent realization that she had been so wrong in judging Marcus's feelings. The blame lay squarely on the pathetic part of her that was a dreamer, always hoping her life would have a Hollywood movie ending. But more disturbing than the reality that Marcus didn't love her were her own feelings for him. She thought she'd long since gotten over her major teenage crush on Marcus Quinn, but clearly she hadn't.

She wished to God she hadn't admitted to him that she'd been in love with him years ago. It was so much harder to look him in the face now, all because she'd opened her big mouth.

In the past week, Alice had entertained thoughts of returning home to her mother and sister, but they would only see her return as proof that she didn't have to leave in the first place. No, as painful as this was, she would stay here until they both felt the threat against her was over. Then she'd move out and go on with her life.

But did that entail moving back to Hollywood? Now, thinking about it, she wasn't so sure. It surprised her to realize she didn't miss Tinseltown, even though movies had been her life for the past thirteen years.

"Aunt Alice?"

At the sound of her name being called, Alice's eyes flew open. The children stood on the stage before her, regarding her curiously. She had been so absorbed in her thoughts, she'd forgotten where she was.

It was Saturday, and while Marcus wasn't at work, he wasn't here either. For the last hour, Alice had tried to tell herself she was glad about that fact, but the truth was, she missed him.

Maybe he was right. Sex had complicated things between them.

"Yes, Mia?"

"I asked if you thought I should try saying this line another way? I'm not sure if it sounds okay."

Mia had been cast in one of the lead roles in the

play, not because she was Alice's niece, but because she'd done so well at the audition that she couldn't be denied the part. Approaching her now, Alice glanced over her shoulder at the script she held. "Which line?"

"This one." Mia indicated a scene where the students first start to wonder if their class is haunted because of strange happenings. "I don't know if I should sound scared, or sound like I'm not taking the situation seriously."

"Why don't you try it both ways, and we'll see."

For the next few minutes, the children rehearsed the scene, after which Mia said she thought her character would be skeptical rather than scared at this point, and Alice agreed.

The rest of the afternoon went smoothly, and Alice felt they'd accomplished a lot. She said goodbye to Mia and Chad and the other parents and children, then stepped outside. The sky was dark and ominous. No doubt it would rain shortly.

She was opening her car door when she heard the sound of screeching tires. Automatically, her head whipped in the direction of the sound. A mere second later, the door to the Jeep flew open and an enraged Terry jumped out. Alice's heart froze as he stalked toward her.

"What's wrong?" she managed, though her voice was merely a croak. She was afraid of him, she realized. He'd never liked her in high school, and he certainly didn't like her now.

"You know damn well what's wrong! I don't know why Tanisha hired you, but you shouldn't be teaching children."

"If you can just calm down . . ."

"Don't tell me to calm down. My daughter looks up to you, but for God's sake, you're a druggie. If you really care about the children, you'll quit as their teacher right now."

Alice was hurt, confused, and enraged at the same time. How dare Terry attack her like this!

"I'm not about to be bullied . . ." He flung something at her, and Alice flinched. Until that moment, she hadn't realized he was holding anything.

"Think about the children you're supposed to care so much about," he said, then stalked back to his car.

When he was gone, Alice allowed herself to look down. An ad for a cigarette company on the back of some paper met her eyes. Trembling, she bent and retrieved the paper. She turned it over—and felt her world start to spin.

It wasn't simply the headline that jumped out at her. It was the picture. A picture she had seen for the first time weeks ago when she'd come to this theater.

Anger flowed through her veins like hot lava. Gripping the tabloid paper in her hand, she stood and charged back into the theater. This time, Tanisha had gone too far. And Alice had finally had enough.

Tanisha looked up from the pile of papers before her as Alice stormed into her office. Her eyes widened in shock.

Alice glanced quickly to her right and scanned the walls. Like she'd known, the picture of her hugging Mrs. Stoffman was no longer there. It was on the cover of the latest copy of *The Intellect* opposite a photo of her since she'd lost her excess weight. The contrast of before and after was startling, which made the crude headline all the more believable to people who didn't know her.

"How dare you?" Alice said, then dropped the copy of *The Intellect* onto the desk.

Tanisha gave no show of being surprised as she glanced down at the paper. Instead, she read the caption aloud: "Miracle Weight Loss or Drug Induced? Desirée's Secret Past Revealed!" Slowly, she raised her eyes to meet Alice's. "What, you think *I* did this?"

"Don't even play games, Tanisha. That very same picture is missing from the wall!"

Tanisha looked in the direction Alice pointed. "Oh, so it is."

"I've been helping you out for how many weeks, yet you seem hellbent on sabotaging my reputation. I know you never liked me, Tanisha, but I won't put up with this."

"I had nothing to do with this."

"You had nothing to do with the gift at my party, nothing to do with my tire being slashed. Poor little Tanisha, always in the wrong place at the wrong time, right? *Bull.*"

"I'm not the only one who has access to this office, Desirée."

"What's this about?" Alice asked. "Marcus? Are you still in love with him or something?"

Tanisha's eyes flashed fire, but she ignored the question. "The parents have access to this office. So do other board members. So does *Marcus.*"

"Marcus would never do anything like this,"

Alice responded without hesitation. "I can't believe you'd even imply that he would."

"I didn't say he did, only that he has access to this office." Tanisha sighed. "Look, I'm sorry this happened. I really am. Why would I do something like this when I've been thrilled that your work here has done so much good for this theater?"

"Because you hate me."

"Emotions have no place in business."

Alice sneered at Tanisha. The woman had an answer for everything. For all Alice knew, Tanisha was deliberately trying to make her look bad. Hadn't Marcus told her just last week how jealous Tanisha had been of her success? This made perfect sense.

"If it weren't for the children, I'd walk away from this right now," Alice told her. "But I promise you, if anything like this happens again, I will."

"Like I said, I know nothing about this."

"Whatever."

Alice spun around on her heel and left Tanisha to chew on that while she coolly walked out of the office.

"Woowee. Mmm mmm mmm. Check out that one, Marcus."

Marcus frowned up at Khalil as he lay on his back on the bench press. "Are you gonna spot me or check out the women all day?"

"Damn, Marcus." Khalil glanced down at him. "Are you in a funk, or what?"

Reaching for the weight bar, Marcus wrapped his fingers around the cool metal. "Don't start with me."

Marcus pushed the bar upward and over its cradle, then lowered it onto his chest. It took every ounce of strength to lift the four hundred pounds once, then twice. By the third repetition, Khalil had to help him return the bar.

Marcus sat up and flexed his arms to ease the burning sensation in his muscles.

"You must have serious woman trouble."

"Why would you say that?"

"You went way over your limit. That's not like you."

It was true that thus far Marcus hadn't bench-pressed more than three hundred pounds, but still Khalil's comment annoyed him. "Why does everything have to revolve around a woman?"

"Hey, I'm no fool. Besides, Tanisha mentioned something about you and Alice."

"Ah, Tanisha. A reliable source of information."

"I wouldn't have believed it if you hadn't been frowning all week at work," Khalil retorted, sounding a tad defensive. "And since the moment you got here."

"I'm sorry. Truth be told, I am a little stressed." Briefly, he explained the situation with the threats against Alice and how she was now living with him.

"No wonder you're in a funk. Living with such a beautiful woman but keeping your hands to yourself . . . I don't pity you."

Marcus could only shake his head at the fact that Khalil had completely missed the bigger picture—that he was worried about trying to protect Alice from an unknown perp.

But then, he realized that Khalil had hit the nail right on the head. Yes, he wanted to protect Alice, but the fact that they'd hardly spoken all week had contributed to his stress factor more than anything else. That and the fact that every time he saw her, he wanted to make love to her. Keeping his hands off her was killing him.

"I'm gonna do some stomach crunches, then head to the shower," Marcus said. "Five minutes all right with you?"

"Sure."

Marcus tilted his head back and drank from his water bottle while he walked to the area of the gym that housed the nautilus equipment. A woman used the abdominal machine, so he stood to the side, waiting.

"Oh," she said when she noticed him. "You're waiting on me."

"Take your time."

She slipped out of the seat. "I'm finished."

There was no mistaking the look in her eyes; she was interested. Marcus wasn't. Smiling politely, he stepped past her and sat at the machine.

She moved away without any further conversation, but when he glanced in her direction, he saw that she was looking at him. She smiled.

And he suddenly pictured Alice, her head tilted slightly to the side, sending a beautiful smile his way. Damn, why should this woman's coy smile make him think of Alice?

Five minutes later, he was in the locker room with Khalil, as promised. They both showered and dressed.

"Want to go for a drink?" Khalil asked.

"Naw." He'd been avoiding Alice much of the week, partly because he sensed she wanted more from him than he was capable of giving. Now, he wanted to head home and make sure she was okay. It was early evening and she should be home from the theater by now.

Khalil hauled his gym bag over his shoulder. "All right. See you Monday." He paused. "I know I bug you a lot about women, but the truth is, I hope you find what you're looking for. My sister wasn't it, and Melissa . . . well, she wasn't either." He shrugged. "Who knows? Maybe Alice will be the one."

Khalil couldn't have floored Marcus more if he'd told him to take up needlepoint. Stunned, Marcus merely nodded. But hearing Melissa's name forced some sense into him. It was important that he didn't lose perspective, didn't start thinking of Alice looking all sweet as sugar. He had to remember she was at his place for one reason—so he could protect her. He'd gotten too close to Melissa and now she was dead.

Marcus slapped Khalil lightly on the shoulder when they reached the gym's front doors. "Take it easy."

"You too, man."

Marcus got in his car and decided to head for home right after he picked up a few things at the first variety store he saw.

"Alice? You up?"

Marcus's deep, sexy voice lured Alice from her nap. Not until she heard it did she realize just how relieved she was that he was home. Today's incident with the tabloid had her on edge. Whether or not someone was out to do her physical harm, they were certainly out to destroy her reputation. Was it Tanisha? And if so, was she only behind the tabloid story, or was she also the one stalking her?

She sat up and finger-combed her hair. "Yeah, I'm up."

"Are you decent?"

Fleetingly, she wondered what would happen if he walked into the room and found her naked. Would he be able to resist her?

That was the last thing she needed to be thinking of. "Yes," she said, straightening her cotton top. "I'm decent. Come in."

The door opened slowly, and Marcus walked into the room, looking as sexy as ever in gray sweats and a white T-shirt. This man could make a burlap sac look sexy, no doubt.

"I don't know how to tell you this," he said.

"If you're talking about *The Intellect*, I saw it."

Marcus stepped further into the room, until he was standing a couple feet before her. "I'm sorry."

"I'll get over it."

He bent on his haunches before her and regarded her with obvious concern—something Alice wished he wouldn't do. It was so much harder for her to quell her feelings for him when he acted like he cared.

"You don't always have to be tough, Alice." He could see the pain in her eyes, and it touched him in a way nothing ever had. He'd do whatever he could to erase that vulnerable, timorous look, and he hoped she knew that. "At least not with me. I know this hurt you."

Alice blew out a ragged breath—one that carried

her resolve to be strong with it. "Yeah, it did hurt. Because this time, it wasn't an angry director in Hollywood trying to save face before people started asking questions about why I left the set. This time, it's someone from my hometown who's deliberately tried to smear my name. I think it was Tanisha."

Marcus considered her words. If Tanisha was responsible for the latest tabloid fiasco, then it was likely that she was the one who had slashed Alice's tire and brought the gift to her house. Based on circumstantial evidence, he could make a case for Tanisha's guilt. She was everywhere the threats had happened. It was the motive that was a little sketchy. Why hire Alice and then try to discredit her? But Marcus had certainly seen stranger things in the years he'd been a cop and nothing would surprise him.

Still he asked, "Why do you think Tanisha was behind this?"

Alice explained the missing picture to him. "Besides, the fact that she hates me? Oh, I don't know."

"I'll question her."

"I already did. She denied it."

"I might have better luck."

Alice let the matter slide. The fight was gone out of her, and knowing that Marcus would deal with this made her feel better.

Better than it should.

He reached for her hand, gently squeezed it. It was meant as a gesture of support, she knew, but a lightning bolt may as well have struck the house, that's how radically the atmosphere changed. The air around them was suddenly electrically charged.

His eyes roamed over her face, as if trying to ensure she was okay. When he looked at her like that, with such concern, it was easy for Alice to believe that he cared about her. His gaze dropped from her eyes to her mouth, and her heart skipped a beat. God, was he going to kiss her?

Slowly, he eased up, edging toward her, and Alice froze. She should move away, say something, but she did neither. Instead, she closed her eyes and waited until his lips met hers.

But they didn't. Instead, Marcus stopped, his face a fraction from hers and moaned softly. "I tell myself I should resist you, but for some reason, I can't," he said. He stood and, taking her hands, pulled her into his arms. "You are so beautiful. Everything about you." He ran one hand over her shoulder and down her back. "The way you feel." He leaned closer, burying his nose in her neck. "The way you smell." He leaned back, yet tightened his arm around her waist. "The way you look."

Alice didn't dare breathe.

Stepping backward, he ran his hands down her arms until he reached her hands. "And your feet. I never understood foot fetishes until I saw those toes."

Alice felt so hot, she wondered if she was in danger of overheating. "My toes?"

"Mmm-hmm," he replied, the sound emanating more from his chest than his lips. Raising her hands, he linked fingers with hers. "And your lips." He urged her closer, rubbed his nose against hers. "I love the way they surrender beneath mine."

Fool that she was, she was putty in his hands. She enjoyed this exquisite foreplay too much to put a stop to it.

"And your breasts. God, I love how they taste."

She couldn't help it—she shuddered as delicious heat flooded her core.

"That's it, Alice." He trailed his mouth along her jaw until his lips found her ear. "I want to feel you surrender in my arms."

The low, seductive whisper in her ear was almost her undoing. She closed her eyes and rode the sweet waves of sensation pulsating through her body. "Oh, Marcus . . ."

He brought his lips to her mouth and silenced her with a kiss. This wasn't a foreplay kiss. This was an I-want-you-right-now kiss. And it left them both panting when he tore his lips from hers.

Marcus was lost. He could no more stop himself from making love to Alice than he could stop himself from breathing. He wanted her. Wanted her with a need that was foreign to him in its intensity. He reached for her shirt and urgently pulled it off her head, then brushed aside the fabric of her bra and took her nipple in his mouth.

She cried out instantly and clutched her hands to his head. God, he loved the way she responded to him. He could spend forever making love to her and not get bored.

Bringing his mouth back to her lips, he moved her body with his until she hit the bed and lay backward. He stripped her of her jeans and panties, stripped himself of his sweats and briefs, then settled himself between her legs, filling her with one eager thrust.

Alice dug her nails into his back while he loved her. Their coupling was urgent, and he wasn't gentle, but she didn't want gentle. She wanted all of him, even if he could only give her that in the act of lovemaking.

And when they skyrocketed into orbit together, both of them gripping each other as if they were the only two people in the world, Alice knew that this was enough.

For now, it had to be.

Nineteen

Two weeks later, the storm over Alice's last feature in the tabloids hadn't calmed. She was used to Terry's animosity, but other parents had also openly expressed their concern that maybe she was doing more harm than good to their children. Their negativity hurt Alice, but she was determined to remain strong. She wasn't going to give in and let the person trying to destroy her life win.

It helped that Marie had supported her, assuring her she didn't believe a word of the rumors. Given all the snide comments her sister had made about Hollywood in the past, she could have used this opportunity to berate her choice of careers once again, but she hadn't. Even more than before, Alice believed that Marie's seeming animosity toward her acting career had nothing to do with Hollywood but with her own frustrations about what she had and hadn't done in her life.

Though Alice hoped the tabloid rumors hadn't reached the children's ears, at every rehearsal since the last story broke, she sensed they were curious about the truth. So when she heard Jeremy bugging Mia about her aunt being on drugs the last time they met, she sat them down and explained her side of the story. If they were old enough to hear the gossip and possibly their parents' distorted views, they were old enough to hear the simple truth from her.

Marcus had been nothing but supportive during the past couple weeks, and the stress that had hung like a cloud over their friendship was gone now. It felt good to laugh and smile again with ease. Perhaps because they'd both given up the illusion that they could live in the same house and keep their hands off each other, they had found a measure of peace. They still made love, and it was always intense, but Alice didn't expect anything beyond the moment. It was easier that way.

They'd made love last night, and Alice had stayed in Marcus's bed long after he had gone to work. She had come close to telling him that she loved him as she'd climaxed, but somehow had held her emotions back. In a way, it was getting harder each time they made love, because he seemed to give of himself so completely that Alice couldn't shake the dream that he loved her but simply wasn't ready to admit the truth to himself.

She rolled from her back onto her side, drawing the bedsheet up to her neck. Inhaling deeply, she savored Marcus's unique scent, mingled with the scent of their lovemaking. It was too late to tell herself that she shouldn't get attached; she was lost.

The phone rang, and Alice stretched across the

bed to the night table to answer it. Marcus often called her during the day to make sure she was okay.

"Hello."

"Desirée, it's Tanisha."

Alice's stomach dropped. Tanisha knew that she was living with Marcus? "Yes?"

"Are you busy now?"

"Right now?"

"Yes."

"Why?" Alice asked. Where Tanisha was concerned, she couldn't help feeling wary. She didn't trust her.

"There's something I'd like to discuss with you, and I'd rather we not do it on the phone. Maybe you can meet me at the theater."

"Anything you have to say to me, say it now. I've got a busy day ahead of me." That was a lie, but she wasn't about to meet Tanisha alone anywhere. After everything that had happened, she didn't trust her. Tanisha seemed the most likely candidate out to destroy her.

"All right. It's about Saturday's rehearsal. I've invited members of the media and city council to view the play."

"You *what?*"

"With all the negative backlash since that article in *The Intellect*, I felt it was the best thing to do. This way, the press can see you in action, see the children perform, and give advance reviews to counter all the rumors."

What Tanisha said made sense, but two days' notice was hardly adequate. "I'm not sure how the kids will react to this, Tanisha. They're used to performing for me, but to suddenly have an audience when they thought they had two more weeks of rehearsals before opening night . . ."

"I wish we had the luxury of time, but we don't. I want to put an end to all the speculation before it permanently hurts the theater's future."

"All right," Alice reluctantly agreed. The children were doing well with their parts, and she was confident they could give a good performance. And if Tanisha was doing this to make her fail, Alice would prove to her that she *would* succeed. "As long as you or I announce ahead of time that this was totally unexpected and not to judge their performances too harshly."

"Of course. I'm glad you understand the importance of this, Alice. The theater's future depends on it."

You should have thought of that before you sent my picture off to the tabloids. "For the theater's sake, I hope this goes well."

"I'll see you Saturday."

"See you then."

The moment Alice hung up the phone, she got the jitters. What if everything went wrong? What if the children forgot their lines? What if the press hated the end product of her weeks of teaching the class?

As she lay back on Marcus's overly large pillows, she told herself that her fears were normal. She'd gotten the jitters before every acting role she'd ever done. Now that she was the director, she carried more weight on her shoulders. This would be an important day for the children, and she wanted everything to go right for them—even more than she'd wished that for her own acting parts in the past. It was only normal for her to expect that the nervous feeling would be even more intense.

But there was another feeling, one of foreboding. That feeling she couldn't explain away.

When Marcus returned home that Thursday evening after work, the first thing he noticed was the smell of vanilla. It filled his house.

The second thing he noticed was the flickering of candlelight on the wall in the living room. Slipping out of his lightweight jacket, he strolled into the living room—and noticed the third surprise.

Alice lay stretched out on the sofa in a white teddy and garters that held up white stockings. The sinfully erotic sight robbed him of his breath.

They'd made love at least half a dozen times, but Alice had never set out to seduce him like this. That she did now had him instantly hot and hard. This was the kind of greeting a man could get used to.

But he didn't want to get used to any such thing. Coming home to a wife and dinner, sex maybe once a week and one day on the weekend? He didn't want that for his life. He wasn't the marrying type, at least not anymore. Marriage changed everything.

Christ, why had thoughts of marriage even entered his mind?

And even if he wanted to contemplate a relationship with Alice, the moment the summer was over, she would high-tail it out of Chicago. Her mother's health had improved dramatically, and soon there would be nothing keeping her away from Hollywood.

The sex was great, as long as they didn't get attached to each other.

"Hey, you," she said in a sultry voice.

"Hey, yourself," Marcus replied, surprised to find his throat was suddenly parched. He swallowed.

"No need to be a stranger," she told him.

Marcus moved toward her and sat on the edge of the sofa. He placed a hand on her thigh. "What's the occasion?"

"Does there have to be one?" she asked, twirling a tendril of her hair over a finger as she met his eyes with a bold gaze.

"No, I guess not." He ran his eyes over the entire length of her body, from the tip of her head to those sexy red toenails he could see through her stockings.

Alice sat up and trailed a finger down his chest. "I figured that after a long day, you'd appreciate a little help unwinding."

"Oh, this is a good start."

"How was your day?"

He could hardly concentrate with her touching him all over his upper body. "It was stressful," he managed. "There was a hit and run. A young mother."

"Oh, God." Alice paused as she regarded him with a serious expression. "Is she okay?"

"She's in critical condition, but she's expected to make it."

"Good." She began massaging his neck. "Anything else?"

"I don't exactly want to talk anymore," Marcus said.

A smile spread across Alice's face. "Hmm. That's the problem with men. They just don't know how to make conversation."

Marcus wrapped his arms around her waist and pulled her onto his lap. "Not when they're tempted by sexy vixens like you."

He covered her lips with his, his tongue delving into her mouth. It was hot and sweet the way it always was. Alice purred immediately, and Marcus went rock hard. The fact that she was so easily turned on when he merely touched or kissed her made him crazy with desire.

"Lie back," he told her when he pulled his mouth from hers. She did as told, bending one leg at the knee and extending her hands behind her head. She was too damn sexy for her own good. He wasn't sure he'd ever tire of her.

"You're trying to torture me, which isn't very nice," he said, in a mock-scolding voice. "Which means I'll have to be ruthless with you."

"Ooh, I love it when you get tough with me. Maybe you should arrest me." She giggled.

Right now, there was nothing he'd like more than to handcuff her to his bed and tease her until she begged him to stop. Alice had him wanting to try all sorts of things he'd never even considered before.

Instead, he lowered his head and used his hands and mouth on her body to make her as hot as she had made him. Finally, she cried out, "Marcus, I can't stand it anymore."

He stripped off his clothes in two seconds flat, then entered her. He controlled the urge to ravage her like a madman, an urge she always brought out in him, and instead led their bodies in a slow, exquisite rhythm.

They reached the stars together, and as Alice gripped his back and softly moaned, he looked down at her. Tears fell from her eyes, down the sides of her face. The vision winded him as surely as a punch in the gut would, but he wasn't sure why.

"I love you, Marcus," she whispered.

And his body went cold.

Three simple words, yet they were enough to fill his world with dread. He didn't want her falling for him. Love was a complication he didn't need in his life. In the past, it had only brought him heartache. He'd always made bad decisions where love was concerned, and he didn't want to make another one.

But it was too late. Hadn't he known Alice was in love with him? Every time he touched her, kissed her, she responded in a way that touched him deeper than in a merely physical way. Still, he hadn't been able to pull away, to stop this affair before it got to this point.

And now, he was going to hurt her. Because he couldn't give her what she needed when he wasn't sure what he needed himself.

Telling Marcus that she loved him hadn't been an accident. She'd been contemplating telling him how she felt for over a week, and with her reason for being in Chicago soon coming to an end, she'd decided to go for it. If he only wanted the wrapping but not what was inside the package, it was better that she learn the truth now. But if he wanted more, it was time she seriously started rethinking her life.

Turning her head, Alice glanced at the digital clock. It read three-sixteen A.M.

A little over eight hours since she had sensed a complete change in Marcus.

He'd still invited her to his bed, and she'd gone, hoping he would repeat the same three words she'd said to him. Instead, he'd talked about an upcoming court case for an impaired driver—like Alice cared about that at that moment! And then when he'd turned off the bedside light, given her a peck on the lips and rolled onto his side with his back facing her, she'd known without a doubt that he'd dismissed her. Not only physically, but emotionally, which was far worse.

Lying on her back, Alice stared into the darkness of the room. Marcus's back still faced her. Several times she'd been tempted to snake her arms around his waist and snuggle up to him, but how long was she going to be a fool? He wasn't interested in more than a sexual relationship, and while she'd thought at one time that that would be enough, she knew now that she couldn't settle.

Not even for Marcus Quinn.

It was all or nothing. It couldn't be any other way.

The next morning, Alice crawled out of bed when Marcus was in the shower, slipped into one of his T-shirts, then made her way to the bathroom. It was like a steam bath when she stepped inside. She could barely see his naked form, so she knew there was no way he would see her through the sheer shower curtains.

She could wait until he was done in the shower,

but by then he'd be dressing and rushing out the door to work. She wanted to deal with this now.

"Marcus."

"Jesus!" he exclaimed, clearly startled to hear her voice.

"I'm sorry. I didn't mean to scare you. But I . . . we need to talk."

"Right now?"

"Yes, right now." She closed her eyes and counted to five, gathering courage. Telling Marcus what was on her mind was going to be the hardest thing she'd ever done.

"Why are you shutting me out?" Alice asked.

"Alice, I'm trying to get ready for work here. Maybe we can talk when I get home."

"No, Marcus. I can't go on like this. I need to know. Now."

"I'm not shutting you out."

"Yes, you are. As soon as I told you I loved you yesterday, you turned into a different person. The same thing happened a few weeks ago after the first time we made love."

"Alice, this really isn't the time."

"Do you love me?"

Marcus didn't answer for several seconds, and Alice had to wonder if he'd heard the question. But she knew he had, and the fact that he didn't answer right away told her more than she was ready to know.

"Do I love you?" he repeated. "What kind of love are you talking about? Friendship?"

Alice's heart did a free fall to her stomach, but still she continued. "You know exactly what I'm talking about. The way a man loves a woman. Or are you able to have sex with me and not feel anything at all?"

"I don't see why we have to talk about this now."

Alice took two steps forward and yanked the shower curtain back. Drops of hot water splashed her, but she didn't care. She deliberately kept her eyes on his face, for looking any lower would be dangerous. "Damn it, Marcus. We've made love several times. Don't you think it's fair that you at least tell me how you feel?"

He wiped water from his eyes and stared at her. After a long moment he said, "Yeah, I suppose it is."

Fear spread through her veins at his words, for it was how he said them, so calm yet so cold, like they had a meaning she didn't want to hear—

"Alice, if it's a relationship you want, I can't give it to you."

Her insides twisted painfully, as though someone had reached inside her body and was actually wringing them with all their strength. For a moment she couldn't breathe. But finally she was able to force down a breath, able to ask, "Why?"

"It's not going to work."

"That's all you have to say?" She couldn't stop her voice from rising. "After everything? That it's not going to work?"

"Alice, I never wanted to hurt you."

A mirthless laugh fell from her lips. "Hurt me? Hurt me! God, Marcus, you've more than hurt me!"

"I'm sorry."

"Don't say that."

"I don't know what else to say."

"So what was this about, then? You getting close to me, acting like . . . like you care for me?"

He dragged a hand over his face, pulling at the already drawn flesh. "I wanted us to be friends again."

"And that's why you seduced me," she said, not caring if she was sounding hysterical. "So that we could be *friends.*"

Meeting her gaze head on, he blew out a long breath, one that sounded full of pain. "I'm sorry about that. It shouldn't have happened."

"Shouldn't have happened?" she cried. She wanted to pull her hair out. She wanted to slap him. She wanted to disappear. "You pursued me like sex was going out of style. Or were you only interested in bedding Desirée LaCroix?"

He didn't respond. Instead, he reached for the soap and sloshed it over his body while he stood beneath the jet stream.

"Oh, God," Alice said in a horrified whisper. "It's true. That's all this was about to you."

"That's not true." He reached for her arm so quickly, it was like a reflex action. And she almost broke down right there, remembering just how thrilling it felt to have him touch her, how he'd made her feel the way no one else had ever made her feel.

Marcus spoke gently. "It wasn't just about sex."

Her heart dared to hope once again. "Then tell me what it was about, Marcus, because I don't understand."

He closed his eyes, and a mix of emotions passed over his face. She couldn't read them. But then, she couldn't read him anymore, either.

"I care for you," he finally replied. "I really do. I always have." He shrugged. "We're two adults who care for each other, enjoying a physical relationship."

"Just friends?" she asked matter-of-factly.

"Yes."

The simplicity of his answer, the fact that Alice had read more into his actions than were really there, crushed her. She'd been stupid to believe in him again, in the impossible dream that he always made her hope for. She jerked her arm free.

"Alice, I never made any promises of love."

"But you knew how I felt about you."

"Yeah, I guess I did."

"And you continued to screw me anyway." She was forcing the issue, because he in fact *hadn't* promised her anything, but she'd held out hope that he would love her—just like she had in high school. That he didn't was almost too much to bear.

"I really am sorry."

The fact that he truly looked contrite made her want to cry. Either that or kick him. "Oh, that's priceless."

"Alice, I know you don't understand, and I know this is going to sound lame, but I'm . . . I'm just not good at relationships. It's better that this all end now, before we both get in over our heads and really end up hurt."

She was already in over her head, but hearing him say the words made her realize just how big an idiot she was. "You prick."

He groaned, like he was hurting, but if he expected her to feel sorry for him, he had another thing coming.

"You're right," he said. "I am a prick. An asshole. But Alice, you have to believe me—I am sorry. I never meant to hurt you. I'm attracted to you, and I let that attraction get the better of me. But it would be wrong to act like I can give you what you want when I . . . I can't. I've made mistakes in the past, and sometimes I'm not even sure I know myself . . ." He blew out a harried breath. "Alice . . . God, I know I have no right to hope this. But do you think we can get past this and be friends again?"

She pulled the shower curtain back into place, obscuring her view of him once again. She couldn't stand to look at him for a moment longer. The place deep inside her, the place she'd tried to bury all the painful memories of her youth, opened up like a freshly dug grave, bringing all the horror of her past to the surface with full force. She was back in high school again. Back at home, with a mother who didn't love her and a sister who didn't have time for her.

He pushed aside the shower curtain. "Alice, let's talk about this when I come home."

Yeah, right. She had to be strong. Some way, somehow, she had to fight the pain. If he didn't even care about her, she wouldn't let him know just how badly he was breaking her heart. So squaring her jaw, she stared at him with a lethal expression. "There's nothing to talk about."

"Yes, there is."

"I won't be here."

"You're not going anywhere," Marcus said in a firm tone.

"You have no claims on me, Marcus. You can't tell me what to do."

Shaking his head, he stepped out of the tub, all six feet, two inches of dripping wet, pure godlike body of him, and a soft whimper almost fell from Alice's lips. After having a chance to love him, how on earth could she go on without him?

"I can't be your friend," she said, surprised at how calm she sounded, considering it felt like her heart was being crushed in a vise. "After everything, how dare you ask me that?"

It was a rhetorical question and judging by his lack of response, Marcus took it as such.

God, he wouldn't even fight for her friendship.

She had to get out of here. Though as she heard his anguished breath, part of her wished, prayed, silently begged him to tell her he didn't mean what he'd said and take her in his arms.

Instead he said, "If that's the way you want it."

And the vise tightened, shattering her heart into a million pieces.

He grabbed a towel and wrapped it around his waist, then simply walked past her as if they'd been discussing the weather and not the fact that he'd broken her heart.

"I guess you're proud of yourself," she said as he reached the door.

He turned around. "Proud of what?"

"Proud of bedding Desirée LaCroix, of course." The words escaped her lips before she could stop them. "Not many men can say they've done that."

As Marcus stared at her with an expression of utter disbelief, Alice thought she saw something else in his eyes. Sadness? Resignation? Pain?

Stop fooling yourself. God, how long was she going to be a foolish dreamer?

She charged past him and down the hallway to the spare bedroom. Somehow her legs supported her. Somehow, she stopped herself from turning around and running into his arms to beg him to tell her he hadn't meant a word he'd said.

But when she reached the comfort of her bedroom, the tough façade finally cracked. She curled up under the covers and threw the pillow over her face, then allowed herself to have a good, long cry.

Twenty

"Alice." Her mother's eyes flashed surprise as she opened the front door.

"Hello, Mother."

Rosa's eyes dropped to the suitcase Alice held in one hand. "What are you doing here?"

Alice didn't answer. Instead, she walked past her mother into the house and placed the suitcase on the floor. "How are you? You're looking really great. Gaining back the weight you lost," she added, even though she'd told her mother this when she'd seen her three days ago. She was rambling because otherwise, she might burst into tears.

"I feel wonderful."

They fell into silence, and Alice wished she could share with her mother her devastation over what had happened with Marcus. But she'd only hear an I-told-you-so from the woman who'd always said she was a dreamer, that Marcus would never love her, and that was the last thing she wanted to hear right now.

"Has anyone called for me?" Alice asked.

"Your agent called. She's left a couple messages. And some reporter has been calling here from a paper in Los Angeles. Wants to interview you about the story in the tabloid."

"When?"

"A couple of days ago."

Alice was going to ask her mother why she didn't call her at Marcus's to tell her any of this news, but at this point, it didn't matter. Dealing with her problems with Marcus was all she could handle right now.

"Alice, is it true? Did you use drugs while you were in Hollywood?"

Alice's mouth nearly hit the floor. "I can't believe you'd ask me that."

"It's the pictures, Alice." While Rosa paused, Alice could only stare at her in disbelief. "I'd understand. If you did."

"You don't understand anything," Alice snapped.

"I understand more than you realize. That's why I tried to shelter you . . ."

"You don't understand anything, Mother. You never understood me, never understood my dreams. Now this? I had hoped that after all this time, I would have finally proven myself to you, but I haven't. And I think it's time I accept the fact that I never will.

"There are times when a daughter simply wants her mother. *Needs* her. I've finally realized that I'll never have that. And that hurts me more than you'll ever know."

Rosa's face tensed. "I'm sorry you feel that way."

Alice chuckled mirthlessly. Not "I'm sorry I didn't believe in you," or "I'm sorry that I hurt you." No, Rosa was putting the blame on Alice for not understanding why her own mother would presume her guilty without asking a single question first.

Alice lifted her suitcase. "I have to make some calls."

"It's a nice day outside," Rosa said, though her voice sounded strained. "I think I'll go for a walk."

That's right, Mother. Call me a drug addict, then go for a walk as if nothing happened.

Shaking her head, Alice made her way up the stairs. Halfway up, she heard the front door close.

Her knees wobbled and she gripped the bannister for support. Lord help her, her life was a mess. Someone was out to destroy her reputation—maybe even do her bodily harm—and her mother couldn't show her any support during this trying time. It was time she gave up the illusion she ever would. Just like she'd finally had to accept that the love of her life would never love her back.

Alice inhaled a deep breath, but it caught in her throat. She wanted to turn around, go back down the steps, leave this house and never return. She almost would have, if she didn't envision Mia's lovely face, followed by the faces of the children at the Bartlett Theater House. They needed her. They depended on her. Her heart swelled with pride at the reality she knew deep inside.

She had made a difference in their lives. It was a special feeling, knowing she had fueled their dreams in a way her own family hadn't done for her. Other than her father. Other than Marcus.

Alice squeezed her eyes shut, willing the image of Marcus naked and wet from the shower out of her mind. She had to forget him, and the sooner the better.

She climbed the remaining stairs, put her suitcase in her old bedroom. She did a quick scan of the room, saw the dresser filled with jewelry and trinkets—and remembered something. She remembered seeing her mother hide her jewelry box beneath a pillow. At the time, that had struck her as odd. Now, an instinct told her that the jewelry box held the answer to so many questions.

Peering outside the window, Alice saw that her mother was nowhere in sight. The next second, she hurried from her bedroom and into her mother's.

The ornate silver jewelry box sat on her dresser in plain view, which made Alice wonder why her mother had bothered to shove it under a pillow in the first place. Still, Alice felt the instinct even stronger. It certainly wasn't a rational feeling, but she just *knew* that her mother had hidden something in this jewelry box that was the missing piece of the puzzle as to why she'd stopped loving her.

Alice paused to listen for any sound downstairs, and hearing none, walked to the dresser. She lifted the box and brought it with her to her mother's bed. Sitting on the bed, she brought the box onto her lap and opened the lid.

Nothing out of the ordinary jumped out at her. There were two strands of pearls, emerald earrings, gold bangles. Alice sifted her fingers through the contents and found only more jewelry. Yet she was determined not to give up.

She dumped the jewelry onto the bed and examined the bottom of the box. Her heart leapt at the sight of another compartment. Slowly, she lifted it.

Inside, she saw a folded and aged piece of paper, which she carefully withdrew. Though a little voice told her she shouldn't invade her mother's privacy, she was about to unfold it to see what it was. But she was suddenly more curious about what she saw below it.

It was a wallet-sized black-and-white picture of a man and a woman. Her mother and father, Alice realized. The picture was taken on the beach with the water behind her parents, who stood in each other's arms, smiling brightly.

Alice had never seen the picture before, and she lifted it for closer inspection. And realized she was wrong. It wasn't her mother and father. It was her mother and Uncle Winston.

Uncle Winston?

How could it be her uncle? *Why* would it be her uncle? In case her eyes were playing tricks on her, Alice closed and reopened them. No doubt about it, it was her uncle, not her father.

She was suddenly winded. Possible explanations for the picture whirled around in her brain. But there was only one explanation that consistently leapt out, and it was something she didn't want to consider.

Even Aunt Sara's comments that she'd had her suspicions about why Rosa was distant, and that Alice should ask her mother about them, lent more credence to the thought that kept surfacing in Alice's mind. But if it was true, what did that mean for her father?

Alice heard the door open downstairs and

quickly scrambled to replace the jewelry. In her haste, she forgot to put the picture back in the bottom of the box. As she was about to do just that, she heard the bedroom doorknob turn.

She shot to her feet.

Her mother's eyes widened as she opened the door and found Alice standing in her bedroom. Her gaze dropped to the bed, and Alice knew her mother had seen the jewelry box. That was fine by her, because she wanted answers. Answers only her mother could give her.

"What are you doing in here?" Rosa asked angrily as she walked into the room.

"What's this?" Alice extended the picture so she could see it.

"You went through my private things!" She snatched the picture from her hand, then moved to the bed where she retrieved the silver box.

"Why are you and Uncle Winston holding each other like that?" Alice said to her mother's back. "Like you're lovers?"

Rosa spun around. "Did you read the letters?"

"No, I didn't."

Rosa turned back to the jewelry box and began inspecting it, as though searching to see if anything was missing. Alice walked to the other side of the bed where she could see her mother's face, not her back. "Were you and Uncle Winston having an affair?"

"Of course I wasn't having an affair!"

"Then why do you two look like it in the picture?"

Seemingly satisfied that all the contents were in the box, Rosa slammed it shut. "I don't owe you any explanations."

"Yes, you do. For once, I think it's time you tell me why you've never supported my dreams, why you've made me feel like such an outcast in this family. What did I do that was so wrong?" Alice felt the familiar pain and disillusionment from years ago tighten her chest. "Why couldn't you love me?"

Her mother's lips tightened, and Alice stopped breathing as she awaited her mother's answer.

The phone rang.

"You should get that," Rosa said. "It's probably for you."

"Let it ring."

Rosa went to the phone beside her bed and picked up the receiver. "Hello? Yes, she's right here."

Damn her mother. Even now, could she not give Alice the answers she needed? If she didn't love her, then it was high time she admitted that so that Alice could give up on that dream altogether.

"It's for you," Rosa said, extending the receiver to her.

"Who is it?"

"I don't know. It's a man."

Despite the situation with her mother, Alice's heart danced. *Marcus.* "I'll take it in my bedroom."

Alice hurried out her mother's bedroom and into her own. When she picked up the receiver, she said, "I got it," and her mother hung up.

"Hello?" Why did the thought of Marcus calling her make all her nerves dance with excitement?

"Desirée."

That wasn't Marcus's smooth, sexy voice. "Who is this?"

There was a soft chuckle. "You've forgotten me already, have you? This is Edmond Minter."

She'd recognized the voice with the mild British accent before he finished speaking, though she was so surprised he was on the other end of the line that she didn't know what to say.

"I hope you don't mind that Connie gave me your number in Chicago."

Alice had been putting off giving Connie a definite yes or no answer as to whether or not she wanted to accept this new role. The truth was, she didn't know why she hadn't said yes immediately, but Connie had no doubt upped the ante by giving Edmond the number to call her directly. It would be harder to say no to him, especially when he was one of the few people in Hollywood Alice truly admired.

"No, I don't mind," she told him.

"Have you received a copy of the script for *After the Moon Rises*?"

"Actually, yes. Connie sent it, but I . . . I haven't had a chance to look at it."

"Oh."

"I don't know if Connie told you, but my mother had a heart attack. My mind hasn't been on the movie business much." At least that was true.

"Understandable, dear. I do hope you'll get the chance to read it soon, and that you'll like it. You'll be just perfect for this part, Desirée. Even Ryan Gray is anxious to work with you."

God, this would be such a fabulous opportunity! "Are you directing?"

"No, I'm merely producing this one. Craig Lewis is directing. If you haven't worked with him before, you'll love him."

Alice had heard nothing but wonderful things about Craig Lewis, and though she'd auditioned for

him once years ago, she'd never had the opportunity to work with him. Now, it seemed as if all the
cards were lining up in just the right way to give her
a dream opportunity that could help her career sky-
rocket.

She wondered if Edmond had heard the latest rumors of her drug use. If he had, he certainly wasn't
concerned. But that shouldn't surprise her. Edmond
was a true gem who had made her life in Hollywood more bearable, considering he was genuinely
interested in her and her career—not in her body.
Which was a relief, since he was pushing sixty. To
her, he was a father figure, and they'd remained
friends over the years.

"Edmond . . . you've heard the rumors, haven't
you?"

"Oh, yes."

"Are you sure you still want me for this role?" she
asked, almost as if she was trying to talk him out of
considering her.

"You don't think I believe that rubbish, do you?"

"No," Alice responded after a moment. Her own
mother didn't believe her, yet this man did. "I just
wondered . . . you know, people might think . . ."

"Wonder no more. All the gossips will soon find
something else to occupy their imaginations. Just
know that Craig and I both want you for this role.
Please read the script and get back to me as soon as
you can. Do you have my home number?"

"No."

"Take it down." Alice grabbed a pen and paper
from the night table and wrote the number Edmond
told her. "Please call me soon."

"I will."

"And take care."

"You too. And Edmond, thanks so much for the call."

"My pleasure."

When she hung up, Alice curled into the fetal position and lay on her bed for a long while, simply staring at her surroundings. For the life of her, she didn't know what she wanted. Did she want her career back? Did she want to start over? If she started over, what would she do? She didn't even have a college degree.

You could continue teaching children how to act.

The voice was so clear, it was almost as if someone had spoken the words aloud.

But she was still confused. If Marcus didn't love her, if her mother didn't believe in her, if someone here was trying to ruin her reputation, what sense would it make to stay in Chicago? She may as well head back to Los Angeles as fast as she could.

And if she did, she'd be running again. God, she was sick of running. The last time she'd run away she hadn't escaped her problems. They'd simply waited for her to return.

She wouldn't run. Not this time. Not until she finally had some closure with her mother and sister.

Tired of thinking, Alice rolled over. Her eyes strayed to the phone. Oh, she was tempted. Really, really tempted to call him. But she fought the temptation, for what would come of it? Marcus had already admitted to her that he didn't love her.

With that thought, a whimper escaped her lips. Her stomach coiled painfully. She closed her eyes and willed sleep to come.

Only sleep would make her forget about Marcus, and the reality that her heart was breaking.

If he never remembered anything else in his life, Marcus would never forget the look of utter devastation in Alice's eyes when he'd told her their relationship wouldn't work.

He felt like a total asshole.

She was right. He hadn't thought about anything more than the here and now when he made love to her. Though he'd wanted to keep their relationship strictly platonic, there was something about her he hadn't been able to resist.

Even now, Marcus didn't like thinking about it. He didn't want to think that he was a man who couldn't control himself around a pretty face.

Yet as he pulled into the driveway of his house and found Alice's car gone, the sight of the empty driveway sent his stomach plummeting to his feet.

What more *could* there be to his feelings? What the hell did he know about love? He knew about attraction and lust, but couldn't trust himself where love was concerned.

Marcus opened the door and stepped out of his car. All day, he'd tried to tell himself that this was for the best. Now that Alice knew they couldn't have a relationship, they had crossed the biggest hurdle. But all day, he hadn't been able to believe his own rhetoric.

He hadn't been able to stop thinking about her. When he'd gotten his morning coffee, he'd remembered sharing a steaming cup with Alice after a night of making love. Later in the day when he'd pulled over a speeder on the JFK expressway, he'd remembered the day he had stopped Alice when she'd returned to town. And when he'd gone to the scene of a serious accident, it was Alice he'd seen on the gurney instead of the actual victim, and he'd wondered about her stalker, if she would be safe from the threat without him by her side to protect her. He had also wondered what he would do if she was no longer in his life.

He pushed that thought aside as he stepped inside his house, but he couldn't as easily push aside the uneasy feeling in his stomach.

As he kicked off his shoes and padded up the stairs, Marcus assured himself the feeling was simply worry. With Alice out of his house, he couldn't protect her the way he wanted.

He could call her at her mother's and make sure she was okay. He sat on the bed and lifted the phone's receiver. Then replaced it. Then lifted it again. He held it in one hand while he punched in Alice's number with the other. Two digits shy of completing the number, his hand froze. Lingered over the keypad. After a long moment, he returned the receiver to its cradle.

Burying his face in both hands, he groaned. He couldn't call her. What was he going to say, other than reiterate how much of a jerk he was?

He didn't know if it was remembering her in his arms, so willing, so trusting, that had him out of sorts. Maybe it was, because being with Alice had been the best experience of his life. He would miss her. Even now, his bed looked empty without her.

Swinging his legs onto the bed, he lay back and stared at the ceiling. Part of him knew what the problem was. The part of him that had always feared getting too close to another woman. It wasn't only his horrible experience with Tanisha that had him jaded. It was the whole sordid mess with Melissa.

Melissa had been another pretty face. He'd fallen for her, and ultimately his lack of restraint had gotten her killed.

Marcus didn't want to think about Tanisha, or Melissa, or his lousy track record with women. Instead, he bounced off the bed and grabbed his sports gear. When he was finished packing his gymbag, he went downstairs to his car.

Yet when he started to drive, he didn't head to the gym. Tonight, lifting weights wouldn't do the trick. What he needed was a stiff drink.

Hopefully that would erase the guilt from his mind.

Twenty-one

As Alice opened the door and entered the theater, she was startled to find Tanisha standing inside the doorway. "Oh," she said, putting a hand over her heart. "You scared me."

"Sorry," Tanisha told her. "Thanks for coming in early."

Tanisha had called her at her mother's house early this morning, asking if she could come to the theater at least half an hour before the children were expected to arrive. Alice had readily agreed. Dealing with the theater would help her forget her problems . . . at least for the afternoon.

And if Tanisha was curious about why Alice was no longer at Marcus's house, she had the decency not to ask.

"There should be a lot of media," Tanisha told her, then turned and rounded the corner into the theater.

Alice followed her, then stopped short when she saw Willie standing a few feet down the aisle. She couldn't be sure if it was simply the unexpected sight of him that had her heart racing out of control. Or fear.

"Hello, Desirée." He walked to Tanisha's side and placed an arm around her waist.

Alice's gaze flew to Tanisha's. Tanisha and Willie were clearly back to being chummy-chummy. Still, why was he here? Did he want his old job back?

Alice asked, "What's he doing here?"

"Oh, did I forget to mention Willie would be here?" Tanisha asked innocently.

"What's going on, Tanisha?" Alice asked.

"It was Willie's idea that we hold this performance, and he wanted to be here."

The explanation seemed reasonable enough. So why did Alice still feel uneasy about the whole thing?

"What was it you wanted to discuss?" Alice asked.

"I was hoping we could go over some of the things you might say to the media," Tanisha replied.

Alice shrugged. "Sure."

"Come on. Let's go to the office."

Willie walked toward the exit while Alice followed Tanisha to the office. Tanisha sat while Alice stood.

"Now, I hope today's performance will ease everyone's mind," Tanisha said. "I figured that once the reporters get here, I'll speak first about the theater, its history, stuff like that. Then, I'll allow you to say a few words. Whatever you want—about the children, how you're enjoying the experience of teaching. I figure there will be a question-and-answer period at the end as well."

"All right." She could handle that.

"I've informed all the parents about what is going to happen today, so they'll most likely stick around."

"No doubt." For their children's sake, Alice prayed none of them expected her to fail.

"I'm hoping this will be a positive experience, but in case someone from the media asks about your drug abuse—"

"I do *not* abuse drugs."

"Well," Tanisha hedged, "if they ask about it—"

"I expect you to steer them back on track. I will only be talking about the children and the play. Understand?"

"Sure."

There was a quick rap on the office door and Alice turned in time to see Willie enter. "The first of the media have arrived," he said.

"Already?" Alice asked. She had a feeling of foreboding, like something would go wrong.

"They're setting up a camera as we speak."

Tanisha hopped up from her chair. "I'll go greet them. You can stay here until I come back for you."

"No problem," Alice said. She was a seasoned performer, used to being in the public eye. But that knowledge didn't help her swallow her fears.

"Can I get either of you some coffee?" Willie asked.

"Coffee would be great," Alice said. Anything to help keep her awake and alert.

"Make a whole carafe," Tanisha told him. "I think everyone could use some today."

*   *   *

Marcus exited the JFK expressway en route to the theater. He hadn't planned on showing up here today, but after Tanisha had called for Alice early this morning and he'd learned of today's performance, he knew he had to be there for Alice.

Besides any possible threat to her life, he wanted to be there to show his support for the first public performance of the play. No, he didn't think she'd be happy to see him, but he hadn't been able to convince himself to stay away. He'd been at all of Alice's performances as a teenager. He wasn't about to fail her now.

Hell, who was he kidding? He simply wanted to see her. He still felt bad about their argument yesterday morning and he hoped that seeing her would ease his mind.

He would see her, make sure she was all right, and then go home. And hopefully after that, his conscience would be cleared.

Alice sat anxiously in the office as she waited for Tanisha to return. Several minutes later, she still hadn't.

She tried not to be anxious. Tanisha was no doubt dealing with the media, as well as parents and children. She'd return soon enough.

At the sound of movement behind her, Alice turned. Willie approached her with a large mug. "Your coffee."

Alice reached for it, thinking that this was her only vice. She didn't do drugs and she could live without alcohol, but life without coffee? She couldn't even imagine it.

"Thank you."

"No problem."

Alice inhaled the coffee before she took a sip, the way she always did. The rich, wonderful aroma filtered into her nose. "Who's here?"

"I think everyone's here," he replied. "Except for a few of the media."

"Oh." Tanisha should be coming for her any minute. "In that case, I'd better drink this quickly."

Willie disappeared and Tanisha finally returned minutes later. "Showtime," Tanisha told her.

Alice stood and inhaled a shaky breath. She wished she wasn't so nervous, but she'd do what she always did. Use the nervous energy in a positive way.

She followed Tanisha out the doors that led to the auditorium, then up the side stairs to the stage. Alice took a mental note of the children sitting cross-legged behind the podium. They all appeared to be there. Mia smiled and waved at her. She waved back.

As she turned to face the audience, Alice's head suddenly felt light. Damn, she didn't realize just how unnerving this was going to be. Perhaps if the theater lights were dimmed so she couldn't quite make out the number of people watching her, she wouldn't feel so on edge.

Tanisha spoke to the crowd, but Alice didn't pay attention to what she said. She could only hear the pounding of her pulse in her ears.

"Desirée," Tanisha said, walking toward her and touching her arm.

"Oh," Alice quickly said.

Tanisha flashed her a puzzled look. "They're waiting for you."

"Oh. Oh, of course." She stepped past Tanisha and found her legs were wobbly. She straightened her spine, hoping she hadn't stumbled.

Why did she feel so . . . odd? She had never felt quite so out of sorts before. She gripped the podium edges for support, then stared out into the audience. As her gaze swept from left to right, she noticed Marcus sitting alone a few rows behind everybody else. Her pulse quickened. What was he doing here?

She continued her surveillance of the crowd, and was shocked as hell to find her mother and sister sitting to the far right about three rows from the front.

Alice suddenly felt queasy. She closed her eyes briefly, then forced a smile.

"Good afternoon, everyone." Her voice sounded weird to her own ears. "I suppose I should introduce myself. My stage name is Desirée LaCroix, but my real name is . . ." Her voice trailed off as the room went fuzzy. She closed her eyes, but the room continued to spin. Something was wrong with her. She forced her eyes open. "My name is Desirée LaCroix. That's my stage name." God, hadn't she said that already? She could barely form a coherent thought, much less coherent speech.

"I have a question, Ms. LaCroix." Alice focused on a man in the audience who was standing. At least she thought it was a man, because the voice was deep. The truth was, she couldn't tell. Damn, she could hardly see.

"I've heard from a source that before every performance, you use drugs to help you get by. Is that true?"

"Pardon me?"

The man continued to speak, but his voice sounded like a warped tape playing inside her head.

Alice's head throbbed as the world around her spun out of control. Somehow, she steadied her eyes long enough to see Marcus's form. She saw him shoot to his feet just before the world slipped away and darkness overcame her.

What the hell?

Marcus watched Alice as she tried to maintain control. She looked good, dressed in a conservative black pantsuit, with her hair swept up in a bun. But it was clear she had lost her faculties, because her speech was slurred and she gripped the podium so hard she gave the appearance that she'd fall if she let it go.

He saw the reporter jump to his feet in his peripheral vision, and could only imagine what they were all thinking. So the question about Alice's drug use didn't surprise him. Right now, Alice indeed looked as if she were high on something.

He waited for her to answer the reporter's question. Saw her wobble and grip the podium harder. Then he stood as he watched her eyes flit about the room, wondering what the hell was wrong with her.

The next second, she collapsed into a heap on the stage. An audible gasp reverberated through the theater and several people stood. Behind her, the children hustled to their feet, rushing toward her.

Dread washed over Marcus. *Please let her be all right,* he prayed, adrenaline coursing through his veins, propelling him with lightning speed to the stage. He forced his way through the crowd of curious children and Tanisha, dropping to Alice's side.

"My God, Marcus," Tanisha said. "She assured me she wasn't taking any drugs."

Marcus silenced Tanisha with a look, then turned his attention back to Alice. "Alice," he said softly. "Can you hear me?"

She didn't move.

His stomach clenched. She was so still, she almost seemed . . . He pushed that thought aside as he felt for a pulse. His shoulders dropped with relief. She had a pulse, but it was weak.

"Alice," he repeated, this time clenching her hand. It was limp within his.

He needed to get her to the hospital. As he gathered her into his arms, he caught sight of a camera crew to his right. They were filming the entire episode.

"For God's sake," he said, lifting Alice. "Shut the damn camera off."

"This is news," a reporter he recognized from a local news station countered.

"So she really is on drugs," another reporter mumbled, then started making notes.

"If you report that," Marcus said in a lethal tone, "be prepared for a lawsuit."

He started past the throng of reporters and parents, and stepped smack into Mia's path. He stared down at her tear-stained face.

"Is my aunt okay?"

The soft little voice was his undoing. Until now,

he'd taken charge the way a cop would, working to get her help while ignoring the reality that the situation might be graver than he imagined. But seeing and hearing Mia's pain made him realize how important Alice was not only to the children here and her own family, but how important she was to him.

God, he couldn't lose her. Not now.

"She'll be okay, Mia," he told her. "I promise you that."

Then he hurried down the steps with Alice and out of the theater.

Her brain was in a fog. She struggled to move her head, but it hurt. She struggled to fight through the haze until she could think again.

A jolt of memory hit her, the memory of where she *should* be—in front of a crowd at the theater—and Alice struggled to open her eyes. Confusion washed over her. Where was she?

Her eyes darted from left to right, and at first all she could see was a blur of light. Then her eyes began to focus, and she made out shapes. A television hanging on the far wall. A window to the right of the television.

"Aunt Alice!"

Hearing the familiar voice of her niece, Alice's eyes flickered to the left. Her mother, sister, and Mia congregated on the left side of the bed.

"Where am I?" Her voice came out in a croak.

"You're in the hospital, baby."

Alice's eyes settled on her mother. Rosa's eyes were red and swollen. Clearly, she'd been crying. "What happened?"

Marie and Rosa exchanged concerned glances before Marie spoke. "We were hoping you could tell us."

Alice drew in a deep breath and blew it out slowly. Man, her head really hurt. Her body felt so heavy, like her limbs were made of lead. "I don't know."

"You don't remember what happened yesterday?" Marie asked.

"*Yesterday?*" Alice exclaimed. "What day is it?"

"It's Sunday."

"Oh my God." Things were becoming clearer, though nothing made sense. "The play. What happened?"

"The performance had to be postponed."

Alice lifted her head in an effort to sit up, but the room spun. She dropped her head back onto the pillow.

"People are saying you were on drugs yesterday, Aunt Alice. But it's not true, is it?" Mia's bottom lip quivered. "You just got sick, right?"

Alice reached for her hand. "I would never do drugs, Mia." Though the way she felt now, she had to wonder if someone hadn't drugged her.

"I knew it," Mia said, sounding relieved. "That's what Marcus told the doctors, too."

"Marcus was here?"

"Uh-huh. He's the one who took you to the hospital."

"Is he . . . here now?"

"He stepped out a few minutes ago to talk to the doctor," Marie responded. She turned to Mia. "Mia honey, you must be hungry."

"Uh-huh."

"C'mon." Marie wrapped a hand around her shoulder. "Let's get you something to eat. Alice, we'll be back in a bit. Mama, you want to join us?"

"No," Rosa said softly.

When Maria and Mia disappeared, Alice faced her mother. "If you still believe that I took drugs, then you may as well leave."

Instead of huffing and stalking out of the room, Rosa did something Alice didn't expect. She reached for her hand. "I'm not going anywhere."

"Don't stay because you feel sorry for me."

"I'm staying because I believe in you. When you told me a couple days ago that you had never touched drugs, I believed you."

For years Alice had waited to hear those words, that her mother believed in her and supported her. But it had taken so long, she wasn't sure she could now trust them. "Why now?"

Rosa heaved a weary sigh. "Because I don't want us to go on like this any longer. And because seeing you pass out on that stage . . . it scared me to death. I don't want any more animosity between us. Life is too short for that."

"Are we supposed to have a touching mother-daughter moment now, Mother?" Alice stared at her in disbelief. "Because it's not that easy. Not after everything."

"I know, I know. But Alice, you're my baby and I love you. If there's a chance we can work past all the misunderstandings, we have to try."

"Because you're my mother." Alice couldn't hide the sarcasm from her voice.

Rosa hesitated, then said, "Yes. Yes, that's exactly why."

Alice rolled her head to the right, glancing away. She couldn't believe how much it hurt to hear what she had longed to hear for years. And her own unwillingness to simply forgive her mother also shocked her. But she had changed.

"Why didn't you love me?" Alice asked, facing Rosa again. "Why didn't you believe in me?"

"I do love you," Rosa said, stressing the words. "Oh, I know I stopped showing it. I realize now that I pushed you away. But I always loved you. Always."

Tears stung Alice's eyes. So her mother knew. Knew that something had been wrong, that somehow she hadn't conveyed to Alice the love she'd so craved. She'd never doubted that her mother loved Marie—tall, slender, beautiful, perfect Marie. But her? She'd never been quite sure.

"Is it because I wasn't beautiful enough?"

A pained expression crossed Rosa's face. "Is that what you think?"

"I don't know what to think."

Rosa moaned softly. "Oh, I guess I can't blame you. You must have been so confused. Ever since you went through my jewelry box a couple days ago, I realized that I should finally tell you the truth."

"About you and Uncle Winston?"

Rosa closed her eyes and nodded slowly.

"So you *were* having an affair."

"No, not an affair," Rosa quickly replied. "But he was the love of my life."

A knot of anger formed in Alice's chest. How could her mother betray her father like this? "What about Dad?"

"I was in love with Winston before your father

and I got involved. We'd dated for a year and I had hoped he would ask me to marry him. But he had dreams of being an actor.

"Oh, sweetheart. Your uncle, he was so obsessed with Hollywood. Nothing would stand in the way of his dream. Not even me. He asked me to go to L.A. with him, but I told him I didn't want to leave Chicago. I thought he wouldn't leave me, but he did. Said he had to go to L.A. to make a go of it. But he promised he'd return for me. Days turned into weeks, weeks into months, and I got more and more depressed. But finally he came home, and it was the happiest day of my life.

"I had no idea he was returning to break up with me. I begged him to try and work things out, but he told me he'd fallen in love with someone else. Someone who understood his hopes and dreams, unlike me."

"Aunt Sara," Alice said softly.

Rosa nodded. "When he left, your father comforted me. And one thing led to another. We ended up married, and the rest is history."

It was finally making sense. Her mother had been afraid of losing her the same way she had lost the love of her life. Unfortunately, where her daughter was concerned, Rosa hadn't learned the error of her past ways, that pushing someone away could backfire. "So, you . . . never truly loved Dad?"

"I loved him, Alice. But not in the same way that I loved Winston. But bless your father's soul, he always loved me with all his heart.

"There's something else you should know. Something I never told you before. Your Uncle Winston died of a drug overdose."

"I know," Alice said softly. "Aunt Sara told me. She wanted me to prepare me for the negative side of Hollywood."

"I see." Rosa glanced at the floor, then back at Alice. "She did the right thing. Maybe knowing the dangers helped you keep a level head." She paused. "Your father and I both thought you and Marie were too young to know the truth, and as you got older . . . the time never seemed right to tell you . . ." Rosa's voice trailed off, and Alice realized that even after all this time, Winston's loss was still painful to her. "When I'd first heard, I was so mad at the world, so mad at Hollywood, so mad at Sara. I could have dealt with losing his love as long as he was still breathing. But I had you and Marie to take care of, so I had to go on. Concentrating on my family helped me get over my broken heart, but I soon started to worry about you. Because you had dreams of acting, like your uncle. Alice, that scared me to death. I did everything to discourage you, and I know that hurt you. But I didn't do it because I didn't believe in you—I could tell from the start that you were talented. I did it because I didn't want to lose you the same way I'd lost Winston."

Alice's heart fluttered. "You thought I was talented?"

"Of course I did. That was obvious."

All this time, Alice had had no clue how her mother really felt. If she had told her once, just once, that she'd believed in her, it would have made a world of difference. Still, putting herself in her mother's shoes, she could understand her mother's fears. Now, everything made sense. "Mom . . ." Alice's voice was strained with emotion. "You don't know how much I wish I had heard those words from you years ago."

Tears filled Rosa's eyes. "I know, and I'm so sorry, Alice. For how I treated you, for not supporting your dreams. For giving you that crazy ultimatum when I really wanted to take you in my arms and tell you how much I loved you. As time passed and you didn't come home, I didn't know how to bridge the gap. I know it doesn't make sense, but I felt abandoned by you, the way Winston had abandoned me, even though I was the one who told you not to come home.

"But even when you were gone, I was so very proud of you. That's why I collected all those articles about your success over the years—and all the photos you'd sent to Marie. It was a way to feel close to you."

"But you were so angry when I came home. So distant."

"I was still hurting. But now I realize I have to accept the blame for that. I brought on that pain—not you." She paused, sighed. "And I'm so sorry that I asked if you'd ever done drugs. When that story came out, part of me wondered—not because I really believed you'd ever abuse drugs—but because I couldn't help remembering your uncle. Oh, I hope I'm making sense."

This was all so overwhelming, Alice's head hurt from supressing her tears. But her heart, finally, felt light. "Yes, Mom. I finally understand."

"If I could turn back the hands of time, I'd do everything differently." When Rosa's voice broke, Alice's heart broke too. She'd seen her mother cry once in her life, at her father's funeral, and Alice now felt helpless. She did all she knew how to do. She extended her hand and when her mother took it, she gripped it as if her very life depended on it.

"I should have been a better mother. I should have been able to help you through all those years when you seemed so lost. But I just didn't want to encourage you, because I didn't want to lose you the way I lost Winston."

"All these years, you never said anything. I never knew . . ."

"That I cared?"

Alice didn't respond, for how could she tell her mother that that was exactly what she'd been thinking? That her mother knew brought tears to her eyes.

"I know we can't turn back the clock, but if you can find it in your heart to forgive me . . ."

"Oh, Mom." Alice squeezed her hand tighter. "I forgive you."

"My sweet baby." Standing, Rosa leaned over the bed and embraced Alice. "I love you."

Tears streamed down the side of Alice's face as warmth filled her heart. "I love you too, Mom."

Alice squeezed her mother tighter, feeling blessed. It had taken thirty-one years, but she finally had the mother she'd always longed for.

"What happened to me yesterday?" Alice asked when her mother pulled back from her.

"You didn't look right from the moment I saw you. Sorta spaced out. You were up on the stage about to speak and you just passed out. Marcus said he's worked on cases before where women have been drugged. He thinks that's what might have happened to you."

Marcus. Making up with her mother had given her a renewed feeling of hope, and knowing that Marcus had been there for her when she needed him most made her believe almost anything was possible.

But where was he now? Had he simply done his good cop deed by bringing her to the hospital?

And if he had, would Alice ever see him again?

Twenty-two

"GHB," the young male doctor explained to everyone in Alice's hospital room. "More popularly know as one of the date-rape drugs."

"I was drugged?" Alice asked. Though that very thought had crossed her mind, the reality still stunned her.

He nodded. "There was a very high concentration of gamma hydroxy buterate in your system."

"You're saying this was deliberate," Rosa said.

"Absolutely. You don't accidentally drink GHB. It's slipped into people's drinks—mostly women's—for the sole purpose of knocking them out."

"My God." Marie looked from the doctor to Alice.

"I was at the theater," she said, more to herself than to anyone else. "About to address a group of reporters and parents. Who would want to knock me out there?"

"Someone who wanted to discredit you, make you look like you were hooked on drugs."

At the sound of Marcus's deep voice, Alice's gaze flew across the room. Her heart soared. He was really here. She wasn't imagining him.

"As I told your husband a little while ago," the doctor continued, "anything's possible. I only know you were definitely drugged. Now, I want to keep you here at least a few more hours for observation, but I don't anticipate any problems. How are you feeling?"

"A little groggy."

"That should pass shortly. I'll be back to check on you in an hour or so, but in the meantime, if you need anything, ring for the nurse."

The doctor excused himself and Alice observed Marcus as he watched the doctor leave. She wondered what was going through his mind. Was his heart racing the way hers was from simply being in the same room with him? Or was he simply here as a cop, thinking and feeling as a cop?

He turned back to her when the doctor was gone.

"Do you really think someone wanted to discredit me as opposed to hurting me?" Alice asked him. "That doesn't make any sense."

Marcus stepped further into the room. "If someone truly wanted to hurt you, they could have done so by now. But with the article in the tabloid about your alleged drug use, and now collapsing in front of reporters—this all seems like a plan to make you look bad."

"Oh my God," Alice muttered.

"All you have to think is motive. Jealousy, greed, revenge. Those are some of the classic ones."

Jealousy—Tanisha perhaps was jealous. Greed? Alice couldn't think of anyone to fit that description. Revenge—revenge for being successful? If that was the case, any of the people she'd known years ago could be responsible—including Tanisha.

Marcus moved to the side of her bed but didn't sit. Professional. Impersonal. Alice's stomach fluttered with disappointment.

"Who did you see when you arrived at the theater?" he asked her.

"Tanisha and Willie. They seemed pretty tight."

"Anyone else afterward?"

"No. I stayed in the back until the children and the media had arrived. You don't think . . . ?"

"You must have consumed this drug in some type of drink. Do you remember drinking anything at the theater?"

"Coffee. Willie made a pot of coffee."

"This is important, Alice," Marcus told her, finally resting a hip against the side of her bed. "Did you stop anywhere along the way to the theater, pick up a soda or a coffee anywhere else?"

"No. Tanisha called me, asked me to come into the theater early. That's it."

"Sonofabitch," Marcus muttered, then stalked toward the door.

"Marcus," Alice called. When he faced her, she saw the anger flashing in his eyes. "Where are you going?"

"To take care of this situation."

Alice was about to ask exactly what he had planned, but Marcus was gone before she could utter another word.

And judging by his demeanor, she could only

pity the person who would be the victim of his wrath.

As Marcus peeled out of the hospital parking lot, he was seething. From day one, Tanisha had been around when every bad thing had happened to Alice. Though he couldn't understand her wanting to hire Alice only to make her look like a fool, he conceded that he'd never truly understood Tanisha and there was no point in even trying.

Now she would pay.

He was so angry, he gripped the steering wheel as if it were Tanisha's neck. He had to calm down. But he couldn't stop envisioning Alice lying in a heap on the stage, seemingly lifeless. He had remembered Melissa, how his body had turned to ice when he'd seen her lifeless body on the kitchen floor. And like that horrible day nearly a year ago, guilt sucker-punched him in the gut. Indirectly or not, he was to blame for what had happened to Melissa, and now he was to blame for what had happened to Alice. If he hadn't crossed the line with Alice, they wouldn't have been at odds—and he would have been there for her. He would have stopped Tanisha from drugging her.

Alice deserved better than him.

A better man would have had regard for her feelings. A better man would have protected her instead of satisfying his lust.

But it wasn't simply lust. Marcus knew that now. Last night, as he'd felt guilty as hell for not being there to protect her, he'd suddenly realized that he felt guilt because he cared and had pushed her away. He was in love with her, probably had been for a long time, but hadn't been able to admit it to himself.

Still, the idea of giving his heart to someone else scared him to death. Would things be different with Alice? He'd thought he'd known Tanisha and had learned that he didn't know her at all. He didn't want to make another mistake.

In his heart, he knew Alice was nothing like Tanisha. But his brain told him he had been burned once. What if a lowly cop couldn't keep Alice happy? Maybe she needed another actor or producer. Someone with clout and money.

Marcus didn't know what to do. Tell Alice how he felt and take another chance on love? Or let her head back to Hollywood, where she could find someone who truly deserved her?

He pictured Alice in Noel Sanders's arms and felt a stab of pain in his heart. He pictured her with Shemar Moore and had the same reaction. Though she might be better off with someone else, Marcus didn't know if he could let her go. Because when he thought of his life, he thought of Alice in it.

But after the way he'd pushed her away, he didn't know if she'd give him another chance. He wouldn't blame her if she didn't.

As Marcus continued to drive, he forced Alice out of his mind. Now he had to concentrate on Tanisha and the fact that she was finally going to get what was coming to her.

"Marcus," Tanisha said breathlessly as she opened her apartment door. "What are you doing here?"

Marcus brushed past her into the apartment. "I'm going to ask you once, and I expect the truth. Why did you drug Alice?"

"Drug her?" Tanisha's mouth fell open. "I did no such thing."

"I'm already pissed off with you, so I have no desire to sit here and listen to you give me a load of bull. Is it jealousy? Is that it?"

"Over you? God, Marcus. You're so incredibly full of yourself."

"Over Alice's success. You never could stand the fact that she'd succeeded where you'd failed."

"I want you to leave."

"Alice was drugged, Tanisha. Someone gave her a date-rape drug that knocked her out. There was such a high level of the stuff in her system, it could have killed her. That's a crime, Tanisha. So no, I'm not going to leave—not without you in a pair of handcuffs."

"What do you mean?"

"You didn't think you would get away with this?"

A sound in the apartment hallway got Marcus's attention. Willie, clad only in boxers, made his way to the foyer.

"What the hell are you doing here?" Willie asked, glaring at Marcus.

Marcus suddenly remembered what Alice had said, that Willie had given her coffee . . . and he wondered if it wasn't Tanisha who had drugged her, but Willie. If Tanisha and Willie were back to sleeping together, maybe this was about him wanting his old job back.

But to go to such extremes? Damn, anything was

possible, especially when he'd been fired and maybe hadn't gotten over the fact that his replacement had done a lot more for the theater in a few months than he'd done in a few years.

"Alice was drugged, Willie. You wouldn't happen to know anything about that, would you?"

Willie glanced away, then back at Marcus. "If your girlfriend is a druggie—"

It took one beat for Marcus to cross the foyer and ram Willie's body against a wall. "It was you, wasn't it?"

"Get the hell out of here."

"No, it makes sense." Marcus knew it, felt it in his gut. Behind him, Tanisha screamed at him to leave, but he ignored her. "Alice said you gave her coffee. You deliberately drugged her so she would look like a fool!"

"She showed her true colors," Willie barked. "Now the whole world knows the truth."

"Sonofabitch!" Marcus grabbed Willie in a headlock. He'd never been so angry. "You could have killed her." He tightened his grip, and Willie grabbed at his arms. But Marcus was the stronger man. He didn't loosen his grip.

"You're going to kill him!" Tanisha cried.

"And maybe that's what he deserves."

"Willie! Tell him. Tell him you had nothing to do with this!"

"You tell the truth, Willie."

"All right," Willie managed. "I'll tell you. Just let me go."

Releasing him, Marcus gave Willie a shove and he landed on the floor. As he stared up at Marcus and

Tanisha, his chest heaved as he struggled to catch his breath.

Marcus crossed his arms over his chest. "I'm waiting."

"Screw you, Marcus."

"That's it," Marcus said, his voice lethal, then started for Willie once more. "You want to do this the hard way—"

"Wait!" Willie cried out, holding up both hands as he cowered. Marcus paused, staring at him hard. Willie gritted his teeth and blew out a frustrated breath. "Okay," he said in a resigned tone. "I didn't mean any harm. I just wanted my old job back."

"So you're admitting it?" Marcus asked, making sure there was no confusion. "That you drugged her?"

Willie swallowed. "Yes."

"Willie?" Tanisha stared at him in disbelief.

"You only fired me because we'd broken up," he told Tanisha. "I know you said I was too clingy, but then we started talking again, getting closer again. I thought you'd realize how much you needed me. You even told me Alice wouldn't be there long, re-member? But the longer she stayed, the more every-one loved her. Including you. I started to wonder if you'd ever give me my old job back, even if she left. I . . . had to make you see that you were wrong about her. That you needed me, Tanisha. That we could be a team again, the way we always should have been."

"That's why you tried to kill her? Because you wanted your job at the theater back?" It took every ounce of Marcus's self control not to strangle the moron to death right now.

"I didn't want to kill her. I just wanted to scare her. That's why I did the things I did. But she wasn't going away. So . . . so I convinced Tanisha to hold a performance for the media, but I only wanted to make everyone believe she was on drugs so she'd have to quit at the theater."

"I don't believe you!" Tanisha yelled. "You're the one who sent that picture to the tabloid?"

"I just wanted her to leave town. So we could run the theater again, baby. Together. The way we did before."

"Don't call me baby. I want you out of here."

"He's going," Marcus said. "With me. Down to the station."

Willie's eyes bulged. "You're gonna arrest me?"

"Stalking, assault charges. You'd better get a damned good lawyer. I'll give you three minutes to get dressed before I drag your ass out of here."

Mumbling under his breath, Willie stood. He didn't look happy as he disappeared down the hallway to the bedroom.

"I'm sorry," Tanisha said when Willie was gone. "I had no clue."

"I'm sorry I accused you," Marcus said. "But you have to understand—"

"I do."

"I'm glad you had nothing to do with this."

Tanisha nodded glumly, then walked to the living room. She dropped onto the sofa and buried her face in her hands.

Marcus went to the bedroom to get Willie, adrenaline rushing through his body. He'd done it. He'd cracked this case.

Now Alice would be safe. She wouldn't meet the same fate Melissa had.

But while the threat was gone, her role at the theater was almost over. And after it was, would she stay here in Chicago, or return to her life in Los Angeles?

Twenty-three

The morning was cooler than forecast, with a light drizzle adding to the already gloomy quality of the day. It reminded Alice of the day her father had died, when all had seemed bleak and hopeless in her life.

Thinking of her father made her think of Marcus, the one other person in her life who had supported her unconditionally. Since her release from the hospital yesterday, she hadn't heard from him. He'd left to "take care of the situation" and she'd thought he would come back to at least tell her what had happened. Had he discovered who'd drugged her?

But more so, Alice had just wanted to see him. She felt like so much was left unsaid between them. He was right, she realized. Sex had complicated everything between them. She wished they could turn back the clock to the time they'd simply been friends.

She'd sensed guilt in him at the hospital, which didn't surprise her, given Marcus's personality. He was so used to trying to save the world, he no doubt blamed himself for what had happened.

She wanted to tell him that she didn't blame him. She wanted to tell him that even if he didn't love her, she wanted them to be friends.

Even if the reality that he didn't love her still broke her heart.

She was in love with him. And there was no cure for that. Only time. But having him in her life as a friend would be better than not having him in her life at all.

It was time she gave up on the dream. The thought hurt her immensely, but didn't all dreams eventually come to an end? Yet the fact that her dream of loving Marcus had come true, if only for a short time, made letting him go hurt all the more.

It hurt more because she'd done more than dream, but had started to believe. Believe that the dream had become a reality. God, how could she really go on without him?

Later that day, Alice was lounging around in her room, too depressed to do anything else. She still hadn't heard from Marcus and was beginning to doubt she would. So when Rosa knocked on her bedroom door and told her that Marcus was downstairs, she was stunned. And elated.

"Marcus?" she asked her mother. "You're sure?"

"I may be old," Rosa retorted. "But I'm not blind."

Still, Alice didn't move from the bed.

"Well, are you going to go downstairs? Or shall I send him up?"

"Mom, why is he here?"

"How should I know? But one might guess he's here because he wants to see you."

Alice was suddenly scared to see him. What if he had only come to tell her about the case and nothing else? And would she find the strength to tell him that she still wanted him as a friend?

"All right. I'll tell him to come up."

"No," Alice said. Finding that she had control of her limbs, she stood. "I'll go down."

While her mother left the room, Alice checked herself out in the mirror. She was dressed in an oversized T-shirt and baggy shorts and her hair was pulled back into a ponytail. She hardly looked glamorous. But what did that matter? Marcus hadn't seen fit to love her when she'd dressed like a knockout.

Still, she couldn't help the rush of excitement she felt as she descended the stairs, the rush of hope.

Downstairs, Alice expected to find Marcus in the hallway, but when she didn't see him there, she opened the front door. There he stood with his back turned. Hearing her, he spun around.

She swallowed. Stared.

He stared back.

"Hi," she said after a moment.

"Can I speak with you?"

"Sure. Come in."

He shook his head. "No. Not here."

"Oh." She flashed him a confused look.

"I was thinking we could go for a drive."

"Uh, sure." She stepped back into the foyer. As

she slipped into her sandals, she called, "Mom, I'm stepping out for a minute." Then she stepped onto the porch, pulling the door closed behind her. Marcus was already making his way down the front steps.

Watching his back, Alice felt the first needle prick her balloon of hope. He was being distant again. Here simply as a cop, no doubt. Why couldn't she accept that he didn't love her?

She met him at his car and he opened the door for her. She slipped inside. Moments later, he was in the driver's seat. But it was soon clear he didn't intend to start the car.

"Marcus—"

"Alice—"

They spoke at the same time.

"Go ahead," Alice said softly.

Marcus stared at Alice, not quite sure what he saw in her eyes. Disappointment? Maybe he'd stayed away too long and she no longer wanted to see him. Suddenly all he'd planned to say fled his mind.

"Willie is the one who drugged you."

"Willie? Oh my God."

Marcus explained the whole sordid situation to her. "Tanisha knew nothing about it."

"You're sure?"

"Yeah."

"Well." Alice shrugged. "I'm glad she didn't betray me like that."

"Me too." Marcus paused. "I was gonna head to the hospital yesterday to tell you, but . . ." His voice trailed off.

Alice looked at him curiously. "But what?"

Marcus shrugged, looking away. "I started driving. And thinking." Thinking that if he wasn't the best man for Alice, he should simply stay away and not hurt her further.

"Thinking about what?" Alice's voice was a whisper.

"Nothing." *Everything.*

"Oh." Alice sounded disappointed.

Marcus glanced at her, but she faced the window. Silence filled the car. There was so much more he wanted to say. After contemplating the pros and cons of whether or not he was the right man for her, Marcus had finally stopped ignoring the bottom line: He loved Alice and didn't want to lose her. But now, he was suddenly insecure. What if he was too late?

Go for it.

"Are you heading back to Los Angeles when the play is over?"

Alice met Marcus's eyes, trying to read the emotion behind the question. Did he care, or was he simply curious? "I don't know."

For the life of him, Marcus didn't know why it was so hard to tell Alice what was in his heart. Just this morning he'd convinced himself to go for it. Alice was so unlike any other woman he'd ever known. If she gave him her heart, he knew it would be forever.

"Marcus?"

"Huh?"

He was staring at her oddly. "Did you want to ask me something else?"

"No. I guess that's all."

She reached for the door handle.

"Wait," he said, suddenly not ready for her to step out of his car. If she did, he knew he'd never have another chance to tell her how he felt. "Did you mean what you said to me at my place? The part about you loving me?"

"Marcus . . ." Exhaling a harried breath, Alice brought her hands onto her lap. "Forget what I said."

"What if I don't want to forget it?"

A tingling sensation spread across Alice's shoulders, and not sure she'd heard him correctly, she slowly turned to face him.

He met her eyes with a hopeful look. "Hmm? What if I said I loved you too?"

Alice's heart went into overdrive. Her throat filled with emotion, making speech impossible. She was too stunned to move, too excited. Since high school, she had dreamed about this moment a million times, but she was so used to this dream not coming true that she wasn't sure she could trust what she heard now.

The excitement fizzled. Of course, this wasn't real. Just days ago, Marcus had told her he didn't love her.

"Marcus, don't pity me. I'm a survivor. Just because you don't love me doesn't mean I'll wither up and die." She hoped to hell she sounded convincing.

"You don't need anyone, do you?"

"No, I don't."

"What if I need you?"

Her breath caught in her throat. "I . . . Marcus, I already told you not to pity me."

"This isn't about pity, Alice. This is about me wanting you in my life. *Needing* you in my life."

She couldn't believe him. This couldn't be true. This was another dream. "Just Friday morning you told me you had no feelings for me other than *friendship*. Don't expect me to believe you've changed your mind in three days."

"No, I haven't changed my mind—"

"See—"

"I just finally stopped ignoring my heart," he finished.

Alice met his eyes firmly, not daring to hope again. She didn't want to set herself up for another disappointment.

Slowly, Marcus moved across the front seat, edging closer to her. Alice didn't dare move. She didn't dare breathe. She didn't dare trust her hearing.

"God, I love that deer look."

She heard the pounding of her heart in her ears. "You do?"

"Oh, yeah." He slipped an arm across her back, gently caressing her nape. "But not as much as I love you."

Her eyes fluttered shut at his words, then opened to make sure he was really here, that she wasn't actually dreaming.

He was there. This was real.

"But you said . . . you said it wouldn't work . . ."

"I was scared then, but not anymore."

She frowned. "Marcus . . ."

"Damn it, woman, you are really going to make me beg, aren't you?"

Alice's eyes widened as she stared at him in surprise. What she saw in his eyes made her heart leap. God, he was really serious. "You . . . you really love me?"

"Yes, damn it." But he smiled. "I don't want you to leave me. Ever. I know that might be asking too much, but I'm hoping we can make a home in Chicago . . . I even figured you might stay on at the theater, teach the children. Since Willie won't be back."

Alice laughed.

"What's so funny?"

"I was thinking the same thing. About staying in Chicago."

"You were?"

"Uh-huh. In fact, just this morning, I called my agent and told her not to send me any more scripts. That I'm not ready to go back."

"You did?" Marcus's heart pounded furiously. If Alice was staying here, they could really make a go of it.

"Marcus, do you really love me?" Alice asked after a moment. "Me, Alice? Not Desirée?"

"I love the girl I got to know years ago, and the woman you've become. I want you in my life, Alice. It's that simple. And I'm hoping you meant what you said last week . . . that you love me, too."

"Oh, Marcus. I've always loved you," Alice admitted breathlessly.

"Then marry me, Alice," he said. "Be my wife."

Alice's eyes filled with tears.

He lifted her hand to his lips. "I'm begging."

"As much as I'd love to see how far you'd go to win my hand in marriage," Alice said, a smile spreading over her face, "that would be pointless. Because I'd only be punishing myself."

His eyes lit up. "So you'll marry me?"

"Oh . . . yes!"

Marcus took her in his arms and kissed her until the car windows were full of steam. They were like two teenagers, making out in his front seat—something Alice had never done before. She giggled.

"You laughing at me?" he asked, nuzzling his nose against hers.

"No. I'm just happy." She paused. "Pinch me, Marcus. Let me know this isn't a dream."

He kissed her instead, and her eyes fluttered shut. "Is that real enough for you?"

"It still feels like a dream."

"Maybe it is. One that's come true."

"It definitely is," Alice said wistfully. For a while she'd given up believing in the power of dreams. So much had gone wrong in her life. But as Marcus held her in his arms, she knew that what her father had told her one summer evening long ago was still true. People held the power to make dreams come true in their lives.

As long as you believed they were possible.

And she did.

Coming Next ...

GOTTA GET NEXT TO YOU

BY

LYNN EMERY

May 2001

The following is a sneak peek ...

It was a glorious sunny day. The sky was still bright blue, but turning darker with touches of orange as the sun set. Cottony white clouds floated along. Bayou Blue was surrounded by lush prairies and bayous. Her grandmother's house, the house she'd grown up in, was three miles from town. Andrea had not really paid attention to the area on previous visits home. But Gran had told her that a group of businessmen were trying to revive downtown. Having the clinic improved and under new management was part of the initiative.

Being home again was part of Andrea's five-year plan after her divorce. She'd been eager to come. The concrete and fast pace of Chicago only served to make her feel more disconnected. After a while, Gran's urging that she come back to her roots did not seem like a bad idea. Andrea wanted to get her life on an even keel.

She walked half-way down one block and stopped within a few yards of a store. Downtown Bayou Blue needed a facelift for sure. The shabbiness of abandoned storefronts contrasted with the beautiful rural setting. Still, the Improvement Committee's efforts did show in a few places. Several historic buildings had been attractively restored. Andrea had fond childhood memories of skipping to keep up with her father's long stride as they walked downtown. Andrea mentally identified the old dress shop where her father had bought her first party outfit. Around the corner had been a combination shoe store and shoe repair shop. It wasn't much of a town by big city standards, but it was well worth saving.

The sound of footsteps brought her back to the present. Andrea realized she'd wandered a good two blocks from where her car was parked outside the clinic. The area was scattered with shabby vacant store fronts. Trash and weeds filled two empty lots to her left.

"Yeah, man. Them dudes crazy. I— Whoa, looka that." A male voice went from conversational to provocative.

Three men wearing low-slung jeans strolled toward her. They seemed to have appeared out of nowhere. Young and lanky, their conversation was filled with profanity. Andrea looked around hoping to see someone else on the street. But what few businesses remained were closed and no one was in sight. She turned around and started back to her car.

"Hey, baby. How ya doin'?" A young man grinned revealing three gold teeth.

"I'm fine," Andrea said without breaking her stride.

"That ain't no lie." The young man rubbed his chin with one hand.

Andrea glanced at him briefly. She'd worked in a Chicago clinic that saw a lot of troubled kids and adults, even gang members. This young man was more bluster than real menace, but the two men with him were another matter. One had a scar along his left cheek that he rubbed as though proud of it. The other, shorter and the color of ebony, wore a red kerchief around his neck. His muscle shirt was hiked up on one side.

They jumped ahead of her on the sidewalk blocking her progress, forcing Andrea to stop as well.

The one with the scar spoke first. "My name's Javon, an' I got what you need," he said with a smack of his lips.

Andrea's throat tightened with fear. "Excuse me, but I'm going to my car."

"You outta your league. Classy lady ain't got time for kiddie stuff. I'm Bo, baby." He let his gaze trail over her body suggestively. Bo wet his lips, his eyes narrowed to slits as he stared at her breasts. He took a step close to her.

Andrea frowned in distaste. "Excuse me." She made another attempt to go around him. When he didn't move, she tried to push her way through.

"Why you in such a hurry? Be friendly." Bo moved closer, until he towered over her. He made a grab for her arm.

Andrea jerked back avoiding his grasp. "Leave me alone."

Bo grabbed her again. "That ain't the way to—"

Andrea knocked his hand aside and kicked his shin hard. Bo yelped at the glancing blow then lunged for her. In a panic, she turned to run and collided with a man's hard chest.

"We gotta problem out here?" a deep voice asked.

Shaking with fear that she was surrounded, Andrea looked up and up. He was at least six feet four with smooth skin like fine milk chocolate. His eyes were a deep brown, like strong Louisiana dark roast coffee as he gazed at them calmly. He wore a light blue cotton Henley shirt and blue jeans that hugged narrow hips. He looked powerful even standing still. Andrea was caught between the aura of masculine strength, palpable as the musky scent of cologne he wore, and the feeling of fear that made her pulse race. Or was it fear? She stared at the strong line of his jaw. This man inspired something more, exhilaration. He surveyed the group of men calmly and Andrea felt as though the cavalry had just galloped across the horizon.

"Nah, we just gettin' introduced," Bo said. He glared at Andrea. "Awright?"

"Funny. Looks like the lady is trying to get away. What about it, ma'am?" He glanced at Andrea.

Bo's whole body was tensed for battle. "Stay outta my business."

"I know y'all can't read, so I'll help you out." Wearing a mild expression, the handsome newcomer pointed to a rectangular sign attached to the stone wall of the clinic. " 'No loitering near entrance,' " he read.

Javon's mouth flapped open as he decided to join in. "You can't tell us nothin'—"

"Come on, ma'am. Let's go inside. The air is

cooler and better smelling," he said with derision. He put a hand under her elbow and guided her inside the clinic.

Andrea was through the door before she could protest but for some reason she did not feel alarmed. This man had a solid, reassuring presence. He radiated confidence with a dash of boldness. She looked at him and felt a shock of warmth travel up her spine. When he fully turned to look at her, warmth turned to a full-blown fire. His full brown lips pulled back in a dazzling smile to reveal gleaming white teeth. This man was more than handsome. The knit shirt seemed to strain across his chest. His muscular arms were even more defined when he put both hands on his waist. His gaze went over her head briefly, checking to make sure the thugs were gone, then back to her face. He was stunning. A dimple in one cheek made the delectable creature near perfect. He glanced around the waiting room.

"Looks like the roaches scattered." He turned around in a half circle.

Andrea said nothing, still taking him in. His dark brown hair was cut short and the tight curls looked like soft wool loops. She had a crazy urge to reach up and touch them. When he faced her again, Andrea blinked rapidly. She must be losing her mind. She looked away, sure that she was gaping at him like an idiot.

Andrea recovered. "Thanks," she said in a restrained tone. "But I've been in tough situations before."

"Sure." Disdain dripped from his voice. He continued to look around.

"I worked in Chicago and dealt with lots of people." Andrea's gratitude was being tested by his know-it-all manner.

"Is that right?" he said. "Well, I'd advise you stay out of this part of town."

"Decent people should be able to go anywhere they want," Andrea said. "We can't let hoodlums dictate what we do."

"Look, lady, use common sense. Unless you want something to happen, don't strut your stuff around here." He eyed her from head to toe.

"If being free to walk in town is 'strutting my stuff' as you so crudely put it, then I've got a right to strut my stuff where I please, when I please." Andrea spoke the words rapid fire like bullets and waved a forefinger at him. "You hear me?"

"Yes, ma'am. Folks for miles around heard you." He swept both arms in an arc.

Two patients, apparently the last for the day, stood staring at them in amusement. Several women were nodding. One woman wearing large hoop earrings that touched her shoulders bobbed her head from side to side.

"Tell him 'bout it baby, that's right."

Andrea lowered her hand quickly. What was wrong with her? Causing scenes, especially in public, horrified her. And here she was, the instigator. She'd spent years trying not to be like her emotional mother. Charlene could create high drama over a broken fingernail.

"Maybe you *could* have taken care of yourself out there," he said, dark eyebrows raised almost to his hairline. A twinkle of amusement lit his eyes.

Something about this man set off strong reactions in her, first attraction then wrath. Every hair on her body seemed raised. And worse she felt strangely elated.

The tingle of desire was pleasurable, and terrifying. She stuck out her hand in a businesslike gesture in an attempt to keep their meeting from becoming too personal.

"Andrea Noble. I'm the new director here."

He shook her hand. "Glad to meet you. I hear they've got plans to fix the place up."

Andrea liked the firm pressure of his handshake. She pulled her hand away quickly, but the warmth of his hand lingered on the soft skin of her palm. She took a deep breath and steadied herself.

"Ahem. Yes, we certainly do," she said.

The man's gaze drifted around again, scanning every inch of the place. He sauntered off and looked down the hall toward the back of the clinic. Andrea's wariness kicked in. Her reaction to his good-looks had temporarily blinded her. Something that had led her to ruin before, she thought sourly. Now she really looked at this man. He seemed to be sizing up his surroundings. Andrea thought about the drugs stored in the small clinic pharmacy. This time she noted every detail of his appearance, in case she had to pick him out of a lineup.

"I didn't get your name," she said.

"Jamal Turner." He spun around and strode to her. "Pleased to meet you."

Andrea fought off the sudden spike of desire when that tall, fine frame loomed over her again. "Mr. Turner."

"Call me Jamal. And I'll call you—"

"Ms. Noble," Andrea cut in. She moved farther from him to avoid more tingling than she needed.

"Well, Mr. Turner, what brings you downtown at this hour?"

He smiled at her formality. "Went to pick up my dry-cleaning and got there five minutes too late," he said smoothly.

Too smoothly, Andrea thought. "Mr. Norman has closed his store at four on Fridays for twenty years. You must not be from around here."

"Actually I am new to the area. But I'm learning fast." His dazzling smile came back, all charm and sex appeal.

This time Andrea was ready for him and his dimple. His explanation had holes in it, smooth or not. "What were you doing on this street? Clotier's is two blocks around the corner."

"I was at the bank and decided to just walk over. Wouldn't make sense to drive such a short distance. Good legs." Jamal slapped his thighs.

Andrea's gaze settled on the well-developed limbs in question. Her gaze drifted a little higher then she blushed and turned away. Her knees felt shaky. So this is what the phrase temporary insanity meant. She had to get control of herself. Jamal Turner's presence spelled trouble for her.

"Thighs— I mean, thanks for helping me." Andrea wanted to sink into the floor. She prayed he hadn't heard the slip. Good God, she was behaving like a sex-starved idiot!

"No problem," he said in a cheerful voice. "Next time you decide to stroll in a high crime area, I'm your man."

Andrea whirled around to set him straight with a sour reply. "Very funny, Mr. . . ." Her voice trailed off and she couldn't think of what to say. Instead of being annoyed, she noticed the delicious curve of his top lip.

"Cease fire," he quipped. "Just be careful, okay?" He titled his handsome head to one side.

"Okay," was all she could manage to murmur.

"See ya, ma'am." Jamal flipped a wave at her and pushed through the glass door of the clinic.

Andrea stared after him, hypnotized by the graceful, loping stride of impossibly long legs covered by dark blue denim. Despite his size, his body flowed like liquid.

She sighed. It was obvious she had a lot of work ahead of her. She was living with Gran until she could find an apartment of her own. Between clearing up the problems at the clinic and apartment hunting, she had no time to fantasize about a handsome player like Jamal Turner. She'd had her fill of that kind of trouble.

Her marriage ended with a bang and work in the inner-city clinic had overwhelmed her. Here she could make a difference. She would put her focus on the clinic and no smiling tower of testosterone would distract her.